A S

"*English Trifle* is a delightful combo of mystery and gourmet cooking, highly recommended."
—*Midwest Review Journal*, October 2009

"**English Trifle is an excellent read** and will be enjoyed by teens and adults of either gender. The characters are interesting, the plot is carefully crafted, and the setting has an authentic feel."
—Jennie Hansen, *Meridian Magazine*

"Whether the situation calls for standing up to a British aristocrat or bribing a security guard with chocolate-dipped macaroons, smart, tenacious Sadie Hoffmiller won't let anything keep her from the truth behind a murder. **Intricate, twisting, and downright tasty**, *English Trifle* will whet your appetite for more of Josi Kilpack's delicious culinary mysteries."
—Stephanie Black, author of *Fool Me Twice*

Lemon Tart

"**Lemon Tart is an enjoyable mystery** with a well-hidden culprit and an unlikely heroine in Sadie Hoffmiller. Kilpack endows Sadie with logical hidden talents that come in handy at just the right moment."
—Shelley Glodowski, *Midwest Book Review*, June 2009

"**I couldn't put it down!** I love, love, love this book. Sadie is more lovable than Regan Reilly, Goldy Bear, and James Qwilleran—all rolled together!"
—Whit Larson, http://www.MormonMomCast.com

"**Lemon Tart was delicious!** Sadie's curiosity, determination, and good old-fashioned pluck made her one of the most delightful characters I've ever met in a book. Finding that all my guesses about whodunit were wrong made for an exciting and clever ending to a satisfying mystery."
—Julie Wright, author of *My Not-So-Fairy-Tale Life*, http://www.juliewright.com

"Josi Kilpack's new book *Lemon Tart* takes everything I love about a culinary mystery—the food, the humor, the intrigue—and blends it all at high speed with a dash of spice in the form of our main character, Sadie. **A must-read for those who enjoy well-crafted mysteries.**"
—Tristi Pinkston, http://www.tristipinkston.blogspot.com

"**Mystery-lovers will be entranced** with Josi Kilpack's cozy mystery, *Lemon Tart*. Amateur sleuth/busybody neighbor Sadie Hoffmiller is funny, quirky, and just the person to uncover the right clues and get her neighborhood back to normal. With a little romance and a lot of yummy baking, I had fun trying to guess whodunit until the very end."
—H. B. Moore, award-winning author of the *Out of Jerusalem* series and *Abinadi*, http://www.mywriterslair.blogspot.com

"**Lemon Tart is an absolutely scrumptious culinary mystery.** It not only kept me guessing, but also had my taste buds demanding I make the included recipes. I'm very excited about this new series by Josi S. Kilpack!"
—T. Danyelle Ferguson, http://www.queenoftheclan.blogspot.com

DEVIL'S FOOD CAKE

OTHER BOOKS BY JOSI S. KILPACK

Her Good Name
Sheep's Clothing
Unsung Lullaby

Culinary Mysteries
Lemon Tart
English Trifle

DEVIL'S FOOD CAKE

A CULINARY MYSTERY
Josi S. Kilpack

DESERET BOOK
SALT LAKE CITY, UTAH

To Chris—*my favorite boy in the whole wide world!*

© 2010 Josi S. Kilpack

All rights reserved. No part of this book may be reproduced in any form or by any means without permission in writing from the publisher, Deseret Book Company, P. O. Box 30178, Salt Lake City, Utah 84130. This work is not an official publication of The Church of Jesus Christ of Latter-day Saints. The views expressed herein are the responsibility of the author and do not necessarily represent the position of the Church or of Deseret Book Company.

All characters in this book are fictitious, and any resemblance to actual persons, living or dead, is purely coincidental.

DESERET BOOK is a registered trademark of Deseret Book Company.

Visit us at DeseretBook.com

Library of Congress Cataloging-in-Publication Data
Kilpack, Josi S.
　Devil's food cake / Josi S. Kilpack.
　　p. cm.
　Summary: When a literary agent dies at a library fund-raiser, Sadie Hoffmiller finds herself on the trail of the murderer. As she digs deeper into the mystery, she discovers connections to a decade-old murder-suicide.
　ISBN 978-1-60641-232-9 (paperbound)
　1. Hoffmiller, Sadie (Fictitious character)—Fiction.　2. Cooks—Fiction.
3. Murder—Investigation—Fiction.　4. Detective and mystery stories, American.
I. Title.
PS3561.I412D48 2010
813'.54—dc22　　　　　　　　　　　　　　　　　　　　　　　　　　　2009046674

Printed in the United States of America
Malloy Lithographing Incorporated, Ann Arbor, MI

10　9　8　7　6　5　4　3　2　1

Chapter 1

"Have you seen Thom yet?" Sadie asked, craning her neck to peer into the corners of the temporary stage set up at the front of the ballroom at the Carmichael Hotel. Thom Mortenson was supposed to have arrived by 6:30, but he'd called to say he was running late. Sadie glanced at her watch: 7:05. So much for starting the program at 7:00 sharp. She was trying not to show her annoyance at men with no concept of time. Detective Pete Cunningham—Sadie's date for tonight—was late too.

"Not yet," Gayle answered from where she sat at Sadie's left. Gayle was Sadie's best friend—and she was dateless tonight, which was a strange occurrence.

"So, did you two read his book, then?" an increasingly familiar voice asked.

Sadie looked past Gayle to the young woman seated next to her—the date of Frank Argula. The girl was Frank's junior by at least thirty years, with thick, brown hair piled on top of her delicate little head. Sadie feared a sneeze might snap the girl's neck completely as her hair had to weigh twenty-five pounds. Sadie didn't know the girl's name—Trixie or Bambi or something like that, she was sure.

"Of course we read it," Gayle answered coolly, shooting Sadie a look brimming with annoyance. It was the fourth time Trixie-Bambi had cut into their conversation in the ten minutes since Sadie had finally been able to sit down. Frank was currently involved in an animated discussion with a city councilman and was therefore paying no attention to his date.

"It must be really good," the girl said with a floating kind of smile as she looked around the room. "I mean, look at all these people who want to listen to him talk about it."

"It is good," Gayle said dryly.

Sadie scraped together the last bite of mashed potatoes from her plate. Truth be told, she hadn't loved Thom's book, *Devilish Details*, which had been published a couple years after Thom had moved away from Garrison. While Sadie was very proud of his accomplishment, the book wasn't really her style.

Gayle turned back to Sadie. "I still can't believe he agreed to come," she said.

"Why?" Trixie-Bambi cut in.

Rather than being annoyed by this interruption, Gayle's eyes lit up at the girl's ignorance. Sadie took a sip of her drink to cover her smile as Gayle turned back to the girl with a very different expression. *Here we go*, Sadie thought. It wasn't that Gayle was a gossip, per se, but she, well, liked . . . being informed and sharing that information with others. Of course, any time Sadie pointed that out, Gayle turned the tables and recalled all the times Sadie had been the one to spill a story.

A server leaned in to take away their plates. "Didn't Frank tell you about Thom?" Gayle asked once the server had moved away.

The girl shook her head.

"Well," Gayle said, wriggling in her seat a little bit and leaning close. "First, his wife, who was mentally ill for most of their marriage, overdosed, leaving him as a single father. Then his son killed himself and his girlfriend after junior prom ten years ago."

The girl gasped and put a hand to her mouth. Sadie felt her stomach tighten. Hearing the details laid out so bluntly was a bit of a shock. Even from Gayle.

"You're kidding," the girl said after lowering her hand. "A murder-suicide? Here?"

Up until last October, when Sadie's neighbor had been murdered, the Mortenson tragedy had been the most recent homicide in Garrison, Colorado. Damon, Thom's son, had only been a couple years older than Sadie's own daughter, so the tragedy had hit close to home. In the weeks following the shooting, the school district brought in grief counselors, and parents no longer hesitated to forbid their daughters from dating the bad-boys. Then Thom Mortenson moved to California, despite the fact that most of Garrison hadn't blamed him for what happened; Damon had been in and out of trouble since he turned twelve, and everyone knew Thom's wife had had problems as well. Lost in her own thoughts, Sadie didn't realize Gayle was still telling the story.

"You can imagine our surprise when a couple years later Thom's name showed up on the cover of a *New York Times* bestseller—"

"And Thom was on *Oprah* after it won the National Book Award," Sadie added. A bestselling novel was one thing, and national awards were amazing, but *Oprah*? Yeah. That was big-time.

Gayle nodded her acknowledgment, but continued speaking as though Sadie hadn't interrupted. "Of course we all knew he'd been a bit of a closet writer before Damon's death, but no one expected this, especially after what had happened."

"Wow," Trixie-Bambi said. She pulled at the top of her strapless gown and looked toward the stage. "Has he written any other books?"

"No," Gayle said, shrugging her shoulders. "Just the one. He's been saying for years that he has another one in the works, though."

"Maybe he'll be like Harper Lee," the girl said. "A common theory in literary circles regarding the fact that she never wrote another book was because she'd written the perfect novel right out of the gate. How do you compete with your own greatness?"

Sadie and Gayle both looked at the girl in surprise. They hadn't expected her to recite scholarly supposition.

"Maybe," Gayle said slowly, obviously caught off guard. In fact, she seemed a bit disappointed that Trixie-Bambi might not be as superficial as they'd suspected.

"I wonder what it's like for him to come back here," the girl added. "I imagine it's hard."

Sadie was reminded of her own surprise when Thom had accepted the invitation. What was there to come back to Garrison for but to face old ghosts?

Her thoughts were interrupted as a server placed a white dessert plate in front of her. Every thought of Thom or Trixie-Bambi disappeared. In the middle of the plate was a most beautiful sight—a thick, black, gooey piece of devil's food cake. Sadie grabbed her fork.

"I thought you were on a diet," Gayle said.

Sadie looked up, fork poised inches from her open mouth, and did her best to feign a scowl at her best friend. Gayle didn't take back the question. In fact she continued to look pointedly at the rich chocolate goodness on Sadie's fork. The rich chocolate goodness that was going straight to Sadie's already ample hips.

Trixie-Bambi turned to say something to Frank, and the clinking of silverware and mingling murmurs of a hundred conversations filled the room. Sadie paid no heed to any of it. Instead, she looked at Gayle and, with emphasized movements, put the bite of cake in her mouth and closed her lips around the fork. Sadie shut her eyes and tried not to groan aloud as the decadent chocolate melted on her tongue.

Gayle snickered, and Sadie feared she'd failed at her attempts to silently appreciate the deliciousness now coursing down her throat. It was just wrong that such an amazing culinary creation should have any calories at all.

"You should really attempt a little more self-restraint," Gayle said when Sadie recovered from her chocolate-induced swoon and opened her eyes. "Everyone knows you made the cake, so you look a little arrogant right now."

No one but Gayle, and maybe Sadie's children, could get away with talking to Sadie like that. However, after twenty years of friendship, there wasn't much they could do to offend each other.

Sadie used the edge of her fork to cut off another bite. "I have no problem with appearing arrogant when I've done something this magnificent."

In truth, it *was* a little embarrassing to lose control like that—especially in public. Sadie prided herself on her humility, and yet she had no control when it came to dessert. She'd returned from England almost six weeks ago and had been existing on salads, fruit smoothies, and baked chicken ever since, hoping to lose not the *seven* pounds she'd thought she'd gained on vacation, but the *twelve* pounds she'd brought home with her. Twelve pounds in two weeks—Sadie didn't know that was even possible.

Unfortunately, the diet hadn't been as effective as she'd hoped—possibly due to the fact that despite her strict meal regimen of protein and leafy greens, she'd been baking scones and crumpets a few times a week. She didn't count that as breaking her diet because perfecting the recipes was actually research. Gayle, of course, knew this.

But then Sadie had been asked to supply the dessert of her choice for the library fund-raiser. Before she'd even hung up the phone, she'd known what she wanted to make—devil's food cake. Since it was commonly understood that diets were left at the door of events like this, she knew it was a perfect opportunity to kill two birds with one stone—she'd make a fabulous contribution to the dinner *and* she'd get a piece of cake otherwise forbidden.

"I swear this is the best cake I have ever made in my life," Sadie said reverently after taking her second bite.

Gayle chuckled, and Sadie couldn't help but join her, knowing that she was being a little ridiculous. She put a hand on Gayle's arm and leaned in toward her friend. "It's a good thing you're sitting next to me," she said, giving Gayle's arm a squeeze. "I'd be liable to embarrass myself otherwise."

Gayle laughed again and cut a bite from her own piece of cake. She paused for a moment after putting it in her mouth and then turned to Sadie. "This *is* incredible."

Trixie-Bambi turned toward them both and nodded, her jaw rhythmically moving as she also chewed her cake. They were now bonded in the devotion to chocolate.

Sadie smiled at them both, glad to be sharing the moment with people who could appreciate it. She took yet another bite and was able to keep from moaning this time—but just barely.

DEVIL'S FOOD CAKE

"How many did you end up making?" Gayle asked, pulling her plate closer as if the cake might disappear at any moment.

"Eighteen," Sadie said. "Thank goodness Shawn arrived last night so he could help me finish up today."

Gayle nodded, but Sadie noted the distracted look in her friend's eyes. Eyes that were green tonight. Gayle's real eye color was mud—Gayle's word, not Sadie's—so she usually wore colored contacts. Green was Gayle's favorite since it went so well with her curly red hair, and her eyes looked particularly good tonight with the green evening gown Gayle had chosen.

"Shawn didn't want to come?" Gayle asked once she swallowed yet another bite.

Sadie shook her head. "He thought spending a Saturday night with his mom at a library fund-raising dinner sounded boring. In fact, I think his exact words were 'dead boring.'"

Gayle huffed in feigned offense.

Sadie chuckled and lifted another morsel to her lips.

The rich chocolate was threatening to make her swoon when her eyes caught movement on the stage. Thom had finally arrived and was fiddling with his wireless microphone, trying to clip it to the lapel of his suit jacket. Another man, shorter and balding, was trying to help. Sadie, however, was intoxicated by chocolate to the point of no longer feeling annoyed by Thom's tardiness.

"Oh, there he is," Gayle said, pointing at the stage with her fork. "I'm guessing the other man is Thom's manager? Mr. Ogreski?"

"I assume so," Sadie said, watching the men with an air of distraction as she cut another bite.

"Thom looks good," Gayle continued in an appraising tone. "He's still single, you know."

Sadie rolled her eyes but couldn't help but smile at the same time. After Gayle's divorce five years ago, the merest hint that she might want to date again had been met with thinly veiled malevolence directed at whoever dared suggest it. And then, about a year ago, Gayle accepted a neighbor's invitation to attend a singles dance at her church. That night, Gayle was officially introduced to middle-age single life and she'd never looked back. Sadie was glad—a woman like Gayle needed people, and people needed women like Gayle.

Gayle opened her mouth to say something, but then straightened, dropped her chin coyly, and looked over Sadie's head. "Speaking of single men," she said, then smiled brilliantly and cocked her head to the side.

Sadie swiveled in her seat, then sat up straight as Detective Pete Cunningham entered the ballroom and headed toward their table. If only she'd been able to fit into her black velvet formal. Instead she was in her navy blue sparkle-dress, which was nice, but not nearly as elegant as the flowing dress Gayle was sporting.

Sadie stood and smiled as Pete approached their table. He undid the button of his tux jacket so it wouldn't wrinkle when he sat down. The man looked downright dapper in his patent leather shoes and bow tie. His well-trimmed silver and black hair and beard were a perfect complement to his formal attire, and for a moment Sadie thought he might kiss her hello; on the cheek if nothing else. Instead he gave her a quick hug. "Sorry I'm late—paperwork."

"Not a problem," Sadie said as she sat back down. He helped push her chair in. He was always such a gentleman—too much of one sometimes. In the three months they'd been officially dating, he had yet to kiss her even once. It was beginning to give Sadie a complex.

Pete had met Gayle twice before and said hello before Sadie

introduced the other people at their table, including Trixie-Bambi, whose real name turned out to be Michele. Apparently she was Frank's niece and an English literature major. Who knew?

Pete shook hands with the people at their table—some of whom he already knew—before finally taking his seat. Sadie was nearly bursting with pride to be the girl on his arm. "I'm sorry you missed dinner," she said. She should probably offer him some of her cake, but she wasn't sure their relationship was at that level. Certainly a little lip-locking was a prerequisite to sharing devil's food cake, right? Instead, she waved to get the attention of one of the servers and then pointed at Pete. The server nodded and headed toward the doors leading to the kitchen. Sadie pulled her plate a bit closer to herself in hopes that Pete wouldn't get any ideas before the server returned with his food.

"They're getting your dinner," Sadie said.

"Oh, good, I'm starving," Pete said. He looked toward the stage. "I haven't missed the main event, have I?"

Sadie shook her head and looked to the stage as well. Thom was still fiddling with the microphone. They had someone from the hotel helping him now. It was weird that they were having problems with it. The microphone had worked fine for Sadie's introduction forty-five minutes earlier. She knew the hotel had a wooden podium with a detachable wired microphone off stage right as a backup. She wondered how long they would keep trying to make the wireless system work before they gave up and moved to plan B.

"He doesn't look much different, does he?" Pete commented, nodding toward Thom.

"Did you know Thom when he used to live here?" Gayle asked, leaning toward them and speaking in a high, sweet voice.

Sadie felt a flash of jealousy that surprised her. Was it her imagination that Gayle was being flirtatious? Or was she just feeling insecure about the no-kissing-for-three-months thing?

Pete looked from the stage to Gayle. "I was one of the detectives on his son's case," he said.

"Oh," Sadie and Gayle said at the same time. Sadie wondered why Pete hadn't told her that before now, but she wasn't about to ask in front of Gayle.

"Maybe you should remind them about the wired microphone?" Sadie heard herself say to Gayle.

"Me?" Gayle said in surprise, dropping her smile for a moment.

"I think they've forgotten about the backup," Sadie said, giving her friend a pointed look. She'd like a few minutes alone with Pete to catch up on the day. Surely Gayle could understand that. And maybe Gayle would have a chance to say hello to Thom in the process. Sadie's motives weren't totally selfish.

Gayle was silent, but put down her fork, correctly interpreting Sadie's look. "Well, I guess I could," she said. Sadie smiled a thank-you. Gayle stood up and put her napkin on her chair before heading toward the front of the room. As she stepped away, a server set down both a dinner and a dessert plate in front of Pete. By the time Sadie looked up again, Gayle had disappeared behind the curtain to the right of the stage. Sadie owed her one.

Michele also stood and excused herself to use the ladies' room.

Sadie nodded toward Pete's dinner. "It's worth the hundred and fifty dollars," she said. "I promise." She only wished she could say she'd made it herself. Feeding the people she cared about was one of her favorite things to do.

Pete smiled and winked at her before using his knife to cut off a piece of prime rib.

Sadie looked up at the stage in time to see Gayle roll the podium out from the curtains on the right and Thom walk offstage left, looking frustrated. The manager must have been backstage as well. A hotel worker helped Gayle plug a wire from the floor into a port on the side of the wooden podium. Sadie took another bite of cake to distract herself from the guilt of making Gayle go up on stage. She wasn't even on the library board this year. Sadie was the one who should be helping out.

Suddenly the stage area was cleared except for the manager and the podium. An expectant hush fell over the crowd, and the manager looked out at the room of people as if just remembering they were there. After straightening his suit coat, he made his way to the podium, which was so tall that the microphone pointed over his head. He reached up both hands to adjust the snakelike microphone holder so that he could speak into it. However, when his mouth moved, the microphone failed to pick up the sound.

Is there a problem with the entire sound system? Sadie wondered. After all their work to pull off this dinner, she would be really, really mad if it all fell apart now.

Mr. Ogreski continued to wrestle with the microphone, which seemed to be stuck. He pulled it free from the holder, but the wire, which should feed through the hole in the podium didn't have much give and he couldn't seem to hold the microphone close enough to his mouth. After a few more seconds, Mr. Ogreski clenched his jaw, adjusted his grip on the microphone, and yanked it toward him, presumably to free the cord that seemed to be tangled within the wooden podium. It didn't budge. He took a breath and planted his feet, poised to pull again.

Sadie let her eyes drift closed, grateful to give herself up to the chocolate ecstasy in her mouth instead of focusing on what was happening onstage for the moment. There were only a few bites left.

In the next instant, a shotgun blast echoed off the walls of the ballroom. Sadie choked on her cake as the people in the room screamed in horror.

Devil's Food Cake

1 cup sour milk (1 cup milk + 2 teaspoons white vinegar or lemon juice OR use 1 cup buttermilk)
2 cups flour
2 cups sugar
⅔ cup unsweetened cocoa
½ teaspoon salt
2 eggs
1 cup vegetable oil
1 teaspoon vanilla
1 cup boiling water
1 teaspoon baking soda

For sour milk, mix milk and vinegar in a small bowl. Set aside for five minutes.

In a large bowl, mix together all ingredients except the water and baking soda. Mix until batter is smooth. Add the soda to the boiling water (kids love this part because it bubbles). Add soda/water mixture to batter. Mix well—batter will be thin.

Pour batter into a greased and floured 9x13-inch pan and bake at 350 degrees for 35 to 45 minutes or until middle is set.

If using round cake pans, grease pans _very_ well and cut a round of wax paper to fit inside the bottom of the pans to prevent cake from sticking when removed. Let cake cool five minutes in pans before turning out onto a wire rack.

Serves 12.

*Shawn (i.e. Mint-aholic) likes a teaspoon of mint extract added to the batter.

CHAPTER 2

By the time Sadie stopped coughing cake from her lungs, the room was in chaos and Pete had disappeared from his seat beside her. Frantic dinner guests had flipped tables on their sides as barricades and a few people ran for the doors. Sadie jumped to her feet and scanned the room, looking for Pete.

"Stay where you are!"

Sadie wheeled around in time to see Pete jump onto the stage and turn to face the audience, looking like James Bond in his tux. "There is not an imminent threat," Pete continued, his voice booming through the room. He held one hand out, palm down. His other hand was in his jacket—likely on the pistol he kept in a shoulder harness most of the time. There might not be an imminent threat, but Sadie knew he wasn't taking chances. "Someone call 911," he yelled.

A hundred cell phones were whipped out of pockets and purses and Sadie put her hand on her hip out of pure reflex. All she felt was the seam of her dress. That's right; she hadn't expected to need her phone tonight, so she'd left it in the car instead of carrying it with her.

Pete turned away from the crowd, walked a few feet, and stopped in front of Mr. Ogreski's body, crouching down to get a better look. It was hard to see anything from Sadie's position at the back of the room. A flash of green toward the right side of the stage caught Sadie's attention. Gayle was screaming hysterically with her hands on either side of her face and staring at the body on the stage.

What on earth just happened? Sadie thought as she picked up her skirts and began making her way toward Gayle. Had it really been a shotgun blast she heard? Or could it have been a bomb? Sadie was getting better at keeping herself together in situations such as this—after all, this was her third dead body in four months—but there was nothing casual in her thoughts or the racing of her heart.

Gayle was still screaming when Sadie reached the stairs so she hiked her skirt up to her calves and moved as fast as her heels would allow. A few people had joined Pete on stage; he was telling them to back away from the body. Thom stood by the curtains on the left side of the stage completely frozen. His face was pale and his eyes were transfixed on the body. Sadie wished she could help him, but Gayle needed her more. Sadie hurried over to her friend who was shaking uncontrollably and put an arm around Gayle's back. She put her other hand over Gayle's hands, which were clenched to her chest. Gayle stopped screaming at Sadie's touch, but her mouth remained open and her eyes wide. Her pale, white face made her green eyes look unnaturally bright.

"It's okay," Sadie said, but then she looked past all the people and saw the body sprawled across the flat gray carpet of the temporary stage. Her stomach turned and she looked away. Why on earth was she saying everything was okay?

She turned her attention to Gayle in hopes to quell the nausea rising in her stomach. "You need to sit down," she said. There were chairs behind the curtains and, without letting go of Gayle, Sadie grabbed the closest one with one hand, turning it away from the grisly scene. A police officer had done something similar for Sadie when Sadie had come upon the body of her neighbor in a field last fall.

"Sit," Sadie said. Gayle sat, but she was still shaking. "I think you're in shock." Sadie rubbed her friend's cold arms. Gayle's hands were still clenched tightly together, but Sadie noticed something hot pink between them.

"What's that?" Sadie asked while gently trying to open Gayle's hands.

Gayle looked down, finally opening her hands to reveal a crumpled Post-It note. Sadie picked it up carefully and tried to smooth it out as best she could.

The handwriting was sloppy, but readable, as though whoever wrote it had been in a hurry.

Backup mic tested and operational.
Plug into floor outlet to use.

"It—it was on the podium," Gayle explained, her voice tight and shaky.

Sadie nodded and smiled at her friend reassuringly. "I'll make sure Pete gets it," she said, patting Gayle's arm again. She looked around the room. Everything was a mess, but the din of screaming had mostly faded into anxiously murmured conversation. People had stood up from behind their barricades and hotel staff members had come through the back doors of the ballroom, looking lost and confused. Apparently they didn't have much specialized training in what to do when there was a shooting in the ballroom. Dishes were all over the floor, and devil's food cake was ground into the carpet, chairs, and tablecloths.

"Sadie!"

Sadie looked up at the sound of her name and saw Pete motioning for her. She glanced at Gayle, who managed a nod and a shaky "I'm okay."

Sadie tried not to look directly at the body as she headed toward Pete. When she reached him, she immediately handed him the pink note. "Gayle said this was on the podium."

Pete looked at it, then nodded and put it in his front pocket. "I'll bag it later," he said. For some reason Sadie hadn't thought of the note as evidence, but realized now that was exactly what it was. She hoped she or Gayle hadn't ruined the evidence by touching it.

Pete touched Sadie's arm. "Get everyone off the stage, but don't let them leave. We'll need statements."

Sadie wasn't sure why he wanted her to do this—she wasn't a trained police officer—and yet she was flattered by his request. Without hesitation, she made shooing motions to the increasing crowd on the stage. "You heard him. Everyone off, but don't leave." She scanned faces, looking for someone she knew well enough to ask for help. "Carl," she called, looking pointedly at another member of the library board. "Get some people to man the doors—no one in or out."

Carl nodded and seemed relieved to have something to do.

As Sadie continued herding people off the stage, she noticed Thom standing at the back of the ballroom.

When did he leave the stage? she wondered.

Carl yelled for another man to help him cover the doors, and Thom seemed to overhear it. Rather than move into the room, like everyone else, he made a break toward the door, taking Sadie off guard.

"Thom!" she yelled, louder than she'd have expected herself capable of doing. He looked at her briefly, as did several other people, but he didn't stop. Instead he slipped through one of the doors left open when the hotel staff had entered, immediately disappearing into the foyer area. The sound of sirens rose above the ruckus of two hundred people trying to make sense of what had happened. She turned back to Pete. "Thom left," she said, feeling panicked.

"We'll find him," Pete said, but his glance toward the ballroom doors didn't seem the least bit casual, reminding Sadie that Pete was the only officer on the scene of a brutal murder with hundreds of witnesses. Talk about pressure. He whipped out his phone and dialed a number.

She looked toward the door Thom had left through. Should she follow him? Why would Thom leave in the first place? Of everyone the police would want to talk to, Thom would be at the top of the list. He'd been right there when it happened and he was the only person who actually knew the victim. In fact, an introduction by Mr. Ogreski wasn't on the printed schedule for the evening—Thomas Mortenson was supposed to give his address during dessert.

Pete ended the phone call and put his phone back in his pocket.

Sadie looked at the body of the man who wasn't supposed to be at the podium at all. "He's dead?" she asked, a lump in her throat.

Pete looked up from where he'd been taking a detailed look at the orientation of the body. He nodded slowly. "He was probably dead before he hit the floor." His eyes went to the podium lying on its back on the ballroom floor, and Sadie looked as well. The front access door was in pieces all over the stage. Set inside—where Sadie imagined the electronic equipment should be—was a gun.

A sawed-off shotgun, if Sadie wasn't mistaken. An elaborate webbing of what looked like string, or maybe a thin cable, was wrapped around the gun, though it was in disarray now and tangled with the thicker cord of the microphone. Had the cable held the gun in place and engaged the trigger when Mr. Ogreski pulled on the microphone? Someone had put an awful lot of thought into this.

"It wasn't an accident," Sadie said. The words had no sooner left her mouth than she realized they were likely the dumbest words she'd ever said in her life. Guns didn't accidentally end up hidden inside a podium.

"No," Pete said. "It wasn't."

CHAPTER 3

Less than a minute later, a stream of police officers entered the ballroom. Pete put one of them in charge of the body and hurried to confer with the others.

Sadie shifted her weight, feeling rather conspicuous standing on the stage waiting for Pete to tell her what she should do next. Then she remembered Gayle. Grateful to have something to do, she hurried down the stairs and to their table where she picked up Gayle's water glass before returning to her friend who was still sitting in the chair facing the right wall of the ballroom. Gayle had regained a little color in her face, but was crying and wiping at her eyes and cheeks, smearing her mascara in the process. Sadie grabbed a cloth napkin from the closest table, hoping no one had blown their nose in it.

"Here you go," Sadie said softly, handing the glass of water to Gayle, who took it with shaky hands. She wiped at Gayle's cheeks with the napkin, but frowned when she only made the smudging worse. After a few more failed attempts with the napkin, she planted a polite smile on her face and put the square of polyester down.

She'd simply have to get Gayle properly cleaned up before she had the chance to look in a mirror.

"I brought the podium out," Gayle said, her voice flat. "I brought it out for him."

Sadie wasn't sure how to respond, but she felt guilty all over again. She'd told Gayle to help with the sound situation because she felt threatened by Gayle's flirting and now her friend might be forever traumatized by the event.

"No one could have known," Sadie said, even though someone *had* to have known. Someone put the gun there. Had that person disconnected the wireless system so the podium would be necessary? Sadie shook her head slowly. Who would go to such lengths to do something so horrible? And in public no less?

"Gayle?"

Sadie turned as Pete approached them. He came around the chair so he was facing Gayle. "I know it's difficult, but I need your statement."

Gayle nodded slightly, but as soon as she opened her mouth, her jaw trembled and she began bawling again. Pete grabbed another chair while Sadie stepped closer to her friend and placed a comforting arm around Gayle's shoulders. Gayle leaned into Sadie; she was glad she'd worn a dark-colored dress so the mascara wouldn't stain.

"I know you've been through a horrific ordeal," Pete said, sounding truly concerned and compassionate. He was such a good detective.

"I-I just can't believe it," Gayle said, trying to sit up straight and wipe her eyes again. "I was backstage, planning to slip out after he introduced Thom—there wasn't any way down on the right side of the stage, you know."

That's right, Sadie realized. The left side of the stage had a door that led out of the ballroom, hidden from the audience by the curtains. But the right side, where the podium had been stored so it would be out of the way, was a dead end. Someone would have to come out from the curtains in order to access the stairs. An instant vision assailed Sadie: what if Gayle had tried to assist Mr. Ogreski with the microphone? She felt her stomach clench, and she hurried to push the horrible thought away.

"Did you see it happen?" Sadie asked.

Gayle nodded and fresh tears spilled out of her bright green eyes.

Sadie wasn't sure crying with contacts was recommended, but then maybe if Gayle cried enough, she'd wash the mascara off completely. One could only hope.

"He—he pulled on the microphone, and then he flew backward, and the . . . cord and the . . . blood." She closed her eyes while Sadie tried to picture the scene from Gayle's perspective, standing only a few feet away. It wasn't pretty.

"The cord," Sadie repeated, focusing on the part that spoke of the mechanical aspect of the trap. "Did you see it come out of the hole on the podium? I mean, it was tied to the trigger, right?" It seemed so Wile E. Coyote.

Pete cleared his throat, reminding Sadie he was there. He gave her a look that made her clamp her mouth shut and then smile innocently. "Sorry," she said after a moment. Pete continued to look at her.

"Perhaps you could let us speak together privately," he said.

"Oh, okay," Sadie replied, trying not to look offended at being left out. After all, she was dating Pete, she was Gayle's best friend, *and* she'd played a part in the investigation of two other murders—which was as many as Pete had investigated in the last ten years.

Arguing those points, however, likely wouldn't work in a high-stress situation like this or help her relationship with Pete.

She turned away, letting her mind race toward what else she could do. Her eyes were drawn to the row of chairs set up on the left side of the stage—the side of the stage where Thom would have been standing when Mr. Ogreski was shot. There was something sitting on the middle of the three chairs. It looked like a small box. Sadie narrowed her eyes, trying to make out what it was, but she was too far away. Immediately she thought that whenever she went somewhere to give a speech, she took a bag with her to hold her notes, lipstick, some breath mints, and a bottle of water in case she became parched. Not that she gave a lot of speeches, but she thoroughly prepared for the ones she was asked to give. Last summer she'd spoken to the ladies' auxiliary club about being a lifelong teacher and the blessings of educating others. She'd done a really good job, if she did say so herself, and had a very nice article about the presentation written up in the weekly paper.

Back to the subject at hand, however—she wondered if what she saw on the chair could be a briefcase. It seemed too small, but Sadie was certain that Thom's hands had been empty when he ran from the room.

Sadie glanced around the room nonchalantly, lifting a hand to rub her neck so it wouldn't seem obvious that she was scanning the room. Assured that no one was paying her any particular attention, Sadie made her way toward the left side of the stage. She was about four feet away when she realized that the item that had sparked her curiosity was nothing more than a copy of Thom's book—*Devilish Details*.

She closed the distance between herself and the book, trying to swallow her disappointment. What important information was she going to get from a book? But she picked it up and looked it over anyway, just in case.

The cover featured what looked like the face of a stone gargoyle, like those she'd seen on the medieval castles in London. Its mouth was open and showing large, sharp teeth. Except that while the face was stone, the eyes were not. Human eyes glared out from the gargoyle's face—kinda creepy.

Sadie, like everyone else in Garrison, had read the book when it came out, excited to have known someone who had actually published a novel. The library had ordered an astonishing five copies—one or two copies of any given title had been the rule until then. But this was an exception to the rule if ever there was one. Thom, though he'd been gone for a couple years by then, was still one of their own. In fact, any lingering negativity directed toward him after what Damon had done seemed to disappear amid the celebrity status Thom had achieved by becoming a published author.

However, despite being a little bit starstruck herself—Thom had been her accountant at one time after all—Sadie had quickly concluded the book wasn't quite her style. The basic plotline involved demonic possession of inanimate objects, like the gargoyle, which then caused havoc for the poor humans in the book. Sadie remembered much wailing and gnashing of teeth and finally closed the cover when she determined the Old Testament had enough of that to suit her just fine. The fact that it wasn't quite her genre, however, did not dispel how proud she was of Thom. Sadie had survived heartache and managed to go on to enjoy her life, and she always wished that same thing for people who, like her, had faced tragedy. Not that losing her husband, Neil, to a heart attack was much of a comparison to what Thom had gone through, but still.

She brought her thoughts back to the present and looked at the book in her hands. Did the book belong to Thom? What about notes for his talk? He was presenting to two hundred people and didn't bring anything but a book with him?

She looked around the area but didn't see anything other than the discarded wireless equipment in a plastic crate by the door. She turned the book over to look at Thom's picture on the back. He was sitting in a leather wingback chair, dressed in a suit, but not wearing a tie, and the top few buttons of his shirt were undone. His hair was grown out but fashionable, and he wore one of those serious, somewhat intellectual expressions. Just once she'd like to see a dust jacket showing an author on a Harley Davidson or fishing or something.

Thom had looked older in person tonight—and tired. Of course, this photo was several years old now, and Thom had been distraught when she'd seen him on stage. Still, the man she'd seen tonight—the man who had slipped out the back door of the ballroom—didn't seem to have much in common with the man on the back of the book.

She turned the book over again in her hands. Why did Thom have a copy of his own book backstage? Was he going to do a reading? Or maybe his notes were tucked inside? Sadie flipped open the book to have a look and lifted her eyebrows in surprise at the words written in black marker across the inside front cover.

I'm sorry.

Chapter 4

Sadie stared at the words, furrowing her eyebrows. "I'm sorry?" she repeated in a whisper. Sorry for what? And why was it written inside the book?

"Mrs. Hoffmiller?"

Sadie whipped around, acutely aware of the book in her hands as she faced a police officer—one she'd met before. "Officer Malloy," she said, trying to smile through her guilt before realizing a smile didn't quite fit the circumstances. Sadie had first met Officer Malloy after Anne's murder. They didn't have the best history; in fact, Sadie had the impression that Malloy viewed her as a bit of a busybody. Sadie wasn't used to being disliked, so it made her uncomfortable every time she encountered him.

His eyes traveled to the book in her hands, and Sadie realized she needed to offer an explanation. "Um, I, uh, found this." She held the book out to him quickly. "I was about to take it to Pete, uh, Detective Cunningham. There's something written in the front cover," Sadie said, unable to hold back the information even though she was pretty sure it would be better for everyone if Malloy discovered it for himself.

Malloy turned the book over in his hands, flipping it open. His eyebrows pulled together.

"I know," Sadie said knowingly. "Weird, right? What do you think it means? Who do you think wrote it?"

"Where did you find this?" Malloy asked, looking between the book and Sadie's face with a decidedly displeased expression.

"On the chair," Sadie said, pointing to the middle of the three chairs.

"And what possessed you to come backstage and pick it up in the first place?"

"Uh, well . . ." Sadie wasn't sure how to answer, wanting to portray herself in the best light possible. "I saw it from over there," she said, pointing toward Gayle and Pete. "I thought it was a . . . briefcase or something." She could tell by Malloy's expression that she was not helping herself.

Malloy glared at her and opened his mouth to say something just as a flash went off behind him. Sadie looked to the source of the bright light, and Malloy turned as well. A dark-haired young man in a tuxedo was snapping photographs. He saw Sadie and Malloy looking at him and held up his camera—a nice one. "Crime scene," he said, pushing his wire-framed glasses up on his nose. "The, uh, lead detective said I ought to take some preliminary photos." He angled his camera again and took another shot.

Was he at the dinner? Sadie wondered, looking again at the tuxedo the photographer was wearing.

Malloy nodded once before turning back to Sadie. "You need to vacate the stage."

Sadie nodded. She actually agreed with him about that. Even though she'd gone backstage hoping to find something—and she had—she was anxious about the message in the book and what it meant. She headed down the stairs, unsure of what to do next, when she saw Pete stand up from where he'd been talking to Gayle. He saw Sadie and moved down the stairs on his side to meet her, smiling slightly, which she appreciated very much.

"You okay?" he asked sweetly when he reached her. It was quite affirming to know that, amid everything else going on, he was worried about her specifically.

Sadie nodded and found herself wanting to *seem* as though she needed comforting, even though she felt she was handling things quite well. "I suppose," she answered carefully, looking up into Pete's dark eyes and wondering if he would pull her close or touch her face if she looked more like a damsel in distress. He didn't and wanting him to made Sadie feel silly. After waiting another moment, she asked about Gayle. Becoming a whimpering female wasn't her thing. She'd have to leave that role for women less interested in details.

"We're still working on Gayle's official statement," Pete said, looking over his shoulder to where Gayle was talking to another officer.

Sadie nodded, scanning the room again, trying to take in all the details. She worried the hotel staff would never get the frosting out of the carpet. "I found a book backstage," she said, realizing that the sooner they figured out what had happened, the better. She met Pete's eyes and instantly realized he wasn't pleased.

"What were you doing backstage?" Pete asked.

Oops.

"Oh, well, I was just—"

"Detective?"

They both turned to look at Officer Malloy who was standing on the stage a few feet above and to the side of them. "CS just arrived. They're on their way in."

Sadie felt very smart to know that CS was short for *crime scene*—the people who would measure and photograph the body, stage, podium, and surrounding area. Their job was really quite intricate and yet they were definitely behind the scenes. She looked back on stage where the man in the tux had been taking pictures. He wasn't there. "Did the photographer go out to meet them?"

"What photographer?" Pete asked, looking at Sadie.

"He was just there," Sadie said, pointing to the stage. "He must have already been at the dinner since he was wearing a tuxedo." She paused, suddenly thinking it was kind of weird that he had his camera with him at a fund-raising dinner.

Pete turned to Malloy. "Was someone taking pictures?" he asked.

"Um," Malloy turned to look over his shoulder as if someone would give him the answer. "He said he *was* crime scene and that the lead detective had sent him up to the stage—that's you, right?"

"The captain hasn't established a lead detective; he's not even here yet," Pete said, his tone brittle. "Did you check his ID?"

"I'm afraid I was busy with something else." He looked directly at Sadie, and she felt her face heat up.

Pete ran a hand through his hair and barked out the names of a few officers who came running up to stand behind him. "What did the photographer look like?" Pete asked Sadie.

It was rather intimidating to look at so many tight faces at once, but she pulled herself together in order to do her best. "Well," she said, focusing hard so she'd be able to give an accurate description. "Young—maybe mid-twenties, with glasses and dark hair—kind of long and blow-dried forward like the kids wear it these days so it kind of hung in his eyes."

"What was he wearing?" Pete asked, seeming unimpressed with

the details Sadie had remembered so far. She'd better make sure to tell him everything she knew.

"A tuxedo," Sadie repeated. "That's why I wondered if he was a guest at the dinner. The tux was the style that buttoned all the way up. He wasn't wearing a bow tie, and his shoes were black leather, but not patent—they didn't catch the light."

"Height? Build?"

"Oh, um, probably about five-ten or so. Not as tall as you, Pete, uh, Detective Cunningham. Small build—lean, you know. Young—maybe mid-twenties? Did I say that already? And he had a nice camera with a neck strap—a Nikon I think." She was pretty sure she'd seen the N and I printed on the strap around his neck.

Pete turned to the officers. "Find him. He's got photos he's not supposed to have."

"And no good reason to have taken them," Sadie added as the officers began spreading out across the room.

Pete turned back to her, looking a little bit annoyed. Not with her she hoped.

"Show him the book," she said to Officer Malloy in hopes of appeasing Pete, whose mood had turned decidedly sour over the course of the last couple minutes. She'd really like to get back to the compassionate feelings he'd been showing toward her earlier. "I already told him about it, but not what it said. Was the message left by the killer, do you think? Who else would write such a thing?"

"Sadie," Pete said suddenly. He took her arm and turned her away from Malloy, who was still standing on the stage—and not retrieving the book like she'd asked him to. "I think it would be best if you go home now," Pete continued when they were a few feet away. He smelled like the Aspen cologne he always wore, but the expression on his face was unfamiliar and equally uncomfortable.

"Why?" Sadie asked, looking up at Pete with surprise. The last thing she wanted to do was go home. She wanted to stay here, help where she could, and be close to Pete.

Apparently Pete didn't agree with her. "It's not appropriate for you to be here."

"But I helped organize this dinner, and I have been here for the whole thing. And I found the book. I can answer a lot of questions, Pete, you know I can. I won't get in the way—I promise." The idea of going home with all this going on was unfathomable.

Pete took a breath. "Look, I appreciate your passion for this kind of thing, but civilians tend to get in the way."

Ouch. "I like to think I'm not just some civilian off the street," Sadie said, trying to sound diplomatic and hide her hurt feelings. Pete looked like he needed some convincing. "I was thinking that whoever rigged this had to have access to the wireless microphone system between my welcome and Thom's speech. That means—"

"Sadie," Pete said, the pressure of his hand tightening on her arm as he leaned close and lowered his voice. "Don't do this."

CHAPTER 5

It was on the tip of Sadie's tongue to argue, but instead she looked into Pete's face. Concerned intensity—that was what she saw in the set of his jaw—as if he were bracing himself for her reaction. She hated him looking at her that way and felt her determination begin to crumble as he continued to explain himself, "This is a very sensitive situation. Plus I think Gayle needs to go home. We'll need to wait on getting a full statement until she's calmed down some. Please, help your friend, and let me do my job."

The pleading tone of his voice took the wind right out of Sadie's sails. She looked past him to Gayle, still sitting several feet away. She was trying to look as though she wasn't crying, but her chin was quivering and she kept wiping at her eyes and nose. She was sitting alone and it made her look vulnerable, which tugged at Sadie's heart. Police officers were everywhere, talking to witnesses and taking notes. To Sadie's left was the stage, and she could just make out the leg of Mr. Ogreski behind a cluster of people. The crime scene unit was securing the stage, getting everyone off so they could do their job. A *job*—something Sadie did not have. All of these official people were here to do a job. Like Pete had said, Sadie was just a civilian.

Humble pie was never a tasty dish, but Sadie nodded, a bit embarrassed by her assumption that she was an integral part of the investigation. She was Sadie Hoffmiller, a widow and retired teacher who had found herself in one too many of these kinds of situations and had forgotten how serious they were.

"The thing is," Pete said, softening his tone a bit, "even though things worked out well in the end, the way you became, uh, involved in Anne's case left a bad taste in the mouths of some people at the precinct."

Sadie looked past Pete at the other officers around the room, truly surprised to hear him say such a thing. How could they have a bad taste in their mouths about what she'd done when Anne was murdered? Sadie was the reason the case had been solved at all. "That's ridiculous," she said, lowering her voice and narrowing her eyes at Officer Malloy, who stood speaking to someone on the opposite side of the room. There was no doubt he was one with that *bad taste*. She moved her eyes back to meet Pete's. "I mean, you defended me, right?"

Pete paused too long, and Sadie gasped slightly. He *hadn't* defended her?

He hurried to save himself. "It's not that *everyone* thinks you're a busybody, but—"

"A busybody!" Sadie repeated, even more offended. Did they all talk about her that way? Was she gossip fodder at the local police station? Granted, she did have certain busybody tendencies, but to summarize her that way was so . . . dismissive of the good she'd done through being a little bit hyper-curious at times.

Pete shook his head and put up his hands in front of his chest, making a calm-down gesture. "Okay, this really isn't the time for this discussion—I'm working a case and I can't seem to find the right words, but it doesn't reflect well on me to have my girlfriend asking questions that could potentially undermine the investigation. I'm sorry. I know you like to be in the heart of things, but everyone is watching you very closely, and neither you nor I can afford to step out of line even a little bit, which is why I need you to go home and lay low, okay?" He flipped a few pages in his notebook. "I'll write you a note so they'll let you leave."

Sadie was still hung up on the word *girlfriend*.

"Girlfriend?" she asked out loud. He'd never referred to her that way before and although saying it out loud made her feel like she was thirteen, she couldn't help it.

Pete blushed slightly—which was darling. "I've got to keep my mind on my work tonight, Sadie. Please."

As opposed to keeping his mind on *her*? Sadie smiled, flattered by the implication that she had the power to distract him.

Pete seemed to pick up the implication as well. He looked around as though making sure no one had overheard, then he rubbed his chin and made eye contact with Sadie.

His beautiful hazel eyes nearly melted her.

"Maybe Gayle ought to stay at your place tonight," he said. "She's had quite a shock and probably shouldn't be home alone. We'll have both of you come in tomorrow, when she's calmed down a little bit, and give us an official statement. We have enough for now."

"Okay," Sadie nodded. The word *girlfriend* replayed in her mind over and over and all her negative feelings had been laid to rest.

Sadie likely could have walked to New York City and back in the time she'd spent pondering her relationship with Pete these last few months. They always had a good time together, but there was a distance he'd never tried to breach. Sadie credited his hesitations to the loss of his wife two and a half years ago; as a widow, she understood that moving on was difficult when you had fully expected to spend your life with the person you married. Even twenty years after Neil's death, Sadie struggled with the fear that letting another man into her life would somehow replace Neil. Empathy for those feelings was why Sadie hadn't pushed for more than what Pete was willing to offer. But the fact that he called her his girlfriend—well, that was big!

"I'll talk to you tomorrow," Pete said, giving her a parting smile as he let go of her arm and turned back toward the stage.

Sadie nodded, still a bit dreamy. After a few more seconds, she headed toward Gayle, who was looking a little more composed. Her eyes were closed and she seemed to be making a concerted effort to take deep breaths. Mascara was still smeared all over her face, and Sadie reminded herself to make sure Gayle had cleaned up before she looked in a mirror.

"It's time to go," Sadie said, her voice rather cheery considering the circumstances. She cleared her throat, hoping to find a more appropriate tone. Gayle opened her red and black-rimmed eyes. "Pete said you should come to my place," Sadie continued. "I think that's a good idea." She put a hand under Gayle's elbow and helped her stand up. "How are you doing?"

"Horrible," Gayle said. "I keep seeing it in my head over and over again."

Sadie patted her friend's arm. "Well, maybe a hot bath and some French chocolate will help," she said, thinking of Gayle's favorite hot beverage of choice. It was a favorite of Shawn's as well.

Shawn!

Sadie's heart sunk. This was Shawn's first trip home since

Thanksgiving. Of all the bad luck—he had to choose the weekend of a murder. She suddenly remembered that her phone was in her purse in the car. What if he'd heard about what had happened and was trying to call her? Suddenly anxious to get home to her son, Sadie headed for the ballroom doors, still holding Gayle's arm. And yet, even in the chaos around her, Sadie couldn't help but wonder how long it would be before she and Pete would discuss this new level of their relationship. The idea made her toes tingle all over again.

Chapter 6

Sadie considered telling the officer posted at the ballroom door that she could be reached at any time if they needed her. The thought embarrassed her all over again. What was wrong with her? She wasn't a detective—but she *was* a detective's girlfriend. The thought made her all fluttery again. As soon as she and Gayle entered the hotel foyer, they were pounced upon by other attendees at the dinner—friends and people in the community worried about Gayle, everyone asking Sadie what was going on in the ballroom. It seemed to take forever before Sadie managed to appease the crowd enough that she and Gayle could move forward.

They were nearly to the front doors when Sadie stopped. "Oh, biscuits," she said in a huff before turning toward Gayle. "I had to bring all those cakes in so I parked around back. We have to go out through the kitchen."

Gayle's shoulders slumped as if she couldn't handle the strain of turning around, but she nodded and headed toward the swinging doors to the right of the ballroom with Sadie. Janet Reese threw her arms around Sadie's neck, causing her to stumble backward before she regained her balance. Apparently Janet had been at one of the front tables; the podium had hit their table when the recoil sent it falling backward. Sadie had no sooner untangled herself from Janet when Denise Braden appeared in front of her; she was worried about her kids at home who she'd left with a sitter. Being a good friend to so many people made Sadie a natural outlet, but now was not the time. She felt horrible putting them off, but kept repeating how she needed to get Gayle home. She finally managed to get Janet and Denise to talk to one another and slipped away.

They reached the swinging doors and escaped the foyer, entering a small utilitarian hallway with chairs and tables propped against the walls. Access doors on the right led to the stage portion of the ballroom while double doors on the left led to the kitchen itself. All of the doors were closed, making Sadie feel cocooned and protected—for the moment anyway.

She pushed open the kitchen doors and encountered a chaos that had been undetectable in the little hallway. Some of the servers talked in scattered groups while others were trying to take care of the leftover food. Andy, the manager of the catering service she'd hired for everything but the cakes, saw them and raised his hands and eyes toward the ceiling as if offering a prayer. He was quite dramatic, which Sadie usually found amusing but wasn't in the mood for right now. She was *trying* to focus on getting Gayle home. It was harder than it looked.

"Oh, Sadie, Sadie, Sadie," Andy said as he hurried toward her, dodging servers as he made his way across the room. "This is just disastrous," he said, throwing his hands up again. "And right while serving your cake too." He shook his head. "What a tragic turn to the evening."

"I know," Sadie said, nodding. "It's all so terrible. I need to take Gayle home. She was on the stage when it happened, you know."

Andy looked at Gayle for the first time and visibly startled at her appearance. Sadie cringed inwardly. No one else had reacted to Gayle's unfortunate makeup situation, and she'd been hoping to keep it that way. Between Gayle's green contacts that made her eyes look almost iridescent against her pale skin and the mascara smears, she looked like a cast member on a low-budget zombie movie.

"Oh, darling," Andy said, putting his hand on Gayle's arm. "You look awful."

"I *feel* awful," Gayle said, her voice flat.

"It shows, believe me," Andy said, his eyebrows creased. "You can't go out looking like this. Let's get you cleaned up."

"What do you mean?" Gayle asked while Sadie winced. "Looking like what?"

"I'll, uh, take the leftover cakes to my car," Sadie said sheepishly as Andy led Gayle to the small hand-washing sink in the corner.

Unfortunately for Gayle—and Sadie—there was a small mirror above the sink. Gayle gasped and ducked slightly upon seeing her reflection. Sadie turned her attention to the cakes in order to avoid the guilt of having allowed Gayle to become so undone. But it wasn't like she'd had a lot of options.

There were three full-sized cakes on the far right counter and one partial. Apparently several women had stuck to their New Year's resolution of not eating dessert.

As she boxed up the cakes, she fantasized about sitting down in a corner and eating an entire cake herself—if for no other reason than to distract herself from everything else. The urge was strong enough that her knees went weak for a moment and her mouth watered. She'd never eaten a full cake by herself, but tonight seemed like a fabulous time to try.

She began moving faster, hoping to ignore the temptation. She picked up a marker from the counter and wrote Andy's name on the box with the partial cake in it so he could take it home to his wife and their two girls. It wasn't much, but Sadie hoped it would let him know how grateful she was for his help. In addition to helping Sadie procure the pink bakery boxes she'd used to transport the cakes, Andy had also walked her through the necessary steps to get a food handler's permit plus a certificate allowing for the off-site preparation of the cakes in the first place. Red tape—what a nightmare!

"I'll be right back," she said a minute later as she turned toward the outside door at the back of the kitchen with the first cake box in her hands. Andy nodded, busy wiping Gayle's face with a dish towel. Sadie hurried to the door, not relishing the scowl she was sure Gayle would send her way as soon as she could.

It was snowing outside—a soft, floating snow that was devoid of wind, thank goodness. Sadie took careful steps, not wanting to slip on the wet pavement, as she headed for the row of cars on the far side of the lot. When she reached her car, she balanced the cake against her hip with one hand and pushed the code into the number pad set beneath the handle on the driver's door. She'd fallen in love with the feature when she'd seen the Ford Taurus on the lot three years ago. To never have to worry about locking her keys in the car again? Priceless.

The locks clicked, and she opened the back door and put the cake on the seat. As she reached to shut the door, she heard the chime of her cell phone alerting her that she'd missed a call.

Shawn!

She hurried to the driver's door and reached under the seat for her purse. Quickly retrieving her phone, she saw that Shawn had texted her four times—each text a little more anxious than the one before. News traveled fast in a small town and she hated that he was worried about her on his weekend home. She slid into the driver's seat and pulled the door shut, trying not to shiver as she typed a reply to his most recent text—sent six minutes earlier.

It seemed like it took forever to text back the message that she was fine and she'd talk to him at home. In addition to the texts, she saw she had a voice mail message. She assumed it was also from her son, but she looked up the call log just to be sure. The call was from a number she didn't recognize with a Denver area code. Who did she know in Denver who would call her tonight?

Glancing at the closed kitchen door, she decided to take a few seconds to satisfy her curiosity about the mystery message. Besides, Gayle might not be ready yet, and Sadie wanted to put off the moment where she apologized profusely a little longer.

The voice in the message was familiar, but not instantly recognizable. "Hi, Sadie, I've got some questions for you. Give me a call as soon as you get this, okay?"

Sadie furrowed her brow and replayed the message, hoping she'd recognize the voice if she heard it a second time. She didn't. It was definitely a woman, though. Obviously, whoever it was expected Sadie to know her since she hadn't left a name.

Shawn texted back saying he'd tried to come to the hotel, but the parking lot was blocked off. Sadie assured him she'd be home within the next half hour and that he should stay home until she arrived. After sending the message, she considered calling the Denver number, but decided against it. She'd call once she was home and things had settled down. She put her phone on the passenger seat, cursing the fact that formal gowns didn't have pockets. After shutting the car door behind her, she hurried back inside to gather the other cakes. She reviewed the phone message in her mind again,

DEVIL'S FOOD CAKE

annoyed that she couldn't pinpoint the voice. It was right there—a wispy memory hovering just beyond her frontal lobe.

Denver? Hmm.

Sadie reached the door that would lead her back to the kitchen, but before she'd even touched the handle, the door flew open, missing her face by mere inches only because she reeled backward, completely losing her balance as she dodged the metal door. Her arms windmilled and her back tensed while she pleaded with gravity to have mercy on her. Just as she realized she was going down, a hand grabbed her arm and steadied her. Relief washed over her until she realized that whoever saved her was also the one who caused her to almost fall in the first place. She looked up into the face of her attacker-slash-rescuer, prepared to give him a reprimand—in the set of her eyes if nothing else—when she realized she'd seen him before. A black camera bag was slung over his shoulder, the word Nikon clearly printed on the top of the leather case.

The photographer!

He was holding a cell phone to his ear with the hand not holding her up.

"Yeah," he said into the phone, barely paying her any attention. "I'll come back for the car. How far away—"

"You?" she said, astonished.

He let go of her arm and looked at her for perhaps the first time, lowering the phone from his ear. "Me?" he asked as his eyebrows came together behind his glasses.

Sadie nodded. "You were taking photos."

He paused a moment, and when he spoke his tone was intent on his words. "What goes around comes around."

"I beg your pardon." Sadie pulled back slightly. "There was a murder tonight and you were snapping photos like some kind of tourist. The police are looking for you." She glanced toward the door, willing an officer to come crashing through it. Though she was quite proud of her Tae Kwon Do skills, she *was* in a dress and heels.

"Looks like there were *two* murders, lady," the young man said. "I wanted proof it had finally come full circle. Maybe the police will actually figure this one out." He looked over his shoulder briefly and then stepped around her while putting the phone back to his ear.

"You here yet?" he said into the phone. A car pulled into the lot and he took long strides away from Sadie. The Carmichael Hotel had a loading dock in back for deliveries and staff that was separate from the main parking lot out front provided for guests. As Sadie watched the car pull up next to the photographer, she looked around and realized how isolated they were—and how perfect the back lot was set up for a getaway. And that's exactly what the cryptic photographer was doing—getting away!

"Wait just a minute," Sadie called to him. She picked up her skirts to follow him, but mincing steps in pinching shoes were no match for his long legs. He didn't even look at her as he snapped his phone closed and slid it into his camera bag. By the time she'd moved a few steps, he'd already reached the car. He pulled open the door, and Sadie startled as the dome light lit up the face of the driver—another face Sadie recognized.

Trixie-Bambi looked momentarily panicked as she met Sadie's shocked expression and then shooed the photographer into the car.

The photographer didn't seem to be in any rush, however. He turned to Sadie and held her eyes. "He's not a good man," he said quickly, folding himself into the front seat of the car. Before he pulled the door shut, he added, "Not all deaths are tragic ones."

CHAPTER 7

The door snapped shut and the engine revved as the car headed out of the lot. Why hadn't the police blocked it off yet? Did they even know it was here? Sadie could do nothing but stand and watch while the snow continued its lazy descent.

"Who wasn't a good man?" she asked herself. *Mr. Ogreski?* What was the photographer's connection to Mr. Ogreski? And did Frank know his niece was involved in this? Whatever *this* was. Sadie thought back to the girl's ignorance about Thom and his book. But obviously she knew more than she'd been letting on at dinner.

"Two murders?" she mumbled to herself as she turned back to the kitchen, deep in thought. What did it mean?

She had to talk to Pete, although she wondered how he'd make any more sense of this than she had. Sadie was nearly to the door of the kitchen when it was thrown open again and she lost her balance for the second time. This time, though, it was a police officer who grabbed Sadie's arm to steady her at the precise instant she realized she was going down.

"Did a man come through here?" the officer asked without even apologizing, looking around the parking lot as if hoping to find who he was after. "In a tuxedo? With a camera bag?"

"Yes," Sadie said with a nod as she regained her balance and the officer let go of her arm. "A car just picked him up. Has there been another murder?"

The officer headed toward the driveway but stopped and looked back at her. "Another murder?" he repeated, clearly confused and a little wary of her question. "What do you mean?"

"The man said there were two murders."

The officer lifted his eyebrows and grabbed the speaker-thing on his shoulder. "Harper to dispatch—cameraman has left the building through the back; told someone there was another murder. Call in Fort Collins. We might have a serial killer on our hands."

"A serial killer?" Sadie looked toward the darkened entryway through which the car had disappeared. That wasn't what she'd meant to imply, but there was no denying what the man had said. Did serial killers wear tuxedos? Sadie thought of Ted Bundy. He'd been the type who would definitely wear a tuxedo . . . *and* take pictures of a corpse.

The officer returned to Sadie and pulled open the kitchen door. "Come with me," he said sternly.

Sadie nodded and followed him, wishing she'd brought her cell phone so she could call Shawn and tell him she was going to be late.

Ten minutes later she was seated in a corner of the ballroom, tapping her foot. Sadie had told the officer about the getaway car, but that didn't stop him from ordering four officers to take up an exterior search. All the exterior doors had been locked to make sure no one came back in since now they were shorthanded. Apparently they believed her enough to keep her close, but not enough to accept that the photographer was halfway to Denver by now.

But wait, Sadie thought, *he said he'd be back for his car.* Did that mean he was staying in town somewhere? If his car was still in the lot, maybe the police could run the plates!

Invigorated by her idea, she looked around to find someone she could tell, but there was no one close by and all the officers were talking to someone else or to each other. She slumped back in her chair and crossed her arms over her chest.

Gayle was still in the kitchen with Andy, and while Sadie was sure her friend was in good hands, it wasn't in Sadie's nature to simply wait around. She needed to finish loading the cakes, take Gayle home, and assure Shawn that she was all right. What she *didn't* need to do was sit here and cool her heels until someone came and asked her the questions they said they wanted to ask her. Urgency was warranted here, and she wasn't seeing very much of it. It didn't help that while she waited, she had to stare at all the plates of unfinished cake set out on the few tables that were still standing. She'd used her friend Sandra's Chocolicious Frosting for the cakes, and it was the perfect accompaniment to the dense devil's food. It was a tragedy for it to go to waste like this, and she wished she dared steal one of the untouched plates. Never mind that she'd have three cakes all her own once she got home.

Pete came toward her, grabbed a chair and spun it around so he was facing her. He had so much finesse. She wondered if he sat this close to everyone he took statements from or if he were purposely sitting closer to her. She preferred to believe the latter. He didn't smile this time; certainly the weight of the investigation was getting to him as the minutes ticked by.

"So, the photographer said something to you on his way out?"

Pete said as he flipped a page of his notebook and wrote some things down. Sadie had an instant flashback to their first meeting in her living room when he'd been asking questions about the death of her neighbor. She'd thought him kind and handsome that day. It was discouraging to realize their relationship wasn't much different now than it had been then. She knew more about him, of course, and they'd spent time together, but as far as levels of relationships went, they weren't much beyond the typical get-to-know-you conversations. How very sad. Was it different now that he'd called her his girlfriend? She tried to note a different expression on his face, a kind of welcome to this new place they were in. However, if anything he seemed more guarded, less at ease.

"Sadie?"

She shook herself back to the moment and smiled to cover up her wandering thoughts. "Yes," she said with a nod, catching up with the question he'd asked. "I spoke with the photographer."

"Please relay to me the conversation," Pete said in a formal tone.

Sadie cleared her throat and sat up straight, attempting to match his professional manner. If this was how he needed to play it, she'd go along with it. "Well, I said 'You?' and he said 'Me?' and I said he'd been taking photos like he was a tourist and then he said there had been two murders and he took the pictures as proof that everything had come full circle." Through the course of murder investigations she'd been involved in, she'd become rather good at giving her statements in as few words as possible. "Oh, and he said Mr. Ogreski wasn't a good man and not all deaths were tragic."

"That's all he said?" Pete looked up at her with a searching expression in his eyes.

Sadie nodded. "He was also on the phone at the same time and talked about the parking lot being blocked off. I'm pretty sure he was talking to the gal who picked him up a minute later: Trixie-Bambi."

"Who?"

"Oh," Sadie said, realizing she'd left that part out. She hurried to describe Frank's niece—Michele—the driver of the getaway car. By the time she'd finished, Pete looked as confused as she felt. "A lot of planning went into this, don't you think?" Sadie prodded.

Pete didn't answer her, and she tried not to take it as a reprimand.

"Where did the serial killer statement come from?" Pete asked, looking back at his notes. "Did you come up with that?"

"Of course not," Sadie said, offended. "It would be a completely unprofessional jump to conclusions for me to make that type of assumption." And though Sadie was prone to conclusion-jumping, it was something she was working on. She didn't appreciate being falsely accused.

"So who said it?" Pete asked.

Sadie didn't want to cast the police officer in a bad light, but didn't see how it could be avoided if she were determined to tell the truth. "The officer who nearly knocked me down," she said. "I asked if there was another murder—you know, because the photographer had said there were two—and the officer seemed to think it meant we had a serial killer. I'm assuming there haven't been any other bodies found?" If there had, she didn't think they'd have let her sit here for so long before they questioned her.

"Two murders," Pete repeated. He tapped his pen on his notes. "We've searched the hotel, if there were other bodies here we'd have found them."

"That's good," Sadie said, trying to sound optimistic.

"Tell me how you found the book."

We're back to that? Sadie wondered. The trace amounts of censure in his voice prickled Sadie's defenses. It was getting harder and harder to give Pete the benefit of the doubt. Still, she *was* trying. "I saw something on the chair and thought it might belong to Thom. I opened the book thinking he might have put notes inside it. He wasn't holding anything when he left the ballroom. Has anyone found him yet, by the way?"

Pete shook his head. "You assume the book belonged to Thom." It wasn't a question.

Sadie considered that. "He's the author," she said with a shrug. It seemed pretty obvious to her. Someone sent Thom a cryptic message written inside his own book—very pointed. But it was still confusing. Who, exactly, was sorry? And for what? Killing his manager? Or was it supposed to have been Thom behind the podium? If that were the case, who was being apologized to?

"Hmm," Pete said. Sadie could hear the caution in his tone. However, she also sensed he was trying to use her as a sounding board. She liked that a lot. After all, she *was* part of organizing the evening and in attendance for the entire dinner, not to mention being a witness to the murder, Thom's suspicious exit, and the photographer's hasty retreat and cryptic words. Sadie wasn't prone to self-adulation, but she couldn't help but wonder what they would do without her. She liked to think that despite Pete's reserved approach with her right now, *he* believed and respected what she had to say, which was why they were still talking.

Sadie spoke up again. "This wasn't Mr. Ogreski's former hometown but whoever arranged this killing went to great pains to make certain it was witnessed by the key members of this community. Maybe someone in Garrison isn't as sympathetic toward Thom as it seems. What about the family of the girl Thom's son killed? Sterling isn't too far away, and Damon left wounds I'm sure have never healed for the family. Could someone have been out for revenge?" Wow, sometimes she impressed even herself with the way she could put information together. But why an apology written inside the book? Wouldn't a killer motivated by revenge feel triumphant, not apologetic?

Pete was taking notes again, and Sadie wriggled forward on her chair a little. She touched his knee lightly, causing him to look up at her. She was instantly taken aback by the flash of *fear* in his eyes. She looked at her fingertips on his knee and pulled them back, thinking that perhaps he was uncomfortable with her touching him when he was on the job. "You said you worked Damon's case," she said.

Pete nodded, his professional mask back in place.

"I'm just curious," she said. "Didn't Damon also use a sawed-off shotgun?" Her recollection of the details were fuzzy, but Pete would know.

Pete pulled back, frowning as he contemplated her question. "I can't tell you that, Sadie."

Sadie felt her eyes narrow slightly but quickly corrected the expression. If the gun Damon had used *hadn't* been a sawed-off shotgun, Pete would have no trouble telling her so. Assured she had her answer, Sadie moved on.

"Two murders," Sadie repeated, leaning toward him, but not touching him this time. "Two of the people closest to Thom are dead. What if Damon's death wasn't a suicide? What if that's what the photographer meant?"

Sandra's Chocolicious Frosting

½ cup butter
2 tablespoons shortening
1 cup baking cocoa
8 ounces cream cheese
3 cups powdered sugar
1 teaspoon vanilla

Melt butter and shortening. Whisk in cocoa and stir until smooth. Let cool until it is cool enough to touch. Add cream cheese and mix thoroughly. Add powdered sugar and vanilla. Mix well.

Will cover two 9-inch layers or a 9x13 cake.

CHAPTER 8

"It *was* suicide," Pete said, shaking his head and sounding a little offended. "I helped investigate Damon's case, and I don't think her family would come back ten years later for this kind of revenge. They were a good Christian family. They were heartbroken, but not vindictive. They moved to Iowa or someplace after the murder to get a fresh start. And they hadn't been in Sterling long enough to put down roots anyway. We'll talk to them, of course, but Damon killed himself. There's no doubt about that."

"No doubt?" Sadie repeated, watching him closely. "Are you sure?"

"Months before that night, Damon had talked to a school counselor about the suicidal thoughts he'd been having. The counselor called Thom and they met with a psychologist from the district who had a few sessions with Damon. In the end, the psychologist concluded that Damon was simply trying to get attention. He recommended Damon get involved in sports and make more friends."

Sadie remembered that now. The psychologist had resigned from his position after the shooting.

"A sawed-off shotgun is an extreme weapon," Sadie said. "Do

you really think it's a coincidence that Mr. Ogreski was shot with the same type of gun Damon used?"

Pete held her eyes for a moment. "I can't tell you anything more, Sadie," he said, his voice nearly pleading.

Sadie didn't want to make things harder for him and was placated by the fact that he'd trusted her with a little bit of information.

Pete cleared his throat, and when he spoke his tone was formal again. "I'm going to need all this in writing," he said, going back to his notes. "Not the supposition, just everything you actually saw and heard—the facts." There was a coldness to his words, and it suddenly felt like a very long time ago that he'd called Sadie his girlfriend. It was disconcerting for her to see him switch moods so quickly. Confiding in her one moment and then talking down to her the next. Maybe it was her own fault. Was she creating an impossible situation for him?

"Do you need it right now?" Sadie asked, following his lead of trying for emotional distance. She looked at the clock on the ballroom wall: 8:18.

"Is that a problem?" Pete asked.

"Well, Gayle is still in the kitchen and I haven't spoken to Shawn yet. He's waiting for me at the house."

Pete let out a breath. "I'm sorry, but we need it before you leave. It will only take a few minutes. I'll have Malloy bring you the form." He stood up and walked away, not saying thank you or good-bye or anything.

Sadie started tapping her foot again, but not with the anxiety of waiting this time. What was she supposed to make of Pete and his convoluted behavior? And people said women were complicated. They'd obviously never dated a widowed police detective. As Pete walked away, Sadie realized that if she wanted a future with him, she

DEVIL'S FOOD CAKE

was going to have to get used to not knowing everything. It was like sand between her toes to face that fact head-on.

Red, hot sand that burned her poor piggies.

Malloy brought the statement form, and Sadie listened politely while he explained how to fill it out, even though she was old hat at these things. She wondered if she should keep her own supply of statement forms on hand, since she seemed to be some kind of murder magnet lately. It might leave a bad impression on people, however, if she whipped out her own forms, especially with the police already deeming her a busybody. No, what she needed to do was play very, very nice so that they could find nothing in her behavior to censure this time around. As Malloy spoke, she slipped her feet out of her shoes that were becoming unbearable. Maybe the stress was making her feet swell.

After Malloy finished his instructions, she borrowed his pen and then agonized over how to give all the details without being too wordy. It was a very difficult balance and in the end she feared she failed since she'd covered the entire lined side, as well as most of the back of the paper. She knew the police didn't like that, but what else could she do? Leaving out details wasn't smiled upon either. She was careful not to add her "suppositions" and stuck to the facts. When she finished, she slipped her feet back into her pinchy heels, stood up, smoothed her skirt, and headed toward Malloy, who was in a discussion with another officer, both of them facing away from Sadie.

"That's what she said. She was supposed to meet with that Ogreski guy after the event," the other officer was saying.

Sadie stopped about three feet behind the two men. It would only take one of them turning his head to see her. She thought small, invisible thoughts in hopes they wouldn't notice her.

Malloy shook his head. "That's all we need—a reporter with an automatic in. It's awfully convenient that the only person who can confirm the meeting is now bleeding all over the stage."

Sadie scowled at the flippant comment.

The other officer snorted. "No kidding," he said with a nod as he crossed his arms. "But she did come up from Denver. She couldn't have made it here so soon if she hadn't already been on her way."

Sadie lifted her eyebrows. *Denver?* She immediately recalled the 303 area code from the unknown caller on her cell phone.

The officer continued. "Then we'd better get ready for an onslaught. Ms. Jane won't be the last reporter looking for some meat to hook her claws into."

Ms. Jane!

That was who'd left the message! Sadie was relieved to have assigned the voice to an actual person, but she had to wonder why Jane would be calling her in the first place.

Jane Seeley, best known as Ms. Jane due to an advice column she wrote for the *Denver Post*, had contacted Sadie last October for help in fleshing out her articles about Anne's murder and the subsequent trial. It had been the first story the paper had given Jane outside of the advice column and she turned out to be a very thorough reporter. On the phone she came across as nice, but a little intense. Sadie wondered what she'd be like in person. What questions did she have for Sadie now? And how did she get Sadie's cell number? Sadie didn't think she'd given it to Jane when they'd spoken before. And Jane was supposed to meet with Mr. Ogreski tonight?

Malloy spoke again, recapturing Sadie's attention. "Piranhas, the whole lot of 'em," he muttered, turning his head to look at the other officer. When he saw Sadie standing behind him, he clamped his mouth shut, which prompted her to take a quick step forward in hopes that it would look like she was just now approaching.

"I finished my statement," Sadie said, smiling in a reassuring manner and using her sweet-and-innocent tone of voice. No busybodies here, no sirree! She held out the paper and pen to him. "Is there anything else you need?"

"No," Malloy said, but he was looking at her suspiciously. Then again, he looked at her suspiciously most of the time. "You're free to leave."

"Okay," she replied brightly, nodding a friendly hello to the officer standing at Malloy's left. "Good luck."

After pushing through the doors of the ballroom, she scanned the hotel lobby where clusters of people were still scattered about, some people were talking to the police while others were filling out statements. She wanted to call Jane back, but her phone was still in the car. Malloy and the other officer made it sound as though Jane were already here. Outside?

Sadie's stomach churned with the desire to go out front and try to find Jane, but the commitments she'd made quickly squashed that idea. Gayle needed to get out of here, Shawn was waiting, and Sadie had been told more than once to go home. Oh, how it burned! But there wasn't anything she could do—or should do—about it. People she loved needed her and that trumped her curiosity over Jane Seeley.

Out of the corner of her eye, Sadie saw Marline Hansen making her way through the crowd. The woman was wonderful, but she could talk the ear off a rabbit. If Sadie stayed in the lobby, she'd soon be inundated with friends again. She wasn't up to it. Pretending she didn't see Marline, and promising herself she'd take over a plate of Turtle cookies—Marline's favorites—to make up for her rudeness, Sadie turned toward the kitchen and increased her steps.

The kitchen was still crowded with staff when Sadie pushed

through the doors. Andy and Gayle were on folding chairs in one corner, talking, and he patted her hand. Sadie stood by the door for a few seconds, not sure what to do, before spying the two cake boxes still on the counter. She picked up one of the boxes and headed for the outside door, all the while wishing she could just turn off her brain. There were plenty of people in the world who could shrug their shoulders and carry on with their lives amid tragedies such as this—why wasn't she one of them? Why couldn't she just worry about herself instead of wanting to see such a big picture? Life would be far simpler if she could.

Sadie transferred the cake box to one hand and pulled on the door twice before remembering that Pete had ordered all the exits and entrances locked. She turned the heavy dead bolt and made a mental note to make sure Andy locked the door behind them when she and Gayle were ready to leave for good.

Moments later she was in the darkened parking lot again and replaying the last conversation she'd had with the photographer. Had she missed anything? Were there inflections that may have said things she didn't hear?

The snow was coming down harder now and she ducked her head, glad that the evening was over and she didn't have to worry about what the snow was doing to her hair. When she smelled cigarette smoke, she looked up and froze as a tremor ran down her spine. When the photographer had made his getaway, she'd realized how secluded the back lot was. Suddenly she felt very vulnerable.

Sadie squinted in the faint glow from the exterior lights, finally picking out the shape of a person leaning against her car. Sadie's heart abruptly began racing within her chest. Fear wasn't something that came easily for her, but finding herself alone in a parking lot with a stranger—and armed with only a devil's food cake—was a precarious circumstance.

The tall, lanky body pushed itself away from Sadie's car and flicked a cigarette, the red ember twirling through the air before sizzling upon the snow-covered blacktop.

"Sadie Hoffmiller," the person said—and not just any person, but the female voice that Sadie recognized from the cryptic message on her cell phone. Ms. Jane herself.

Tina's Turtle Cookies

1 cup all-purpose flour
⅓ cup cocoa powder
¼ teaspoon salt
½ cup butter, softened
⅔ cup sugar
1 large egg, separated, plus 1 egg white
2 tablespoons milk
1 teaspoon vanilla extract
1 cup pecans, chopped fine
14 soft caramel candies, unwrapped
3 tablespoons heavy cream

Preheat oven to 350 degrees. Line 2 baking sheets with parchment paper or silpat liners. Combine flour, cocoa, and salt in a bowl. Set aside. In a large bowl, beat butter and sugar with an electric mixer on medium-high speed until fluffy. Add egg yolk, milk, and vanilla. Mix until incorporated. Reduce mixer speed to low and add flour mixture until just combined. Refrigerate dough until firm, at least 1 hour.

Whisk the 2 egg whites in another bowl until frothy. Place chopped pecans in another bowl. Roll dough into 1-inch balls, dip in egg whites, then roll in pecans. Place balls 2 inches apart on prepared baking sheets. Using a teaspoon measuring spoon, make an indentation in the center of each ball. Bake 10 to 12 minutes until set, switching and rotating sheets halfway through baking.

While cookies are baking, microwave caramels and cream in a bowl, 1 to 2 minutes, stirring every 30 seconds until smooth. Once cookies are removed from oven, fill each indentation with ½ to 1 teaspoon caramel mixture. Cool 5 minutes, then transfer cookies to wire rack and cool completely.

Makes 3 dozen cookies.

CHAPTER 9

"Can I help you?" Sadie asked, intimidated by the circumstances of this introduction but trying to play it cool. She squinted through the snow, reaching for visual recognition that would make this exchange a lot less creepy.

By the time the woman was within ten feet of her, Sadie was feeling less threatened and more confused. Ms. Jane's picture accompanied every one of her advice columns—a picture of a fine-featured, sweet-faced blonde with a shoulder-length bob. But the woman standing in front of Sadie was at least six feet tall, with black hair combed flat to the front and sides of her head. Her hair was spiked at the crown and tipped with bright red—if the light of the parking lot wasn't creating some kind of optical illusion. Aside from the strange but trendy hair, the woman had a lean face and large, dark eyes. She wasn't wearing any makeup except for red lipstick that seemed a bit too much on her otherwise ordinary face. Despite the lipstick, there was a mannish quality to the woman's features. Sadie wasn't sure she was beautiful, exactly, but there was definitely a striking quality both to her features and the way she held herself with impenetrable confidence.

"And you were at the dinner tonight?" the woman mused, half her mouth pulling up in a sticky red smile. "You've just made my job a lot easier."

"And you are?" Sadie finally asked, trying to equalize the dueling impressions of this woman in her mind.

"Jane Seeley," the woman said, smiling. "I know. I look nothing like my picture."

Sadie shook her head, "No, you don't."

Jane shrugged. "It was a joke."

"What was a joke?" Sadie said, trying to keep up. Did she mean she was joking when she claimed to be Jane? But the voice matched.

"The picture," Jane explained. "I'd been writing freelance for the paper, covering everything from junior high basketball to the increase in eastern religious practices in the rural areas of Colorado. Everyone at the *Post* knew me by name, but I'd never met any of them thanks to e-mail and telephones and I couldn't seem to crack into anything but bit pieces. So, on a whim, I submitted the Ms. Jane column idea—and included a picture of my half-sister, Becca. She was far more the 'look at me and sigh' girl in my family. I meant the whole Ms. Jane thing to be a little tongue-in-cheek but I couldn't help but wonder if being a blonde bombshell would help my chances. What do you know they snapped it up and printed the first one before I had a chance to explain. After that, they felt it would be unprofessional to swap the picture so it stayed. But it's all good. I can be plain Jane and she can be beautiful Becca as long as it's my words people read."

"Oh," Sadie said. Plain was not the word she would use to describe this woman. Intimidating, maybe. They were silent for a moment while Sadie tried to decide whether or not she believed the story. She wondered if it would be rude to ask for ID.

"I'm glad to meet you in person," Jane said. "Did you get my message?"

Sadie didn't answer the question directly. "How did you get my cell number?" She looked from Jane to her car and then back again. "And how did you know that was my car?"

"The same way I get everything else—Google."

Sadie was stunned silent. Her cell number and car information were available through Google?

Jane laughed softly. "About three years ago you headed up a fund-raiser for a youth orchestra. You put your cell number on the flier that they attached to the website for people to download. It was a few pages into the search results so it's pretty buried, but, well, digging is what I do." She pointed her thumb over her shoulder toward Sadie's car. "I had your license plate number on file from when we spoke last fall. I always do backgrounds on my sources."

Even scarier, Sadie thought.

"I'm hurt you didn't recognize my voice, though" Jane said, putting a hand to her chest and pulling her mouth down in a pout. "Most people do."

"We only talked a few times," Sadie said. She was uncomfortable with Jane's assumed familiarity. And that was saying something since Sadie generally made friends with, well, everyone.

"You called me almost two hours ago," Sadie said, getting back to the point. "Why?"

Jane shrugged. "You're the only person I know in Garrison. I thought I'd ask about Thom Mortenson and whether you knew him when he lived here. Did you, by the way?"

"Not very well," she said carefully. "But I thought you were meeting with Mr. Ogreski, not Thom?"

"News travels fast," Jane said, dropping her chin so she was looking down on Sadie in a way that made her want to fix her hair or adjust her dress. "I *was* going to meet with Mr. Ogreski, and now I'm trying to figure out who kept him from our appointment." Jane looked at Sadie intently. "How did you know I was meeting with Mr. Ogreski? I didn't think he'd told anyone, not even Thom."

Why did Sadie feel like she was being set up for something and needed to defend herself? "I heard some police officers talking," she said simply. "You know Mr. Ogreski's dead, right?"

Jane gave a dismissive wave to the comment, her blue fingernail polish catching what little light there was. The flash of color was unexpected, like tiny bolts of blue lightning. Jane fixed Sadie with a piercing look. "Were you actually in there when Mr. Ogreski was shot?"

Sadie felt a shiver run through her at the directness of Jane's questions. "I was there," she finally said. "Did you really have a meeting scheduled with him?"

"At nine-thirty," Jane said with a nod and a frown. "I arrived early and thought I'd catch the end of the lecture. I made it into the parking lot before the police closed it off, but imagine my surprise when I learned my contact had been killed. Blasted cops wouldn't let me inside the building."

"I believe they were comparing reporters to piranhas." She hoped to put off Jane without taking the blame for it.

Instead of defending herself, Jane snapped her teeth together twice and smiled even wider. She looked past Sadie toward the door behind her. "Is that the kitchen? Is the door unlocked?"

Sadie looked over her shoulder to verify they were talking about the same door. Then she turned back to Jane. "What are you doing out here?" Sadie asked, cutting to the chase. "Why find me?"

"You're Sadie Hoffmiller," Jane said evenly. "I read about what happened in England, and I know from talking to you before that you have an eye for detail. I've got to find another way to get the information I need for my story. You could help me."

Sadie wasn't sure whether to feel offended or flattered to be seen as a source of help and information. Maybe a little of both was appropriate. There had been some articles here and there about the events in Devonshire, but it had been two months ago and wasn't big news in America like it had been in the United Kingdom. People didn't talk about it much anymore, which was fine by Sadie. She didn't want bad things to happen around her. She didn't like the idea of people getting hurt or murdered.

"Well, you're welcome to come to my house and talk with me in about half an hour," Sadie offered, curious enough about Jane to be willing to put up with her a little longer, but on her terms, not Jane's. "I'm just leaving."

"I was hoping you could help me get inside," Jane said with a conspiratorial smile.

Sadie shook her head before Jane finished. "You know I can't do that," she said, looking up at the reporter—a reporter who knew the rules about things like this. "It's a crime scene. No one in or out without permission from the police." Except Sadie, it seemed. Pete had planned to write her a note for her to leave the hotel, but he'd never given it to her. Besides, there wasn't a cop at the back door to check for permission anyway.

"I only want to look around and get a visual for the article I need to write. Have they arrested anyone or made noises about who they think would do something like this?"

Sadie shook her head. "No."

Jane glanced at the back door. "Please let me in," she said, but it was more a demand than a request. "I came all the way from Denver to talk to Mr. Ogreski and everyone is treating me like any other stringer hungry for a story. Besides, I've already got the story—or most of it anyway—that's not the problem. What I want to understand is why it ended like this."

Sadie felt the familiar surge of excitement course through her. Jane had a story *before* the shooting! And she'd had a meeting no one was supposed to know about with the man who was now dead on the hotel stage.

Go home, a voice said in her mind. It sounded a lot like Pete's voice, which may have been why it was so easy for Sadie to push it away. "What do you mean, you've got the story?"

Jane narrowed her eyes slightly, as if taking Sadie's measure. "Well, for one thing, Thom's still here." She nodded toward the building behind Sadie.

"What?" Sadie asked. Thom was still at the hotel? How would Jane know that? Though why had Sadie assumed he *wasn't* there?

"They rented a black Camry from the airport Hertz last night," Jane said, her eyes fairly twinkling as she imparted this knowledge. "It's in the lot, but the police are still looking for Thom, right? Without a car, he couldn't get far, especially in the snow. And, quite frankly, the man can't even tie his own shoes these days, let alone escape the dragnet this town has dropped over him."

Sadie was stunned. Jane knew the time and place Thom and Mr. Ogreski had rented their car? Did she get that from Google too?

"What do you mean Thom can't tie his own shoes?"

Jane shook her head. "Oh, come on, that's old news. Thom's had a serious drinking problem for the last few years. It's why he rarely does events anymore."

It wasn't old news for Sadie. "Is that the story you had?" she asked, reviewing in her mind how Thom had looked that night. She admitted he did seem . . . worn out and anxious, but his agent had just been killed right in front of him. Thom was a drunk? No. Sadie didn't see how that could be true. She didn't *want* it to be true. She wanted Thom to be the man who had overcome his tragedies, not fallen victim to them.

"Oh, no," Jane said with emphasis. "What I've got is way better than that, I assure you. But the alcoholism does factor in." She looked at the cake in Sadie's hands. "Do you need help with that?"

Sadie glanced down at the cake box she'd forgotten she was holding. There was a thin layer of snow on top of the cardboard. She was grateful for the turn in conversation because it gave her an excuse to move forward and think about what Jane had said.

"I need to get this cake in the car," Sadie said, still skeptical of this reporter but willing to take her offer of assistance. Jane stepped aside to let her by.

Jane followed her while Sadie transferred the cake to one hand so she could type in the door code and unlock the car, careful to shield the number pad from Jane's eyes. One could never be too careful. Once Sadie had unlocked all the doors, Jane pulled the back door open and made a dramatic bow.

"Thank you," Sadie said as she leaned in, positioning the box squarely next to the other one on the backseat. She took her time, thinking about what to say once she returned to the conversation. With the cake box properly placed, Sadie stood up to ask Jane another question about the story, only to find herself once again alone in the parking lot. She looked to her right and her left. No one was there.

"Jane?" she asked.

The slightest movement by the back of the hotel caught her eye—the kitchen door falling closed.

Chapter 10

As soon as Sadie entered the kitchen, she scanned the room for Jane. The woman only had a few seconds' head start. However, Andy made a beeline in Sadie's direction. She had no choice but to give him her attention though she continued to look for the rogue reporter.

"I got most of the mascara off with some olive oil," Andy said. "But she really should use a good cleanser. Those pores need to be opened up as soon as possible."

Jane wasn't in the kitchen, which meant she'd already made it into the hallway.

"Did you see a woman come in?"

Andy let out a breath and looked annoyed. "People have been in and out all night. What I'm worried about is Gayle."

Sadie turned to look at Gayle, who was still seated near the sink, several feet away from them. Her face was shiny and free of makeup, though her eyes were still red and puffy. But then Sadie caught sight of a woman with short, dark hair in the back of the room. The woman turned—not Jane.

"Sadie? Are you listening to me?"

Reluctantly, Sadie looked back at Andy, whose face showed his frustration. "Vitamin C," he said in slow, clipped tones. "Do you have a vitamin C-based cleanser she can use?"

"Um, yes," Sadie said even though she'd never heard of a vitamin C-based cleanser. Orange juice mixed with sugar, maybe? She looked past Andy again and focused on the doors leading to the hallway. Every second she waited allowed Jane to get further away. "I'm sorry, Andy, but I really have to do something. I'll be right back." Sadie didn't meet his eyes as she passed him. He let out an audible sigh, obviously frustrated with her. She hated that, but what could she do?

Sadie hurried into the hallway. Empty. She bit her lip and considered her options. On the one hand, she wanted to go home and let Jane get caught on her own. But Jane wasn't supposed to be here, and she'd tricked Sadie to get inside, which was a sure sign that the reporter couldn't be trusted.

Sadie groaned and took a breath as she headed for the doors to the main ballroom. She didn't have time to search the hotel—and it wasn't her job anyway—but she had to tell Pete, regardless of how much she dreaded having to talk to him again after being dismissed twice already.

All the lights in the ballroom had been turned up, all the better to put the absolute mess on display. It was horrible. Sadie feared that if the staff didn't start cleaning soon, they'd all be there until two o'clock in the morning. She finally saw Pete on the stage, discussing something with two important-looking men. A gurney stood off to the side with a big, black lumpy bag strapped to it. Little tented pieces of paper were all over the place. Evidence markers, Sadie guessed.

She walked to the bottom of the stage stairs, waiting for Pete to notice her. He didn't. She shifted her weight, anxious to get it over with. He still didn't see her. With another sigh, she picked up her skirts and climbed the steps with heavy feet before stopping a few feet away from the three men. After waiting a few more seconds in hopes Pete would perhaps *feel* her presence, she gave up and cleared her throat. He didn't notice. She cleared her throat again—much louder. This time Pete turned around. The two men with him looked in her direction as well. She was immediately reminded that she'd been out in the snow for several minutes. Her hair must be a sight—and not a good one. She forced a smile and lifted a hand casually to her hair, attempting to re-lift the roots which were decidedly flattened. So much for wooing Pete's good favor through her stunning good looks.

"Sadie," Pete said with forced politeness.

She smiled and motioned him to come toward her. After a slight hesitation, he excused himself from the other men and walked toward her. When he drew close, he took her arm and walked her down the steps. She could feel the tension in him and hated that she was adding to it.

"Why are you still here?" he said, leaning toward her as he spoke.

"I need to tell you something important." She gave him a strong look that she hoped would communicate how important this was and that she wouldn't interrupt him otherwise. "I was taking a cake out to the car and I ran into a reporter."

"There are dozens of reporters here," Pete said, putting one hand in his pocket. Even though she couldn't see it, she knew it was clenched in a fist. "If you would leave, they'd stop bothering you."

"She wasn't bothering me," Sadie said, hating his dismissive and annoyed tone. She knew it seemed as though she kept sticking her nose in the case, but she wasn't doing it on purpose. "Well, I mean she *was* bothering me, but that's not my point. She said—"

"Detective Cunningham?"

Pete turned to look up at one of the men on the stage. The man had a thin face and heavy eyebrows in serious need of a trim and which served to give him a decidedly severe look. He wasn't in a uniform, but Sadie felt sure he was very important all the same. Maybe he was a plainclothes detective, like Pete.

The man lifted his eyebrows in an unspoken question: Were they going to get on with their discussion or not? Sadie expected the man wasn't the type who took well to waiting. She could relate and hoped he could count to ten or something. She put her hand on Pete's arm to get his attention. If she could just get the words out, she could leave and go home like Pete had asked.

"This reporter," Sadie said. "Ms. Jane, she's—"

"Look," Pete said, cutting her off. He attempted to smile, perhaps to soften his tone, but the stress and strain of the situation made the smile rather ineffective. "The medical examiner just arrived from Fort Collins and the captain is here. I *really* can't talk to you right now." He looked over his shoulder at the two men who had gone back to their discussion. A discussion Pete obviously wanted to be a part of.

"But you need to know that this reporter—Jane Seeley from the *Post*—is here. She's inside the hotel." Sadie leaned close to him and whispered the rest of what she had to say. "She was supposed to meet with Mr. Ogreski tonight." She pulled back, nodding knowingly. That was important information, right?

Pete looked at her, not registering any enthusiasm for what she'd said. "Okay," he said tightly, "I'll take care of it."

The flippancy was impossible to ignore. "Did you hear what I said?" Sadie asked. "A reporter is here. She came in through the kitchen when I was taking cakes out to my car—"

That got his attention. "The doors are supposed to be locked," Pete said.

"Well, I had to unlock it so I could take my cakes out," Sadie said, though she was reluctant to admit she'd been part of the reason Jane had come in. "But I didn't *let* her in," Sadie hurried to explain. "In fact I told her she *couldn't* come in. But then I turned to put the cake in the car and she snuck inside."

Pete's jaw clenched, and he didn't speak for a few moments.

"I'm sorry," Sadie said. "And I'm going home, but I wanted to make sure you knew about Jane being here."

When Pete spoke, his voice was tight. "Go home, Sadie," he said, and she suddenly felt like a disobedient puppy. "Your interest in this case is *not* normal and it *has* been noticed. You are creating a problem that is becoming an issue." He nodded slightly over his shoulder at the man with the wiry eyebrows. "I'll call you tomorrow, okay?"

Sadie didn't know what to think so she just nodded and turned away, feeling foolish for interrupting Pete in the first place, especially if people felt she was interfering. She wasn't trying to be a bother; she was just trying to do the right thing. And Pete didn't seem to even care about Jane. It didn't matter that Jane was in the building and that *Sadie* had been the one ordered to leave? Humph.

Go home, Sadie. Pete's words repeated in her mind, and she was determined to do exactly that. She didn't want to talk to Pete or anyone else anymore. Nothing was going to get in her way. She would take Gayle home where she'd relieve Shawn's worries and leave this whole case behind. With new determination, she hurried across the ballroom and through the side door, coming into the hallway at the same time Andy pushed through the doors of the kitchen. They met in the middle.

"Sadie!" he said, exasperated. "Either you take Gayle home right now or you get her a room at the hotel. She has got to be off her feet. Shock can cause an awful lot of swelling and it would be a shame for that to happen to her pretty little ankles! I think the woman's had enough trauma for one day, don't you?"

"We're going," Sadie said without a backward glance at the ballroom. She'd done what she could. Where Pete took it from here was up to him. However, if it were *her* case, she'd kick Jane out of the hotel, put an officer on the kitchen door to prevent random reporters from sneaking in, *and* she'd listen to the lady who had so much great information. But, since it wasn't her case, she'd just go home and fix herself some kibble like a good girl.

Woof.

CHAPTER 11

"I've got some lounge pants and a T-shirt you can change into," Sadie said as she pushed open the back door of her house and ushered Gayle inside and out of the increasing snowstorm. It was good to be home. She'd ended up giving Andy one of the full cakes by way of apology and handed the partial cake to one of his employees, leaving her with only the two that she needed to bring in from the car. She'd do it in a minute. "Are you sure you don't want to stay with me?" she asked, giving Gayle one more chance to change her mind.

"No, I'll go to Amber's. It will be fine."

Gayle had called her daughter, Amber, as soon as they left the hotel, and Amber had insisted her mother come stay at her house. She was running to the grocery store for milk and could pick Gayle up from Sadie's house on her way back. Gayle could take the time to change into something more comfortable so she wouldn't be stuck in her evening gown all night. A gown saturated in the trauma of the evening.

"You can stay in Bre's room," Sadie added while leading the way into her bedroom.

"I'm fine," Gayle said. "I don't want Amber to have hurt feelings." Sadie pulled open two drawers before finding her favorite pink-and-black plaid lounge pants. They were three sizes too big but insanely comfortable. She moved to the closet in search of a roomy T-shirt. There wasn't much to choose from. A pox on the Salvation Army drive last month!

"Thank you for the offer," Gayle said as she sat on the edge of the bed, absolutely exhausted. "And thank you for the clothes. But spending a night at Amber's will help me pull myself together much quicker."

Staying at Amber's didn't sound very restful to Sadie; she'd met Amber's kids. She smiled at Gayle's ironic tone, though. It was nice to see a small spark of her old self, though her eyes still had a blank dullness about them.

"She said it would be about twenty minutes," Gayle said, rubbing at her forehead.

Sadie finally found a T-shirt. Last fall, all the Red Cross volunteers had received matching shirts for their help with the blood drive at the Baptist church. The shirt was white, which would match the lounge pants, but the words Got Blood? were printed on the back in red lettering. Sadie frowned. The shirt was definitely not appropriate, but after a quick twice-over through her closet, Sadie realized it was the only shirt she had that would fit over Gayle's—ahem—voluptuousness. Whereas Sadie held her excess weight in her hips, Gayle held hers a bit higher.

"Mom!"

Both women looked toward the door. Sadie offered a comforting smile to her son, Shawn, who nearly filled the doorway. If she and Neil had had any idea they'd have a son of his magnitude, they'd have built their house with ten-foot ceilings throughout. But life had a funny way of throwing you curveballs. Sometimes those curveballs were devastating strikes—like Neil's early death—and sometimes they were home runs—like adopting a beautiful son who, though built like a truck, was as sweet and cuddly as the proverbial teddy bear.

Shawn's eyebrows pulled together as he looked from Sadie to Gayle. "Is Gayle okay?"

"I'll talk to you in a minute," Sadie said, giving him a strong look.

He nodded and backed up to allow Sadie to enter the hallway. She turned to look at Gayle, who was simply staring at the floor and holding the plaid lounge pants to her chest.

"Is there anything else you need, Gayle?" Sadie asked from the doorway, wishing there was more she could do. Then she remembered the French chocolate and felt better. It was Sadie's Aunt Melinda's recipe and perfect for entertaining. There was no party tonight, of course, but something a little fancy seemed like good balm for all the tender emotions of the evening. Plus, it would give Sadie something to do.

Gayle looked up. "I'm good," she said. "I'll be right out."

Sadie smiled and pulled the door shut, taking one last look at the T-shirt she'd laid on the bed. "Wait," she said, opening the door again. "I bet Shawn has a better T-shirt."

"Um, my clothes are still in the wash," Shawn said a little sheepishly from the doorway. It was just like him to bring an entire suitcase of dirty clothes with him on the plane. "Two birds with one stone" is what he called it. Sadie called it "Get Mom to do my laundry any chance I get."

The shirt couldn't be helped, she supposed. She quietly shut the door again, and immediately found herself nearly lifted off the floor in a bear hug from her baby—a two hundred and eighty pound baby. After a moment he returned her to the floor, and looked at her with those soft, brown eyes she'd fallen in love with the day they picked him up from the hospital where his birth mother had left him.

"I'm okay," Sadie said as he let her go. He was Samoan or Tongan by birth—they weren't certain which—and likely had some African-American blood in his genetic pool as well, which accounted for his tightly curled hair that he liked to pick out so it surrounded his head like black foam. "I'm sorry you were so worried. How did you hear about it?"

"Crab has a—"

"Jonathan," Sadie cut in automatically, disappointed that the nickname was still dogging her former student. She'd hoped it had been a third-grade thing he'd grow out of when he stopped pinching everyone during recess, but the name had stuck.

"You're the only one who calls him that," Shawn said with a grin. "Well, other than bill collectors, I guess. Anyway, I was helping him install new speakers in his car when his dad came out and told us. His dad's a volunteer with the fire department so he listens to the scanner all the time."

"You must have been worried sick," Sadie said sympathetically. "I left my phone in the car all night."

Shawn nodded. "The police wouldn't let us in the parking lot so Crab brought me back here. I've seen a couple breaking news reports on TV since I got home, but no one is saying much. So, what happened? I was totally freaking out."

Sadie couldn't help but feel the annoyance in Shawn's voice was a fair turnabout. How many times had she grilled him with the same questions when he had come home late?

"And you said library fund-raisers were boring," she chided.

Shawn put both of his huge hands up in mock surrender. "I take it back. What *happened?*"

"I don't know where to start," Sadie said with a shake of her head. It was amazing how much could happen in a short span of time. "I promised Gayle I'd make her some French chocolate," she said, heading to the kitchen. Shawn was more than a foot taller than Sadie and stood to the side, but it was still a tight squeeze past him in the hallway. "She was backstage and saw the whole thing."

"It happened backstage?"

"No," Sadie said, kicking off her shoes, which meant her skirt pooled on the floor. She grabbed a clothespin from the odds-and-ends drawer. Why people paid so much money for those plastic bag clips when they could get fifty clothespins for two bucks was a mystery to her. She gathered up her skirt so it was a few inches off the ground and used a clothespin to hold it in place on one side. Before heading for the fridge, she grabbed another pin and clipped up the other side. There hadn't been time to change, and besides, Gayle was still in Sadie's bedroom.

"Will you get the hot fudge from the pantry?" she asked as she pulled open the fridge in search of whipping cream. Front and center, however, was what was left of the Angel Snowball cake she'd made a couple days earlier to celebrate Shawn's first weekend home in months. The cake would go great with the French chocolate, and since she'd never finished eating her devil's food cake at the fundraiser, she felt she deserved a slice herself. Of course, she had two full devil's food cakes sitting in her car, but she wasn't sure she or Gayle wanted the reminder right now.

After putting the Angel Snowball cake on the counter, she returned to the fridge for the whipping cream. She shut the fridge at the same time that Shawn thumped the jar of hot fudge on the counter.

"Mom," he said as if running out of patience. "Will you please tell me what happened?"

"Oh, right," Sadie said. While she assembled the things she needed for the French chocolate, she gave Shawn the condensed version of the evening. By the time she finished the account, the milk was heating on the stove, the cream was in the bowl ready to be whipped, and the hot fudge had been softened in the microwave.

Shawn sat down on one of the kitchen chairs and stared at his mother. "You saw it?" he breathed, leaning forward, his eyes wide.

Sadie shook her head. "Not exactly. I was savoring cake, but Gayle was only fifteen feet away when it happened."

"Oy," Shawn said, sitting back in the chair.

She took advantage of the pause in the conversation to start up the electric beaters, whipping the cream into a froth. As she added the powdered sugar and vanilla, she glanced at the clock in the living room. It was 9:12. Two hours ago Mr. Ogreski was alive and well. She wondered if he had a family. How many lives had been changed forever because Mr. Ogreski had chosen to do an introduction? Or had Mr. Ogreski been the intended target all along? And what had prompted Jane's meeting with him?

Jane.

Sadie was still terribly unsettled about that woman being in the hotel, but she tried one more time to talk herself out of it. This wasn't her business, and she needed to stop obsessing about it.

"So what happened next?" Shawn asked, cutting off Sadie's internal reel of unanswerable questions.

Sadie told him about her running to Gayle, and then Pete asking her to clear the stage, and then Thom running from the room. "That's when I found the book," she said.

"The book?" Gayle asked from across the room.

Sadie looked up from where she had been spooning the thick and frothy French chocolate into individual cups. Shawn stood up and helped Gayle to a chair at the kitchen table as if she were an old lady, which, at fifty-one, she certainly was not. But Sadie was impressed by his chivalry. Gayle smiled a thank-you at him as she sat down.

"How are you doing?" Sadie asked with concern. Gayle's color was better, but she still had a bit of the deer-in-the-headlights look about her.

"What book were you talking about?" Gayle asked, ignoring Sadie's question.

"Thom's book." Sadie tapped off the spoon on the side of the third mug, then turned to remove the now-hot milk from the stove. "Well, a copy of it anyway. I found it backstage after the, uh, shooting." She grabbed a ladle from her utensil drawer and carefully poured hot milk into the first of the three mugs.

"It was on the podium next to that pink Post-It note," Gayle said in quick words. Sadie looked up at her friend, splashing hot milk on the counter in the process. "The podium was pushed up against the backstage wall, and when we pulled it out, the book was right on top. Mr. Ogreski picked up the book and gave it to Thom."

"This was right before the shooting?" Sadie asked, thinking through the timeline. "Are you sure?"

Gayle nodded. "I didn't think about it before."

Who did the book belong to? Sadie wondered. "Did Thom open it? Did he read what was written inside?"

"What was written inside?" Shawn and Gayle asked in unison.

DEVIL'S FOOD CAKE

"Oh, didn't I tell you that already?" Sadie asked. "The words 'I'm sorry' were written on the inside cover."

"'I'm sorry'?" Shawn repeated. "Sorry for what?"

Sadie shrugged. "That's what I wondered. I don't know."

"They meant to kill Thom," Gayle said weakly. "I just know it!"

Sadie made a maybe-shrug and began stirring the milk and cream together in the mug. "Do you know if he read it?" Sadie asked Gayle. "When you saw Thom take the book, did he open the front cover?"

Gayle looked at the table in concentration, then shook her head. "I don't remember. He held the book, and then that poor man was on the floor and everyone was screaming."

"But you said Thom left the room," Shawn said to Sadie, leaning his forearms on the edge of the table.

"He did?" Gayle asked, reminding Sadie that, while Gayle had been an eyewitness, she'd still missed a lot of details of the evening. Sadie quickly brought her up to speed on the rest of the story.

"Maybe he ran out because he thought he was the target," Shawn offered.

Sadie picked up a mug in each hand and took them to the table, putting them both down. Gayle wrapped her hands around a mug and hunched over it slightly, as if drawing strength from its warmth. Shawn picked his up and took a quick sip before putting it down and getting back to business. "But seriously, why leave?" Shawn said with a glint in his eye that was a little too familiar to Sadie and threatened to fan the flames of her own insatiable curiosity, which she was barely keeping under control as it was.

Shawn continued, "I mean, his manager gets whacked, and the guy makes a run for it?"

"Like you said, maybe he was scared," Sadie offered. She pulled three plates out of the cupboard and grabbed a knife to slice the cake.

"Or maybe he had something to do with it," Shawn said, putting Sadie's wondering into words. "He was either running in fear or making his getaway."

Gayle shook her head. "I can't believe he's guilty of anything," she said with a sense of finality in her words. "Did you see him tonight, Sadie? He didn't look as good up close, did he?"

Sadie thought back to what Jane had said about Thom's alcohol problem. If it was as bad as Jane said, was he capable of making a rational decision after such a traumatic event? "No, he didn't look good," Sadie agreed. "But Shawn might have a point. If he was somehow involved—"

"I can't believe that," Gayle interrupted, shaking her head.

Sadie and Shawn exchanged a look. It was time to change the subject, but Sadie was sure Shawn was filing away the discussion for later. Maybe it wasn't such a bad thing for Gayle to go to Amber's, Sadie mused. She and Shawn could share ideas a bit more openly once they were alone.

Sadie finished slicing the cake, placed a fork on each plate and slid them next to the mugs on the table. Shawn ate his cake in three bites. Gayle poked at the creamy chocolate filling, but put the fork down. She really had been traumatized if she was passing on chocolate.

"So anyway," Sadie said, after taking a couple bites of the delicious cake. Maybe she'd have another piece after Gayle left. "After I picked up the book, a police officer came and I gave it to him. Then we saw this photographer on stage who said he was crime scene, except he wasn't, and later he came barreling through the parking lot when I was taking cakes out to the car and said something about there being two murders and that everything had come full circle and then he drove off with Trixie-Bambi."

"Who?" Shawn and Gayle asked at the same time.

Sadie blushed at the internal nickname she'd given the girl and couldn't seem to shake. And she was critical of people calling Jonathan, Crab?

"Sorry, I mean Michele. She sat at our table," she explained, looking at Gayle. "With the hair and the dress." She pretended to pull up the bodice of a strapless gown.

"Frank's niece?" Gayle said, looking stunned. "She picked up the photographer?"

Sadie nodded. "Remember how she excused herself to go to the ladies' room? She never came back, but of course I didn't think about it until I saw her in the car with the photographer. She didn't only leave the ballroom, she left the hotel. The photographer said he couldn't get his car because the lot was blocked off, which means Michele left before the police even arrived."

"It's like some kind of conspiracy," Gayle said, her eyes wide.

"Yeah, I know," Sadie said. "But to kill a man so . . . dramatically? And in Garrison of all places?"

"It was meant for Thom," Gayle said again. "I just know it."

"Two murders?" Shawn cut in. He leaned forward even more. "The photographer said that?"

Sadie nodded, feeling her excitement building again. "The police searched the building but didn't find any other bodies." She took a long sip of her chocolate while replaying the short exchange she'd had with the man.

He'd also said that it was about time things came full circle. And what did that mean?

The comment hinted at a wait of some kind, or why else say

it was "about time"? Plus the words "full circle" denoted revenge or vengeance, which brought her back to the question of who the intended victim really was: Thom or Mr. Ogreski. Since she didn't know anything about Mr. Ogreski, she couldn't help but think of what she *did* know about Thom. He was a former accountant and a single father of an only son who had had a history of extreme behavior before he killed himself and his girlfriend. One of the reasons given for Damon's problems was that his mother, Thom's ex-wife, had a history of mental illness that had ended with an overdose when Damon was little. Sadie was once again saddened by the thought of Thom falling victim to alcoholism after so many trials. She so wanted him to have a happier life.

But who would want Thom dead now? Who had reason to exact some kind of revenge on a novelist who didn't even live here anymore? It brought her back to the discussion she'd had, or rather tried to have, with Pete. "The girl," she heard herself say out loud. She looked up from where she'd been staring into her chocolate and saw Shawn watching her. He'd always been very expressive and she could see he'd been watching her closely, both curious and eager to hear her thoughts. Gayle was still hovering over the cup in her hands, which she raised to her mouth every twenty seconds or so to take a small sip of the rich beverage. She wasn't paying attention to either one of them.

"What girl?" Shawn asked.

"The girl Damon shot," she said. She wondered if Pete had contacted the girl's family yet. Would he tell her what he learned, if anything?

"Damon?"

"Thom's son. About ten years ago he killed his girlfriend and himself after prom. You don't remember?"

Shawn shrugged, but looked thoughtful. "A little bit," he said. "I was in sixth grade. I remember the police coming and giving an assembly on gun safety. I was all freaked out when Uncle Jack asked me to go hunting with him the next fall."

Sadie nodded. "I remember that. You were worried just touching a gun could make it go off."

Shawn's dark skin darkened even more. "Pretty dumb, huh?"

"Being overly cautious is never dumb," Sadie said in her schoolteacher voice, smiling at the memory of the little boy who depended on her to assure him that hunting with his uncle was okay, but throwing water balloons at girls because they were, well, *girls* was unacceptable.

"Damon was a junior that year, like Amber," Gayle cut in. Her zoned-out state had given Sadie the impression she wasn't listening. But of course she was. She was two feet away from them.

"She saw them at the dance that night," Gayle continued. "It was really hard for her when, well, you know. When he did what he did."

The three of them were silent as they contemplated the tragedy all over again. "So, Damon was two years older than Bre?" Shawn said, using his sister as a gauge to give both himself and Sadie a point of reference.

"Yeah, I guess so," Sadie said. Breanna had still been in junior high school, giving Sadie's family a bit more of a buffer between themselves and the tragedy. Shawn nodded thoughtfully before standing up and leaving the room. Sadie watched him go with a questioning look, but her attention was quickly redirected when Gayle spoke.

"Is there any chance you have some Tylenol PM?" Gayle took another sip of her hot cocoa. She returned the mug to the table and raised one hand to rub her forehead with her thumb and fingertips.

"I've got a horrible headache, and I'm worried I won't be able to sleep."

Sadie headed for the cupboard next to the fridge where she kept all her over-the-counter medications and picked out the bottle of Tylenol PM. "I'm sure we could call Dr. Bernard and he could get you something stronger. At least for a couple nights," she said as she filled up a glass with water.

"I'll try the Tylenol," Gayle said. "I feel like I could sleep for two days straight even without it, my brain is so exhausted." She put her elbows on the table and dropped her head down so she could massage her temples.

"I can only imagine," Sadie said with sympathy. Poor Gayle. Sadie put the water and the pills on the table as Shawn came back into the kitchen, a large hardbound book in his hands. He dropped it on the table with a thud, making the mugs and plates shake. Some French chocolate splashed out of Sadie's mug, and she scowled at her son before grabbing a paper towel to clean it up.

"Oh, sorry," he said, making an apologetic face and lowering himself into one of the kitchen chairs. About five years ago, Shawn had leaned back in one of Sadie's old Victorian chairs and the thin legs covered in ornate designs had practically disintegrated beneath him. The chair hadn't stood a chance against the starting linebacker for the Garrison Gator's football team. And he wasn't getting any smaller. The week after the disaster, Sadie had gone on the hunt for a more sturdy dining room set and eventually found one made of solid walnut. Since then she hadn't worried about him breaking furniture. Well, at least not as much.

"A yearbook?" Gayle asked after scanning the covers, her forehead scrunched up in confusion.

Sadie was confused too—for about .02 seconds.

Melinda's French Chocolate

1 jar (16 oz.) hot fudge sauce (Mrs. Richardson's is the best)
1 pint whipping cream
¼ cup powdered sugar
1 teaspoon vanilla extract*
3 quarts milk, heated (amounts vary)

   Heat hot fudge in the microwave until warm and thin enough to pour, but not too hot. In a mixing bowl, whip the whipping cream and add powdered sugar and vanilla when cream begins to thicken. When cream is at the soft-peak stage, slowly add the hot fudge sauce, continuing to whip the cream and chocolate together. Serve by spooning desired amount of French chocolate mixture into a mug and adding heated milk. Stir until combined.
   Serves 8.

   *Can use mint, orange, or almond extracts in place of vanilla. (Shawn prefers mint—no surprise!)

CHAPTER 12

Shawn flipped the yearbook open. "If Damon is two years older than Bre, he ought to be in her seventh-grade yearbook, right?" He looked up at his mother.

"Right," Sadie said, leaning toward him as he flipped pages. There was only one junior high and one high school in Garrison, so while the kids in town attended any one of four elementary schools, once they hit seventh grade, they were interacting with every other kid their age for the rest of their public school career.

"I just wanted to get a visual," Shawn said, still turning pages.

"The girl was from Sterling," Gayle said, sitting up in her chair, but making no attempt to look at the book. Sterling was a town not much bigger than Garrison, about forty miles to the east.

After the murder-suicide, there had been candlelight vigils and counselors to help the kids in both Garrison and Sterling cope with the tragedy. Thom had Damon buried in California, where he'd buried his wife several years earlier. Everyone had been surprised when Thom returned to Garrison, but after a few months, he moved away for good. The town had been mostly sympathetic for his situation. Few people blamed him once the level of Damon's mental instability came out into the open, but sympathy was a weak balm for such a trial, and there would always be those who held Thom accountable for not having done more. It wasn't surprising that he wanted a new start.

"Here he is," Shawn said a moment later. "He even looks like a psychopath, doesn't he?"

Sadie looked at the photo above Shawn's finger. The boy in the picture looked surly and arrogant, with long hair and what appeared to be the barest trace of peach fuzz on his upper lip. He wasn't smiling.

"He's, what, fourteen in this picture?" Sadie said, surprised by her own defensiveness. "I bet there are two dozen other boys with the same expression."

"Yeah, but only one of them took out his girlfriend and himself."

Two murders, echoed in Sadie's brain again. *Full circle. It's about time.* And yet Pete insisted Damon's death was a suicide. Maybe the two murders referred to the girl and Mr. Ogreski—could it be that simple? But what would the connection be between them?

Only one connection came to mind—Thom.

The doorbell made her jump. Then she remembered that Amber was coming to pick up Gayle.

"I'm going to use the bathroom and then get my things," Gayle said, pushing away from the table. "Can I get these back to you next week?" She pulled at the flannel lounge pants she was wearing.

"Of course," Sadie said. She lifted one eyebrow and looked sideways at her friend. "I know where you live if you try to keep 'em."

Gayle managed a smile on her way out of the kitchen. Sadie cringed at the Got Blood? written on the back of the T-shirt and she hoped Gayle hadn't noticed it. Once Gayle disappeared into the hallway, Sadie headed for the front door.

"Hi, Amber," Sadie said as she moved to the side so the younger woman could come in. The snow was coming down harder than before. Thank goodness she didn't have to go out again tonight; the roads would be messy.

Gayle's daughter was dressed in pink velvet sweats at least one size too small with rhinestones lining both edges of the zippered jacket. Her blonde-streaked hair was pulled into pigtails. Except for the beginning of crow's feet around her eyes and the voluptuous figure that took after her mother, she could have been a thirteen-year-old on her way to a slumber party.

"Hey, Amber," Shawn said from the table, looking up to smile at her before going back to the yearbook in front of him. Amber was five years older than Shawn, but they were acquainted with one another through their mothers.

"Hi, Shawn," Amber said before turning to Sadie. "How is she?" she asked in a whisper after Sadie shut the door.

"Well," Sadie said, wanting to be honest, but kind. "She's a bit traumatized, as anyone would be, but she's holding it together all right. It was nice of you to invite her over."

Amber nodded. "Of course," she said dismissively. "Besides, I've got two junior basketball games tomorrow, and I was going to ask her to babysit anyway."

Sadie thought the last thing Gayle needed right now was to babysit. And the last thing Amber needed was a recent trauma victim watching over her children. After a moment, however, she offered a polite smile and tried to convince herself it was none of her business.

"What's this?" Amber asked, moving toward the table and leaning toward the yearbook open on the table.

"Shawn wanted to see a picture of Damon Mortenson," Sadie

explained, walking behind the younger woman. The word "Princess" was appliquéd on the rear of Amber's sweatpants and Sadie forced herself to look away. "He was pretty young when it all happened and doesn't remember a whole lot." Shawn pushed the book toward her and Amber gave him a grateful smile.

"I wish I didn't," Amber said.

Suddenly, Sadie realized Amber was the perfect person to put a little more flesh on the bones of the boy's memory. She glanced at Shawn who winked his silent agreement. No wonder he'd relinquished the book so quickly. He'd already figured out that Amber was a good resource.

"Um, Shawn, honey," Sadie said sweetly. "Would you mind getting the two cake boxes from the backseat of my car? I'm sure Amber's family would love to take one home."

Amber looked up at Sadie and smiled. "That is so generous of you," she said. "Thank you."

"Don't mention it," Sadie said, waving away the younger woman's thanks, despite the fact she was counting on that gratitude to serve her well.

Shawn gave his mother an annoyed look, but did as he was asked.

"So," Sadie said casually once Shawn had left and Amber had turned back to the yearbook. "You were in the same grade with Damon, weren't you?"

"Yeah," she said with a nod, still scanning pages.

"Did you have any classes with him your junior year?"

Amber was quiet for a moment before she nodded, still turning pages. "He was in my English class—well, until he dropped out." Amber giggled, pointing at her ninth-grade picture. "Can you believe my hair? It's a good thing I didn't smoke. I could have incinerated myself if the hairspray had caught fire."

Sadie kept to herself that dried hairspray wasn't very flammable, since it was the alcohol content and propellant that would feed a flame, and most of that would be evaporated by the time hairspray was dry. "You said he was in your English class," Sadie said, drawing the topic to Damon again.

"Yeah," Amber said, turning the page and chuckling at someone else's picture.

"What was he like?" Sadie heard the back door open as Shawn let himself in. That was fast, but then he wouldn't want to miss this conversation either. Shawn placed the two pink boxes on the counter.

"Damon?" Amber asked, squinching up her face as if trying to remember. "Well, he was . . . weird."

"Weird, how?" Shawn asked. He returned to his seat at the table, but was watching Amber with just as much interest as Sadie was. She hoped he didn't blow their cover by acting *too* interested. It was hard to balance the right amount of casual interest and Sadie wasn't sure he was well enough trained to do the job right.

Amber took a breath. "Well, he was always doing these creepy drawings in his notebook—like devils and skeletons and stuff. He was totally Goth and didn't talk to anyone. But Mrs. Veeter loved him—that was weird too."

"Diane Veeter?" Sadie asked, her thoughts shifting ever so slightly. Diane Veeter had won the Colorado Teacher of the Year award right around the time Sadie herself had returned to teaching. They'd met at different functions throughout the years and developed a casual friendship. Unfortunately, Diane had been killed in a car accident eight or nine years ago. It had been a tragic loss not only for Diane's husband, Brian, and their grown children, but for all the students she supported so passionately over the years.

Amber looked up. "Oh, that's right, you were a teacher too, huh?"

Sadie nodded, not wanting to get too far off topic. "I wonder what it was Diane—I mean, Mrs. Veeter—liked about him so much."

Shawn had clasped his hands on the table, looking a bit too studious. Sadie would need to give the boy lessons when this was all over.

"Well, for all his strangeness, Damon was a great writer," Amber said casually, turning another page. "Mrs. Veeter read a couple of his things out loud in class and they were really good—deep, ya know? But it totally embarrassed him when she did it so she stopped." Amber looked up at Sadie. "Why so many questions?"

"Well," Sadie said, settling on the truth, or most of it anyway. "A man was killed tonight, and he's connected to Damon's father. I think a lot of people are going to be asking questions about Damon." She glanced at the hallway, wondering when Gayle might appear and thus bring the conversation to an end.

"It's weird he went to the dance," Shawn interjected. Sadie threw him a little smile of encouragement. Good segue. "I mean, with him having dropped out of school and everything."

"I know, right?" Amber looked at Shawn, a more serious set to her face, and then back to Sadie. "It was intense. To find out they were both dead the next day was awful. Josh really beat himself up over the fact that he'd left them up at Pearson's Pond. But his date had a curfew."

"Josh?" Sadie repeated.

"Yeah," Amber said. "Josh Hender. He was Damon's best friend, well, only friend really."

Josh Hender, Sadie repeated in her mind. She knew a lot of people from having lived in Garrison for so many years, but Hender didn't seem familiar.

"Was Josh your age too?" Shawn asked.

Amber nodded. "Here, I'll show you his picture." She flipped a few pages in the yearbook and Sadie moved closer to her while Shawn stood up from the table and headed back down the hallway—again. Now where was he going? But Sadie couldn't allow herself to get distracted.

Amber turned one more page and ran her finger down the names on the edge of the page. She stopped and tapped at the photo, turning the book so Sadie could get a better look.

She squinted at the picture of a skinny, fourteen-year-old boy with a flattop and metallic smile. Sadie tried to recall if she knew this kid, but she came up blank. The black-and-white picture was old, and yet there was *something* familiar there.

Shawn returned holding yet another yearbook. He put it on the table and sat down, cracking open the book immediately. After a few seconds, Shawn pushed the book in Sadie's direction, pointing at one specific picture.

A shiver ran down Sadie's spine as she stared at the photo. It was Josh Hender's senior picture. He was wearing a tux and, although his hair was shorter and lighter in the photo, his skin a bit tanner, and he wasn't wearing glasses, Sadie was almost positive Josh Hender was the photographer who'd nearly knocked her on her tush earlier that evening.

Chapter 13

It took a few seconds for Sadie to get over her shock, and she shot Shawn a look she hoped would communicate to him that she'd made a powerful discovery.

"What's Josh like?" she asked, trying to keep the eagerness out of her voice.

"Oh, I haven't seen him in years," Amber said, turning another page and scanning more photos. She leaned down and put her elbows on the table, causing her backside to stick out. Sadie, again, tried not to look. It was not a flattering position. "But in high school he was okay—kinda quiet. We had a couple classes together, but weren't really in the same social group, ya know."

"What group was he in?" Shawn asked.

"Well, I was a cheerleader." Amber shrugged her shoulders as if that explained everything. "Josh was into art and video games." She looked up at them and made a face. "Not my thing."

"So they were both artsy," Shawn summed up. "Damon and Josh."

"I guess," Amber said. "But not in the same way. Josh was just kind of in the background, but Damon was creepy—everybody thought so. Did you know he brought his backpack to the dance? They think he had the shotgun in there the whole time. Thank goodness no one hassled him. Can you imagine?"

"It would have been horrible," Sadie said, remembering how the backpack detail had been a big deal in the papers. It was also the reason why the school board ruled that no bags bigger than a purse were allowed at school dances anymore.

"Damon didn't hang out with any other kids?" Shawn asked.

"Nope." Amber casually turned another page. "Unless you count the times he got beat up. I heard some guys stuck his head in the toilet just before he dropped out. Maybe that's why he brought the gun to the dance." She clucked her tongue and turned another page before laughing out loud again. "The Dog Squad," she said, shaking her head at the drill team photo. "Seriously, they look like a bunch of cross-dressers."

Sadie shook her head at the reality of Damon's life back then. Kids just didn't understand. The shooting at Columbine High School, only a few hours away from Garrison, had occurred only a couple years before Damon's shooting. One would think a tragedy that close to home would have taught more of a lesson. But high school was high school, for better and, too often, for worse. It sounded like Damon's experience was certainly worse than most.

"What did Josh do after high school?" Shawn asked.

Amber shrugged. "Dropped off the face of the earth pretty much. I remember him talking about going to art school back East, but the kid barely passed the geometry class we had together. I don't see how he'd have the discipline for college. Not everyone is college material, ya know. Anyway, I didn't keep up on him, and he didn't come to the five-year reunion."

But he was in town tonight, Sadie thought. Interesting.

Gayle suddenly appeared in the doorway, drawing everyone's attention. Her green pumps were peeking out from under the lounge pants and her dress was thrown over her arm. "Sadie's feet are too small," she said when Amber made a face at the heels. "I can't fit into any of her shoes."

Difficult though it was, Sadie put her thoughts about Josh Hender on the back burner and moved to give her friend a hug good-bye. "She's going to ask you to babysit in the morning," Sadie whispered in Gayle's ear while they embraced. Gayle groaned softly. "You can tell her we have plans if you need to." Gayle nodded as Sadie pulled back. Sadie looked her friend over, not wanting to argue in front of Amber but wishing she could convince Gayle to stay. A good night's sleep and a full breakfast would be far more beneficial than having her monster grandchildren nipping at her heels.

"I'll be okay," Gayle assured her, answering Sadie's questions without tipping off Amber. "I'll call you in the morning."

"Or sooner if you need anything." *Like a rescue mission via helicopter,* Sadie thought.

"I will," Gayle said.

Within a minute, Amber's car pulled away from the curb. Sadie shut the door and turned to face her son.

"Josh Hender was the photographer," she said as quickly as she could.

"Damon's best friend?" Shawn looked back at the yearbook in front of him. "Are you sure?"

Sadie came to stand behind him in order to see the picture again, but like the first time she'd seen it, a shiver raced up her spine. "I'd bet you an Evil Chicken dinner that's him."

Evil Chicken was exactly that—evil, and destined to clog arteries and send blood sugar levels through the roof. And yet the chicken and bacon dish was oh so delicious. Not to mention one of Shawn's favorites.

Shawn looked back at the picture, almost convinced. "This was taken, like, ten years ago," he commented.

"Nine," Sadie clarified. "And did you miss the part where I bet you an Evil Chicken dinner? And I'll make it tonight."

Chapter 14

"You're sure you're sure?" Shawn asked again as he stood up from the table.

"Yes," Sadie said, putting her hands on her hips. "Why are you doubting me?"

"It's just . . . not something you'd want to get wrong." He turned toward the computer desk in the living room. "Let me Google him. Maybe we can find a more recent photo."

"That's fine," Sadie said, humoring him. She had a better idea, however.

According to Amber, Josh didn't live in Garrison anymore. But Josh had said he'd be getting his car later, which meant he'd have to stay in town until they opened the parking lot unless he wanted to try to convince a cop to let him pick up his car. Sadie didn't think that was likely, since every police officer had his description.

Sadie moved to the counter and picked up the phone book. It was nothing like the four-inch-thick phone books compiled for larger cities. Instead, Garrison was combined with several other small towns into an inch-thick volume listing all the residences and businesses in Logan County.

"Hender," she whispered while flipping the book open with one hand and turning pages with the other.

When she reached "H" she ran her finger down the column until she landed on "Hender, D." It was the only Hender in the book and Sadie tried to suppress a smile of success. Mothers always knew where to find their children.

"Josh Hender comes up with 700 million links to Josh *Henderson*," Shawn said from where he was hunched over the keyboard.

"Who's Josh Henderson?" Sadie asked as she tapped the name in the phone book and considered her options. What would she say if Josh answered?

Shawn sucked in a large breath. "Blasphemy!" he said with dramatic flair. "Josh Henderson is a brilliant actor, of course. He's featured in Ashley Tinsdale's music video, didn't you know?"

"Who's Ashley Tinsdale?"

Shawn shook his head as though disappointed. "I'll keep looking. The point is that the name Josh Hender is so close to Josh Henderson that it makes it hard to find the guy we're looking for." He leaned back in the office chair, and Sadie tried not to cringe as the chair creaked beneath his weight. He had far more faith in furniture than Sadie did. "Who are you calling?" he asked, nodding toward the phone book.

"Well, I'm thinking about calling Josh's mother. At least that's who I think this number is for. There's only one Hender in the phone book."

"You think he might be there?"

Sadie shrugged one shoulder. "Maybe. But even if he isn't, I might be able to verify he was in town. It would be nice to have someone else confirm he was in Garrison tonight. It would make what I tell Pete more credible, right?"

"Why not," Shawn said.

He wasn't really asking her a question, but she answered it anyway. "Well, I'm pretty sure Pete doesn't want me doing this kind of stuff."

"Really?" Shawn said as though not getting the point she was trying to make. "Wouldn't it help him?" His face lit up. "Facebook would be a better place to try to find this guy." He spun back around to face the computer, leaving Sadie to make the decision herself. She hated being the one who had to make all these choices! Then again, she hated it when people made these types of choices for her, too.

The fact that she was vacillating, however, was proof that she knew the right thing to do was pass on what she'd learned to Pete—the real detective. After allowing herself a moment of internal venting about how unfair it was that she was sharing what she knew when Pete wouldn't reciprocate, she gave in and picked up the phone. But instead of calling D. Hender like she wanted to, she called Pete. His cell was lucky number seven on the speed dial on her cell phone. She held her breath while it rang five times before going to voice mail. She hung up without leaving a message and texted him instead. She suspected that he wouldn't take the time to call his voice mail, but a text message would take all of four seconds for him to read and respond to.

I know who the photographer is. Call me.

After sending the text, she waited a full minute for his reply, tapping her foot and drinking French chocolate while she watched the seconds tick by on the big clock in the living room. After the first minute had passed, she waited thirty more seconds for good measure. While she waited, the certainty that she was right about Josh continued to build in her mind. Her annoyance at Pete for ignoring her text grew too.

Shouldn't he take her information seriously? Didn't it reflect poorly on the entire investigation if he let this slide? And then her thoughts pushed even further. Maybe Shawn was right and she'd be doing Pete a favor by verifying her information first. He had all those statements to collect and officers to manage, not to mention the medical examiner and the severe-looking man with the eyebrows. She thought of how Pete had blown off what she'd told him about Jane. If he were *that* busy, would it not be a good thing for Sadie to take this teeny little part of the investigation and figure it out for him? She was his girlfriend after all. Didn't people who were committed to one another help each other out?

Why, just last week she'd returned home from the library meeting where they'd fine-tuned the details of tonight's dinner and found Pete shoveling her driveway, his cheeks rosy and his fingers numb. It had been such a sweet thing for him to do. Calling Josh Hender's parents would simply be paying him back, right?

Thoroughly convinced, and unable to stand the waiting any longer, Sadie moved to the wall phone, picked up the receiver, and dialed the number. She'd figure out the exact wording of how she would present all this to Pete later.

The phone rang twice.

"Hello?" the woman said, sounding a little breathless.

"Hi, is Josh there?" Sadie said in her official you-can-trust-me voice. The tone had worked wonders for her in the past.

"Um, he's not here," the woman said. She didn't sound young, rather she sounded older and distressed. She sounded . . . like a mother whose son had been at an event that ended in murder.

Bingo!

CHAPTER 15

"Do you know when he'll be back?" Sadie asked.

"I have no idea," the woman said, and Sadie heard tears in her voice.

The shooting had taken place more than two and a half hours ago, and surely the whole town had heard about it by now. Any mother with a child in that building would be worried sick. Especially a mother whose child hadn't returned home.

"Was he at the library dinner?" Sadie asked, bracing herself for the answer, even though she knew she already knew it. Feigning ignorance was an important trick in her detective tool belt. One of her favorites if truth be known.

The woman was silent, but then Sadie heard a definite sob. "Yes," the woman said. Sadie's heart went out to her, but she didn't interrupt. "He isn't answering his cell phone and I . . . I don't even know if he's all right."

"I was at the dinner," Sadie said, hoping to soothe at least some of the woman's fears, despite knowing that the woman's distress was far from over. "And I think I saw him there. He was fine." If Josh hadn't gone to his parents' house, then where was he?

The woman on the other end of the line sucked in a breath. "He was all right? Are you sure it was Josh?"

"I think so," Sadie said, looking back at Josh's photo in the senior yearbook. "Black hair, square jaw, wire-framed glasses, and blue eyes, right? He was wearing a tux—but the kind without a bow tie."

"Yes," the woman said as she exhaled loudly. "That's him."

"Did he take his camera with him?"

The woman sniffed. "Yes, he was supposed to take some new pictures for Thom's website," she said. "Thom paid for his flight and everything."

Sadie chewed on that information for a moment and covered up the mouthpiece of the phone. "Shawn," she whispered loudly. "Look up Thom Mortenson's website."

"Who are you again?" Mrs. Hender asked. Apparently her relief at knowing her son was okay had faded enough that she was wondering why Sadie was asking about her son in the first place.

Sadie considered hanging up right then—she had what she wanted to know—but her number had likely come up on Mrs. Hender's caller ID. It would only worry Josh's mother if the line went dead.

"My name is Sadie Hoffmiller," Sadie said, wishing she had some kind of connection that would be helpful in gaining a relationship of trust with this woman. Alas, Sadie didn't think their paths had ever crossed.

"What do you want with Josh?" she asked, suspicious now.

Sadie scrambled for an answer. "Uh, what with the evening ending so tragically—and the fact that he'd been such good friends with Damon, well, I . . . worried it would bring back some memories."

Mrs. Hender was silent, which Sadie hadn't expected. She

thought Josh's mother would agree with her concern. Instead she seemed deep in thought.

"Mrs. Hender?" she asked after a couple seconds.

"I'm sorry," she said quickly, a sob in her voice. "I just don't understand why he hasn't called me."

"You know kids," Sadie offered. "They don't have any idea how much we worry. I assure you he was fine when I saw him." She felt like she needed to extend some type of excuse in hopes to offer relief. "Maybe he was giving his statement to the police. They were talking to everyone." The lie didn't sit well with her and she wished she hadn't said it, even if it had been the nice thing to do.

"Oh, I hadn't thought of that," Mrs. Hender said, her voice sounding lighter.

Shawn finished on the computer and came back into the kitchen. He leaned against the wall by the phone and folded his arms across his chest, listening carefully to Sadie's side of the conversation with his eyebrows knit together in concentration. He looked rather foreboding when he stood that way, even when he didn't mean to.

"So, Josh and Thom have been pretty close over the years, huh?"

"Thom's been good to him," Mrs. Hender said, sounding more relaxed and open.

Sadie knew that sometimes people needed to talk about things when they were worked up, and she was happy to listen, especially now that Mrs. Hender's suspicion seemed to have abated for the moment.

"His father left us when Josh was nine. Thom sort of filled that role in his life. After Damon died, well, Josh really worried about Thom and they became even closer."

"I see," Sadie said. "It's wonderful they could remain friends." She thought it was a little bizarre, too, but she didn't want to say that out loud. Josh was a grown man, and yet he and Thom were still close. Sadie wouldn't have expected that. "Do they see each other much?"

"No," Mrs. Hender answered. "Josh lives in Virginia now."

Sadie knew Thom lived in California, which was a long way from Virginia. "Right," she said, trying to pick her way carefully through potential questions. "I heard Josh had gone to a good art school after high school."

"Oh, yes," Mrs. Hender said in her proud-mama voice—every mother had one. "He got a full scholarship with housing and everything to the School of Art Institute of Chicago."

Scholarship? Sadie repeated in her mind.

Mrs. Hender continued. "Now he's working for a magazine. He's in charge of—"

A click sounded on the line. Sadie's first reaction was that someone was listening in. An instant later, however, she realized it was simply the call waiting on Mrs. Hender's phone. Paranoia was beginning to set in.

"Oh, it's him," Mrs. Hender said, her voice higher with relief. "I've got to go. Thank you for letting me know he was okay."

"Wait!" But the line was dead before Sadie could get the words out. Shoot.

Sadie returned the phone to the cradle. "He called on the other line," she said dismally.

"But you got what you needed to know," Shawn asked. "Right?"

"I guess so," Sadie said, but she was discouraged. "I mean, his mother verified Josh was in town tonight, and that he's friends with Thom Mortenson, but . . ." Despite all she'd learned, it wasn't enough. She wanted more and looked past Shawn to the computer. "Did you find anything?"

"Facebook never fails," Shawn said, motioning her to the computer where a black-and-white photo of Josh Hender stared back at them. His hair was a little shorter in this one, and he didn't have glasses in the photo either.

"It's totally him," Sadie said.

Shawn nodded. "Yep. You were right."

Sadie hit him playfully in the arm. "Told you so."

Shawn rolled his eyes. "I also found Thom Mortenson's website," he said, clicking on another open tab. A moment later a website with a gray background and basic black type came on the screen. The title was simply "Thom Mortenson." There were a couple of photos of Thom speaking back when he looked a whole lot younger and healthier, as well as a cover for *Devilish Details*.

"I'm assuming Josh's mom didn't give you a motive for why her son was snapping pictures of the dead guy?"

"She said Thom had asked Josh to come and take pictures for his website," Sadie said, no more satisfied with the answer than Shawn was.

Shawn clicked on the "Events" tab and then frowned at the blinking words on the screen: "Website under construction. Come back soon!" He went back to the home page.

"I hope they hired a web designer to work on a new layout along with the new pics," Shawn said. "There's not much here."

"Except that the pictures Josh ended up taking were pictures of a murdered agent."

"Okay, so it doesn't make him perfectly legit, but it explains him at least being there—he's friends with Thom. It's a start, right? So he called on the other line when you were talking to his mom?"

"Yeah," Sadie said, turning away from the computer. "I wish she'd have put me on hold and then come back on the line. I mean, where is he? Why didn't he call her sooner? What's he been doing all this time?"

"You really think she'd have told you all that?" Shawn said, turning his chair around to face her.

He made a valid point—Sadie was a stranger to Josh's mother. Why would she want to tell her anything? But then again . . . Sadie's eyes drifted to the Angel Snowball cake still sitting on the counter. There were only a few slices left, but how many pieces of chocolate mousse-filled cake did a divorced mother need to convince her that Sadie Hoffmiller was concerned for her welfare—which she was—and that she was also willing to listen to anything she had to say about her son?

People lowered their defenses pretty fast when chocolate was on the line. She only needed a little more information and then she could hand over a nicely wrapped package to Pete.

Her eyes went from the cake to her own son and she raised an eyebrow. "How fast can we get to Morning Glen Road on the west side of town?"

Angel Snowball Cake

1 loaf angel food cake, sliced into ½- to 1-inch slices (day-old cake is easier to slice)
1 8-ounce package semi-sweet baking chocolate
3 tablespoons water
3 tablespoons powdered sugar
5 eggs, separated (room temperature)
½ teaspoon vanilla
1 pint whipping cream
¼ cup powdered sugar

DEVIL'S FOOD CAKE

Line a 4 to 6 quart bowl with wax paper. Line the bottom and sides of the bowl with slices of angel food cake. In a double boiler, break up chocolate and melt on low heat, adding water and 3 tablespoons powdered sugar when chocolate is mostly melted. Stir until smooth. Remove from heat and add egg yolks, one at a time, stirring well after each addition. Set aside.

In a separate bowl, beat egg whites until stiff. Add vanilla. Carefully fold the egg whites into the chocolate mixture, stirring until combined. Pour chocolate mixture over the sliced cake. Cover bowl with plastic wrap and refrigerate 12 to 24 hours.

An hour before serving, carefully invert bowl onto a large platter. Remove wax paper. Whip whipping cream and ¼ cup powdered sugar. Frost the cake. Refrigerate until ready to serve. (You can refrigerate leftovers for up to four days.)

Serves 12 to 18.

Chapter 16

It wasn't until Sadie was trying to negotiate her slick front steps in her heels with her purse and a plate of cake in one hand and her clothespinned skirts in the other that she realized wearing an evening dress for this meeting wasn't the best idea. Muttering under her breath, she handed the cake and her purse to Shawn while turning back to the house.

"I've got to change," she called. "Start the car. I'll be right out."

"Okay," he said right before she closed her bedroom door and began fighting with the zipper on her dress. She eyed the purple velvet sweat suit still lying on her bed from that morning. The outfit had been a birthday gift a few years ago from Sadie's brother, Jack—a man with no sense of color at all. Purple emphasized the blue tones in Sadie's skin, which tended to wash her out. However, while the color was all wrong, the clothes were incredibly comfortable and had deep pockets. Sadie appreciated that since many sweat suits were definitely subpar when it came to adequate pockets. Because she refused to buy new clothes to accommodate the weight she'd gained, the outfit that had sat in a drawer for so long had been put to good use these last six weeks. She also didn't have time to try on anything else in hopes something would fit better tonight than it had this morning.

She threw on a white T-shirt before pushing her arms and legs into the velvety fleece. She grabbed a pair of socks out of her drawer and hopped toward the closet on her left foot while pulling on her right sock. She then switched legs and had chosen her slip-on clogs by the time both feet were properly socked. As she ran through the front door and down the steps a minute later, she used her fingers to fluff up her hair despite the fact that it was still snowing. Multitasking—she'd never get anything done without it, and while this wasn't an emergency, Sadie was a big believer in striking while the iron was hot. Besides, Pete could call her back at any time and he'd tell her to stay put. But if she was already on her way . . .

"Phew," she said as she closed the passenger door mere milliseconds before Shawn began pulling out of the driveway. "I must have set a new world record."

He'd put the plate of cake on the dashboard, and Sadie moved it to her lap to keep it from ending up all over the car when he made his next turn.

"Two minutes is hardly anything to brag about, Mom," Shawn said, looking over his shoulder. "I can go from turning off the shower to fully dressed in thirty-six seconds. My roommates timed me."

"Whoop-de-do," Sadie said as dryly as possible. Two minutes was still impressive for a girl. She flipped down the visor so she could check her makeup and hair. Just as she'd feared, the purple was playing havoc with the circles under her eyes. She fluffed her hair again. It didn't help much. With a grunt, she flipped the visor back up and pretended she hadn't looked. Glancing down, she realized she'd chosen white socks. Adding them to her purple sweatsuit and her brown clogs was not going to win her any fashion contests, that was for sure.

The wind had picked up and the snow was coming at the windshield at a angle, making it look like they were traveling at warp speed on the USS *Enterprise*.

"Have you called your boyfriend about any of this yet?" Shawn asked.

Sadie's stomach sank at the reminder, and she worried a little over how quickly she could forget all about Pete. But she knew why. Thinking about him automatically reminded her that he'd asked her to stay out of this and she wasn't. But, she quickly rationalized, she had called him *and* texted him. He hadn't called or texted her back. What was she supposed to do? She'd like to see what the police thought of her sitting at home twiddling her thumbs while Josh Hender jumped on a plane for Switzerland!

"I was hoping to wait until I had more answers," Sadie said.

"Hey," Shawn said as though defending himself. "It's all cool by me. I'm just saying he might be ticked or something. You know how cops can be."

Sadie worried what kind of example she was setting for her son if she didn't call, and so, while trying to hide her hesitation, she pulled her cell phone out of her purse and typed out another text to Pete.

PLEASE CALL ME!

She spent the rest of the drive alternately wishing he'd call her back and hoping he wouldn't. She also pondered the information she'd learned about Josh, wondering if it might come in handy in the next few minutes: Damon's best friend; parents are divorced; Mom never remarried since she was still listed under Hender; Josh lives in Virginia; Mom says he had a full-ride scholarship to art school . . . but Amber said he barely graduated high school at all. Hmm.

DEVIL'S FOOD CAKE

"So what are we going to do when we get there?" Shawn asked as he leaned into a right-hand turn faster than he should have. Sadie held the cake plate on her lap with both hands and looked at her son with reproach. He was squished into the driver's seat and looking rather miserable. Sedans were not made for a man of his size. She decided not to give him a hard time about his driving and instead took comfort in the knowledge that since all the police in town were likely at the hotel, Shawn's chances of getting a speeding ticket were slim.

"I just want to talk to her," Sadie said. "See if I can get any other information about Josh or where he might be now."

"Here's Morning Glen," Shawn said, putting on his left-turn signal and slowing down. "It only took us six or seven minutes to get here." He was obviously very proud of himself.

"The house number is 1318," Sadie said, leaning forward in an attempt to see through the snow. "Slow down so we can read the addresses."

There wasn't really a need to slow down. The fourth house on the right had its porch lights on, illuminating the numbers 1318 placed above the door. The house had a single-car garage, but a brown Honda Accord was parked in the driveway and covered with at least an inch of snow. Sadie suspected that Mrs. Hender's garage was too full of stuff to park her car inside it. She could sympathize; her garage was stuffed too.

"Drive past," Sadie said quickly, hitting Shawn's arm to ensure he was listening to her.

"Stop it," Shawn said when Sadie didn't stop hitting him as they passed the house.

She dropped her hand. "Sorry." She craned her neck to watch the house. "Drive to the end of the block and turn around. And kill the lights."

"Bond, James Bond," Shawn said with a British accent as he turned around. He switched off the lights, pulling to a stop across the street and two doors down from 1318. "Seriously, I thought you were bringing her some cake. Why the subterfuge?"

"I'm just trying to take in my surroundings," Sadie answered, watching the front door of 1318. After a few more seconds, she opened her car door. She'd come all this way, now was no time to hesitate.

"Whoa," Shawn said, reaching over and putting a hand on her arm. "What's the plan?"

"Well," Sadie said, giving grave emphasis to her words as she met her son's eyes. "I thought I would get out of the car, cross the street, go up to the front door, and knock. What do you think?"

Shawn narrowed his eyes at her attempt at humor. "And I wait here?"

"If I'm not back in five minutes, come after me." She smiled at him as she pushed the door open, then shut it quickly, cake in hand. Her right foot was poised to step off the curb when the Hender's front door opened. Caught off guard, Sadie glanced around quickly, looking for somewhere to hide so that their meeting would be on her terms. She spotted a tree a few feet away and darted for it—never mind that the trunk was no more than six inches in diameter. Good thing the streetlight was several houses away. She hoped the snow would help hide her as well. She needn't have worried, though. A woman in what looked like her late-forties—Mrs. Hender, Sadie assumed—stepped onto the covered porch and she wasn't looking for people hiding behind skinny trees.

The woman had a heavy bag thrown over her shoulder and she walked toward the steps, then paused and put the bag on the porch with a thud. Sadie wondered where Mrs. Hender was going in such a hurry. Mrs. Hender went back in the house, leaving the door open. She must have forgotten something. Keys to the snow-covered car perhaps?

Sadie stepped out from behind the tree, looked both ways, and crossed the street in hopes she could intercept Mrs. Hender when she came back out. She hurried up the steps, looking through the front door as she stood under the porch covering and shook the snow from her hair. She didn't see anyone inside, so she glanced at the bag on the porch. It was a duffel bag. A large black one.

"Hello?"

Sadie looked up at the woman standing just inside the door. She had long, brassy blonde hair, pulled into a ponytail at the base of her neck and she wasn't wearing any makeup. Even her clothes—a buttoned-up, purple-and-pink striped shirt and baggy jeans—looked tired. When a woman worked too hard, it showed, and Mrs. Hender was most certainly a woman who had worked very hard.

"Mrs. Hender?" Sadie asked, straightening up and smiling.

"Y-yes," Mrs. Hender said with confused hesitation and a hint of anxiety. "Can I help you?" She glanced quickly at the bag sitting on the porch behind Sadie and her anxiety rose up a notch.

Sadie held out the plate of cake, still smiling. "I'm Sadie Hoffmiller," she said, her tone light. "I was talking to you on the phone a little bit ago. After you hung up, I couldn't stop thinking about the stressful evening you'd had. So I brought you some cake." It sounded really stupid when she said it out loud. The expression on Mrs. Hender's face seemed to communicate that she thought so too.

She glanced at the plate of cake and then back to Sadie, looking more confused than tempted. "Um, that's very nice of you," Mrs. Hender said rather dismissively. "But now isn't really a good time."

"Oh, I'm sorry," Sadie replied, equal parts embarrassed and curious. "Is everything okay? I'm assuming Josh was all right?"

Mrs. Hender stared at Sadie for a moment before her jaw clenched. "Everything's fine," she said, but her words were clipped. "Now, if you'll excuse me."

Sadie wasn't sure what to do now. She had hoped to learn something by coming here, but now she realized the circumstances didn't facilitate her asking the questions she wanted answers to. But she *had* brought the cake and even if she wasn't going to get what she wanted, she could still do that part. She held the plate out to Mrs. Hender. "I'll just leave this with you then."

Mrs. Hender began shaking her head, but then looked at the cake again. She tilted her head to the side a bit and seemed to reconsider. "Is that filled with pudding?"

"Mousse actually," Sadie said, reminding herself that she should never underestimate the power of Angel Snowball cake. "It tastes as good as it looks, I promise, and you'd be doing my hips a favor if you'd take it. I've already eaten way too much."

"I'm not sure my hips need it any more than yours do," Mrs. Hender said with a small smile, but she was still looking at the cake, battling with her willpower. It was a fight Sadie knew Mrs. Hender's willpower would lose. She reached the plate closer to the woman.

"Well, it does look delicious," she said. "And I have to admit it's been a difficult evening."

Sadie glanced at the duffel bag again as a thought crossed her mind. Women took luggage or overnight bags when they went somewhere. Not heavy, overfilled duffel bags. Was Mrs. Hender taking the bag to Josh?

Mrs. Hender reached out her hand for the cake when something inside the house caught her attention. She turned her head and pulled back her hand for just a moment. But it was the same moment Sadie released the plate into Mrs. Hender's grasp. Both women gasped and stepped back as the cake fell to the threshold between them. Sadie reached for it but was too late. As though in slow motion, the plate turned upside down in the process of the fall and landed on its top—spraying whipping cream, cake, and chocolate mousse all over the entryway of Mrs. Hender's home, not to mention the woman's tennis shoes and Sadie's pants. Plastic wrap could only withstand a certain amount of abuse.

"Oh, I'm so sorry," Sadie said, bending down to pick up the plate—carefully so she didn't make a bigger mess. Mrs. Hender looked at the mashed cake in what Sadie interpreted as mourning over having lost the dessert. "Do you have some paper towels?" Sadie asked, trying to get as much chocolate off the tile of Mrs. Hender's entryway as possible. She tried using the plastic wrap to keep her hands as clean as possible, but it didn't help as much as she would have liked.

"Oh, uh, yes," Mrs. Hender said. She turned back into the house and a moment later Sadie stood up, having cleaned all she could until the paper towels arrived. She looked around as though she might find a towel hanging on the porch railing, but of course there was nothing on the porch with her other than the duffel bag, which had received a fair dose of splattered whipping cream as well. Sadie hadn't been invited in, but had little doubt Mrs. Hender would have done so if she hadn't been in a hurry to get the paper towels. She took a few steps into the house, looking around the rather plain living room that spoke of economy and a lack of interest in interior design.

"Mrs. Hender?" she asked, looking toward the left end of the room where a dining room set stood near a doorway that Sadie could only assume led to the kitchen.

Sadie took a step toward the dining area, but then stopped as she heard the hinges of the front door moving behind her. She spun around and then swallowed as she stared into the eyes of Josh Hender.

Chapter 17

"We've got to stop meeting like this," Josh said as the door snapped shut. He wasn't smiling.

Sadie kicked herself for not anticipating the possibility that Josh might be home. She needed to be more careful about jumping to conclusions. At least it looked like she had surprised him with her arrival as much as he had surprised her. His shoes were untied and he shrugged his shoulders to straighten the Broncos sweatshirt he'd apparently just thrown on. That was good. Surprise could work in her favor so long as she played her cards right. She chose to ignore the fact that he was blocking her way out.

"By *this* you mean in your mother's living room with you barricading the door? I'm pretty sure this is the first time this particular *meeting* has occurred," Sadie said.

Mrs. Hender came into the room with a roll of paper towels in her hand. Her steps slowed as she approached them.

Sadie didn't break eye contact with Josh despite wishing she could call a time-out and bring his mother up to speed on their earlier encounters.

"You know this woman? This Mrs. Hoffman?" Mrs. Hender asked Josh, coming to a stop several feet to Sadie's left.

Sadie bit her tongue to keep from correcting her last name.

Josh ignored his mother. "Every time I turn around you're there." Anger flashed over his face, showing how much Sadie had thrown off his plans. His mother was in the room, so he wasn't going to hurt Sadie, but he was having to think fast. "You're not a cop, which means this has nothing to do with you."

"You're not a cop either, but it has everything to do with you, doesn't it?" Sadie felt that by mentioning the police, he was acknowledging he'd done something illegal.

Josh shook his head. "Lady, you don't have any business—"

"Who paid for your schooling?" Sadie asked, cutting him off and cocking her head to the side as she threw another wrench into this confrontation. If her hands hadn't been covered in chocolate mousse, she'd have put them on her hips for emphasis. Instead she had no choice but to hold the plate and stare him down. "Your mother said you got a full scholarship, and apparently you got the education, but where did the money come from?" She turned to Mrs. Hender, who looked confused. "Didn't you ever wonder how Josh got a full ride? Academics and sports are the only variables that entice schools to pay for everything."

"Art schools don't care about sports or academics," Josh said through his teeth, drawing Sadie's attention back to him. There was panic in his tone that told Sadie his defense was not completely sincere. Even if he was telling the truth about art schools having different criteria for scholarships, she was on to something. She knew it. His increased anger made her nervous, but not enough to slow her down. Shawn was outside, and while she'd been kidding about him coming in for her after five minutes, she was hoping he took it more seriously than she'd said it.

"Well, I'm not sure how that all works," Sadie said, hoping it covered her ignorance. "But I'm seeing a lot of little things that don't add up. Like you being Damon Mortenson's best friend ten years ago. Like telling people you had a scholarship when you nearly flunked out of high school. And let's not forget the fact that you were taking pictures of a dead man."

"What is she talking about, Josh?" Mrs. Hender asked carefully.

"Nothing," Josh said, shaking his head with frustration.

"Josh," his mother said in a nervous tone. "What does—"

"Nothing, Mom," Josh said, shooting his mother a warning look before glaring at Sadie once again.

Mrs. Hender didn't say anything else, but rather than look scared or embarrassed at having been shut down by her son, she glared at Sadie as if *Sadie* were responsible for Josh's poor manners. As if!

"Look," Sadie said, not liking the way this conversation was going. "Whatever it is you're a part of is unraveling. You know it, I know it, and the police know it. If you go to them instead of them coming for you—which they will—things will go much better for you."

Josh looked past Sadie, toward his mother. She couldn't read his expression, but heard Mrs. Hender put the paper towels down on the dining room table.

Sadie kept talking. "You've gotten involved in something much bigger than yourself, Josh. It happens, and the police understand that, but if you don't go in now, someone else will get through the door first and then you lose your advantage."

"Someone else?" Josh said, meeting her eyes again.

DEVIL'S FOOD CAKE

"Trix . . . Michele, perhaps? Or someone else involved in this." She really wished she knew what *this* was, however. It was disconcerting to be saying such bold things when she didn't know the answer to the quandary about college or why Josh had been taking pictures of Mr. Ogreski. But showing her ignorance wouldn't work either. He had to believe that his capture was inevitable—that the gig was up, so to speak.

Josh raised a hand to his forehead and closed his eyes as he turned to the side. He was cornered and he knew it. Sadie allowed herself a moment of victory. And then he threw his hands up and yelled, "This is crazy!"

Sadie startled at the fervor behind his words, but tried to quickly pull herself back together. He was certainly moments away from giving up.

"So do the right thing," she said.

"The right thing?" Josh repeated, turning to face her, his jaw clenching. "And what is the right thing?"

"Go to the police and tell them what you know. Tell them who's involved, and why you were taking those pictures."

Josh shook his head. "You don't understand."

"So explain it," Sadie countered with equal frustration. "Help me understand." She held her breath and begged in her mind that he'd simply tell her everything he knew.

"And why on earth would I do that?" he said.

Suddenly he cupped his hands in front of him and looked to his mother, nodding slightly.

A split second later, something sailed over Sadie's shoulder, causing her to duck. She looked back and met Mrs. Hender's eyes before whipping her head around to see Josh throw open the front door, a set of car keys in his hand. He snagged the shoulder strap of the duffel bag on the porch and ran down the front steps. It didn't seem nearly as heavy when he carried it as it had when his mother had brought it outside.

Sadie paused for another half-second before taking off after him. However, with him in sneakers and her in clogs, it wasn't an even match. And that wasn't counting the thirty-year advantage he had on her or the messy plate she was still holding in one hand.

By the time Sadie reached the bottom of the stairs, he was already at the driver's door of his car. The click of *two* car doors opening caught Sadie's attention and she looked across the street to see that Shawn had pulled closer to the house while she had been inside. He'd opened the driver's door and was stepping out of the car at the same time Josh was pulling his door closed and turning the key in the ignition. Sadie looked from Shawn to Josh.

"Follow him!" Sadie yelled at Shawn.

"Wha—"

"It's him," Sadie yelled, pointing at the car peeling out of the driveway, the windshield wipers clearing away the snow. "We need to know what he knows."

"But—"

"Go," Sadie yelled in order to be heard over the car's engine, waving her messy hands in a shooing motion. "I'm fine. Don't let him get away. And be careful."

Shawn hesitated another moment before scrunching himself back into the car and pulling the door shut. Josh was in the street by then, shifting into drive as the car jolted forward. Shawn was right behind him, and Sadie watched as both sets of taillights disappeared around the corner within seconds. Her stomach tightened as she questioned her decision to send Shawn after Josh at all. She should have specifically told him to call the police with his location and not take any unnecessary risks. He'd be careful, though, right?

Right?

With her heart in her throat, she reached into her pocket for her phone so she could call the police to go after him. She smeared cake and mousse everywhere in the process, but she wasn't worried about staying clean anymore.

Her phone wasn't in her pocket. She slapped her other pocket, making an even bigger mess. Empty.

With a groan she realized she'd left her phone in her purse, which was still in the car. Perfect. Tingling with adrenaline, she turned around to see Mrs. Hender standing on the threshold, looking stunned.

"Mrs. Hender," Sadie said as she headed back up the steps. She tried to keep her frustration to herself as much as possible. "I'm really sorry about this, Mrs. Hender, but Josh is in big trouble and giving him the keys just made it worse." Sadie paused at the top of the steps, mindful once again of not having been invited inside.

Mrs. Hender bit her bottom lip as she looked past Sadie at the tire tracks in the snow on her driveway. Her eyes were confused and scared.

Sadie couldn't get a line on this woman. She seemed clueless about far too many things about her son, and yet she'd thrown Josh the keys with only a look.

"I don't know you," Mrs. Hender said as though that were enough to explain everything that had happened in the last few minutes.

Sadie let out a breath. She did not have time for this conversation. "I need to use your phone."

"To call the police?" Mrs. Hender asked, looking nervously back at Sadie.

"A man died tonight, Mrs. Hender, and your son took pictures before leaving the scene." Sadie could feel her anger rising. As a teacher, she had always struggled with those parents who refused to see their children objectively. And yet, because of her history with this type of parenting, Sadie also knew anger would get her nowhere. "I'm sorry this has happened, Mrs. Hender, but please do the right thing for Josh. If he's innocent, the police will clear his name and he'll be fine."

Sadie held her eyes, begging her to see reality. After a moment, Mrs. Hender looked down and stepped aside. Sadie took the action as an invitation and entered the house.

She headed toward the doorway she had previously suspected of leading to the kitchen. Everyone had a phone in the kitchen. There were dishes in the sink and a few bags of chips on the counter, but otherwise, the room was pretty tidy. The phone was on the far wall, next to the back door, but Sadie stopped at the sink, dropped the plate and messy plastic wrap into it, and then turned on the water with her forearm so she could rinse her hands. The front of her jacket, as well as the lower portion of her pants were covered with whipping cream and mousse. Between the crushed cake and her white socks that seemed blaringly obvious against her purple pants, Sadie was not the least bit proud of her current appearance.

Without looking up, she noticed Mrs. Hender come to the doorway of the kitchen. Should she say something else? Continue the lecture? But she felt as though she'd made her point. The paper towels were still in the dining room, so she flicked the water off her fingers and turned her attention to the phone. The sooner she got the police involved, the better for everyone.

DEVIL'S FOOD CAKE

While crossing the last few feet, Sadie wondered if she should be angry and demanding, or soft and humble. Which approach would better capture Pete's attention? And should she call Pete directly or just call 911? Regardless of who she called, she'd be sitting here with Mrs. Hender for several minutes waiting for the police to come. She should probably try to ease their relationship a bit so the wait wouldn't be quite so awkward. "I really am sorry about all this, Mrs. Hender. This is not why I came over tonight," she said, reaching for the phone.

She picked up the phone, then hesitated when she realized she didn't have Pete's cell phone number memorized. She'd programmed it into her cell phone as lucky number seven on her speed dial so she hadn't dialed it by hand in months. What did it start with—691, something, 7, maybe?

She heard a sound behind her and with the phone to her ear, Sadie turned. She had barely opened her mouth when the words froze in her throat at the sight of Mrs. Hender clutching the handle of a frying pan with both hands as she swung it toward Sadie's head.

CHAPTER 18

Sadie's instincts kicked in and she managed to duck and spin out of Mrs. Hender's reach, dropping the phone while Mrs. Hender's momentum spun her in nearly a full circle. The frying pan came close enough that the wind it created whooshed through Sadie's hair.

"Mrs. Hender!" she screamed as she scrambled backward trying to keep an eye on her attacker as well as look for a way to escape. The kitchen ended in an alcove set with a table and chairs and the back door was now parallel with the crazy woman wielding the frying pan. Sadie had no choice but to move as far from Mrs. Hender as she possibly could, even though it, literally, put her in a corner. Sadie's heart was racing. "Let's calm down and talk about this," she said, trying to be diplomatic.

"Leave my son alone!" Mrs. Hender shouted, holding the frying pan over her head as if she were going to swat Sadie like a fly. Mrs. Hender's face was red and her eyes were wide. "He's been through enough!" She brought the frying pan down even though Sadie was well out of reach.

Sadie bumped up against the table while Mrs. Hender continued to move forward, flapping the pan as she went. Sadie scrambled around the table, nearly falling when her foot got caught on the caning of a chair.

"Mrs. Hender," she said, putting one hand out in a calming motion. "Maybe I didn't explain myself very well. I'm here to help Josh, not hurt him."

The table was between them but Sadie was still trapped. There were windows on both sides of the alcove, but she didn't think she could simply dive through one of them like they did in the movies and survive to tell about it.

"Do you have any idea how hard he's worked to get where he is?" Mrs. Hender said. "He went to college! He's got a good job! And you want to take that away from him."

Sadie shook her head quickly. "No, I don't."

Mrs. Hender circled one side of the table, which meant Sadie also moved in the same direction in order to keep the table between them. Seeing the retreat, Mrs. Hender moved back to the center. Sadie did the same.

"He was taking pictures of a dead man," Sadie said. "Don't you wonder why?"

Mrs. Hender shook her head and tightened her grip on the handle of the pan. "Josh is a good boy," she said. "I won't let you hurt him—I won't!"

Sadie scanned the room again, trying to find a way out. There were two doorways leading to other areas of the house, the one Sadie had entered through at the far end of the room and the one to her left. It looked as though that one led to a hallway. It also had the benefit of being directly opposite the front door of the house.

"I'm sorry for coming here, Mrs. Hender," Sadie said, hoping she sounded more sincere than scared, though she felt both. She tried to ease toward the left side of the table. Mrs. Hender moved to cut her off. "I shouldn't have gotten involved."

"No, you shouldn't have," Mrs. Hender repeated.

Sadie's heart was racing and she could hear the blood pumping in her ears. There had to be a way to reason with this woman. "What can I do to help you?" Sadie offered, putting her hands up in surrender. "I'll do whatever it takes."

"To help?" Mrs. Hender asked, lowering the pan slightly.

Sadie nodded, eager to diffuse the intensity of the moment. "This is just a mess, isn't it? You're upset. Josh is scared. There's got to be something we can do, right? Something to help him?"

Mrs. Hender was only a few feet from the back door, leaving the door to the hallway unguarded.

Mrs. Hender lowered the pan a little more, and Sadie took the chance to make a run for the hallway, pushing over a chair as she rounded the table in hopes it would give her a few more seconds to make her escape.

Unfortunately, she underestimated the spryness of a mother-bear protecting her cub.

Mrs. Hender lunged toward her, dodging the chair without a problem.

Sadie made it to the hallway and took two blessed steps onto the carpet before the frying pan made contact with her skull.

CHAPTER 19

Sadie realized she could still breathe before she dared open her eyes. The sound of a door shutting reminded her of where she was. Unlike how it was usually portrayed in the movies, she remembered everything leading up to her being rendered unconscious. She remembered trying to duck and feeling the bottom of the frying pan make contact just above her left ear. She even remembered the floor coming at her before everything went black.

It wasn't black anymore. Instead, light pulled at her eyelids. She'd have considered the possibility she might be dead if not for the fact that if she were in heaven, her head wouldn't hurt like this. She was sure that was mentioned specifically in the Bible somewhere. Someone moaned as she tried to lift her head, and she froze, thinking Josh's mother was standing over her, ready to take a second swing. Then she realized she'd made the painful sound herself. Oh, her head hurt!

The sound of a very loud engine rumbled to life somewhere outside and the noise set her heart to hammering once again. The garage had been toward the back of the house, on the side near the kitchen. Was there another vehicle in there after all? Was Mrs. Hender leaving?

Sadie could only hope. Then she wondered if it was a neighbor's car she'd heard. What if Mrs. Hender was still here?

The thought helped Sadie's blood start flowing again even though her body was still slow to respond to her commands. Sadie managed to open her eyes enough to look across the carpet squished against her face. The frying pan sat abandoned on the kitchen floor. If Mrs. Hender was still here, she was unarmed. Sadie turned her head the other way—cringing in pain as she did so—and found herself looking through the one-inch gap below the partially closed door of a room. Bringing her hands up to shoulder level, palms down, Sadie pushed herself up, her head screaming at her to stop and return to the floor where she belonged.

She painfully brought herself to a crawling position, then reached for the wall and sat back on her knees, allowing several seconds for the hallway to get over its teetering tantrum before she dared try to stand. Even then her equilibrium wasn't steady and she had to hold onto the wall. With one hand on the frame of the door in front of her, she lifted her other hand to her head, worried she was bleeding. She wasn't, but a large goose egg was forming. She'd read somewhere that the longer someone was unconscious, the longer it took for them to become fully oriented again. Since Sadie knew where she was, how she got there, and remembered the entire recipe for her Heavenly Hot Wings, she assumed she must have been out for only a few seconds, otherwise she wouldn't have come to quite so well.

Once on her feet, Sadie glanced left and right. She felt vulnerable standing in a strange hallway in a strange house. What if Mrs. Hender hadn't actually left? What if she'd just made it look as though she had so she could sneak up on Sadie unawares?

Sadie wrapped her hand around the edge of the door frame and

DEVIL'S FOOD CAKE

carefully slid inside the room before pushing the door closed, stopping it right before the latch caught. Sadie surveyed the room, looking for something she could defend herself with in case Mrs. Hender was still in the house, but she was quickly distracted by the room itself.

Each wall was a different color—terra-cotta, sage green, chocolate brown, and mustard yellow. Sadie couldn't decide if it matched or not, but the tones seemed to work together okay. Across from the doorway, a huge M. C. Escher print hung on the mustard-yellow wall, an optical illusion made up of stairways she knew would make her sick if she studied it in too much detail. The twin bed was unmade, clothes were on the floor, and there was a DC shoe company sticker in the lower corner of the mirror above the dresser.

Sadie realized she was in Josh's room. Instantly, she thought that maybe she could find something important in this room—a clue! And yet the room had a kind of emptiness that confirmed Josh was only a visitor these days—he didn't live here anymore.

Weapon, she reminded herself, focusing on the most important thing first. She needed to be able to defend herself. As she scanned the room, the spine of *Devilish Details* on a bookshelf caught her eye. She moved across the room, the throbbing in her skull quieted somewhat by her brimming curiosity.

She wasn't surprised to find the book in the room, considering that Josh maintained a close relationship with the author. She pulled the book—braced by fantasy novels on either side—from the shelf and looked at the cover. She couldn't help but think of the other copy she'd opened backstage a couple of hours ago and the note written inside of it. She opened the cover of Josh's copy, wondering if there was a note in this one too. There was! She immediately noticed, though, that the handwriting in this copy was not the same as the handwriting in the one she'd found backstage.

Josh,

Sometimes the hardest things we do provide us with the greatest opportunity. Here's to a triumphant future for both of us.

Thom Mortenson

Sadie read the inscription twice, wondering if that was the kind of thing authors typically wrote in books. She flipped to the copyright page, running her finger down the paper until she reached the year of publication: 2003. She looked up at the bulletin board where a ribbon said "Class of 2003." The book had been published the same year Josh had gone off to an expensive art school. When Sadie had asked Josh who had paid for his schooling, he'd become defensive enough to tip Sadie off that it hadn't been the scholarship his mother was so proud of.

Sadie closed the book and returned it to the shelf, catching sight of a pair of wire-framed glasses on the next shelf up. She'd already known her unexpected arrival had interrupted Josh's preparations to leave. Had he left something else behind besides his glasses?

Did she have time to look? Her head was killing her, and she had no idea whether Mrs. Hender was coming back. And Shawn!

Her stomach sank all over again, and she questioned why she had sent him after Josh at all. But she'd thought she'd be calling the police within minutes, then she'd call Shawn, or have them call Shawn, and they could all figure out where he was so the police could take over the pursuit. How long had it been since he'd left? Five minutes? Ten? She couldn't be sure and felt horrible she hadn't thought about him sooner. Having her kids in college and not a part of her daily life was no excuse. What kind of mother was she?

She had to get to the phone.

On her way to the door, however, fear washed over her again. Was Mrs. Hender out there? Remembering, again, that she'd come into this room in search of a means of defending herself, she made a final scan, hoping she would stay focused this time. She couldn't afford to be distracted.

There was a lamp on the bedside table. She headed toward it, but didn't look where she was going and tripped over a pile of clothing heaped on the floor. She managed to catch herself on the edge of the bed and reached down with her other hand to untangle her ankles, only then realizing that she'd tripped over the tuxedo Josh had been wearing at the fund-raiser. He apparently hadn't had time to hang it up. Consequently, she did not have time to be slowed up by it.

As she threw the trousers of the tux away from her, however, a key tumbled to the floor. Sadie lifted her eyebrows and then reached down for the key. Apparently Josh hadn't thought to double-check his pockets before he ran from the house. The top of the key was encased in an orange plastic cap with the numbers 649 printed in white letters. The first thing she thought of was the lockers at the community pool. They had pins through the top, though, and this one didn't. She turned it over and saw there were more numbers written in black marker on the back. She brought the key close to her face so she could read them: 29184. *What is the key for?* Sadie wondered, looking back at the pants in her hand. If Josh hadn't checked his pockets for the key, could something else have been left behind?

She slipped the key into her jacket pocket before searching the pants pockets. They were both empty. Sadie moved on to the tux jacket. The two inside pockets were empty, but as she went to lay it over the bed to keep it from becoming even more wrinkled, her fingers found a lump of some kind. It took a little investigating before she realized that whatever it was had been put in the small pocket on the front of the jacket. Sadie had always thought that one was mostly for decoration. She reached in and pulled out a silver disk about the size of a nickel but three times as thick. It seemed extremely heavy for its small size and looked a lot like a large watch battery, though without the little engraved numbers.

She moved to put it on the nightstand, but at the last moment she reconsidered and dropped it in her pocket with the key—just in case. The police bagged everything, even if they thought it was unimportant. She should do the same.

Ready to make her exit, she picked up the lamp, removed the shade, and turned the lamp upside down to make a better weapon of the pewter stand. She pulled the cord from the wall, allowing it to trail after her while she eased into the hallway, her breath coming in short, shallow bursts as she anticipated what she might find on the other side of the door. After looking both ways and listening for any noises that might indicate someone else was in the house, Sadie moved toward the kitchen. She paused, listening once again, and then stepped into the kitchen.

The phone that had been mounted on the wall was now in a heap on the floor, the multicolored wires sticking out of the wall haphazardly. Why hadn't Mrs. Hender used the phone to call the police? Sadie was in her home; she had cause. Sadie leaned to the left and looked out the window. The door to the garage was open, revealing the cavernous interior. Mrs. Hender did have a second car. She'd knocked Sadie out and left her in the hallway. Why?

DEVIL'S FOOD CAKE

Sadie wasn't sure she wanted to know.

It was time to leave and bang on a neighbor's door. Sadie didn't even pause this time, didn't allow herself to feel any regret at leaving behind Josh's house and the information it might hold. She'd been here too long already! Still holding the lamp out in front of her, Sadie headed for the front door with small, quick steps. The promise of being outside put extra motivation beneath her feet.

She was almost to the front door when someone knocked.

Sadie nearly tripped over herself in an attempt to stop her forward motion and managed to bang the lamp into her knee. Ouch. The recognition of pain, however, was short-lived, lost in the sudden and intense fear that hit her full-on, sufficiently hijacking her thoughts.

Someone was here!

Who?

It was nearly 10:30. Who came knocking at this time of night? She didn't know what to do. Run to the back door and slip out that way? Hope they'd go away if no one answered? Hide, in case they came in?

She didn't realize how long she stood there analyzing her options until the doorbell sounded, startling her. Sadie proceeded to the door with caution, paused, and then peered through the peephole while trying to summon some optimistic thoughts. Maybe it was the police come to save her, thanks to a tip from Shawn—or to arrest her, thanks to a tip from Mrs. Hender. But the face pulled out of proportion by the peephole lens wasn't that official. Sadie had to take a second look.

"Thom?" she whispered.

Heavenly Hot Wings

½ cup soy sauce
⅓ cup packed brown sugar
1 tablespoon vegetable oil
½ teaspoon minced fresh ginger root (or 1 teaspoon ground ginger)
¾ teaspoon garlic powder
½ teaspoon cayenne pepper*
1 teaspoon Tabasco sauce (optional)
½ teaspoon crushed red pepper flakes (optional)
2 pounds chicken wings (or legs)
Blue cheese or ranch dressing (for dipping)

In a medium bowl, combine soy sauce, brown sugar, oil, ginger, garlic powder, and cayenne pepper. (Add Tabasco sauce and red pepper flakes if you like your hot wings <u>hot</u>.) Stir until sugar is dissolved. Put chicken in large zip-top bag and add marinade. Coat chicken completely with marinade. Marinate at least 3 hours (overnight works great).

To cook, pour contents of the zip-top bag into a 9x13 baking dish. Cover with foil and bake at 375 degrees for 35 minutes. (Baking without foil makes for crispier, but dryer, chicken.) Remove foil, turn and baste chicken, and bake uncovered for an additional 15 minutes.

Serve with blue cheese or ranch dressing.

Serves 6 as an appetizer; 4 as a main course.

*Double the cayenne for Jack or Shawn!

CHAPTER 20

What on earth is Thom doing here? Sadie asked herself as she studied the man on the front porch. His hands were shoved into the pockets of his suit, and he kept looking over his shoulder nervously.

As well he should be nervous! If the police had found him, he'd still be talking to them. They never would have let him go so quickly. She was still staring through the peephole when Thom looked directly at her and leaned forward. She immediately pulled back.

"Josh?" Thom asked.

Sadie didn't dare look through the peephole again, but she leaned forward so she could hear him through the door better.

"Donna? Please let me in. I've got to talk to Josh."

Had he walked here from the hotel?

"Look," Thom continued a moment later, "my phone's not working and Mark's dead. There's going to be trouble. I know you're there. Please let me in."

Trouble? Sadie repeated in her mind. Thom and Josh were in cahoots somehow. Who was Mark? In the next instant she realized it must be Mr. Ogreski, seeing as he was the dead man of the evening.

The doorknob started to turn and she took a step back, her heart leaping into her throat. She didn't know if anyone had locked it after she'd come inside to use the phone. It was too late now. She scanned the room in search of somewhere to hide. There were several pieces of furniture, but none of them offered a good hiding place. Then she saw the curtains.

She sprinted the four steps it took for her to reach the floor-length cotton drapes on the left side of the picture window at the front of the house. She pulled them back from the wall so she could step behind them, and then held her breath as the fabric—and a good amount of dust—settled over her and the lamp she still held against her side. She was sure the cord was still showing but she could only hope he wouldn't notice. She heard the door swing open across the tiled entryway as she sneezed internally. She was going to need some Benadryl after this.

The door clicked closed, then there was a pause, and then the sound of muted footsteps. Sadie tried to take careful breaths to avoid filling her lungs with dust as she listened carefully, trying to track his movements as best she could despite the blood rushing in her ears.

"Josh?" Thom called, though not too loud. "Donna?"

No one answered, of course, and he called their names a second time, sounding like he was closer to the living room this time. Sadie held perfectly still, listening to every whisper of his steps and movements. Thom cursed under his breath, sounding even further away from Sadie's hiding place. Then everything went quiet.

Sadie strained to hear something, anything, that would alert her to his location, but heard nothing until what sounded like a drawer slamming shut caused her to jump. The sound wasn't close, thank goodness, just loud and unexpected. After the second drawer slammed, Sadie dared herself to pull back the curtains. It took a double-dog-dare before she crumbled under her own challenge. The living room was empty and she let out a sigh of relief that he wasn't standing there watching her emerge from her hiding place.

What on earth am I supposed to do now? she asked herself as she stepped out from behind the curtain. Dust stuck to her velvet sweats, and she scowled while trying to brush it off, not that it made much of a difference. The whipped cream and mousse wasn't yet dry so the most she managed to do was mix the dust in with it. Beautiful.

Another drawer slammed, prompting Sadie to turn toward the front door she now knew was unlocked. She should leave. And yet her eyes slid toward the hallway where the sounds were coming from. Thom was looking for something. What?

Almost against her better judgment—the justification that she was helping Pete by staying on the case was still fresh in her mind—she turned away from the front door and toward the hallway she'd exited not long ago. She moved carefully, pausing to listen to Thom's movements between each step until she realized he was in Josh's bedroom. The door was partially open and Sadie didn't dare move any closer in order to look inside. However, through the gap between the hinged side of the door and the door frame, Sadie could see Thom's hands fumbling through what looked like a bunch of boxer shorts. She grimaced at the idea of rummaging through someone's underwear, even if it was clean underwear, and wondered what Thom was after.

He slammed another drawer shut and headed for the bookshelf, passing the gap and causing Sadie to freeze in hopes he wouldn't notice her watching him. She could hear the sound of books being moved on the shelf and then the sound of crumpling paper. What she really needed was a mirror that would allow her to see beyond the door frame—or a periscope! That would be perfect! Where was Shawn's junior detective spy kit when she needed it?

The crinkly paper sound had disappeared by the time Sadie focused her attention again, but Thom was still looking for whatever it was he was looking for. He crossed the door again, initiating another "freeze tag" response from Sadie. She moved to the left, trying to get a clearer angle and hit her head on the frame of the door. Apparently the swelling from the previous attack had thrown off her usually exact perceptions of how much space she took up in the world.

Whether it was the thump or the soft gasp of surprised pain that Sadie couldn't stop in time, the movements in Josh's room stopped.

If you are quiet enough, she told herself, *and still enough, he'll blow it off as the heater kicking on or something.* At least, that was her hope. But she'd no sooner thought up the possible excuse for the sound she'd made when she heard Thom's shoes pivot on the carpet.

"Donna?" Thom said, his voice closer than it should have been.

CHAPTER 21

Sadie blindly stumbled backward, looking for somewhere to go. Thom came around the door before she managed to escape, and his eyes went wide as he stopped in the middle of the hallway and stared directly at her.

Sadie made an attempt to stand straight. "Thom," she said in an authoritative voice, lifting her chin and putting her hands on her hips for emphasis while her mind reeled forward in search of something intelligent to say. Unfortunately, she came up with nothing and had to settle on what she really wanted to know. "What are you looking for in there?" she asked, removing one hand from her hip in order to point at Josh's bedroom.

The two seconds they stood staring at each other were among the most uncomfortable two seconds of Sadie's life.

Thom's expression turned from surprise to confusion. "M-Mrs. Hoffmiller?"

"Call me Sadie," she said automatically. He looked terrible. His nose and cheeks were red, but his face was otherwise quite pale, almost like wax. His hair hung limp and wet across his forehead. He'd obviously been outside for quite some time and, while that could explain a lot about his current appearance, Sadie couldn't discount what Jane had said about Thom having an alcohol problem. Looking at him now it was a pretty easy assessment to make. He was not a well man. Though she'd known Thom several years ago, it had been a business relationship. She didn't really know *this* Thom. Back then, Thom had never been a man someone would call confident or outgoing, but he'd had depth to him—a latent strength Sadie had a hard time seeing right now.

"What are you doing here?" she asked.

"Well, I—" Thom looked quickly to the side and then back at Sadie. He was incredibly nervous. "I-I was looking for—um, what are *you* doing here?"

Sadie ignored his question. "You're supposed to be talking to the police."

"I, uh . . ." He ran a hand through his hair, and Sadie noticed that his hand shook slightly as he did so. He continued to look around, seemingly uncomfortable meeting her eyes for more than a moment at a time. "Are you with the police?" he asked, and his voice was tinged with fear.

"Sort of," Sadie said, secure with her honesty since she was doing their job for them. "Everyone is looking for you."

"I know," Thom said, running the same shaky hand through his hair again. After a moment, he glanced at her with a hopeful look in his eyes that triggered the sympathy Sadie had been attempting to hold back. There was something so . . . vulnerable about him. "Do you know Josh? Do you know where he is?"

"He's, uh, gone," Sadie said, surprised Thom had so quickly stopped questioning what she was doing there.

Thom's shoulders slumped. "Do you know when he'll be back?"

Sadie didn't like the idea of giving Thom too much information,

DEVIL'S FOOD CAKE

and yet sharing information was what developed trust—and she'd like him to trust her. "I don't think it will be any time soon. He took his bag with him and left in a bit of a hurry."

"Oh," Thom said, his shoulders slumping even more. "And Donna? Did she go with him?"

"I have no idea where Donna is," Sadie said truthfully. Where did pan-wielding bludgeoners go after incapacitating their prey? Sadie couldn't begin to guess, but she was awfully glad the woman had left. Trying to come up with something to say—preferably something that would break this weird small-talky stuff they were doing at the moment—Sadie noticed the front of Thom's jacket bulging slightly. A tiny sliver of white stuck up from the small front pocket.

He ran his hand through his hair again, and the movement made the object in his pocket shift and crinkle—a sound very similar to the one Sadie had overheard when Thom had been in Josh's room. Whatever paper Thom had found had been shoved in the front pocket of his suit coat. What was important enough that he'd walk two miles in the snow and then rummage through Josh's room? Was it a reasonable expectation to think Sadie could find out?

Maybe if she kept the frying pan close—in case Donna Hender came back—she could stay here for a couple minutes and see what she could learn.

Sadie softened her expression and smiled. "Donna will be back soon," she said, though she hoped that wouldn't really be the case. "You look a little chilled. Can I get you something to drink while we wait? Coffee, hot cocoa, tea?" Assuming Mrs. Hender had those things in her kitchen, Sadie felt she could justify taking over another woman's kitchen—it was for a good cause, after all.

"Oh, uh," Thom said, looking at his watch.

"Hot cocoa ought to do the trick," she said, wishing she'd

thought to bring a thermos of French chocolate with her. "Come into the kitchen with me and we'll get you taken care of. It will only take a few minutes. Are you hungry?"

Thom hesitated as though unsure that going into the kitchen was a good idea. "I don't—"

"Nonsense," Sadie said. She stepped forward and took Thom's elbow. The arms of his jacket were wet and cold. "I'm sure Donna will be back any minute, then you can ask her all about Josh." She pulled on his arm and he didn't fight her. That was always a good sign. She gave him another tug and he fell into step behind her as she made her way back to the kitchen, swallowing her discomfort with acting so much at home. Once there she ushered Thom into a chair at the table. Thom sat down like an obedient child who didn't know how to protest. Which was pretty much exactly what Sadie was looking for. However, it was a little worrisome how easy it was to convince Thom to do things her way.

Once she was certain he wouldn't bolt, Sadie began opening cupboards in search of hot cocoa mix. *Come on, Donna*, she grumbled in her mind. *You owe me one!* But the woman didn't keep her cupboards well-stocked. However, Sadie did find a partial can of baking cocoa way in the back of one of the cupboards. Sadie grabbed it, mixed it with some sugar she found in a sugar jar, a pinch of salt, and then added it to half a mug of water. While it heated in the microwave—which was easy to operate, thank goodness—Sadie opened the fridge and found some coffee creamer. Perfect! Breanna had learned to make a homemade cocoa mix in Girl Scouts several years ago and it had become a Hoffmiller staple ever since. Of course, Sadie had to improvise in Donna's kitchen, but at least the basics were there. Within two minutes of depositing Thom on a kitchen chair, Sadie was able to push a steaming—but not too

DEVIL'S FOOD CAKE

hot—mug of hot cocoa in front of him. It wasn't French chocolate, but circumstances, and the sparse pantry of the Hender home, didn't lend themselves to such a decadent drink anyway.

"Thank you," he said quietly as he wrapped his hands around the mug.

"Oh, you're very welcome," Sadie answered. "You didn't arrive at the fund-raiser in time for dinner, so you must be hungry." She scanned the counter before her eyes rested on a half-full bag of corn chips. She'd seen cheese in the refrigerator and, even if she didn't find anything else, that was a meal right there.

"Killer nachos," she said, smiling at Thom as he lifted the mug to his lips.

"What?" Thom put the mug down, startled.

Sadie had already grabbed the bag of corn chips. "Killer nachos," she repeated. "You'll love 'em, and it should only take a couple of minutes to throw them together." There were plates in the cupboard by the fridge and olives hiding behind the enchilada sauce. A can of green chilies was also hiding in a corner, and upon closer inspection, Sadie realized that Donna Hender wasn't all bad—she had three kinds of cheese.

"Do you like onions?" Sadie asked, popping her head up over the refrigerator door. "Not everyone does. And then there are people like my mother, who smelled like onions for forty-eight hours whenever she ate them."

"Um, I like onions," he said flatly.

Sadie gave him another wide smile and went back to the fridge. There was half a tub of sour cream on the second shelf. Perfect! As she worked, she paid careful attention to what Thom was doing when he thought she wasn't looking. He removed the paper from his pocket and smoothed it out on the table while Sadie assembled her ingredients. She wished she could see his facial expression, but he was too far away and had his head down, studying the words. She tried to close the door to the refrigerator quietly so as not to remind him she was even there, but once he heard the click, he quickly folded the paper and put it back in his pocket.

Classic Cocoa Mix

*Bre's recipe
2 cups non-fat dry milk powder
1 cup white sugar
¾ cup unsweetened cocoa
1 cup powdered non-dairy creamer
Dash of salt
Dash of cinnamon

Combine all ingredients and store in an airtight container. To make cocoa, add 3 tablespoons of mix with 1 cup hot water. Stir until combined.

*Bre loves a scoop of vanilla ice cream added to her cocoa, though Cool Whip works in a pinch.

CHAPTER 22

After putting the paper away, Thom patted down his suit, removing four mini bottles from the interior pockets of his suit coat and lining them up one by one on the table.

Sadie bit her lip, unsure of what to do. He really shouldn't be drinking, but if his alcohol problem was as bad as Jane had said it was, withdrawal symptoms could be horrible, and Sadie suspected Thom hadn't had a drink for at least a few hours.

Thom twisted the top off the first bottle and tipped it to his mouth. It was gone in one swallow and Sadie cringed. She'd never understood how people could slam hard liquor like that. He replaced the cap and put the bottle back in line with the others.

"So," she said as she spread a layer of corn chips on a large plate. "You and Josh have stayed close all these years, huh?"

"Josh?" Thom repeated, as if not sure who Sadie was talking about. Then he nodded quickly. "Oh, yes," he said simply as he twisted the top off the next bottle in the lineup.

Was he going to drink all of them? She'd heard of people who used whiskey and the like to heat up—maybe that's what he was doing. But she wrestled with the morality of letting an alcoholic drink.

Sadie found the cheese grater in the third drawer down next to the sink while Thom put the second empty bottle back in line. "I hear Josh is doing quite well for himself," Sadie said, though it was a complete jump to conclusions on her part. She needed to get Thom talking without broaching any of the sensitive topics too overtly.

He began twisting the lid off the third bottle.

Sadie couldn't stand it. "I don't think you should drink that," she said, taking a few steps closer to the table. "You've already had two and while I know it makes you *feel* warm, alcohol actually *lowers* your core body temperature, which is really not a good idea for you right now."

He looked at her and surprised her by smiling. "It's sweet of you to care." He returned the bottle to the table. "Maybe I will wait a little while."

He looked at his watch and Sadie glanced at the clock on the microwave. It was 10:38.

He folded his hands and placed them on the table, which Sadie took as a good sign. Moving as fast as she could, Sadie assembled the first layer of chips, cheese, and toppings before putting the plate in the microwave for forty seconds. The cheese was mostly melted when she removed the plate, so she assembled the next layer of nachos while assessing the next layer of investigation she was approaching.

As the tray spun and the machine hummed behind her, she turned away from the microwave and leaned against the counter. "That was a very nice thing you did, Thom." Sadie pretended not to notice Thom's confusion and continued speaking. "He's lucky to have had such a benefactor."

"Who?" Thom asked, his voice timid.

The microwave dinged, and Sadie removed the plate of nachos and added one more layer, this one with extra cheese. She cooked it for an entire minute this time, wanting to make sure all the layers of cheese were adequately melted. At home she baked them—it was really the best way to keep the chips crunchy—but there wasn't time for that now, of course. She turned to face Thom once again.

"Josh," Sadie said with a little laugh, as though it were obvious. "That was very generous of you to pay for his college."

Fear and surprise jumped into Thom's eyes before he looked away.

Sadie continued to smile as she reassured him both in words and in tone that he had no reason to be fearful of what she knew. "There aren't many people who can look past their own pain enough to ease someone else's burden."

"Well, uh . . ." Thom said, though he sat up a little straighter. "Josh is a good kid."

Is he? Sadie wondered. The microwave dinged one last time, and Sadie removed the plate from the microwave, retrieved the paper towels from the dining room table—she hadn't found any napkins—and took the plate to Thom who, despite his reluctance in the beginning, couldn't take his eyes off the heaping plate of melty deliciousness.

"It's a little messy," Sadie said as she slid the plate of nachos in front of him and tore off a couple paper towels from the roll. "Would you like to take off your coat? I don't know who does your dry cleaning, but I know I always have problems with them treating grease stains properly. It makes me crazy because if they try and fail, the stain never comes out at all." She didn't comment that his suit was soaking wet and he'd never warm up if he stayed in it. And she'd never get the paper out of his pocket.

Thom nodded and shrugged out of his jacket. Sadie eased it off his back and casually slung it over her arm. The moisture quickly seeped through her own jacket, but she pretended not to notice.

"Would you like a glass of milk?" she asked, trying not to let her excitement at having Thom's coat show too much.

"Yes, thank you," Thom said as he gingerly lifted the first chip, a string of cheese refusing to let go as he lifted it higher and higher.

Sadie nodded and went to the fridge. Behind the cover of the open refrigerator door, she slid the damp paper out of Thom's suit pocket and into the pocket of her sweats. It was almost too easy. She grabbed the jug of milk from the fridge and a glass from the cupboard next to the sink. She returned to the table and laid Thom's coat on the chair beside him at the same time he returned the third empty bottle to the lineup.

He glanced at her with a guilty look and then went back to his meal. "This is wonderful," he said. "I can't remember the last time anyone cooked for me."

Sadie felt her heart soften a bit, despite herself. She looked at the empty bottles and back at his face. What she saw was a broken human being. Not a famous author or a person of power, just a lonely old man with no one in his life but his dead son's best friend and his agent—who was now dead too. No wonder the drink had gotten to him.

"I'm so sorry about Mr. Ogreski," she whispered, not wanting to shatter him further and yet feeling compelled to offer her sympathy.

Thom's movements slowed and he put down the chip he was holding. He didn't respond for a few seconds. Then he reached for the fourth bottle.

"Please don't," Sadie said, putting her hand on his arm. "Just eat. You need some food in your stomach."

He looked at her hand on his arm and then up at her face, making her wonder if he was as hungry for physical touch as he was for home-cooked food. He didn't speak, but just nodded and picked up the chip again once Sadie removed her hand.

DEVIL'S FOOD CAKE

She pulled out the kitchen chair across from him, searching for questions she could ask about tonight when the sound of a very loud—and far too familiar—engine rumbled up the driveway behind her. Immediately she stood ramrod straight and took a quick breath.

"This is delicious," Thom said with his mouth full and a string of cheese stuck to his chin.

The engine went silent.

She turned to look out the window in time to see Mrs. Hender appear at the side door to the garage, a roll of what was either duct tape or a very ugly bracelet in her hand. Mrs. Hender caught Sadie's eye through the window. For an instant they both froze. Then Donna hurried toward the steps leading to the kitchen door six feet from where Sadie stood.

"I think Donna's back," Sadie said as she spun toward the doorway that would take her out of the kitchen before Donna could come inside. It wasn't until Sadie was at the front door that she realized she should have locked the kitchen door to buy herself a few more seconds. Too late now.

Sadie reached the front door, threw it open, and hurried down the steps after pulling the door closed behind her. Mrs. Hender was dangerous and Sadie wasn't willing to chance another injury.

She didn't know where to go once she reached the end of the driveway. She looked left and right down the sidewalk in front of the house. There was a car parked next door and she thought she could hide behind it if she needed to, even though she was fully aware she might be overdramatizing this whole thing. Mrs. Hender would probably be satisfied with Sadie being out of her house. The duct tape was probably for . . . repairs.

The snow had changed from light and dry to heavy and wet, melting the snow that had been sticking to the roads earlier and leaving a layer of slush behind. Surely Mrs. Hender wouldn't want to come after her in such icky weather. However, the sound of quick footsteps made her turn around. Donna Hender was racing down the steps straight for her. It was one thing to confront Sadie in her house, but to chase her down on the streets? The woman was not playing with a full set of fondue forks.

Sadie immediately turned right and broke into a run, glancing over her shoulder only long enough to see Donna's rage-filled face twenty yards behind her, the roll of duct tape in her hand.

Seriously? Sadie thought to herself. This was insane, but Sadie kept going, moving her legs as fast as she could, though it wasn't fast enough. Sadie's head was throbbing and her clogs kept sliding on the slick pavement. Donna Hender was at least twenty pounds heavier than Sadie, though, and she could only hope that would work to her advantage. What was it they said—every excess pound was five pounds of pressure on your joints?

"I won't let you send my son to jail!" Mrs. Hender yelled from behind Sadie.

Sadie didn't bother answering. She needed all her energy to continue forward. By the end of the block, Sadie was panting heavily and her head felt as though it had split right open. She could feel Josh's key bouncing in her jacket and was grateful for deep pockets. As she rounded the corner, she glanced over her shoulder. Mrs. Hender wasn't gaining anymore, but she wasn't giving up either. The woman gave new meaning to the term overprotective parent. Sadie dropped her head and pushed forward even harder as ragged breaths ripped from her haggard lungs.

Knowing she couldn't keep up this pace much longer, she looked around in hopes of coming up with a new plan. What were her options other than letting Donna catch up or running until she collapsed? A few houses ahead of her there was a long RV parked in a driveway, the back extending almost to the street. It blocked her view of the front porch of the house behind it, but she could see a couple of windows on the side of the house. They were lit up so Sadie figured someone must be home.

Swallowing the inevitable embarrassment she was sure to feel as she burst in on some poor family, she ran around the RV and then made a sharp turn toward the front porch. With the trailer offering some protection, Sadie barreled up the stairs and grabbed the doorknob at the same time as she threw her full weight into the door. She pictured something like out of an action movie would happen as she burst inside, shut the door behind her, and then explained herself to the surprised occupants of the house and demanded they call the police. She'd give them the shock of their lives, but it would be a great story for them to tell at work on Monday!

Unfortunately for Sadie, the owners of this house did not share the sense of community safety Sadie had. The door was locked.

Worse, Sadie's full-speed run did not react kindly to the solid oak door barring her way and she bounced off the heavy door like the green tomatoes Shawn used to throw at the side of the garage. After hitting the door with her shoulder, she ricocheted back against the metal porch railing which hit her hip-high and she flipped head-first over the bar. She managed to twist to her side, crushing the same shoulder she'd smashed against the door and landed on what felt like a pile of sticks. The air had been knocked from her lungs and she rolled off of whatever she'd landed on and flopped onto her back. It was impossible to scream without air but as she struggled for breath, Pete's words came back with great clarity: *Go home, Sadie.*

Oh, if only it were that easy.

Killer Nachos

1 pound hamburger
1 packet taco seasoning
¼ cup water
1 bag corn tortilla chips

Toppings
4 cups of cheese (a combination of Monterrey Jack, cheddar, mozzarella, and Colby work the best)
1 (4-ounce) can diced green chilies
1 (4-ounce) can sliced black olives
1-2 diced fresh tomatoes
¼ cup diced onions
Sliced jalapeños, to taste (optional)

Garnish
½ cup guacamole
½ cup sour cream

Preheat oven to 350 degrees. Brown hamburger, drain, and add taco seasoning and water. Simmer and stir until water is well incorporated. Layer half of the corn chips in a 9x13 pan and bake for ten minutes to make chips crispy. Remove from oven and add a layer of hamburger mixture, cheese, and other topping ingredients as desired. Cover with the remaining chips and bake 6 minutes, until cheese begins to melt. Remove from oven and top with remaining toppings. Bake an additional 8 minutes, or until cheese is melted. Garnish hot nachos with a dollop of guacamole and sour cream and serve immediately.

Serves 4 to 6.

*Nachos can be made in the microwave, but the chips won't be as crispy.

CHAPTER 23

Pounding footsteps approached from the direction of the sidewalk, causing Sadie to open her eyes in panic. In her oxygen-deprived state she had no means to defend herself. However, she'd apparently landed on some kind of shrubbery—an evergreen by the looks of it since it was still green and blessedly thick in February. Though it was mangled by her fall, the bush might hide her from Donna Hender's view.

Sadie rolled onto her right side and the movement jarred her left shoulder. She had to bite her lip to keep from screaming out in pain despite the fact that she could still hardly breathe.

Moisture from the wet ground began seeping into her clothes fast, and it seemed she'd lost a shoe. She laid her head on the dirt in resignation as her body began shivering from the cold. There was nothing like pain and cold to overwhelm all her high ideals of justice. She'd pushed too hard and made a mess of everything. Some people might even say that being ground into the dirt like this was exactly what she deserved. She took as deep a breath as she felt she could, grateful for the oxygen and hoping it would clear her mind sooner rather than later. She felt on the verge of passing out, but worried if she did, she'd never wake up.

The hinges of a door creaked open above her and light spilled out of the doorway of the home she'd thought would be her refuge. In a sense it still was, but not like she'd hoped.

"Hello?" a male voice called out into the night.

Sadie wanted so badly to yell out that she was down here, beside his porch, and that she was in serious need of medical attention and a hot bath. But she didn't dare. Donna Hender had to be close by.

"Can I help you?" the man continued.

Sadie looked up to see if the man was talking to her, but she couldn't even see him. She put her head back on the ground and closed her eyes. She felt like she'd been hit by a truck.

"I was . . . looking . . . for . . . someone," Mrs. Hender said and her ragged breaths made Sadie feel a little better about her own physical condition.

"No one's here but me. Uh, are you all right?"

His voice sounded closer, and Sadie dared open her eyes. She couldn't see much except the side of the cement porch and the metal railing she had flipped over. Then he took a step forward and put his hands on the rail, affording her a look at the man who would have been her rescuer if not for the paranoia that had led him to lock his door.

He looked to be in his forties or so—a good ten years younger than Sadie—and had long, brown hair pulled into a ponytail at the base of his neck. A scruffy-looking beard covered the lower half of his face. He was wearing a black, long-sleeved T-shirt with what looked like the Ford logo on the front. Sadie would bet dollars to donuts he had a motorcycle in the garage.

"It was . . . a woman," Donna continued between gasps.

"Which I am not," the man continued, sounding more humored than annoyed.

Sadie's pain threshold was being seriously challenged so she closed her eyes again and relaxed her neck, hoping the man and Donna would finish their conversation so she could crawl home in shameful surrender. What she would do once she got there was a mystery. She needed to call the police . . . She hoped Shawn was okay.

"But . . . she was . . . right here," Donna said.

"Well, she ain't here now," the homeowner said. "Can I help you with anything else?"

Donna muttered something Sadie couldn't understand, her voice sounding further away. Sadie was relieved, but felt little victory. She hoped she wasn't going to go into shock, but her right side was numb with cold and her left shoulder was burning with pain. After waiting several seconds for the door of the house to shut so she could attempt to stand, she opened her eyes to see the man of the house looking down at her with dark blue eyes and a curious expression wrinkling his forehead. He was holding her missing shoe in his right hand, his forearms resting on the railing. His hair and beard had just enough flecks of gray to prove he might be closer to fifty than she'd previously thought. She'd been right about the Ford logo on his shirt though. If only getting those details right were enough to wash away some of her embarrassment.

He cleared his throat as though he didn't already have her full attention. "I don't know how you got down there, but I'm thinking you could use a little help getting out."

Chapter 24

The man's name was Eric. Sadie didn't catch his last name. Five minutes after he'd discovered her in the bushes, Sadie was wrapping her hands around a hot mug of lemon water. He'd offered coffee, which she'd refused. Sadly, Eric had no cocoa or chamomile tea; in fact, he had never heard of chamomile. Finally, Sadie asked if he could simply heat up some water for her in the microwave. She needed warmth. Adding lemon was his idea; apparently hot lemon water was a liver detoxifier. Sadie did not ask why he knew this or why he thought she might need to detoxify her liver. It didn't seem pertinent and her head was throbbing and overcrowded with enough thoughts already.

After being unsuccessful in remembering Pete's cell phone number, Sadie had simply called 911 and explained that she needed to get a message to Detective Cunningham. Now all she had to do was wait for Pete to call her back. Without her cell phone, though, she'd been forced to leave the number to Eric's house, which meant she couldn't leave until Pete called back.

Sadie took a sip of her liver detoxifier and relished the heat coursing through her body while wincing at the pain that shot down her arm when she moved her shoulder. She put her left arm on the table in hopes to stabilize it and took another sip, using only her right hand. The feeling in her toes was returning, and she rehearsed what she would say when Pete called. She wanted to tell him what had happened in as straightforward a way as possible.

Eric pulled out a chair on the opposite side of the table from Sadie and sat down. She tried not to be bothered by his amusement. Although she was grateful for all his help, it was a bit unnerving how casual he was about the whole thing. It was almost as though finding wounded women in his bushes was not an uncommon event. Sadie hoped that wasn't true because that would be very, very weird indeed.

"He should be calling me back any time," Sadie offered with a polite smile as she took another sip.

"No worries," Eric said, smiling at her across the table that was covered with newspapers, bills, and a dish full of loose change and metal parts she didn't recognize. It was a perfect match for the rest of his house which was also in a state of comfortable disarray. Sadie surmised with little doubt that Eric was a bachelor.

"You ready to tell me what had you in my shrubbery tonight?" Eric asked, leaning back in his chair and lacing his hands behind his head so that his elbows stuck out.

She'd been wondering at what point he'd ask her what was going on. "Well," Sadie said, setting down her mug, "I wish I could tell you, but I'm afraid it's confidential."

Eric's eyebrows went up. "Really? Sounds intriguing."

Sadie nodded. It *was* intriguing, but she felt duty bound to protect the information until she'd told Pete. "I'm sorry," she said. "I really can't talk about it."

"Are you like a cop or something?" Eric asked.

"Or something," Sadie said. She shifted, causing her shoulder to protest, and she winced. "Do you by any chance have a bandana or something I can tie my arm up with? I think if I could immobilize it a little bit it wouldn't hurt so much."

Eric looked at her arm that she was hugging to her chest. "It's your shoulder, right?" he asked, standing up and moving to a cupboard in his kitchen.

"Yes?" Sadie said, realizing it sounded like a question.

After several seconds of rummaging, Eric returned with what looked like an actual sling and an Ace bandage.

"I don't throw many things away," he said by way of explanation, which Sadie did not find to be very surprising. It was good to note, however, that his pack-rattyness had worked in her favor. "We'll need to remove your jacket," he said, nodding toward the zipper.

Sadie hesitated, feeling oddly vulnerable, but then used her good hand to unzip. She couldn't fix herself up without help. Eric leaned forward and helped her ease the sleeves off her arm. He smelled like coffee and sweat—not a great combination.

Once he'd removed the jacket, Sadie tried to smooth out her horribly wrinkled shirt while Eric adjusted the sling. He eased her arm into it and she tried not to whimper as he fiddled with the strap that went around her neck.

"Sorry," he said. "I swear it will feel better in a few minutes."

Sadie hoped he was right. After the sling was in place, he explained that, in order to immobilize the shoulder, he needed to lash her arm to her chest. Sadie agreed and then winced some more as he adjusted the bandage, trying not to show how uncomfortable she was with him being so close to her as he did so. She wasn't used to being . . . touched by a man. The thought made her blush since it sounded so wanton, but it was the truth. Not even Pete did much more than put his arm around her when they watched a movie. She immediately felt silly for thinking those types of thoughts at all. Eric was younger than she was and had hygiene issues. *And* Sadie had a boyfriend. Maybe.

By the time Eric had finished wrapping her arm, Sadie was exhausted. Between the pain and the sheer stress of everything, it suddenly felt like it was one o'clock in the morning. She was ready to go home with or without hearing from Pete. Then she remembered the paper she'd taken from Thom's pocket. Maybe she should at least look at it before she threw in the towel.

"May I use your restroom to clean up a bit?" she asked, coming to her feet slowly. With her arm bound, she felt a little off-balance. She picked up her jacket from the table with her good hand.

Eric pointed to the hallway off the kitchen. "Second door on your left," he said, still watching her as if he might be able to see what it was she knew if he looked long enough. "Please don't judge me too harshly. I'm not home much."

He was certainly home enough to make *the mess,* Sadie thought to herself, then felt bad for being so judgmental. Just because she was a bit neurotic about having a clean house didn't mean everyone was. Although, it would be nice.

Sadie found the door easily enough: it had a red "Danger" sign on it. Wonderful. She took a breath and used two fingers to push open the door. Her first thought was that it could have been worse. At least there were no bugs or dirty underwear amid the excessive collection of stray hairs, half-full personal care items, and the kind of dust indigenous to bathrooms—the kind that glued itself to the floor when not swept up in a timely manner.

Sadie pushed the door closed and then fumbled with her jacket until she managed to remove the paper from her pocket. With nowhere to safely put her jacket down, she put it back on, the left sleeve hanging empty at her side.

She moved to the counter and vacillated for a moment before gingerly moving some cologne, shaving cream, and deodorant by lifting the bottles by their lids. Then she got some toilet paper wet and wiped down the cleared section of the counter with her good hand. If she had a little extra time—and two working arms—she'd clean the whole room. Alas, time was of the essence.

It was tricky trying to smooth the paper out on the blue Formica with one hand, and she knocked over a tube of toothpaste, which hit the shaving cream and started a chain reaction along the countertop clutter that eventually sent a bottle of mouthwash to the floor.

"Everything okay in there?" Eric asked from the other side of the door while Sadie tried to keep her balance as she squatted down to pick up the mouthwash.

"It's all good," she called back, then paused to listen as he moved away. She cleared a bit more of the counter and then flattened her palm over the paper to keep it flat enough to analyze it. The paper turned out to be a typed letter, written in full block form. The return address in the upper right-hand corner was from New York. Her eyes roamed down the page—looking for the meat—when they zapped back to the name written above the sender's address: Mark Ogreski.

A letter from the dead man!

What was it doing in Josh's room?

Her eyes were drawn to the date printed above the salutation—it was dated more than ten years ago.

A letter from a dead man written ten years ago found in the room of a young man who'd taken pictures of the deceased and then pinched by the client of said dead man.

Huh?

Sadie moved on to the actual correspondence, hoping it would have some answers.

> Mr. Mortenson,
>
> Thank you for sending the query and first three chapters of your book. I am very intrigued with your premise and writing ability and would like to review the manuscript in its entirety. My agency requests that you give us exclusive rights to review your manuscript for the period of two months so that we may determine whether or not it's a good fit for us. We look forward to receiving your full manuscript as soon as possible.
>
> Sincerely,
>
> *Markus F. Ogreski*

Could this be Thom's acceptance letter for *Devilish Details*? But the book hadn't come out until almost three years after the date on this letter. And why would Josh have it? Sadie read it through again and asked herself what she'd learned. Not much. Mostly she had more questions. She closed her eyes and let out a breath. She was tired of questions. They were wearing her out. Glancing up from the letter, she startled at her own reflection in the toothpaste-flecked mirror. There was a purple bruise on the left side of her head where Donna's frying pan had tried to teach her a lesson and a smudge of dirt across her cheek from the tumble into the bushes. She rubbed at the smudge with the back of her hand before making another attempt at fixing her hair, which felt like dirty straw and didn't look any better. The last thing she needed right now was a mirror. What Eric must think of her!

Forcing her eyes away, she read the letter one last time before folding it up and returning it to her jacket pocket. As she did so, her fingers touched Josh's key and she took it out of her pocket. She had some experience with mystery keys and cryptic letters—not all of it good. Could she trust either one this time? She'd have to. It was all she had to go on.

The ringing of a phone interrupted her pondering and she hurried to replace the key and straighten her jacket, the left sleeve dangling as though she were an amputee. By the time she reached the kitchen, Eric had already answered the phone.

"She's right here if you'd like to tell her yourself—oh, I see." He looked at Sadie and lifted an eyebrow as he listened to whoever was on the other end of the line. Sadie didn't like the sound of this. "Right. Okay, I'll give her the message." He returned the phone to the cradle and offered Sadie an apologetic smile of his own. "That was the detective you'd left the message for. He said to tell you to go home and he'll call you later. He doesn't have time to talk with you right now."

CHAPTER 25

Sadie's shoulders fell even as her anger rose in her chest, completely overriding her earlier professionalism. "That man is impossible," she said, attempting to cross her arms. It didn't work very well since her one arm was under her jacket and bound to her chest. She settled for putting her good hand on her hip. "All I have done from the very beginning is attempt to help him. And I *would* be helping him if he would drop his blasted pride for point three seconds and listen to just the tiniest bit of what I have to say!"

Eric raised both eyebrows this time and stared at her in such a way as to break through her self-righteousness enough to let some embarrassment filter in. Dang it anyway. She preferred self-righteousness.

"Well, then," Eric said, giving her a half-smile that only managed to annoy her more, "I don't imagine you're ready to tell me what it is you're doing, are you?"

Oh, how Sadie wanted to tell him what she was doing! If for no other reason than to get back at Pete for being so dismissive. But quite honestly, she didn't know where to start. Did Eric even know about Mr. Ogreski's murder? And who was Eric anyway? Could he be trusted?

The fact was that two wrongs—Pete dismissing Sadie, and Sadie confiding in Eric out of spite—would not make things right.

"I'm sorry," she said again, her tone deflating just as easily as it had intensified moments earlier. "I just can't."

Eric shrugged his acceptance and moved to the kitchen counter where he started rummaging through a pile of clutter. She took a deep breath and attempted to get control of her momentary lapse in conduct. She worried Eric was mad, but then he turned to face Sadie with a set of keys in his hand. "I'm assuming you need a ride," he said, smiling valiantly.

Sadie opened her mouth to tell him she'd have Shawn pick her up, but that thought brought another pang of conscience.

"Shawn!" she said.

"No, Eric," he corrected.

Sadie shook her head, filled with maternal panic. Sharing what she'd discovered about Josh Hender was part and parcel to having the police find Shawn. If the police refused to listen to her, she couldn't get help for her son, whom she'd sent on a fool's errand. "Not you," Sadie said, looking away from him so she could think things out without distraction. "My son, Shawn. He—he has my car, but he's out there somewhere." She watched the snow fall outside Eric's kitchen window. "I need to call him," she said, looking at Eric. "Can I use your phone again?"

"Sure," Eric said. He took a few steps to the table and picked up the cordless phone, holding it out to her.

"Thank you," she said, taking the phone and turning away as though that would give her a little more privacy. She dialed the area code—Shawn had gotten his own plan when he moved to Michigan for school. Then her finger hovered over the keys. Shawn was number three on her speed dial, she hadn't typed in his number by hand since she'd put it in her phone two years ago. She knew it was 566 . . . something. Argh! She clenched her eyes shut and concentrated hard.

Harder.

After a few seconds she groaned and opened her eyes. "I can't remember his number. It's programmed into my phone—which is currently in the car with him."

"So, couldn't you call your phone?" Eric offered.

Sadie blinked at him. Yeah. That could work.

The phone rang five times before it went to voice mail where her voice told her to leave a message. Did she really sound so whiney?

She didn't leave a message and instead called her phone a second time. It went to voice mail again. What did that mean? Why wasn't Shawn answering? Was he simply ignoring it? Or was he out of the car and unable to hear it? Or was he bleeding to death on the side of the highway somewhere? The last thought made it hard to breathe. She'd told him to chase Josh. What kind of mother puts her son in such a dangerous situation? She wished she'd given him more instructions. Would he call the police on his own? Would he try to confront Josh himself? The idea made the room spin slightly.

"Are you okay?"

Sadie shook her head, trying to swallow the anxiety building in her throat. "What have I done?" she said under her breath.

"You tell me," Eric said.

She was glad to see he wasn't smiling this time. They looked at one another for a few seconds before Sadie looked away, once again embarrassed to be there, to have Pete dismiss her to this man, and to have not kept better track of her son.

What do I do now? she asked herself, thinking through her options. Pete wanted her to go home—but that was impossible. She couldn't leave Shawn out there, and she couldn't pretend she didn't know what she knew. Which meant she only had one option, even though the thought made her wilt inside. It wouldn't be pretty.

"Can you take me to the Carmichael Hotel, please?" Sadie asked, not liking the sound of surrender in her voice. She needed to make Pete listen to her, she knew that, but she dreaded facing him again. Based on his reaction when she tried to tell him about Jane, as well as the fact that he'd told her via Eric to go home *again,* she had little doubt it would be an awkward discussion. She could only hope that once she got the words out, Pete would realize why she had to go to such great lengths to make sure he heard what she had to say.

"The hotel where the shooting took place?" Eric asked.

"You know about the shooting?" Sadie asked, looking quickly at him.

"It was on the news." He pointed his thumb at the TV set in the living room. The picture was still on, but he had muted the sound. "Is that what this is all about?"

CHAPTER 26

Strangely enough, though Eric's house was a disaster area, his car—a Jeep Cherokee—was clean enough that she was able to relax for the first time that evening. The scented air freshener smelled like vanilla. She liked that; it reminded her of baking.

"There's a loading area around back," Sadie said as they approached the hotel. There were easily a dozen news vans lining the road beside the main parking lot, which was still blocked off.

The snowstorm had gotten worse since her fall into the bushes. Wind whipped through the naked tree branches and the snow was coming down fast and hard through the darkened night, making the roads quite treacherous. She was glad Eric's car had four-wheel drive.

He followed her instructions, pulling to a stop at the back lot entrance as an officer stepped out from his car that was parked nearby. "Thank you for doing this," Sadie said quietly as they waited for the officer to reach them.

Eric smiled. "Letterman's a rerun," he said with a shoulder shrug. "Besides, now I'm curious. I'm still hoping to figure out what exactly is going on."

Sadie felt guilty about that. Didn't he deserve to know? Especially since he was driving her around?

The officer reached the door, and Eric rolled down the window, allowing snow to come into the car.

"The hotel's on lockdown," the officer said.

"She needs to see Detective Cunningham," Eric said with authority.

Sadie did a double take. How did he know she was coming to talk to Detective Cunningham? Then she remembered he'd seen the news, listened to her 911 call, and talked to Pete himself.

Eric continued with confidence. "He needs to hear what she has to say."

The officer hesitated. "I'll need to get permission," he said, grabbing for his radio.

"I know where Thom Mortenson is," Sadie yelled across the seat, causing both men to look at her in surprise. "Or, at least where he was twenty minutes ago. I tried to call Detective Cunningham, but he . . . didn't seem to understand what I was trying to tell him. I really need to speak with him."

"She really needs to speak with him," Eric repeated, speaking calmly as though he knew all the details. He was so comfortable that she couldn't help but wonder if he knew more than she thought he did. But how could he? He was a random homeowner of a random house she'd run to for help. She shook her head in hopes of shaking the suspicion from her mind.

Meanwhile, the officer spoke into his speaker-thing and then leaned back into the window.

"What's your name?" he asked.

"Sadie Hoffmiller," she said.

He nodded and went back to his speaker-thing for a few more

seconds before turning back to the car. "Go in. They're waiting for you in the ballroom."

Sadie couldn't hide the triumph in her smile as Eric nodded and pulled into the parking lot. There were two police cars back here now, and most of the cars that had been there earlier were gone—probably staff who'd been allowed to go home. Sadie wondered if Jane was still inside.

Eric pulled into a parking spot and Sadie climbed out, trying to ignore the constant pain in her shoulder. These murder investigations always seemed to end up a little brutal on her poor body. She was surprised when Eric met her at the back of the car.

"Come on," Eric said with a rueful grin, which emphasized the laugh lines around his eyes. "You didn't think I was going to let you go in alone, did you?"

Sadie was torn between offense and kindred-spiritedness. He was curious just like she was. At least she hoped that's what it was and not that he was simply feeling protective of her. She could take care of herself, but had learned that no one ever believed you when you tried to convince them of that. An appropriate reply did not present itself, so she merely smiled politely and headed for the door. Eric fell in step beside her, matching her stride. No one had come in or out of the back door in some time; the thin layer of snow was intact on the blacktop.

The kitchen door was locked, but after they knocked, an officer let them in. Sadie thanked him, and he nodded before leading the way through the empty and quiet kitchen. All the lights were off except for those above the triple sinks, and Andy, his staff, and the catering equipment were gone as well, which was somewhat unsettling for Sadie—though she couldn't imagine why it mattered. Eric followed her into the hallway, where the officer showed them to the door that led to the ballroom. Sadie paused and looked at the door before taking a breath and pushing it open. This was the moment of truth. She didn't know what she'd do if Pete refused to listen to her this time.

The ballroom was still a mess. The poor hotel employees were going to be up all night. She stopped just inside the ballroom to better survey the scene and get her bearings.

There weren't many people left in the room, just a handful of officers and some plainclothesmen she skimmed over. She was looking for Pete, but she didn't see him. The man with the wiry eyebrows looked at her briefly, however, then nodded to Officer Malloy, who was talking with another officer near the stage. Sadie frowned as Malloy approached her. Where was Pete? Malloy had made it painfully obvious he didn't like her. She'd rather not make her report to him.

When Malloy was about six feet away from her, he reached behind his back, and Sadie felt herself stiffen. Something about this was all wrong.

Moments later Malloy held a pair of handcuffs in one hand. Sadie stared at them and then up at Malloy. He couldn't be serious. But his expression proved he was, in fact, completely serious. Sadie's eyes immediately whipped around the room again, desperately searching for Pete. Where was he? Did he know this was happening?

Malloy grabbed her right wrist and snapped on the handcuffs.

"Wait a minute!" she spat as rage and humiliation shot up her spine and the back of her head. "Wh-What are you doing?"

Malloy didn't answer, though he had the decency to look uncomfortable.

This was ridiculous, unnecessary, and . . . rude. She looked around the room for Pete one last time.

"Are you *arresting* me?" she demanded.

"Sadie Hoffmiller, you are under arrest for interfering with a police investigation. You have the right to remain silent. Anything you say can and will be . . ."

Chapter 27

Shock and anger were the only reasons Sadie did what Malloy said and remained silent. But after a few seconds—around the part in the Miranda warning where Malloy was telling her about court-appointed attorneys—Sadie determined that she was not going to do this their way. Every minute they wasted was more time she didn't know where her son was. While Malloy tried to figure out what to do with the other cuff since her left arm was strapped to her chest, Sadie took a deep breath and yelled as loudly as she could, "Thom Mortenson was at the home of Donna Hender twenty minutes ago!"

Every head in the room turned to her, and she closed her eyes in hopes of blocking out the absolute mortification she felt at having had to resort to such measures. Her reputation as a respectable member of the community was officially on the line. Despite the fact that she was right, outbursts like this simply were not looked upon as trustworthy behavior.

Malloy gave up on cuffing her other arm, but yanked her good arm toward the door, sending a jolt of pain through her shoulder that caused her to gasp. Malloy didn't seem to notice.

DEVIL'S FOOD CAKE

Sadie felt she had no choice but to continue. "Donna Hender lives at 1318 Morning Glen Road! She's the mother of Josh Hender, the man who was taking photographs of Mr. Ogreski earlier this evening—"

"That's enough," Malloy said, pulling her forward and causing her to stumble a few steps. She opened her eyes and gave him the dirtiest, angriest look she could manage. He didn't even flinch as he continued pulling her toward the exit. She took another breath. Even if no one believed her, they couldn't pretend they hadn't heard what she'd said. Eventually they would have to look into it and then they would prove her right. She wondered if they would apologize.

She attempted to stop her forward momentum by pressing her heels into the floor, but her clogs simply slid across the flat, gray carpet.

Eric stood just inside the door, his eyebrows raised as he watched her humiliating arrest. Housekeeping skills aside, he was a nice man and must think she was an absolute loon.

Sadie only had eight more feet before Malloy would shove her out of the room. She took full advantage of those eight feet and screamed as loud as she could, "Josh escaped through the back parking lot, and Frank Argula's niece—Michele something—drove the getaway car. Josh Hender was best friends with Damon Mortenson!"

Malloy, still holding her arm firmly, reached forward to open the ballroom door. Sadie put her left foot out, pushing it against the doorway. Malloy swore but Sadie kept yelling, cramming her words together in order to fit as many in as possible. "Josh barely graduated from high school, but he told everyone he was on scholarship and less than an hour ago my son chased after him when he tried to run and then Thom showed up at Josh's house after Mrs. Hender hit me in the head with a frying pan and—"

Malloy grabbed both of Sadie's upper arms from behind, causing her to gasp in pain as her shoulder ignited all over again. Malloy forced her through the door while she yelled, "And I found a letter and a key!" The door shut in her face. Sadie tried to catch her breath in the eerie silence of the hallway.

"What on earth was that?" Malloy roared, spinning her around to face him. Another razor of pain shot through her arm and shoulder, and she tried to suppress a grimace. Malloy's red face looked ready to explode. She hoped he didn't taser her. She'd seen that on YouTube and it looked awful.

"I'm done," she said as calmly as possible, hoping he would follow suit. Besides, she *was* done. She'd said what she needed to say and had no reason to continue shouting. "I had to get the words out," she said. "No one will listen to me." She glanced around quickly. They were alone. Eric hadn't followed her out of the ballroom.

"That's because you are certifiably insane," Malloy said, shaking his head in disbelief as he held onto the other half of the handcuffs connected to her right wrist.

"You would need a psychiatrist to make that determination," Sadie said, hoping she sounded intelligent and not defensive. She tried to shift her shoulder, which was hurting quite a bit since Malloy had grabbed her. Moving it only made it worse though, and she bit her bottom lip. After the pain passed, she let out a breath and met Malloy's eyes again. "When no one will listen, sometimes you have to scream."

CHAPTER 28

At that moment, one of the questions rolling around in her brain came to the forefront. Why would whoever killed Mr. Ogreski go to such pains to make it public? To scream it, so to speak.

Rigging up the shotgun and disabling the microphone were not easy and simple considerations. The planning behind this murder was intense, which meant the reason for it must have been equally so. If Mr. Ogreski was a mistaken target, whoever set up the murder would have been horrified. The plan would have failed. Would Josh Hender have taken pictures of the wrong body if he were part of a plan that had gone awry?

Malloy was looking at her, his jaw working as if he were biting back all kinds of things he wanted to say.

Sadie lowered her chin and glared at him with extreme malice. "I know you don't like me, Officer Malloy, and I can live with that. I also realize that my relationship"—saying that word stung her heart a little bit. What on earth would Pete think of her when he heard about this?—"my relationship with Detective Cunningham has earned me cautious treatment. But despite how you feel about me, you have to ask yourself why would I make this stuff up? I know it makes me look foolish to keep pressing these issues, but I can promise you that I would not have put my reputation on the line if not because, like you, justice is my primary goal. Josh Hender drove away from his house an hour ago, and my son is pursuing him. I have a key and a letter in my pocket—both of which I found in Josh's room. It's wrong for you to ignore what I've discovered simply because you don't want me to know it." She took a deep breath as her quick monologue had left her a little light-headed. "Now, I need help finding my son. Where is Detective Cunningham? I need to speak with him."

"He's not the lead detective on the case," Malloy said, his eyes narrowing slightly. "And you can thank yourself for that. He's been sent to look into other things."

Sadie swallowed the lump forming in her throat. Pete was being penalized because of her? That was horrible, and yet it didn't make her information any less important. "Then I need to speak to the lead detective. You can't ignore me, Malloy, and neither can he. Justice demands you hear what I have to say."

Malloy stared at her. He still looked angry, but there was a question in his eyes, a question she could almost read letter by letter. *What if she's right?* As much as he didn't want to consider it, he couldn't help it. She stared back until he looked away. A moment later he moved to the wall where several folding chairs had been stacked. He grabbed one, unfolded it, and waved her to it. "Sit," he said simply.

"With these cuffs and everything?" Sadie asked, begging him with her eyes and her tone of voice. She had too much pride to come right out and ask.

He ignored the request and pulled her forward—rather roughly, in her opinion—and clipped the empty cuff to the side of the chair.

Sadie frowned at the chair she was now partnered with. Malloy didn't say another word as he went through the door of the ballroom, leaving her alone in the hall. She hoped he was going to talk to the lead detective, maybe even try to convince the other officers to consider the things Sadie had said. She hoped they would see reason and stop this before it went any further.

Please listen to him, she begged in her mind. *Please, please, please, listen to him!*

After a few more seconds, she gave into the inevitable wait and sat down on the chair. Between the sling and the handcuff, she had to wriggle around to get even a little bit comfortable.

She kept her eyes trained on the ballroom door, waiting for Malloy to return and let her know her fate. But the sound of a door opening from the other direction caused her to turn her head.

Eric poked his head through the doors leading to the common area of the hotel, then put a finger to his lips. He looked around as if making sure they were alone and then entered slowly and carefully. His stealthy behavior was a little creepy and Sadie found herself leaning away from him as he approached.

Her eyebrows came together in confusion. "What are—"

"Shh," he said, cutting her off and squatting in front of her so close she could smell him again. She tried not to make a face. Did he know how badly he smelled? If she didn't know better, she'd think he hadn't had a shower in a week.

"You said you have a key," he said, looking at her intently.

"What's it to?"

"I don't know," Sadie said warily. "I found it."

"Can I see it?" Eric asked.

Sadie hesitated, watching him closely. She didn't know this man.

Why would he want to see the key? That didn't seem like a smart decision.

He watched her for a moment, waiting for her answer. When she didn't move, he reached into his pocket and pulled out his car keys. He separated a small key from the others on the ring.

It was a key Sadie recognized from past experience, and her eyes widened in surprise. "You have a handcuff key?"

Eric nodded and took hold of the wrist shackled to the chair.

"Wait," Sadie said as soon as she realized what he was doing. "Don't—" But the ring fell off her wrist, clanging against the metal chair. Sadie stared at it for a split second before her eyes snapped back to her uninvited rescuer.

He was smiling, looking quite pleased with himself.

Sadie's whole body flushed with heat, and she glanced quickly at the ballroom door. "Put it back on!" she demanded, trying to do it herself, but it was impossible since the wrist she needed to cuff was connected to the hand that had to do the work.

"Put it back on? Why?" Eric asked.

"I'm under arrest," Sadie said in a panicked whisper, afraid someone would overhear. "I can't just leave! Don't you understand—they already hate me." She fumbled with the dangling cuff.

"Sadie," Eric said as though they'd known each other for years. "Do you deserve to be arrested?"

"Of course not," Sadie said. "But this won't help."

"Sure it will," Eric said. He reached out and grabbed her upper arm, pulling her to her feet. She looked at him with a mixture of fear and confusion. "They're arresting you because you're bothering them. I mean, come on, interfering with a police investigation? That's just silly. They'll just put you in a corner of a cell and wait until they have nothing better to do, then they'll slap you on the wrist and send you home. Why not find your son, get your shoulder checked out, and get a good night's sleep. And *then* go to the police, let them slap you on the wrist and send you home. If they're not going to listen to you either way, then why allow them to do this?" He waved at the chair with the handcuff attached.

"It's not that easy," Sadie said. "M-Maybe they want me to come to the police station so they can listen to what I have to say."

"They haven't listened so far."

He had a point. Sadie scrambled for another reason. "They'll be so mad at me."

"What are you—six?"

Sadie looked at Eric, frustrated by how casually he was treating this situation. Was he a good guy or a bad guy? She honestly wasn't sure. She sat back down, determined to do the legal thing. "Please put it back on," she said, picking up the cuff again.

Eric just looked at her, an expression of disappointment on his face.

She shook the cuff at him. "Put it back on!"

He turned and started to walk away. "I pegged you as a bit more determined than this, Sadie Hoffmiller."

Sadie didn't like that at all. Who was he to make those kinds of judgments about her anyway? "I'm trying to do the right thing," she fired at his back.

Eric stopped in front of the kitchen doors and turned to look at her. "Do you believe in coincidence?" he asked, his voice a little calmer as he crossed his arms over his chest.

Sadie wasn't sure now was the time for such an esoteric conversation. However, the look on Eric's face was sincere. After a few seconds, Sadie shook her head. "No," she said. "I never have."

Eric smiled slightly. "Neither do I. I'm a locksmith—keys and locks are what I do. If you show me the key, I might be able to help you figure out what it goes to."

Sadie lifted her eyebrows, but she wasn't quite convinced. "It's important," she said. "We'll both be in a lot of trouble if I don't give it to the police."

"The same police who are ignoring everything you tell them?" Eric said. "The same police who want to tuck you in a corner so that you don't bug them anymore? Look, I've had my own experience with people not listening when I have something important to say. I can help you be heard—if you want."

Be heard, Sadie repeated to herself. That was all she wanted.

Eric watched her for a few more seconds before he smiled and nodded in a forgiving kind of way, perhaps trying to show his understanding of her decision, even if he didn't agree with it. "Good luck," he finally said. "I hope they do listen to what you have to say sooner rather than later. For your son's sake, if nothing else."

The doors swung shut a moment later and Sadie watched them flap back and forth on their hinges. The handcuff was still in her hand. How was she going to explain that when Malloy came back? Eric's parting words rang over and over in her head. *For your son's sake . . .*

Sadie didn't know what to do. Shawn was still out there, and she couldn't deny that Eric was probably right about the police simply wanting to get her out of their hair. She knew she didn't deserve to be treated that way; she knew she was only trying to help. She clenched her eyes shut and dropped the handcuff. It clanged against the metal chair and echoed off the cement walls, reverberating in her head and reminding her of the sound of jail cell doors being pulled closed. When she opened her eyes again, she looked at the kitchen doors. They weren't swinging anymore. Eric was likely in the parking lot by now. Her chance to leave would disappear with him, and he was the only person willing to help her.

Sadie glanced one last time at the ballroom doors and at the handcuff now hanging useless against the side of the chair. She bit her lip and tried to stop the butterflies in her stomach from taking over as she stood up. She had only moments to make a decision and it made her sick. Pete had said that the other police officers didn't trust her. That point had been proved without a doubt over the last five minutes. She liked to think Pete would understand once she explained everything, but as she moved to the kitchen doors she couldn't ignore the possibility that Pete might very well never forgive her for this.

Apparently, it was a risk she was willing to take.

CHAPTER 29

Sadie ran for the outside door of the darkened kitchen and nearly screamed when Eric's voice caught her off guard.

"Took you long enough," he said, a bit of humor in his lowered voice.

Sadie squinted into the shadowed area around the door. The police officer who'd let them in ten minutes earlier wasn't there any longer—one point in their favor.

Eric pushed away from the wall of the kitchen and pulled open the outside door for her. A thousand snowflakes swirled through the doorway.

Sadie looked from the snow to Eric. "I just need a ride home," she said. "So I can find my son. Then I'm going to the police station."

"Fine," Eric said. "But you'll go back on your terms, in a position of power." He waved at the door. "But if we don't hurry you won't get that chance."

Sadie had so many questions—chief of which was why Eric cared that she went to the police in a position of power—but there was no time. What she was doing was bad enough, the idea of being caught before she actually got away was unfathomable. She hurried through the door. Eric was right behind her.

The footprints they'd left on their way into the hotel were all but filled in, and they practically ran through the curtain of snow for Eric's car. Sadie held her injured arm with her good hand to keep the jostling to a minimum. As it was, though, the pain was getting harder to ignore.

As they approached the exit, Eric waved at the officer who was sitting in his car again. Sadie's heart raced. If Malloy had discovered she was gone, wouldn't he tell all the other officers? But it seemed luck was still on her side. The officer smiled, seemingly grateful they didn't slow down, thus requiring him to get out in the storm. Her disappearance must not have been discovered yet.

It took another block before Sadie could relax against the seat of the car. She shifted around in hopes of finding a better position. After a few seconds, she gave up. She just hurt. There was no way around it.

"Where do you live?" Eric asked as he rolled through a stop sign.

"Peregrine Circle," Sadie said. "It's on the east end of town. Are you familiar with Horrick Elementary?"

Eric shook his head.

"Oh, well, follow Center Street east until you get to Highland, then turn right."

"Got it," Eric said with a nod. They were silent for a moment at a red light.

Sadie couldn't keep her eyes off the side mirror, waiting for a police car to come up behind them. As they waited for the light to turn green, she lined up her thoughts according to priority. Shawn was at the top of her list, which reminded her of something Eric had said. She turned to him. "You said you knew what it was like when no one listened—what did you mean?"

The light turned green and Eric drove through the intersection, not looking at Sadie. "Three years ago my daughter went on spring break and never came home."

"That's horrible," Sadie said. She couldn't imagine if something like that happened to Breanna.

Eric nodded. "For the next six months the police did everything they could, but with no leads other than the fact she took a cab back to her hotel, it fizzled out. Everyone thinks she's dead and because of that, no one will help me."

"I don't know what to say," Sadie said. "I can't imagine what it must feel like to wake up to that every day."

Eric kept his eyes straight ahead. It was obvious he was uncomfortable with the discussion. "I've tried to keep the case alive, tried to keep up the fight, but it's hard." He looked at Sadie briefly as they stopped at another light. "And it's even harder when people won't listen. As much as I respect the police and what they do, they deal with these things all the time. They can't care the way I can, and they're limited in ways I'm not. So I'm the advocate my daughter deserves to have. The police aren't listening to you and that will hurt this case. And possibly your son." He looked back to the road. "If we can find a solution to both of those things, everyone will be better off, right?"

"I hope so," she finally said when she remembered it was her turn to speak. "I'm so sorry." Sadie watched him for a few more seconds until he caught her staring. Was everyone more than they seemed to be upon first impressions?

"Thank you," Eric said, inclining his head slightly as he drove through another intersection. "But we can talk about that another time, right now we need to get to work. You needed to track down your son, right?"

"Right," Sadie said, forcing herself to take his lead. "I have his number written down at home, I think."

Eric leaned forward so he could reach under the seat of his car and straightened a moment later with a phone book in his hand. "Does he have a friend you could call?"

"Good idea," Sadie said, impressed. She kept last year's phone book in her car, too, and it had helped her many a time. He handed her the book and she put it on her lap so she could flip to the R's in search of the home number of Jonathan Rodriguez, better known as Crab. There were three listings for Rodriguez. It was after eleven o'clock, way past polite phone call hours but Sadie had little choice, so she took a breath and called the first one. No one answered. The second one was a Hispanic woman who cussed her out with words Sadie didn't understand, though the meaning could not be disguised by a simple language barrier. After apologizing profusely, Sadie dialed the third number and held her breath. If no one answered, or if it wasn't the right one, she'd have to come up with a new idea. And she was fresh out of new ideas.

The phone was picked up on the second ring by a man who didn't seem much happier than the last lady had been. "Hello?"

"Is Jonathan there?" Sadie asked.

"Who?"

Sadie paused for a moment, remembering what Shawn had said about everyone calling him by his nickname. "Crab?" Sadie asked instead, hating that she was giving in. "Is Crab there?"

"Let me get him," the man grumbled. It appeared even Jonathan's parents called him Crab. How sad.

A few seconds later, a new voice came on the line.

"Hello?"

"Jonathan?"

There was a pause. "Don't you guys have rules about how late you can call?"

"It's Mrs. Hoffmiller—Shawn's mom and your third-grade teacher."

"Oh, hi, Mrs. Hoffmiller," he said carefully. "Sorry about that. Nobody calls me Jonathan anymore. I thought you were a collection agency."

"I'm sorry to bother you but, well, I don't have my phone where I programmed Shawn's phone number and I really need to call him. I wondered if you had it?"

"Shawn's cell?" Jonathan repeated.

Sadie didn't remember him being so slow in the third grade. "Yes, Shawn's cell."

"Well, yeah, I've got it. Hang on a minute."

Sadie covered the mouthpiece and turned to Eric. "Do you have a pen?"

Eric flipped open the glove compartment, producing a pen just as Jonathan returned to the line. She wrote down the number he gave her on the cover of the phone book and then read it back to him.

"That's it," Jonathan confirmed. "Uh, Mrs. Hoffmiller?"

"Yes, Jonathan?" Sadie replied, keeping the urgency in her voice so he would know she was in a hurry.

"What's going on?"

"Shawn will have to fill you in on that a little later, dear," she said sweetly. "I'm afraid I haven't the time right now. But Shawn's fine, if that's what you're worried about."

"I'm not worried about Shawn," Jonathan said. "He's not the one they just issued an APB for—you are."

CHAPTER 30

"What?" Sadie said, her pulse speeding up again. She hoped it wasn't bad for her heart to react so quickly all the time. If so, she'd likely have taken five years off her life tonight. Eric must have heard what Jonathan said as he turned to face Sadie quickly, his eyebrows raised.

"It just came across the scanner," Jonathan said. "The police are calling you a person of interest in the hotel shooting."

Sadie swallowed. "Oh," was all she could think of to say, though it seemed terribly inadequate.

Jonathan continued. "Don't worry, Mrs. Hoffmiller, I won't turn you in or anything."

"Th-thank you," Sadie said, wondering why she should be surprised by the APB. Of course the police would want to bring her in. The question was, why? Were they going to lock her away? Or did they simply want to confirm the information she'd spouted out in the ballroom? Unfortunately, Sadie's trust level of the police was at an all-time low and she was unable to give them the benefit of the doubt.

Eric tapped her arm. She realized he'd come to a stop along the curb at the corner of Highland Drive and 1500 West. He pointed both directions and shrugged, needing directions on where they were going.

"I've got to go," Sadie said into the phone. "But I promise to have Shawn call you and tell you everything as soon as possible, okay."

"Sure, Mrs. Hoffmiller. Whatever it is you're doing—good luck."

"Thanks," Sadie said before hanging up. She needed all the help she could get.

She shut the phone and stared out the front windshield. "I'm a person of interest," she said, humiliated to have her name attached to such a title. Would they put that on her permanent record?

"Now that you've got Shawn's number, where are we going?" Eric asked, completely ignoring her pity party as he pulled back into the street. "Your place or mine?"

"I beg your pardon!" Sadie said, turning to face him.

He looked over at her and chuckled. "I need Internet access," he clarified. "To determine where the key is from. We can go to my house and use my Internet or go to yours, assuming you'll let me use your computer." He nodded at the phone in her hand. "You can call your son now, right?"

"Oh," Sadie said, looking away with embarrassment. "The police are probably on their way to my house," she said, swallowing. This was unbelievable. "I guess we should go to your house—if you're sure you don't mind."

"I don't mind," Eric said, turning right.

"I'll call Shawn," Sadie offered aloud, glad to have something to do instead of obsess on her current status with the police. She dialed the number and was relieved when he answered it immediately.

"Shawn!" she said with almost a gasp. "You're okay?"

"Sure," he said easily. "We're fine. Where have you been? I've almost finished making the Evil Chicken, which means you still owe me since I had to make this batch myself."

"What?" Sadie asked in confusion. "You're home? And you're cooking?"

"Yeah," Shawn said as if that were obvious. "Since we didn't really figure out a meeting place, I figured you'd have to come home sometime."

"Where's Josh?" Sadie asked, trying to figure out what had happened on Shawn's end of things since they parted ways. If he was almost done with the Evil Chicken, then he'd been home for awhile. Had he lost Josh that quickly? Was Josh already on his way to Switzerland?

"He's right here," Shawn said.

Sadie startled in her seat. That was not what she'd expected to hear. "Right there!" Sadie repeated too loudly. "At the house?"

"Sure," Shawn said. "Like I said, I've been waiting for you to come home. Didn't you have all kinds of questions you wanted to ask him?"

CHAPTER 31

Sadie was too stunned to speak.

"Mom?" Shawn asked. "Are you there?"

"I-I'm here," Sadie said. "But I'm very confused. Josh is with you?"

"Yep," Shawn said in an I've-already-told-you-that-three-times tone of voice.

"He was okay having me ask him questions?"

"Well, I wouldn't say *that*. But he was easily convinced that coming without a fight was better than having me stuff him in his duffel bag and haul him in."

Sadie felt her stomach drop and her hand tightened around the phone. "Please tell me you're kidding. You didn't . . . make him come, did you?"

"Like I said, I *convinced* him to come," Shawn said, not picking up on Sadie's alarm. "I can be quite convincing, Mom. It's a gift."

Sadie closed her eyes and braced herself for the answer to her next question. "Is he tied up?"

"Tied up?" Shawn repeated. "No, he's not tied up. He's more like strapped in."

DEVIL'S FOOD CAKE

Sadie tried to take a deep cleansing breath, but it didn't work. "You have got to be kidding me!" she yelled, causing Eric to flinch and the car to veer right sharply enough that Sadie fell against the door. She took the phone from her ear and hit Eric's arm with it. "We need to go to my house," she said quickly before putting the phone back to her ear to finish chewing out her son. "Shawn, you can't just convince people to come with you against their will. It's against the law!" The words had no sooner left her mouth than her own actions of the evening flashed through her mind at warp speed. It was a brutal realization.

"I didn't hurt him," Shawn defended. "Besides, isn't that what you wanted? To talk to him? Isn't that why you had me go after him?"

"No," Sadie said. "I'd hoped you'd call the police so they could catch up with him. I didn't want him to get away without him talking to the police first." She moved the phone away from her mouth again while Eric rubbed his arm with his other hand, looking at her strangely.

"Fifteen Peregrine Circle." She put the phone back to her ear. Eric made a U-turn and Sadie had no choice but to brace herself against the door since she couldn't hang onto anything.

"I figured *you'd* call the police," Shawn said. "Besides, we only made it a couple of blocks. He turned onto Carson's Road—you know, the one that looks like it goes under the freeway, but gets cut off by the railroad? He's been out of Garrison for awhile I guess. So as soon as he tried to turn around, I ran up to the car and convinced him that coming with me quietly was a better option than my making him do it."

Sadie could imagine her enormous son banging on the window and offering Josh a choice. No one in their right mind would invite

Shawn to use force. She closed her eyes and shook her head, sympathetic to the terror that must have been running through Josh's veins.

Eric came to another stop sign and once again looked to Sadie for directions. She pointed straight ahead.

"What's Josh doing?" Sadie asked into the phone.

"Looking through the yearbooks," Shawn said. "I haven't talked to him much. He said he was hungry when I asked if he'd eaten, and I was starving, so it all worked out. Listen, I really need to go—I don't want the brown sugar to turn into toffee on me."

"I don't think you have any idea what you've done," Sadie said, wanting to crawl into a hole and die for fear of what would happen next. She'd been arrested and fled the scene, and now Shawn had kidnapped Josh Hender. And yet, if Josh was the murderer, it was better that he was at Sadie's house instead of making a getaway, right? She forced herself to calm down a little bit, but she suspected she'd need the rest of the drive to complete the task if she were going to confront her son without going ballistic on him.

"We're a couple of minutes away," she said flatly. "Go back to your meal. We'll deal with this when I get there."

After hanging up Eric's phone, Sadie leaned back against the seat and tried to wrap her brain around what was happening. What had started out as a fund-raising dinner had turned into an absolute mess. This was the third murder investigation she'd been in the middle of in the last four months. That was not normal and it was hurting the people she loved. Why did this keep happening to her?

Eric cleared his throat, reminding her he was still there. "So are you going to tell me what's going on?"

"Right," Sadie said, nodding at the wisdom of his request and glad to have something else to think about. They passed Cypress

Road, which meant she had a few blocks to give him as many details as possible. Lucky for Eric, Sadie could compact a lot of information into very few words when necessary. Lucky for Sadie, Eric was a very good listener, nodding as the details were laid out like stepping stones.

They rolled up to Sadie's house a few minutes later and both looked at the illuminated kitchen window. The sheer drapes were pulled, which limited their view inside.

"We've likely only got a matter of minutes before the police catch up," Eric said. "What do you want to do?"

Sadie didn't have an answer to that. "Maybe I should let them arrest me," she said. "If they find Josh here, then it lends credibility to what I told them, right?"

"And slaps a kidnapping charge on your son," Eric summed up.

Sadie's mouth went dry. Seriously, what was Shawn thinking? She stared at the house for a few more seconds. "I have no idea what to do," she said, deciding there was no reason to be anything but perfectly honest. "I'm in trouble. My son is in trouble. And I'm getting you in trouble too. I should just take my lumps and get out of this mess. Maybe if you and Shawn went to your place, I could convince the police to go easy on you. But . . ."

"But . . ." Eric prompted her.

She couldn't help but take the bait. "But I *do* want to ask Josh some questions. I want to know what he was doing on stage, what he meant when he said there were two murders. He could very well be the person everyone needs to find. He could be the murderer."

"Well, he's definitely connected," Eric said.

Sadie nodded. "And maybe if I can figure out his connection, the police will be a little more understanding of the means I employed to get me to that end." The truth was that Sadie really, really, really didn't want to go to jail.

"Maybe," Eric said. Sadie couldn't tell if he was placating her or being sincere. "What about this? We take him with us to my place for thirty minutes or so, see what you can learn. I'll try to figure out that key you say you've got. Then you can take Josh and turn yourself in at the same time. Shawn and I can follow a little later after you soften up the cops."

Sadie considered that plan. "If nothing else it would give me the time I need to make an absolute decision rather than acting in a heightened state of anxiety."

Eric nodded. "Anxiety rarely leads to good decisions."

Sadie was impressed with how similar his thoughts were to her own. "Right," she said, nodding.

"But you've only got a few minutes to get the heck out of here," Eric said.

Satisfied with the way that came together, Sadie let herself out of the car. They both ducked their heads and hurried through the snow. Sadie glanced behind her as she headed up the front steps, grateful there were no red and blue lights on the road just yet. Eric followed.

At the front door, she took a breath and ushered Eric into the house, quickly shutting the door behind them. Then she turned to look at the two young men looking back at them. Shawn was at the stove with a wooden spoon in hand. He was wearing Sadie's "If Mama ain't happy, ain't nobody happy" apron, though it barely came below his waist. She was surprised he could tie it around his back. Josh was sitting at the kitchen table, his hand frozen in the process of turning a page in the yearbook that sat in front of him. The black duffel bag wasn't too far away. Sadie was glad someone had thought to grab it as she suspected the camera was inside.

At first glance, the scene looked almost normal—well, other than the apron—but on closer inspection, Sadie realized that Josh's ankles were lashed to the legs of the chair with what looked like belts, and his right hand was tied behind his back somehow. What a horrible situation!

"Dude," Shawn said, looking at his mother with alarm. "What happened to you?"

Sadie glanced down at her arm lashed to her chest beneath her jacket, the empty sleeve at her side, and remembered the purple welt on the side of her face, not to mention her hair or the dried cake on her clothes. What she wouldn't give for ten minutes to make herself presentable. "I'm fine," she said. "I'll tell you later."

Shawn seemed to accept that, though not easily. Then his eyes slid over Sadie's shoulder.

"Who's that?" Shawn asked, pointing his wooden spoon at Eric.

"This is Eric," Sadie said. "He's helping us out."

"Helping us with what?" Shawn stirred the pan while still appraising Eric.

"Oh," Sadie said, her mind rewinding to why Eric was there. She reached into her pocket and pulled out the key she had found in Josh's room. "This," she said, lifting it up.

Josh's eyes widened as he instinctively grabbed the front pocket of his jeans with his free hand.

"How did you—" he started.

"Never mind that," Sadie said, waving off his questions and putting the key back in her pocket. "We've got to get out of here."

"What?" Shawn asked, drawing her attention away from Josh. "Why? The rice isn't done."

Sadie moved to the rice cooker and unplugged it. "We'll take it with us," she said. "As for why, that's an even longer story, but suffice it to say that we've managed to get ourselves in quite a bit of trouble."

"We?" Shawn asked.

Sadie nodded toward Josh.

"Oh, right," Shawn said, finally seeming to understand that bringing Josh home might not have been entirely smiled upon by the local police.

"We're going to Eric's for a little while, just to get our thoughts together." The rice cooker was too heavy for her to lift with one hand, and she nearly dropped it. Eric came to her rescue and picked it up for her. She smiled at him gratefully and then nodded toward Shawn. "Put the chicken in a dish and bring it with us." Shawn continued to stand there. "We need to hurry," she repeated. Then she looked at Josh, feeling horribly guilty that he was there at all. But, she reminded herself, he was involved in a murder. That reminder gave her enough cause to keep going, even though it was hard to justify. "I'm assuming you'll come willingly again?"

Josh looked from her to Eric and then to Shawn, who scowled at him. "I think it's in my best interest," he said evenly.

"Oh, good," Sadie said with relief. She was not up for any more drama. She turned to Eric, "My car won't do so good on these roads. Is it okay if we all go with you?" Not to mention that the police would be looking for her car.

"Sure," Eric said, a hand already on the doorknob.

Shawn quickly scooped the contents of the pan into a dish. "By the way, Mom," he said. "Your phone's been ringing." He nodded toward her purse on the kitchen counter. "I brought it in from the car for you."

Sadie gave him a tired look. "If you'd have answered it, a lot of this mess could have been avoided."

"Answer *your* phone?" Shawn said as he grabbed a rubber scraper to get the last of the sauce from the edges of the pan. "Why would I do that?"

Evil Chicken Dinner by Laree

<u>Dieters beware!</u>

1 pound bacon, cut into bite-sized pieces*
½ to 1 pound boneless, skinless chicken breast, chopped into bite-sized pieces (one large chicken breast will usually do the job)
3 tablespoons chili powder
1 cup brown sugar
Up to ½ cup water, as needed
Cooked rice

In a large pan, cook bacon over medium-high heat until nearly done. Do not drain. Stir in chicken and chili powder. Continue cooking, stirring occasionally, until bacon and chicken are fully cooked. Add brown sugar and cook until sugar is dissolved and sauce begins to thicken, about 4 to 5 minutes. (Be careful once the sugar is added not to let the sauce turn into toffee.) Add water if necessary to thin the sauce, but keep in mind the sauce is more of a coating. Serve mixture over hot rice.

Serves 6.

*Bacon is easier to cut if it's partially frozen.

CHAPTER 32

Just a block past Sadie's house, they saw a police car heading toward them. It passed them by, but Sadie watched it in the side mirror as it turned into the circle. Her throat had gone dry, but she chose to see the fact that they got away as a good thing.

By the time they reached the first light, her stomach was growling. She hadn't thought she was hungry until she was stuck in a car with three men and a pot of Evil Chicken on her lap. The rice cooker was between her feet where she could keep it from rolling around while they drove.

She had to shift her entire body to look over the seat to check on Josh, and winced at the discomfort in her shoulder. For the most part she could ignore the pain when there were other things to focus on, but she could never quite forget.

Josh looked back at her with cold, but slightly fearful eyes. Shawn had unfastened him from the chair, but then lashed his hands together with one of the belts. They sat next to one another in the backseat, Shawn holding the end of the belt like a leash. The black duffel bag was on the floor next to Shawn.

She was determined to make every minute count from here on out.

"Why were you taking pictures of Mr. Ogreski's body?" Sadie asked point-blank.

Josh turned his head slowly until he faced her. "Posterity," he said after a few seconds' pause.

"You want your future children to see pictures of a man publicly executed?"

"Executed," Josh repeated slowly. "I hadn't thought about it like that, but it's probably not too far from the truth."

"And what is the truth?" Sadie asked, wanting an actual answer instead of Josh's little word dance.

When he didn't reply, she realized it was time for a little shock factor.

"You killed him," Sadie said bluntly. She'd hoped for a jolt or a look of horror, but he made almost no reaction at all, just continued looking at her.

After a moment, he let out a breath and relaxed against the seat. "No, I didn't kill him," Josh said, sounding almost disappointed. "But I'd love to raise him up just to shoot him again."

Sadie was unable to hide her surprise at such a malicious statement. "Why? What did he do?"

Eric took a corner a bit faster than she'd have liked and, without a hand to brace herself, she fell against the door. He glanced at her, but didn't apologize. His manners were intermittent at best.

Josh continued to stare out the window, not answering.

"Listen, young man," Sadie said, turning to look at him as squarely as possible as she moved up to the tough-cookie level. "You had better start talking."

"Or what?" Josh challenged, swinging his head around. "You'll get mad? I hate to break it to you, lady, but the stuff I'm dealing with is a lot bigger than you." He sat back in the seat, looking somewhat smug.

"Dude," Shawn said, nudging Josh with his shoulder. "She's like freaky when she gets mad. You ought to tell her what she wants to know."

Sadie enforced Shawn's comment by giving Josh her best evil eye. When he didn't answer right away, she offered up something else. "Thom showed up at your house after you left," she said.

Josh jolted slightly at the mention of Thom's name and the arrogance disappeared from his face.

"He did?" Josh leaned forward in his seat. "Was he okay?"

"Yeah," she finally said, thinking about his shaky hands and blank stares. "I mean, I guess he was okay." She paused before she decided to move forward. "I'm surprised his alcohol problem hasn't been a bigger deal in the media."

Josh looked out the window for a few seconds before he decided to speak. "It's gotten worse these last few years," he said with a degree of sadness in his tone.

"And why is that?" Sadie asked.

Josh faced her again, his eyes narrowed and the arrogance back. "Because life is hard, okay? Just 'cause he's some fancy-schmancy author doesn't mean his life is all peachy keen. His wife and son are both dead and he's been tethered to Mark Ogreski ever since. His life pretty much sucks."

"But he had you," Sadie said, watching him closely so she could gauge his reaction. "Certainly that helped."

"Except that he has no power in his own life," Josh said. "He wanted to move closer to me, but Mark wouldn't let him. Said California was the new New York for publishing and he needed to keep a presence there. Like Thom was going to get all better one day and start writing again."

"He stopped writing?" Sadie asked. "I thought he'd been working on a sequel to *Devilish Details* for awhile."

Josh grunted and turned back to the window. "I'm done talking about Thom," he said. "His life isn't any of your business."

"Sounds like it wasn't his own business either," Sadie said. "Why would he let Mr. Ogreski rule his life like that? Or did it just happen as the years went by?"

"I'm done talking about Thom," Josh repeated.

Sadie wanted to shake him! Not to hurt him, just to get his barriers down. He had information she needed yet refused to share it. The longer he held out, the worse things were going to get for everyone. "Okay, then, maybe you can explain why your mother attacked me with a frying pan."

"Dude!" Shawn said, looking horrified. "Is that what happened to your head?"

"Not now," Sadie said, shooting him a very quick, but very loaded, look.

Josh turned to look at her again, staring specifically at the side of Sadie's head that bore proof of Mrs. Hender's cookware.

"She's going to be in a lot of trouble for it," Sadie said, ignoring for the moment the trouble she herself was in. She grimaced; twisting around to look into the backseat was murder on her shoulder. "Your mother's involved now. And then there's Thom, who isn't well, and let's not forget Michele, who picked you up in the parking lot."

Surprise flickered across Josh's expression before he shut it down again.

"Michele was sitting at my table," Sadie explained. "The interesting thing is that she acted as though she knew nothing about Thom Mortenson at all. Then she excused herself just before the shooting and didn't come back until she picked you up. Quite the cast of characters, don't you think? And here you are with the opportunity to make it easier on everyone by coming clean and yet you refuse."

Josh's expression had returned to the bored blankness it had shown before she mentioned Michele. "You think I don't know that sooner or later you're going to take me to the cops anyway? There's no reason for me to spill my guts to you when it isn't going to do me any good one way or another."

He had a point. A rather good one. Lucky for Sadie, she was saved from having to reply as Eric turned into the driveway of his home. He threw the car into park alongside the RV and turned to face the backseat.

"The key to wisdom is knowing all the right questions," he said, looking directly at Josh. "And sometimes, the right questions are answered by a key."

He glanced pointedly at Sadie, but it took her a few seconds to realize what his poetic explanation meant.

"Oh, right," she said, shifting the dish of Evil Chicken so she could reach into her pocket and extract the key. Eric smiled even bigger, letting Sadie know she'd picked up on his not-so-subtle instruction.

Josh looked at the key and clenched his jaw.

"What's it to?" Sadie asked.

"Like I said, there's no reason for me to tell you anything."

"That's what I thought you'd say," Eric replied. He turned to Sadie. "You're all welcome to come on in and make yourselves at home. Don't mind the mess." With that he turned off the car and opened his door.

Sadie quickly thought about how they were going to get the answers Josh didn't seem all that motivated to hand over. Her eyes were drawn to the duffel bag. She looked at Josh and smiled sweetly. She had more than just the key she could hold hostage, but she didn't bother saying so out loud.

CHAPTER 33

The rice cooker was plugged in, the Evil Chicken was deemed warm enough to eat without having to reheat it, and Josh was retied to a chair before Sadie had a chance to open the duffel bag. She'd taken it into the den around the corner from the kitchen so she wouldn't squirm under Josh's disapproving stare. The camera bag took up half the space inside the duffel and it was tricky to wrestle it out of the bag with one arm, but she managed. She set it on the floor and tried to determine what they should do next. Wait for the rice to be done, or get right to the questions?

"Mom," Shawn called from the kitchen. "Your phone is ringing again!"

Pete!

Sadie struggled to her feet and hurried to the back door where she'd hung her purse on one of the hooks. The other hooks held a variety of grocery sacks, jackets, and an old pair of work boots tied together at the laces.

The phone was on its fourth ring by the time she dug it out of her purse, both terrified and hopeful it was Pete.

It wasn't.

The area code was 303 and Sadie immediately thought of Jane. After hesitating another moment, Sadie pushed the talk button milliseconds before Jane would have been sent to voice mail. Even as she put the phone to her ear she hoped taking this call wasn't a bad idea.

"Hello?" Sadie turned her back on the three men watching her and walked back to the den. And a well-lived-in den at that. She accidentally kicked an empty pop can across the floor, and after assessing that the furniture wasn't going to easily offer her a comfortable place to sit, she chose to stand.

"Sadie?" Jane asked, sounding relieved. "I've been trying to reach you forever."

"I've been a little busy," Sadie said dryly.

"Yeah, well me too," Jane said as though they were in some kind of competition. "And I need a little help."

"From me?" Sadie asked. "The woman you duped into helping you get inside the hotel? I think you've used up all my favors."

Jane was silent for a moment. "I'm sorry," she said, sounding like she meant it. "But I'm in trouble. It's freezing out here, and I don't have anyone else I can call."

For the first time, Sadie picked up on the shiver in the other woman's voice. "You're outside?" She looked out the window at the falling snow. According to last night's ten o'clock news, the storm wouldn't let up until early morning.

"I left the hotel about thirty minutes ag-go," Jane said. "But my car is in the lot and it's still blocked off. I thought I could find a restaurant where I could hunker down and wait it out, but I swear everything in this town closes at ten. Is there any way you could come pick me up?"

Sadie's sympathy button was officially triggered despite herself.

The last thing she wanted to do was go back outside, but she couldn't leave anyone out in a snowstorm like this. Not even sneaky reporters who took advantage of Sadie to further their own agendas. There was also that part about Jane's mysterious meeting with Mr. Ogreski. She couldn't help but wonder if Jane could confirm some of the things Sadie had learned or perhaps even add to them. "Where are you?" Sadie asked.

"Um," Jane paused. "I'm behind Shopko. They have a loading dock that's at least covered so I'm out of the worst of the snow."

"I know where that is," Sadie said, surprised that Jane had made it almost half a mile away from the hotel. "Hold on a minute."

Sadie put the phone against her stomach so Jane wouldn't be able to overhear and went back into the kitchen, searching for Eric. He, along with Shawn and Josh, were sitting at the table, eating. Apparently dinner was ready.

"It's awesome, huh?" Shawn said with his mouth full.

Both Eric and Josh nodded as if they were all friends enjoying a meal, instead of strangers thrown together in such bizarre conditions.

"Eric," Sadie interrupted, "I need to pick up a . . . friend. Could I, uh, use your car?"

"Are you sure that's a good idea?" Eric asked.

Sadie realized they'd taken Eric's Jeep to the hotel and a wave of guilt washed over her at what she'd put this poor man through. "They could be looking for your Jeep," she said. "I shouldn't have asked you, I'm—"

Eric shook his head. "I'm not worried about that. If they were tracking the Jeep, they'd have caught up to us by now. I'm just wondering if you're okay to drive."

Sadie forced herself to stand a little straighter. She may only have one arm, but she was fully capable. "I can drive," she said. "It's just that she's out in all this"—she waved toward the window—"and she's kind of a part of everything."

Eric nodded. "Sure, it's fine with me. I was going to get started on the key, but would you rather I drove you somewhere?"

"I think it would be better to figure out that key as soon as possible," Sadie said. She kept to herself that she still had concerns about Jane's character and didn't want to complicate things by having someone else Jane could try to manipulate.

"I can go with you," Shawn said after he swallowed another bite.

Sadie shook her head. "No, you stay here with . . ." She was going to say "him" but it seemed so impersonal, but saying his name sounded so familiar and she wasn't sure that was appropriate either. "With Josh. I'll be fine."

It took a few more seconds of assuring Shawn she was okay to go by herself before Sadie returned to the den and put the phone to her ear.

"I'll be there in a few minutes," she said to Jane. "Look for a green Jeep Cherokee."

"Thank you," Jane said, her voice very different from the arrogant woman Sadie had first encountered in the parking lot. "I owe you one."

Sadie hung up the phone and put it in her jacket pocket, but Jane's words continued to play in her mind: *"I owe you one."*

Sadie was counting on it.

CHAPTER 34

The huddled form in the corner of the loading dock was impossible to mistake for anything other than a nearly frozen Jane Seeley. Sadie pulled up next to the stairs as Jane came rather slowly to her feet. Her black-and-red hair was plastered to her head and every stitch of clothing she had on looked wet and frozen. As Jane made her way to the car, Sadie reflected on the fact that Thom was lucky he'd come inside when he had. She wasn't sure he could have made the same walk now. As it was, Sadie had shifted the Jeep into four-wheel drive within a block of leaving Eric's house. The roads were awful and the plows hadn't been out yet.

Jane opened the door and slid into the seat. She pulled the door shut and wrapped her arms around herself.

Sadie turned up the heat and closed the vents on her side so all the warm air would go to Jane. She also made a mental note that the seat would be wet and Eric would probably need a shop vac to get the water out.

"Oh, sweetie," Sadie said, sympathy overwhelming her hesitation. "You're soaked to the bone."

Jane rested her head against the seat and closed her eyes. "Thank you for picking me up," she said, her voice shaking.

"Maybe you should have stayed at the hotel," Sadie said, pulling away from the building. During the drive over, she'd kept a sharp eye out for police cars, but hadn't seen any, thank goodness. She hoped her luck would hold as well on the ride back.

Jane shook her head, her eyes still closed. "The police were in a frenzy. They'd arrested some lady and she'd gotten away or something. I managed to slip out the back, but my car was around front and the press vans were clogging the street. I was worried the police would want to interrogate me since I never got one of those ticket things they were giving everyone who was cleared to leave. I really didn't think it would be a big deal to wait out the barricade, but it got cold real fast and so I started walking and calling you. I'd thought your phone had gone dead or something, but then you didn't answer at your house either. I'm so glad you finally answered."

They drove in silence for a minute. Jane began shaking, a common effect of extreme cold.

Sadie pulled over to the side of the road. "Maybe Eric has a blanket in the back," she said. "Hold on." She let herself out of the car.

It took some finagling, but she eventually got the back hatch open. Sure enough, there was a blanket in the back. It was one of those velour types popular at cheap motels, but it was soft and warm and that's what mattered. Even though she had used her good arm, it about killed her shoulder to close the back door. She had to pause to catch her breath while the pain subsided. She climbed back in the car, kicking as much snow as possible off her shoes before closing the door. There was nearly two inches on the ground.

"Unfortunately," Sadie said as she pulled back onto the snowy street, "as long as you're in those wet clothes the blanket won't do much good."

"I-I'm okay," Jane said, wrapping up in the blanket with a grateful smile. She looked at Sadie's empty sleeve. "What happened to your arm?"

"Oh," Sadie said, "let's just say it's been an adventurous evening for both of us. It's not too bad though." That was a lie—it hurt terribly—but Sadie didn't want to get into that.

Jane didn't press the topic of Sadie's injury. "I owe you an apology."

Sadie couldn't deny she was surprised to hear that. She didn't pretend to be ignorant of what it was Jane was referring to. "You got me in trouble with one of the detectives," Sadie said, leaving it at that for now. While she couldn't blame Jane for her own arrest, interrupting Pete's meeting had certainly affected Sadie's credibility with several people within the department.

"I'm sorry," Jane said again. "I get carried away sometimes." They both fell silent for a minute. "I know you don't owe me any more favors, but is there any way I could go to your house and warm up? Maybe borrow something to change into?"

Sadie shifted uncomfortably. "Normally I'd say yes, but I'm afraid I can't go home right now." Quite frankly, Sadie didn't know what to do with Jane. She hadn't thought beyond rescuing her from certain death. Would it be unfair for her to take Jane back to Eric's house? Shouldn't she ask Eric's permission first? And yet, what other options were there? Even if she took Jane to a hotel, Jane had nothing dry to wear. There were really no options other than taking Jane with her. Boy, she was going to owe Eric big-time for all the help he was giving her. Maybe she'd clean his house once she had both hands. That was a payback he certainly couldn't refuse. "I'm staying at a . . . friend's house. You can come there for a little while."

"Thank you," Jane said.

Sadie nodded her acceptance of the gratitude. Anyone would have done as much. She hoped that if Eric did any household chores, it was laundry so Jane could get out of her wet clothes.

"Did you find anything that helped your story?" Sadie asked as she looked both ways at a four-way stop. The roads were empty, many roads not even showing tire tracks in the deep snow. Most people were home—which is exactly where Sadie wanted to be.

Jane let out a breath. "Not really," she said darkly. Some of the softness she'd had in her earlier comments was decidedly gone. Tough Jane was back.

"Oh," Sadie said, hoping her own disappointment wasn't too obvious. If Jane hadn't learned anything, she couldn't share it. "I'm sorry to hear that. You've certainly put a lot into this story."

"Yes, I have," Jane said. She paused for a moment before continuing, her voice taking on an angry urgency. "I'm good at what I do, Sadie," Jane said, sounding strangely defensive. Sadie wasn't sure what Jane needed to defend herself against in the Jeep, but she didn't interrupt her. Emotional venting was often full of valuable information. "I went to their rooms but—"

"Rooms?" Sadie interrupted.

"Yes, the hotel rooms for Thom Mortenson and Mark Ogreski."

"You got into their rooms?"

"Well, not really," Jane said, frustration lacing her words. "The police were already there, and so the best I got was to overhear that Mr. O has some serious problems."

"What do you mean?" Sadie asked.

"One officer was reading off like eight medications." She reached under her shirt and produced an only slightly wet notepad with Carmichael Hotel stamped on the top. "Prozac, Xanax, Ambien, and codeine. Okay, that's only four, but still."

"Those are heavy-duty medications, aren't they?" Sadie asked, looking at Jane again.

"Yeah," Jane said. Her tone was a bit dismissive, however, telling Sadie that Jane didn't think the meds were all that important. "But right then another cop came around the corner and got after me. I said the hotel manager had sent me up to see if they needed anything, but I had to go back downstairs. I had really hoped that . . ." She stopped herself and Sadie looked at her quickly.

"What?" Sadie asked. "Hoped what?"

Jane was silent for a moment, and Sadie concentrated hard on sending out "you can trust me" vibes.

After a moment, Jane let out a breath. "I'm a good reporter, Sadie," she said again. "And the Ms. Jane column is a good gig—I'm not complaining—but it's not me. The picture isn't even me. And while I'm grateful for the work, I don't want to spend the rest of my life telling coeds whether or not to pay their bum boyfriend's cell phone bills. I've been trying so hard to break out of the mold I put myself in, but the paper's fighting me. They've let me do a story here and there, but nothing exclusive, nothing earth-shattering. And then here I am, in the perfect place at the perfect time with the perfect exclusive that only needs a little fleshing out and I'm stuck. I get into the hotel—a crime scene—and I get two feet from their room, for heaven's sake, and I end up with nothing. My contact is dead, my sources are used up, and every other journalist in the country is swarming over my story like flies. After weeks of research, I'm going to end up telling the same overdone story as every other newspaper in the Midwest because I can't get my facts verified. Yet I've worked so much harder than any of them. It's so not fair."

"I'm sorry," Sadie said, still aware that Jane had yet to tell her what her story was about. Even though she didn't necessarily support Jane's methods, she could relate to hard work coming to nothing. That was never fun—even when that hard work was illegal. She tried to phrase her next question as casually as she could. "What exactly were you researching all these weeks? It must have been big to have taken so much of your attention."

"It was big," Jane said, sounding discouraged. "Huge—if I had verifiable facts to support it, which I can't seem to find."

"What kind of verifiable facts?" Sadie finally asked, once again in search of the perfect tone of voice that communicated interest without triggering Jane's defenses.

Jane turned her head to look at Sadie, and Sadie continued to look out the windshield as though she didn't notice the other woman watching her.

She tried to reframe her question. "I mean, maybe I can help you figure it out." She hesitated. How much did she want to say about what she'd discovered tonight? She decided on bits and pieces. "It's been kind of an interesting night for me, too. Maybe I have something that would help you."

"What?" Jane asked, an edge to her voice. It was hard to believe this was the same woman who'd been humble and apologetic a few minutes ago. "What do you have?"

Sadie glanced at her and hoped she was playing her cards correctly. "What do *you* have?" she asked back.

Jane was silent, but she straightened in the seat. "You won't just tell me what you know?"

"You won't just tell *me* what *you* know?" Sadie countered. She came to a stop at a stop sign less than two blocks from Eric's house. She didn't continue through the intersection after she'd paused for her required three seconds. Instead she looked at Jane and lifted her eyebrows expectantly.

Jane narrowed her eyes and lifted her chin. "I'll trade you," she said. "You tell me something I don't know, and I'll do the same."

That sounded good to Sadie. She went first, a show of good faith in her opinion, but she only told what she knew would be well-known once she went to the police. "There was a young man at the hotel taking pictures of Mr. Ogreski's body. He said he was with the crime scene, but he wasn't. I found him in old yearbooks. He was Damon Mortenson's best friend before Damon died."

Jane looked impressed. "What else do you have?"

Sadie shook her head. "Your turn."

"Okay," she said, looking thoughtful for a moment. "*Devilish Details* is going out of print. The publisher filed a notice, but it hasn't been made public yet."

Sadie lifted her eyebrows. "Wow. That must be hard for Thom."

Jane shrugged and waited expectantly.

"I found the original letter requesting the full manuscript for Thom's book. It was dated a few months before Damon died." She didn't really know why that detail might be important, but it was a discovery she could take credit for.

Jane, however, looked rather skeptical. "Really?" she said, her tone doubtful.

"Yeah," Sadie said. She kept to herself the fact that she had the actual letter in her pocket at that very moment. "Your turn."

Jane paused and then took a breath. "Thom Mortenson didn't write *Devilish Details*."

Chapter 35

It was a good thing Sadie was already stopped. "What?" she breathed, staring at Jane, who, despite her shivering, seemed rather pleased with Sadie's reaction. "What do you mean Thom Mortenson didn't write it?"

"Trade," Jane said, then continued before Sadie had a chance to respond. "What's this guy's name? The photographing-former-best-friend of the deceased Damon Mortenson."

"Josh Hender," Sadie said.

Jane dug a pen from her pocket and quickly scribbled the information in her notebook.

Sadie didn't wait for Jane to finish writing before she fired her next question. "If Thom didn't write it, who did?"

"I don't know," Jane said, frowning slightly and tapping her pen against her notebook. "That's what I planned to find out from Mr. Ogreski tonight. But that letter you found is part of the fraud, I guarantee it. They've worked very hard to keep it a secret."

"If you're right, and they worked so hard to hide the truth, why would Mr. Ogreski suddenly decide to talk to you?" Sadie asked. If

Thom didn't write *Devilish Details*, it was big news. Very big. Too big to just hand over to some advice columnist at a regional paper. Jane smiled, looking very pleased as she turned to face Sadie. "Because I asked. And he knew I'd find the answer sooner or later."

"Wait," Sadie said, putting up a hand. "This isn't working. We're both getting jumbled answers. Just details, not the full picture. Let's cut to the chase. You said you've been researching this for weeks—why? What triggered it? What started the search?"

"Come on, Sadie," Jane said, shaking her head slightly. "You're asking me to give up my story. Journalists don't do that."

"What if I made it worth your while?" Sadie said, not taking her eyes off the other woman. It was time to pull out the big guns.

"And how would you do that?"

"Give you another story," Sadie said. "And maybe, with your journalistic wiles, you can help fill in some of the blanks that are making me crazy." She wriggled forward in her seat, suddenly eager to impart what she knew to someone as interested as she was. "While you've been in the hotel poking around and finding nothing, I've been all over the city. I tracked down Josh Hender, got attacked by his psycho mother, and made nachos for Thom Mortenson. Then there's a guy, Eric . . . something or other, who's trying to figure out the lock that this key I found will fit in, and my son is holding Josh Hender until I can figure out what's going on." It sounded pretty impressive when she said it all at once like that.

"Holy cow, woman," Jane breathed, looking at Sadie with surprise and perhaps a little admiration too. "You did all that tonight?"

Sadie nodded, trying not to come across as too proud. In truth, proud wasn't the right word anyway. She was rather embarrassed by all she'd been a part of, and terribly worried about what was going to happen to everyone involved. But still, it was nice that someone seemed to appreciate what she'd done.

"What makes you think Thom Mortenson didn't write *Devilish Details?*" she asked.

"Because Diane Veeter said so."

For the second time in three minutes Sadie was completely stunned.

"Diane Veeter?" Sadie said, certain she'd missed something. "That's impossible. Diane Veeter is dead."

"I know," Jane said. "That's what made this story so irresistible." There was a longing tone to her voice that spoke of her surrender to the fact that things were not going to work out as well as she'd hoped they would. She paused and took a breath before continuing. "Before I tell you this, you have to swear you won't talk to any other reporters about it. There's a chance I can still salvage what I've learned into a story that will at least have something different than everyone else's. I need your word."

"I don't even know any other reporters," Sadie said. "Well, except for Linda Knight. She writes up the Garrison pieces for the *Logan County Journal,* but she mostly focuses on quilting groups and motocross, so I don't think she'd even know what to do with this kind of thing. But I promise not to tell her anyway."

Jane nodded and began speaking. "About two months ago, I threw a tantrum about wanting a new office. I'd been sharing one with a couple sportswriters who were continually predicting the imminent end of life as we knew it if LeBron didn't make his foul shots. I simply couldn't take it anymore. I got the new office, but it had no windows and had been used for storage—mostly personal stuff previous employees hadn't taken with them when *their* tantrums didn't end up as profitable as mine did. I didn't care—I had my own space and I was happy.

"For a few weeks I just let the boxes sit there, but then I decided I'd rather have a LoveSac than these stupid boxes full of junk. So I got permission to go through them. Mostly I threw things away—although I found a sweet Montblanc pen that's the bomb." She paused, realizing she was off track, and then picked back up again.

"Anyway, about halfway through these boxes I found a stack of mail for a reporter who hadn't been with the *Post* for years. Apparently, the mail had come after the reporter left and was thrown in the box, waiting for her to come back and get it—which obviously she never did. Most of the mail was bills and ads, but there was this hand-addressed envelope marked confidential." Jane chuckled. "Well, if there is one way to get a reporter obsessed, it's to write *confidential* on an envelope. So, I, of course, open it up and find a letter from a woman named Diane Veeter who is telling this reporter that she knows Thom Mortenson didn't write *Devilish Details* and that she can prove it and she wants a face-to-face meeting to discuss it."

"When was the letter written?" Sadie asked, barely able to breathe as she hung onto Jane's every word.

"Like I said, years ago," Jane said. She didn't seem to like being interrupted. "So I go look up this Veeter woman and find out she's dead—like *days* after she'd mailed the letter."

"Oh, my gosh," Sadie said, leaning against the door, her thoughts spinning. Just as she opened her mouth to say something, she caught the flash of headlights coming up behind her. She straightened and looked in her rearview mirror, nearly swallowing her tongue when she saw it was a police car. She quickly looked both ways and drove through the intersection while chanting *Not yet, not yet, not yet,* in her head.

When the police car turned left instead of following her, she could breathe again. There was a church ahead on the right, and Sadie pulled into the parking lot and around the back. She killed the lights and turned back to Jane. "Are you implying Diane's death wasn't an accident?" Sadie asked, picking up where she'd left off.

Jane shrugged. "I don't know. I've gone through the original accident report and there's no evidence that it was anything *but* an accident—too much wine, bad weather, and unfamiliar roads is the official report. She was visiting her sister in California and on her way back to the hotel after they'd met for dinner, she apparently drove right off the canyon road."

Sadie nodded. She remembered all those details, every one of them part of the tragedy.

Jane kept talking. "I dug as deep as I possibly could into the stuff the police knew, but nothing turned up. So I turned to her husband, but he wouldn't talk to me. So then I shifted my focus to Thom Mortenson instead. Diane had said she could prove he didn't write the book, which meant there had to be some evidence out there that supported her claim. I learned that Thom had entered a couple writing contests before his book was published. I was able to get copies of those entries, which I compared to *Devilish Details.* They sounded like two completely different writers."

"But writers have different styles for different types of books," Sadie said, disappointed Jane didn't have more conclusive evidence that Thom hadn't written the book. Besides, Sadie had a letter in her pocket from Mark Ogreski asking for an exclusive on the book. "Ray Bradbury, for instance. He sounded completely different in his science fiction than he did in *Dandelion Wine.*"

Jane shook her head. "No, he didn't," she said, leaning forward. "If you analyze the syntax of his sentences in his science fiction against his more literary works, you'll see they're almost identical. And even though his semantics may differ because of the genres he's writing in, there's enough of a parallel through the use of modifiers and iambic to make it obvious even to the casual observer that the same person authored both types of works, despite those works using different formulas indicative of the genre models. That's not to say growth isn't identifiable in a writer's subsequent works, but increased skill at the craft doesn't override style to that degree."

Sadie called Uncle. Jane was using words Sadie had never heard before in her life.

"But Diane Veeter said she had proof," Sadie said, returning to more stable ground. "How would she, of all people, know that Thom hadn't written the book?" As soon as Sadie asked the question, though, her brain made a connection as a completely new thought spun into center stage in her mind.

Jane didn't miss Sadie's sudden reaction and she narrowed her eyes. "What?"

Sadie locked her gaze with Jane's. "Diane Veeter was Damon Mortenson's English teacher."

"She was?" Jane nearly yelled.

Sadie pulled the letter out of her pocket and opened it up. Jane leaned in and Sadie turned the paper so they could read it together. It was addressed to "Mr. Mortenson" and had been sent a couple of months before Damon's death. Sadie had assumed Mr. Mortenson was *Thom* Mortenson. But what if it wasn't? Could Damon have written *Devilish Details?* That question led to another one—Did Sadie believe what Jane had told her? Did she believe that Thom *hadn't* written the book? Apparently, she did. That was somewhat disturbing in and of itself, but not as disturbing as considering the possibility that Thom had published his son's book as his own. The very idea raised yet another set of questions that dangled in front of Sadie like cobwebs in the attic.

"No way," Jane said, as if reading Sadie's thoughts. She sat back in her seat and shook her hair-plastered head. "No way a kid wrote that book," she said. "If that's what you're thinking."

Sadie didn't bother answering as she scanned the letter again. There was nothing in the letter that proved it wasn't written to Thom, but Diane had been Damon's teacher—his *writing* teacher. If *Diane* had proof, it wasn't a far stretch to assume she had some of Damon's writing—or even part of the original manuscript if, in fact, Damon had written the book. She'd have had to have held onto it even after Damon had died, though, since Diane wrote the letter to the *Post* almost two years after Damon's death, which was shortly after *Devilish Details* had come out. The big question was, had Diane's husband kept this proof after Diane died?

After some thought, Sadie folded up the letter and put it back in her pocket. Then she leaned forward and wrestled the phone book from under the driver's seat of Eric's car—uh, Jeep. She put it on her lap so she could use her good hand to flip the pages. There was only one Veeter listed in the phone book, and she read through the address twice—thank goodness she wasn't dealing with any Smiths or Johnsons tonight.

She handed the phone book to Jane while glancing at the dashboard clock—it was nearing midnight. Too late to be knocking on anyone's door, but with Josh Hender hog-tied at Eric's house, the police trying to find her, and potential answers just out of reach, Sadie was willing to abandon yet more social protocol. She put the car back into drive and pulled out from behind the church. At the road she turned on her left blinker. Brian Veeter didn't live very far away, which she appreciated as the roads were becoming more treacherous by the minute.

"He won't talk to you," Jane said emphatically, after glancing down at the phone book that was still open to the Vs. She held onto the dashboard throughout the next turn as the Jeep's back tires slid despite being in four-wheel drive. "I tried every angle," Jane continued. "And left literally dozens of messages. He finally answered one and said he'd sue me for harassment if I ever contacted him again."

"That's just it," Sadie said, glancing at the younger woman, who still looked like a drowned rat. "You don't need an angle. You simply need a reason to talk about something that hurts."

"If it's not news, then it's a waste of my time," Jane said, shaking her head. "And this crazy idea you've got is a total waste of time. I'm telling you that a kid did *not* write the book."

"You don't know that," Sadie said, shaking her head at Jane's stubbornness.

"Yes," Jane said, her voice even stronger, "I do know that. *Devilish Details* is very well-written. No teenage kid writes with that kind of skill and symmetry. Especially not some high-school dropout who later whacks himself and his girlfriend. Good writing takes years to develop, and there isn't a sixteen-year-old on the planet who can pull off anything of that caliber, never mind a kid who's m-mentally ill."

The stutter reminded Sadie that Jane was still at risk of developing hypothermia. "I'll take you to Eric's house first," she said, though she hated the delay. The Veeters' street was approaching, but she switched her signal to turn right, which would take her toward Eric's house instead. "Then I'll come back."

Jane was silent, but not for long. "N-no way. If you're going, I'm going with you. I'm just saying it's a waste of our time."

"And yet you want to be in on it," Sadie said, giving Jane a knowing look. Even if Jane didn't believe it was possible, she couldn't stand the idea of something happening without her. Sadie knew how that felt.

Sadie turned left onto the Veeters' street. She squinted at the mailboxes until she found one with the house number that matched the listing in the phone book. The brick mailbox resembled a lighthouse and the name Veeter was etched into a stone inlay on the front. She pulled into the driveway and looked up at the large, brown stucco home. The house was easily twice the size of Sadie's, but Sadie had always preferred paid off and cozy to expensive and vaulted. She wished there were some lights on. She hated the idea of waking anyone up, and yet she didn't feel this could wait.

She reached for the door handle, but then turned to Jane. "When I get back, maybe you can tell me how long you've been working on *your* book." She smiled smugly at Jane's expression and let herself out of the car. "Now, stay here. You've already managed to make a pest out of yourself with them and I don't want you undermining this, okay? Are you sure you wouldn't rather go to Eric's?"

Jane folded her arms over her chest and turned away like a petulant child. No matter. She likely needed a time-out anyway.

CHAPTER 36

Sadie hurried up the wide cobblestone steps, hunching over to keep the snow off her face. She was glad Jane hadn't argued with her about staying in the car. For one thing, Jane was still freezing. In the car she could huddle around the heat vents and at least ward off hypothermia better than she could if she had returned to the cold, even for a minute or two. The other reason, however, had everything to do with the idea of "the angle" Jane had mentioned. Jane was a reporter, a stranger stalking a story. Sadie was a friend of Diane's, asking questions for what were very different reasons. She could only hope it would make a difference to Brian.

Thank heaven for covered porches, Sadie thought as she reached the top of the steps, which was blissfully dry and snow-free—though freezing cold. She took a breath, wishing there was even one light on inside the house. But she didn't dwell on it long enough to back out of it. It had to be done. She rang the doorbell and then knocked hard on the heavy oak door, hoping the double announcement of a midnight caller would spark the urgency she wanted Brian to feel.

After counting to fifteen she knocked again, then put her ear to the door, gratified to hear footsteps. A light flipped on, and Sadie took a deep breath and a step back, straightening her back as best she could as she prepared to face Brian and ask if she could come in. But Brian didn't answer the door. Instead, a thick yet petite woman no older than her early thirties, Sadie guessed, with shoulder-length, brown hair and tired eyes pulled open the door about six inches. She was dressed in a nightgown with a robe over the top.

Sadie panicked. Did she have the wrong house?

"Um, I'm sorry to bother you so late at night," she said. "But I'm looking for Brian Veeter."

"Dad's not here," the woman said, still blinking herself awake.

Sadie was relieved to at least be at the right house, but that did little to soothe her disappointment. "He's really not here?" she asked. "Will he be home soon?" Maybe he'd run to the store or something. At midnight. In the snow.

"Do you have any idea what time it is?" the woman asked.

"I do," Sadie said. "And I'm really sorry. If it weren't of utmost importance, I wouldn't be here. Do you know when your dad's going to be back?" Maybe she could come back in the morning.

"He's on his honeymoon," the woman said flatly. "He won't be back until next Thursday."

Sadie could feel the surprise showing on her face. "Honeymoon?"

The woman didn't smile or act giddy about her father's good fortune. Her expression stayed blank as she nodded, which said plenty. Clearly, she was not supportive of this marriage.

"I'm sorry," Sadie said to explain her reaction. "I didn't know."

"Few people do," she said. "But *she* will be moving in when they get back, so you won't be able to miss her. She's about twenty-eight and looks like Pamela Anderson, but not as classy. They met online a few months back and got married in Vegas two days ago."

Sadie cringed at the knowledge that Brian Veeter had become

a very sad and disappointing statistic. She was pretty sure he was pushing sixty-five.

"Can I help you with anything?" the woman asked.

Sadie was fully prepared to tell her no, but then realized that given the circumstances, Diane's daughter might be more helpful than Brian would be. Chances were good he wouldn't want to talk about his first wife with the new Mrs. Veeter around.

"Well, maybe," Sadie said. "I needed to ask some questions about your mom."

The woman's expression became even more guarded, and she closed the door an inch.

"No, no, please don't shut the door," Sadie said, putting out her good hand, her fingers beginning to tingle from the cold. "I'm afraid some questions have been raised tonight that only Diane may have known the answer to. My name's Sadie Hoffmiller, and I was a friend of Diane's. Can I please ask you a few questions?"

The woman hesitated, and then opened the door. A hallelujah chorus sang in Sadie's mind as she hurried over the threshold. How on earth had Jane survived outside for so long?

She stepped inside and immediately noticed several boxes in the otherwise beautifully decorated living room. Some empty boxes were stacked at one end of the room, but several opened boxes were lined up in the middle of the floor. The woman had said the new Mrs. Veeter was moving in—was this her stuff?

"Thank you," Sadie said, smiling gratefully as the woman shut the front door behind her.

"Who are you again?" she asked as she walked further into the house and faced Sadie again.

"Sorry, my name is Sadie Hoffmiller," she said. "I was a teacher too."

"You taught with Mom?"

"Well, no, not really," Sadie offered with a smile she hoped would help convince this woman to give her the benefit of the doubt. "But we taught some of the same students, and we knew one another through district events and things." But not well enough that Sadie knew the names of Diane's children. And right now she sure wished she did. Based on Diane's age, and the age of the woman standing in front of Sadie now, she took a chance. "You're Diane's youngest daughter, right?"

"Tina," the girl answered, nodding carefully.

Sadie smiled. "Right," she said, relieved to have guessed correctly. They both looked at each other for a few more seconds before Sadie realized she should be the one doing the talking. She looked at the boxes again, but forced herself not to ask about them. It wasn't her business. "I'm here in hopes that maybe your mother kept some of her students' papers—favorite students."

This time it was Tina who looked at the boxes, then back to Sadie. "You came here at midnight to ask about old student papers? After all these years?"

Couldn't anyone just smile and give her what she needed? Sadie tried to come up with an answer that would be quick and yet to the point. She glanced at the boxes and then did a double, or rather a triple, take. She squinted in order to read the words written in magic marker on one of the boxes closest to her.

DIANE—CLOTHES

She looked up at Tina, who was watching her. "You're going through your mother's things?" What strange timing.

Tina took a breath and sighed. "Dad told us about the wedding two weeks ago, then he hauled up these boxes. He was going to throw them out. I asked if I could go through them first. He agreed, but he wants it all gone by the time he and Cat get home."

"Cat?" Sadie asked.

Tina's eyes narrowed. "Yep." She didn't say anything else. She didn't need to.

"I'm sorry," Sadie said again, forcing her mind to slow down. "I can only imagine what this has been like for you."

Tina shrugged, looking tired. "So, what is it you need?" she asked. "Why are student papers important after all these years?"

Sadie glanced at the boxes again. Some of them looked like they held files. She looked back at Tina and decided against getting to her point in a roundabout way. "I'm looking for anything that might be related to Damon Mortenson."

Tina furrowed her brow. "Why?"

Another quick glance at the files—right there in front of her—helped her decide to be as honest as possible. "Before your mother died she sent a letter to a reporter at the *Denver Post* that claimed she had proof Thom Mortenson didn't write the book *Devilish Details*, which had come out a few weeks earlier."

Tina's eyes went wide. "Mom said that?"

Sadie nodded. "Unfortunately, the letter was lost until just recently. Now that we have it, we're trying to find her proof."

"We?" Tina asked. "Who's we?"

Shoot, why hadn't Sadie watched her pronouns a little better? "A friend of mine," she finally said. It was the second time that night she'd called Jane a "friend," and she wasn't entirely comfortable with that label. "She works at the *Post*."

"She's the one harassing my father!" Tina's voice rose in pitch and her tired face was instantly animated—but not in a good way.

"She called him twelve times in one day, demanding that he meet with her to talk about Mom. If you ask me and my sisters, she's the *exact* reason my dad decided to marry that bimbo." She stopped for a breath, and Sadie tried not to show her fear at the intensity of Tina's reaction. "My dad had a very difficult time coming to terms with my mother's death. We were all relieved when he finally started dating again. We didn't want him to be alone for the rest of his life. But then he got involved with that girl online and we knew it was a disaster. We were able to convince him to take things slow and not rush in to anything. Then that reporter starts harassing him, bringing all the emotions he felt after Mom died back to the forefront. He's tired of hurting so much, but this *friend* of yours wouldn't let up. Lo and behold a week later he announces he's getting married. He's starting a new life and he wants Mom's stuff gone—no more reminders. Your *friend* has no idea what she's done."

Sadie put up her one hand, hoping to ease the tension that had suddenly filled the vaulted foyer of the home. "I'm not like the reporter and I completely agree that she pushes too hard," she said quickly. "I'm also very sorry about your father's marriage. I can imagine it's very difficult, and I can see why you're angry." Sadie thought it was a bit much to blame the wedding on Jane, though. "I'm here because I know Diane wouldn't have made that kind of accusation against Thom Mortenson without good reason."

Tina shook her head. "Mom was a teacher. I don't know why she would send that letter to the newspaper, and I'm not convinced she really did. She never said anything about Thom Mortenson's book to anyone else and reporters lie about stuff like that all the time."

Sadie could feel herself running out of rope and decided it was time to compact her information. "Your mother showed a special interest in Damon Mortenson, and I think it might be because *he* wrote *Devilish Details*, not his father. I think the proof she mentioned in her letter might very well be right here." She waved toward the boxes of files.

Tina looked at the boxes and then back at Sadie.

"Please," Sadie said, trying not to beg, but finding it nearly impossible not to. "I'm not trying to add more heartache to your plate, I swear."

Tina didn't look convinced, and Sadie wished she hadn't brought Jane up at all.

Sadie made one more plea. "Your mother knew something important. Please."

Tina watched her for a few more seconds, then looked around the room as if searching for something. "I have to ask my dad. Hold on and I'll call him." She made a face, obviously not looking forward to it.

Sadie forced a polite smile. It wasn't a no—not yet—and that was a good thing. Tina exited through a doorway, probably heading for the phone. Sadie's attention immediately locked on the boxes of files, and she carefully glanced back and forth between the boxes and the doorway Tina had disappeared through. After a few moments she could hear Tina's muted voice on the phone.

With Tina occupied, Sadie took a closer look at the multicolored files in the boxes. They were organized alphabetically; the first box she looked at was marked A-F. She looked past it to the next box— G-L. There was a stack of files—a dozen at least—on the couch. Sadie assumed they were the ones Tina had decided to keep.

Glancing at the doorway, Sadie took a few steps closer to the couch and looked through the stacked files. Nothing stood out to her, so she crouched down and thumbed through the files still in the boxes, trying to get a feel for what they contained. Adams, Melissa. Arrington, Dallon.

Sadie knew Dallon Arrington—he'd been one of her third-grade students many years ago. Good kid. She pulled out his file and flipped through it, smiling at Diane's sprawling handwriting and her notes like "Great characterization!" and "You made me run for the Kleenex, Dallon. Well done! I'd love to keep this for my files."

Mixed in with the student files were files for things like allocution exercises—whatever that meant—and Beetzer Phonics programs. But mostly the files were names of students, which meant the possibility of Damon Mortenson having a file of his own was a very real possibility. But where were the rest of the boxes? These ended at L.

"What are you doing?"

Sadie jumped to her feet before realizing she still had Dallon Arrington's file in her hand. She felt her face heat up as she stammered an apology and quickly returned the file. When she stood again she was unable to meet Tina's eyes and didn't know how to explain herself.

"My dad said no," Tina said after a few intolerable seconds. She pointed to the front door. "Get out now before I call the police." Whatever benefit of the doubt she'd given Sadie was gone.

Sadie was so embarrassed she couldn't bring herself to argue. "I-I'm so sorry," she said, turning toward the door. "I guess I got carried away." Wasn't that exactly what Jane had said after apologizing for sneaking into the hotel and getting Sadie in trouble?

"Go now," Tina said menacingly.

Sadie moved as fast as she could out the door and down the steps. First she vented like an idiot at the hotel, and now she got caught peeking at private files in someone else's home? What was happening to her? She got back in the car and shifted into reverse.

"So?" Jane asked. She had the blanket pulled up to her chin, but was still shivering despite the fact that the car had to be ninety degrees.

Sadie couldn't even put the experience into words. She just shook her head and looked in her rearview mirror, anxious to leave.

However, just as she was about to put her foot on the gas, she caught a glance of the Veeters' big, black garbage can tucked under the eaves of the double car garage. The lid wasn't closed all the way.

She narrowed her eyes, finding it difficult to make out details through the snow. Then she turned on the headlights and recognized a rainbow of files sticking out over the side of the stuffed garbage can.

The intense evaluation of her morality would have to wait at least another fifteen minutes.

CHAPTER 37

Jane was quiet as they drove back to Eric's house. Sadie couldn't blame her for being annoyed. If Sadie could have done it herself, she'd have dug out a backseat worth of files from the garbage can alone. Unfortunately, in her disabled state, she had no choice but to ask for Jane's help. Dumpster diving soured her dramatically—no pun intended.

The interior of the car was smelling rather sour as well—those files hadn't been the only things in the can. Sadie was definitely going to have to get the Jeep detailed after this. She hoped Eric would understand.

"I appreciate your help," Sadie said for the sixth time.

Jane snorted for the sixth time.

They remained silent for a little longer and Sadie wondered what would happen from here on out. She was bringing a surly reporter back to what was basically their headquarters. Was that such a good idea? She'd learned that while Jane could be soft and charming, she had an edge to her. That edge made it difficult for Sadie to trust her fully, and yet Jane had given her so much information. It was very confusing trying to figure people out sometimes.

"There's something else we ought to talk about before we get to Eric's," Sadie said, shifting in her seat in preparation for a difficult conversation. "I know you're used to being the one who calls the shots, and while I have no problem taking you with me, I need two things from you in exchange."

"I already told you about Diane Veeter's letter, that Thom didn't write the book, *and* I dumpster dived for those files. What more do you want from me?"

Sadie stopped the car in the middle of the road and turned to face her companion. "I want you to take a step back and not try to dominate the situation." Sadie kept her expression tight, but inside she wriggled. She didn't like strong-arming people any more than she liked it when other people strong-armed her. And yet, it had to be done.

"You promised me a story," Jane said again, her eyes narrowed through the hair still stuck to her forehead.

"And if you can work as a team with the rest of us, and respect the circumstances we all find ourselves in, you'll get more than you'd ever get otherwise."

"What circumstances?" Jane questioned, seeming to soften a little bit.

Sadie hedged, but then realized she was too far in to start backing out now. "You said when you left the hotel they were going crazy trying to find someone, right? Well, that someone was probably me. They kind of arrested me for interfering, but then I got away. Meanwhile, my son had grabbed Josh Hender and tied him up. We're trying to gather together as much information as possible in the hopes that we can clear ourselves once the police catch up." Sadie paused. "Come to think of it, maybe you'd rather not come. You might end up in just as much trouble if you do. I could call you and tell you what I find out, if you'd rather do that."

"Huh," Jane replied, watching Sadie thoughtfully. "I have to say you're a lot more interesting than I ever imagined you'd be. I'd called you in hopes of getting a little history on Thom Mortenson, and instead I get all this."

Was that supposed to be a compliment?

"I need your assurance that you can be a part of this team, and that you know what you're getting into," Sadie said.

Jane nodded. "I get it. And I am at your command."

Sadie felt she had no choice but to accept Jane's agreement to her terms. She nodded and started driving again, not realizing until they turned on Morning Glen that she'd pass the Hender home on her way to Eric's. She sunk in her seat a little when she saw a police car parked in the driveway. Luckily, there was no one in the car at the moment. Which meant they were inside. Was Thom still there? What was he telling them about the woman who had made him nachos? Was he drunk from those blasted mini-bottles?

Her heart was pumping, but she also felt a shot of validation. Someone had listened to her and sent an officer to the Hender home. Hopefully, that would give her more credibility when it came her time to face the local law enforcement.

She pulled up beside the RV in Eric's driveway and turned off the car. "I'll have Shawn bring in the files," Sadie said to Jane as she opened her door. "And I'm sure Eric will have some dry clothes you can change in to."

"I can't wait," Jane said in a cheery voice.

Sadie was disturbed by the wide grin on Jane's face. Why did Sadie feel like she was adding jalapeños to cake batter by bringing this woman here?

CHAPTER 38

It took almost ten minutes for Jane to take a quick shower and change into a pair of Eric's sweats and a flannel shirt. Meanwhile, Sadie explained to Shawn about the files—outside of Josh's hearing—and sent him to bring them into the house and put them in the den. Josh was at the kitchen table reading through last week's newspaper. Shawn said Josh had eaten every bite of his Evil Chicken. Sadie was glad he'd liked it and hoped it would foreshadow his cooperation once she was ready to start talking to him. When she'd left to pick up Jane, she'd had no idea she'd be gone for nearly an hour. Sadie imagined that if Josh had ever thought he might one day be kidnapped and held against his will, he would have never guessed it would be quite like this.

She was watching Josh when Eric stole her attention. "I found the lock."

He'd spoken so quiet and casual that it took a moment to realize what he'd said and why it was important.

"You found the lock!" She hurried to stand behind him so she could look over his shoulder at the computer screen. There was a small, square photo in the upper corner with a picture of what could have been the exact key she'd found at Josh's, other than the numbers were different.

"That's it!" Sadie said.

"I know," Eric replied. "That's why I said I found it."

Sheesh, he was suddenly so sensitive. Sadie leaned in, trying to get a feel for this website. "What is this?"

"Locksmith nerd heaven," Eric said, typing into a message field at the bottom of the screen. "It offers repair information, changes in lock technology, and a message forum for other things—like trying to track down a specific type of key."

"Wow," Sadie said, rather impressed. Who knew locksmiths had these kinds of resources? "So what does the key go to?" She glanced at Josh. He was watching them carefully. She straightened and directed her next question to Josh rather than Eric. "Unless you'd rather tell us."

Josh shrugged and went back to his paper, shaking it out slightly as if to verify his extreme interest in the events that had happened in Colorado last week. "Knock yourself out," he said. The tightness of his shoulders and the glance he stole when he thought Sadie had already looked away betrayed that he was paying very close attention. Why?

As she turned her attention back to the website, she noticed Jane standing in the doorway.

"Good, you're done," Sadie said, smiling a smile she didn't feel as she wondered how long Jane had been standing there. She tapped Eric on the shoulder, "I'll be right back."

Eric nodded and kept typing.

Sadie led Jane into the den where Shawn had set a huge pile of rainbow-colored files in the middle of the floor, which, Sadie noted, really needed to be vacuumed. Stray papers were everywhere and she frowned. This could take awhile, but at least having an extra pair of hands would speed up the process.

"Jane, this is Shawn, my son. He could use your help going through the files. We're looking for one on Damon Mortenson."

Jane looked over her shoulder, toward the doorway that led to the kitchen. "I'd really prefer to talk to Josh."

"I'm sure you would," Sadie said. "But right now I need you to go through the files."

Jane shifted her focus to Sadie's face, held her eyes for a moment and then shrugged. "Whatever you need, boss." There was no sarcasm in her tone, but Sadie felt it in her word choice anyway.

"Okay then," Sadie said. "Let me know what you guys find."

Jane sat cross-legged on the floor and reached for the top file, her back toward Sadie.

Sadie waited until Shawn looked up at her, then mouthed the words "Watch her" and pointed at Jane.

Shawn nodded, then looked at Jane carefully as he took a file too.

Satisfied the situation was under control, Sadie returned to the kitchen. "Sorry about that," she said as she moved to stand behind Eric. "Now, where were we?"

"I was getting to the good part—where I tell you what the key goes to."

"Oh, right," Sadie said, unable to keep the excitement from her voice. She noticed Josh's eyes were trained—unmoving—on the paper. He wasn't reading. He was listening. "So, what's it to?"

"A storage unit," Eric said triumphantly. He turned the key over and pointed at the numbers on the back. "I'm betting this is the code to the exterior door. It's not very secure, writing it on the key, but I'm not complaining."

"Do you know which storage company it's for?"

"Advanced," Eric said. "But they used to be owned by Sunrise, whose logo was orange, hence an orange key. This storage unit must have been rented before the sale, which is why the key still matches Sunrise, not Advanced, whose colors are blue and gold."

"I thought storage units required you to provide your own lock?" Sadie asked while mentally trying to remember where Advanced was located. By the railroad, she thought. Then she had another thought: Josh was only twenty-six, so why did he own a storage unit?

Eric shrugged. "*Self*-storage usually does. But Advanced is just storage. And it's inside units rather than outside ones. More secure, but not as easily accessed."

"Do you know when Advanced bought Sunrise?" Sadie asked.

"Six years ago," Eric said.

Eric continued discussing protocol for re-keying storage units when businesses changed hands, but Sadie was watching Josh, waiting for him to react to their discovery, maybe even try to stop their discussion. Strangely enough, he made no protest at all, but seemed deep in thought instead. After a minute she put up her hand, cutting Eric off.

"You didn't know it was to a storage unit, did you?" she asked Josh.

Eric looked at the young man at the end of the table as well.

Josh tried to shrug off her question.

"You don't," she concluded. "Where did you get the key?"

His jaw moved, but he didn't answer.

"Look," Sadie said, feeling her frustration rise. She stood up straight and put one hand on her hip. "You're in the soup, so to speak, and holding out on us isn't doing you any good at all."

"Except I'm not helping you, which totally works for me."

"Why?" Sadie asked, exasperated with his stubbornness. "You said you didn't kill Mr. Ogreski. What else is there to hide from us? Why insist on being so unforthcoming?" She wasn't sure that was actually a word.

"Um, well, let's see," he said, making an exaggerated face and tapping his chin with his free hand. "I was kidnapped, and now I'm currently tied up and being held prisoner by a bunch of total psychos. Geez, I can't imagine why I wouldn't want to make things easier for you. Weird, huh?"

Sadie narrowed her eyes. "We are not psychos," she defended. "We're trying to do a good thing here."

"By breaking the law?" Josh asked. "You're like this modern Bonnie and Clyde vigilante gang, honking about justice and truth while ducking the cops yourself. And now you want me to answer all your little questions just to be nice?" He shook his head and raised the newspaper again. "I don't think so."

Sadie needed to come at this from another direction. Then she remembered the camera bag. "I guess it's time to pull out the big guns," she said ominously.

"More guns?"

Sadie looked up at Jane, standing in the kitchen doorway. She tried to swallow her irritation at being interrupted.

Jane raised both eyebrows. "We found something you need to see." She turned back to the den before Sadie had a chance to answer.

Eric pushed away from the table. "We're not going anywhere, Bonnie," he said.

Bonnie? It took Sadie a moment to get the reference.

"I think I'll finish off that chicken stuff. It was really good." He looked at Josh. "Wanna split it with me?"

Josh looked torn between the lingering power of his refusal to cooperate and the temptation of Evil Chicken. The Evil Chicken won out and he nodded.

"I'll be right back," she said to Eric, turning away from her captive and hurrying into the other room. If they'd found Damon's file already that might help this whole process.

Jane plopped herself back on the floor once they reached the den. Shawn sat on the edge of a recliner a few feet away from her. The sticky smell of garbage now permeated the room and Sadie wrinkled her nose. Shawn and Jane seemed to be used to it, though, and Sadie hoped she'd quickly acclimate as well. It really stunk.

"Did you find Damon's folder?" she asked.

Shawn shook his head and held out a file.

"No?" She was confused. What was more important than finding Damon's folder? She took the file from Shawn and turned it over so she could read the handwritten tab.

After reading it once she blinked and read it a second time, wanting to make sure she had read it right.

Mark Ogreski–literary agent

Why on earth did Diane have a file on him?

CHAPTER 39

She flipped the file open. The first paper was a purple flier of some type. It was for a writer's conference in Denver that focused on novel writing—and was almost twelve years old. Had Diane wanted to write a book too? The theme of the conference had been "Dream Building" and Sadie's eyes quickly focused on the name of the keynote speaker: Mark Ogreski of Anderson Literary Agency. Diane had known Mr. Ogreski before Damon or Thom ever did. Behind the flier were pages of notes in Diane's handwriting. From the conference, Sadie assumed.

Sadie skimmed over words like *query* and *synopsis* before turning to the next paper in the file. It was a letter typed and addressed to Mr. Ogreski himself with the word "copy" written in the upper right-hand corner. There were little handwritten marks and arrows in the body of the text, lighter gray than the type, which made sense if Diane had saved the copy instead of the original.

"What is it?" Shawn asked. "You look excited."

"It's a letter to Mr. Ogreski," she said. "I think Damon wrote it."

"Serious?" Shawn said.

She cleared her throat and read the letter. "'*Demon Fire* is an urban thriller set in San Francisco at a time when the gates of hell have been flung open, allowing demons to come to Earth. Unable to possess humans, the demons are forced to take refuge in inanimate objects, literally giving life to things that have never lived. What then happens is terror and turmoil beyond comprehension as the demons seek to obliterate the human population so they can have the world all to themselves.'"

Sadie made a face, reminded again of why she'd disliked the book, but there was no doubt the story described was, in fact, *Devilish Details.* "The title's wrong," Sadie said aloud, confused. "It's not called *Demon Fire.*"

"Probably the working title," Jane summed up. "Publishers change the titles most of the time."

"Oh," Sadie said, looking further down the page. "Diane wrote something at the bottom: 'Good start. Figure out a hook and include the word count.'"

"So she was helping him write the query letter," Jane said, looking thoughtful.

Sadie flipped to the next page in the stack—the copy of the revised query, with a few more edits from Diane, though not as many. Damon's name and address was in the upper right-hand corner of this one, removing any doubt that he was the owner and author of the query. At the bottom Diane had written, "I think you're ready to send this off, Damon. I'm so proud of you! Let me know how it goes."

Sadie scanned up to the date: the October before Damon's death. The same time Damon would have been in Diane's class.

Sadie turned to the next paper in the file and read the first few lines. Like the other letters, it was marked "copy" in the top corner. "Is this the letter you found?" she asked Jane, handing her the page.

"She kept a copy?" Jane said. "That's weird."

Sadie took it back. "I keep copies all the time of letters I send. You never know when it might be important." She shook the paper for emphasis before putting it back in the folder and moving to the next letter in the stack. This one captured every ounce of her attention and she read through the opening paragraph before looking up at Shawn and Jane who were watching her intently.

"The reporter at the *Post* isn't the only person she wrote to," Sadie said, hearing her voice speed up as she spoke. "She wrote a letter to Mr. Ogreski too." She cleared her throat and read out loud, "'I will be visiting with my sister in Chula Vista from the eighth to the thirteenth and would like to meet with you and Mr. Mortenson during my trip to discuss *"Thom's"* book. Please call me as soon as possible to schedule a time we can meet. I can only promise discretion for a little while longer.'"

"When did she write the letter to the *Post*?" Jane asked.

Sadie quickly turned back to the letter Diane had sent to the newspaper. "The day before she left on her trip. Maybe to make sure someone else knew about it."

"And maybe to make sure she followed through. Knowing the reporter would be calling her about the letter would make sure she didn't chicken out," Shawn offered.

Sadie thought that was definitely a possibility. Both letters made it clear that Diane was not taking this situation lightly.

"So she just happened to die in a car accident during the trip where she planned to meet with Thom and Mr. Ogreski?" Sadie said out loud.

Silence reigned once again. Sadie looked at Jane. "Didn't the accident report say she'd had too much wine and that, combined with unfamiliar roads, is what caused the accident?"

Jane nodded. "She'd been at a restaurant located up a canyon. It was raining, too, which certainly didn't help anything."

"Who was she at the restaurant with?" Shawn asked, leaning forward with his elbows on his knees, his eyebrows pulled together in concentration as he took in the facts he was hearing for the first time.

"It was her last night in California and she'd treated her sister's family to dinner," Jane said. "They were in separate cars, though, and finished up around 7:30—long before it got dark. Diane's sister reported that Diane had said she was going to use the restroom before heading back to her hotel. The police determined that Diane stayed in the bar—maybe waiting for the rain to stop?—and had a few more drinks before deciding to leave. By then it was dark and the roads were really wet."

"Did she pay for those drinks herself?" Sadie asked. "Do the police have proof of that or is it just conjecture?"

Jane furrowed her brow, obviously uncomfortable not having the answer. "You know, I'm not sure," she said.

Sadie stared at the letter. It looked like she'd reached the end of the file, but she turned over the letter to Mr. Ogreski just in case. There was a pink message slip dated October 1—almost a week after the date on the letter—stuck to the back. The message slip was very similar to the slips used by the school Sadie had taught at for so many years and the note was written in Diane's handwriting.

Meet Mr. O at Rancho Hills at 8:00 on 10/12.
Call his office to make any changes.

"What day did Diane Veeter die?" Sadie asked Jane.

"October thirteenth," Jane said. "Or at least that's when they found her car off the road."

Sadie read the message a second time. In her mind she pieced it together as best she could. Other than her letter to the *Post*, Diane had been careful about who she'd told about her suspicions. If the meeting with Mr. Ogreski was the real reason she'd gone to California, she'd disguised it by visiting her sister. After setting up the meeting with Mr. Ogreski, Diane had offered to treat her sister's family to dinner on the same night—before her meeting. Probably to get comfortable in the environment before Mr. Ogreski arrived. Maybe she did have more wine, maybe she didn't, but how hard would it have been for Mr. Ogreski to slip something in whatever it was she drank that night? Something that would kick in while she was negotiating turns on a wet, unfamiliar canyon road in the dark? It would look like an accident. And with the alcohol in her system, well, why would the police look any further than that?

"Oh, Diane," she said, leaning against the couch as tears pricked her eyes. "All you wanted to do was the right thing." How was it that Mr. Ogreski had all the luck on his side, and Diane Veeter had so little? It wasn't fair.

The room was silent for a moment, then Sadie let out a breath. "We have to tell her family," she said, looked at Jane, whose eyes were on fire with excitement. "Before it makes the papers."

Jane looked away quickly. Sadie waited for the reporter to say something, but she didn't.

"Now?" Shawn asked.

Sadie looked out the window. It was pitch-black outside. Only the snow falling closest to the glass was illuminated enough to see clearly. She didn't know how to answer Shawn. Part of her definitely wanted to go over to the Veeters' house right away. Not only to tell Diane's daughter what had really happened to her mother, but also to redeem herself for snooping and stealing the files. Wait—then she'd have to admit to stealing the files, wouldn't she? Her stomach rolled at the idea of confessing to Tina; she already thought so poorly of Sadie. But was self-preservation a worthy justification for not sharing this information immediately?

"I don't know," she said, shaking her head and putting her good hand up to her forehead. "I have no idea what to do next."

"Well, we're still looking for Damon Mortenson's file, right?" Jane grabbed another file. Shawn picked up one as well.

Sadie hesitated for a moment, but then remembered Josh and Eric in the other room. It was long past midnight and there was still much to be done. With the painful realization of Diane's death still fresh in her mind, Sadie turned back to the kitchen and saw Josh's camera bag sitting by the doorway.

This game had stopped being fun a long time ago, and Sadie was tired of playing. She needed answers. She grabbed the camera bag and continued into the kitchen, taking a deep breath as she prepared for the next item on her agenda. She had to find out what Josh knew and why he had taken those blasted pictures.

Sadie put the camera bag on the table in front of her as she sat down across from Josh, new vigor behind her pursuit of truth. Things were coming together fast. The bag blocked her view, so she moved it to the left slightly in order to make eye contact with Josh.

"Eric," she said, though she was still looking at Josh, who returned her stare with a boiling one of his own. It seemed the camera was the exact motivation she'd needed all along. When Eric didn't answer, she called out, "Hey, Clyde," giving Eric a little smile when the nickname caught his attention. He smiled back and seemed to understand they were going to be playing this out as a team. "Will you look up this camera? It's a—" She had to break eye contact with Josh in order to wrestle the bag open and look at the camera.

"A Nikon D300s DX. It says 12MP here—I think that stands for mega-pixel."

Josh's eyes jumped from Sadie to Eric, looking concerned, and maybe a little confused.

"I'm curious as to how much a camera like this costs," Sadie said nonchalantly. "It looks expensive."

"It is expensive," Josh said quickly, leaning forward. His bindings, however, kept him from moving very far. "And it's not a toy."

Sadie hefted the camera with her one hand and braced her elbow on the table, holding the camera flat on her palm.

Josh looked at the camera longingly.

"So," Sadie said slowly, maintaining control of the situation even while battling her discomfort with such blatant dominance. "You have information we need. And I have your camera. Are you willing to trade?"

CHAPTER 40

Josh didn't answer her, just continued to glare. She hoped the belt Shawn had used was good and thick because Josh looked ready to pounce across the table at any moment. You'd think they hadn't fed him any Evil Chicken at all for the anger on his face.

"It's heavier than I'd have thought," Sadie said, making an exaggerated act of hefting the camera in her hand.

Eric cleared his throat. "It retails for about two grand," he said, whistling slightly. He leaned toward Sadie. "Does it have a battery grip?"

Sadie had no idea what a battery grip was, but Eric looked at the camera and nodded.

"It does," Eric said. "Add a couple hundred more to the price—assuming that's the stock lens and not a specialty lens he swapped it out for."

Josh's face paled and his voice took on a kind of forced calm when he spoke again. "Please. Just put it back in the case."

Sadie ignored him because he wasn't yet offering his cooperation. "How do you work this thing, anyway?" she asked, looping the strap around her neck as though she were preparing to take some photos. She turned the camera in her hands, looking at all the buttons and gauges. It seemed to her that having to adjust so many things would suck all the fun right out of taking pictures. She accidentally popped off the lens cap and noticed Josh tense.

"Don't," Josh said quickly, then clenched his mouth shut and took a breath. The anger was morphing into a begging kind of fear. "Please don't touch anything."

Eric scooted his chair closer to Sadie, looking as curious about the camera as she was. "My brother used to have a fancy camera like this," Eric said. "See if there's a latch or a button by the bottom of the lens. It should allow you to change out the different lenses—though, unfortunately also exposes all those sensitive innards of the camera itself."

Sure enough, there was a tiny button. She pressed it and the lens popped off a fraction of an inch.

"Cool," Eric said, twisting the lens free from the rest of the camera. Sadie and Eric looked at Josh at the same time. "Shall we continue?" Eric asked. "You've got a lot invested in this thing, right? Your career, your future. Are you sure it's worth not telling us things that are going to come out anyway?"

"Okay," Josh said in surrender, reaching his free hand toward the camera. "I'll tell you what I know, just leave the camera alone."

Eric snapped the lens back on, and Sadie removed the strap from around her neck. She put the camera back down on the table, pushing it closer to Josh, but not so close that he could take it from her. In reality, she was relieved he'd given in. There was no way she'd actually damage something so important to him. Had he not agreed to cooperate he'd have figured that out eventually and called her bluff and then she'd be out of luck.

Sadie laid her one good arm on the table, wishing she could lace her fingers together and stare at him menacingly. It didn't seem to work as well with the sling, but she did her best with what she had to work with. "Who killed Mark Ogreski?"

Josh was silent, his nostrils flaring. It was very hard to not show her discomfort. "I don't know," he said.

Eric reached forward and took hold of the camera strap, pulling the camera a couple of inches toward himself.

"I swear," Josh said, putting his hand out in a stopping motion. He strained at the belts before giving into the futility of it and sat back once more. "I don't know who arranged the shooting. I didn't have anything to do with that."

"That's really hard for me to believe," Sadie said. "You were up there taking pictures of a dead man. To do something like that you'd have to be involved."

"Well, I guess I am involved—kind of," Josh said with a nod. "But not with the shooting. I came to the dinner to take photos for Thom's website—that's what Mark asked me to do."

Sadie noted that he was on a first name basis with the deceased. "Then why did your mother say Thom invited you?" Sadie asked, lining up questions in her mind as quickly as she could. She didn't want to miss anything.

Josh shrugged. "Same thing—Mark controls everything. He's the one who asked me to come and agreed to pay the expenses. Thom was glad to have me there, though. I haven't seen him for a long time."

"And so when Mr. Ogreski ended up dead on stage, you just decided to snap some pictures and pretend to be a crime scene photographer?" Sadie asked, definitely missing the logic of such a choice. She turned to Eric and resorted to sarcasm, "Sounds perfectly reasonable to me, how about you?"

Eric nodded and lifted his eyebrows, answering her with equal sarcasm. "I'm sure I'd have done the same thing."

The way they worked so well together helped bolster Sadie's confidence that they could get what they needed. She was suddenly feeling very grateful for Donna Hender. Without that crazy woman, Sadie would never have met Eric at all.

"It wasn't like that," Josh said, letting out a haggard breath. "I took the pictures to prove to myself—and to Thom—that it was real. I admit it looks bad, but I'm a photographer. I chronicle life through pictures. It's what I do, and it just sort of . . . happened."

"I don't believe you," Sadie said, shaking her head. "You break the law and put yourself center stage—literally—to prove something both you and Thom already witnessed? That's just . . . stupid."

Josh glared at her. "Well, I guess I'm stupid then."

Sadie leaned forward. "But that's the thing. I don't think you are stupid, which means you have another reason to make yourself vulnerable—like . . ." She reviewed all the motives of murder she'd come up against these last few months, but unfortunately revenge and self-preservation didn't fit this situation. But greed did. "Profit," she said out loud. "How would Mr. Ogreski's death be profitable to you either personally or financially?"

Josh said nothing, but his jaw tensed.

Sadie was on to something.

After waiting a few moments for Josh to defend himself, Eric scooted his chair back to his computer and started tapping keys. "I wonder . . ." he said, letting his voice trail off. "What would someone pay for those photos? My brother—the one with the fancy camera—used to work as a stringer in college. He'd make a few hundred bucks if the newspaper bought his shots."

Isn't that what Peter Parker did in the Spider-man comics? Sadie thought, wrinkling her nose at the idea of someone selling pictures of a dead man. Even though she was the one who suggested a profitable motive, she couldn't imagine who would want to see something so grotesque. She was about to argue her point, maybe suggest finding another hypothesis, when she noticed Josh's neck had turned red. It took a few moments for her thoughts to catch up. "Really?" she said out loud. "You were going to sell them?"

Josh looked at the table and wriggled in his seat for a moment. When he spoke, his voice had lost some of its heat. "There are literally millions of people out there trying to live by their lens, and most of them eat mac and cheese for dinner every night."

"You went to the Chicago Institute of Art," Sadie reminded him, in case he'd forgotten his own credentials. "And your mom said you've got a good job."

"My mom would be just as proud of me if I was taking photos at Walmart. The truth is, I'm one of three assistant photographers at a regional magazine that's talking about cutting their staff by fifty percent this summer," Josh said. "I can make a year's salary off those shots." He nodded toward the camera. "Any other photographer in my situation tonight would have done the same thing. We see the whole world through our lenses. Letting an opportunity pass by isn't in us."

Sadie tsked and shook her head. "That's disgusting."

"And illegal," Eric said.

"Wanna bet?" Josh said, meeting Eric's gaze head-on. "Those guys who shot photos of Michael Jackson being put into the ambulance made bank. Last year, I was doing a layout for a new high-end resort in Virginia Beach and I got a picture of Catherine Zeta-Jones without any makeup on. Sold it to the *Star* for four grand and paid off my car. Every photographer I know does the same thing, always looking for the shot that will make all the difference."

"So if you were going to make money off these photos," Sadie said carefully, "then you have a motive for murder."

Josh shook his head quickly. "No, no, no. No way. I told you—I was there to take photos for the new website and see Thom. I didn't—"

"Website?" Sadie cut in, suddenly remembering the "under construction" note on the site she and Shawn had looked up earlier. "Why is Thom building a new website anyway? Isn't the book going out of print?"

"No one's supposed to know the book is going out of print," Josh said after a moment.

Sadie shrugged that off. "Well, I know, and obviously you know too. So why a new website when the book is about to disappear?"

Josh was quiet again, but in a confused way rather than a defensive one. "I don't know."

Sadie glanced at Eric, who looked as unconvinced as she felt.

"Okay, so your story is that you were asked to come take photos for a new website, even though the book is going out of print, and when a horrible public murder happened, you jumped on stage and took some shots you hoped to sell for a million dollars?"

Josh's expression seemed to say he realized it didn't sound so good.

"You can't blame us for finding that rather weak," Sadie added.

"Weak character, maybe," Josh said, his voice sounding more humble than it had all night. He met Sadie's eyes. "But I didn't kill him, and I don't know who did."

Eric cut in. "Didn't you say in the car that you were glad he was dead?"

Sadie nodded, glad that Eric had brought that up. "And that you'd raise him up and shoot him again if you could."

Josh paled slightly. "It's not that I'm . . . *glad* he's dead, but he was not a good man. The world is a better place without him in it, and Thom will have a better life, now. Finally."

"Why?" Eric asked.

"Mark was not a good man."

Sadie forced a smile and spoke calmly, cocking her head to the side and giving him a come-on-already look. "You can't just keep saying that," Sadie said. "*Why* isn't he a good man? *Why* is the world a better place without him in it? *Why* is Thom better off without him? Didn't Thom need him? Wasn't Mr. Ogreski kind of Thom's caretaker?"

CHAPTER 41

Josh paused, looking torn. Seeing that he was still unsure about what to say ignited Sadie's sense of urgency. She leaned forward and decided to offer him an olive branch by filling him in on what she knew in hopes it would then be easier for him to fill in the gaps rather than feel responsible for divulging the bigger secrets.

"Look, I know Thom took credit for Damon's book. Diane Veeter knew about it, too, and I suspect that Mr. Ogreski may have had something to do with the accident that killed her. I also know Thom's an alcoholic, that he paid for your college, and that Michele, Frank Argula's niece, is a friend of yours and she's a part of this too."

Josh looked absolutely stunned, as did Eric, reminding Sadie that she hadn't updated Eric on everything she'd figured out. She continued, "What I want to know is how those pieces came together and how exactly they turned into murder. In the meantime, I'm willing to give you the benefit of the doubt and accept that you didn't kill Mr. Ogreski and that your motives are purely based on greed, but you've got to help me with that belief because it's starting to feel a little shaky."

Josh blinked. "But . . . how do you know all that?" he asked after a few seconds of silence.

Sadie leveled him with a look. "Funny thing about secrets, Josh, is that they eat at you. For some people they're like acid, chewing them up rather quickly one day at a time. For other people, secrets are more like wind, eroding their soul little by little, day by day. Eventually—whether it's acid or wind, or some combination of the two—they break through and then those secrets are nothing but facts, like salt in the wounds they leave behind."

Silence prevailed once again and Sadie felt her frustration rising. Josh didn't even seem to appreciate her poetic symbolism. She had to find another way around his barriers. The quickest way to do that was make Josh defend himself. "Thom paid for your college, right? Hush money?"

Josh shook his head. "No," he said emphatically. "It wasn't anything like that."

Sadie raised her eyebrows, encouraging him to convince her.

Josh hesitated a moment longer before he let out a breath and leaned back against the chair. "Yes, I knew the book was Damon's and, yes, Thom paid for my college, but the two things aren't related." He seemed to realize how ridiculous that sounded so he continued talking.

Sadie felt herself relax a little.

"Thom had a college fund for Damon. After Damon died, Thom and I stayed close. I think it helped Thom to have me around so he didn't get so lonely. I wasn't sure I would even go to college, but then Thom offered me the money—money that would make it possible for me to get a good education without being in debt for the next fifteen years. Remember how I told you most photographers eat mac and cheese?"

"And you lied to your mother about a scholarship?" Sadie asked. "Why lie to your *mother?*" If he wasn't the murderer, then he should have a conscience in there somewhere.

"My mom's a little . . . overprotective sometimes."

Sadie could attest to that, her head was still throbbing, though it was hard to separate that pain from the pain of her shoulder. Thank goodness the adrenaline seemed to numb everything a little bit.

Josh continued. "And although she was understanding of Thom's relationship with me, it was still threatening to her sometimes. Thom giving me fifty thousand dollars would be hard for her to swallow. So we made up the scholarship thing and gave her something to brag about. Had she thought about it as much as you have, she'd have realized she never saw an actual award letter and that my grades would have scared pretty much any school away—even an art school that didn't care about academics. But she wanted to believe good things and so she did."

"And you didn't feel guilty about that?" Sadie asked.

"I did," Josh said, his voice lowering. "But I wanted to make something of myself and I needed a good education to do that. I made a choice—for better or worse."

Sadie nodded and crossed that question off her internal list. "How about going along with the story that Thom had written *Devilish Details*. Did you ever feel guilty about that?"

"Not at first," Josh admitted, surprising Sadie with his candor.

But then Sadie remembered that she had been the one who had compared secrets to acid. Purging oneself of the poison of poor choices was often a very liberating experience. She was glad to have remembered that. It made her feel a lot better about the things she'd been doing tonight when she thought of it as helping people.

"When Thom first talked to me about it," Josh said, "he said how publishing the book would immortalize Damon and allow his story to live on. Damon was so proud of that book." Josh smiled a little, though it faded quickly. "Mark had explained to Thom that with Damon's name on it, the book would never be published. Publishers don't publish books by dead authors who can't promote their work or write sequels. And even if someone *did* publish it, everyone hated Damon for what he did. With Thom's name on the cover, though, Thom would be able to quit his job, he'd have a foundation to get his own writing published, and in this one way Damon would live forever."

"But you and Thom would be the only people who knew Damon was the real author," Eric pointed out. "How does that immortalize Damon if no one knows?"

Excellent point, Sadie thought as she nodded her agreement.

"Thom and I were probably the only two people in the world with any positive feelings about Damon," Josh said. "And we were the only two who could look past what he'd done and see the good that was in him. He was a gifted writer and that mattered to us. As I got older, I was more uncomfortable with the whole thing, and I understood better what exactly Mark and Thom had done, essentially *stealing* Damon's book. But by then I could see the toll it was taking on Thom too. Sharing my feelings would have made that worse. I was the only friend Thom had left. Thom had thought it would be an easy thing to do—we both did—but the lies were so hard for him to tell over and over again."

"And you blamed Mr. Ogreski for that," Sadie prodded.

Josh's eyes narrowed slightly. "Absolutely," he said. "He was the one who came to Thom with the idea. And then when Thom started struggling under the weight of the lies, Mark wriggled his way into every corner of Thom's life, taking over bit by bit until Thom was completely dependent on him. Thom's drinking got worse, and it was Mark who kept the whisky handy."

Eric leaned forward. "You blame the agent for Thom's drinking? That's a bit of a stretch."

"No," Josh snapped, "it isn't. I've watched this for ten years but I still didn't see the stranglehold Mark had on Thom until the last nine months or so. When I finally went to Mark and asked him to get Thom help, he fed me all kinds of sympathetic comments, promised to see what he could do, and then did nothing at all. The next time I brought it up, he hedged around and passed the phone off to Thom. That's when I realized Mark couldn't let Thom get well because that might mean Thom would tell someone the truth. Mark would lose everything if the truth came out, so he simply kept Thom sauced most of the time." Josh paused. "And you said you already knew Mark killed Diane Veeter. What more proof of a man's character do you need?"

Sadie nodded, accepting the point he was making. She could still picture Thom in her mind, lining up those mini-bottles. He was in bad shape, and if Mr. Ogreski helped him get to that point, it was horrible. But she wasn't going to allow Josh to pass the buck quite that easily. "So you knew Mr. Ogreski was allowing Thom to self-medicate with alcohol and—"

"Not allowing," Josh said, leaning forward again, his blue eyes snapping with anger. "He encouraged it. He supplied every drop. Thom hasn't been able to drive for years, but Mark's made sure Thom had enough whisky to drown in."

"Okay," Sadie said, letting that one go. "But you *also* knew Mr. Ogreski was responsible for Diane Veeter's death and said nothing. How do you justify that?"

CHAPTER 42

Josh's ire deflated. "I didn't know about Mrs. Veeter until a few weeks ago," he said. "And I have racked my brain trying to figure out what to do ever since. The problem was that if I turned in Mark, the police would have to come up with a motive and the motive was protecting the secret about Damon's book, which would destroy Thom."

"How did you even find out about Mrs. Veeter in the first place?" Eric cut in.

"When Mark refused to get Thom into treatment, I started suggesting Thom check himself in. The idea paralyzed him, so I had to be careful, but I brought it up as often as possible. I knew that if Thom could get himself away from Mark, he could get well. After awhile, Thom started becoming more open to the idea, but he felt horrible about leaving Mark, even though the relationship was a sick one. Thom was convinced he couldn't take care of himself.

"When Thom told me he had to go to Mark's office to sign some papers about the book going out of print, I told him he should try to find his social security card and birth certificate—Mark had taken them for safekeeping a few years ago—all part of his taking control.

I told Thom that finding those documents wasn't a commitment to leave Mark, just a first step in getting some power back over his own life. Thom trusted me, so he did what I'd told him. Only he didn't find his documents. Instead, he came across a letter Mrs. Veeter had sent to Mark and an article about the accident. Thom hadn't even known she'd died, but Mark had an article? It wasn't hard to guess what had happened based on the dates and how paranoid Mark always was about anyone learning the truth."

"So that was the other murder you were talking about when you told me there had been two murders and you hoped the police would figure out this one?" Sadie asked.

Josh nodded. "For a few minutes tonight I thought it would all work out and I wouldn't have to be involved at all. So much for that."

"Did Thom know Mrs. Veeter had helped Damon submit the book?" Eric asked.

Josh shook his head. "I didn't even know about it. Thom didn't find out about Damon submitting until months after Damon died, when Mark called to update Damon on how things were going with the book."

Sadie considered that. It made sense that none of them would have known about Diane. They believed they were the only ones who knew the secret. And with the three of them bound together by their shared guilt, the secret was safe—until Diane sent a letter to Mark Ogreski telling him she knew the truth. He then chose to save himself through drastic measures.

"So Mark called Thom, found out Damon was dead, and said, 'Hey, let's just put your name on it,'" Sadie said.

"No," Josh said. "It didn't happen like that. Mark was very sympathetic when he learned what Damon had done. He called Thom a few times over the next month or so to see how he was doing. Thom was extremely vulnerable. It was only after they became friends that Mark brought up the idea of publishing the book under Thom's name."

"And then Thom found out about Diane's death and he told you?"

Josh nodded. "Thom was terrified, but I saw an opportunity. With the book going out of print and the rights reverting back to Thom, he could finally be free of Mark forever. Plus, now he had a very good reason to sever all ties. Thom was ready, but he felt he needed to do this library fund-raiser first."

"He wasn't worried about coming clean?" Eric offered. "Like you said, getting well might mean telling the truth."

"But see, that's the thing," Josh said, excited now that Eric and Sadie seemed to be seeing the motive behind his involvement. "It doesn't matter anymore. Thom is flying back to Virginia with me tomorrow afternoon. I paid for his ticket so Mark wouldn't find out. Monday morning we are going to the police and telling them what we know, then Thom is checking into a treatment center I've arranged for him. There will be consequences for what we've done, of course, but Thom will get well. And that's all I wanted in the first place."

"But then Mr. Ogreski turns up dead days before Thom is supposed to go into treatment," Sadie reminded him. "Interesting timing."

"If Thom were afraid of Mr. Ogreski," Eric mused as he deftly continued the questions, "wouldn't it be easier for Thom to knock him off himself rather than have the fear of Mr. Ogreski's revenge hanging over him?"

Josh looked at Eric with confusion. "You weren't there tonight, were you?"

Eric shook his head and Josh turned to look at Sadie. "You've seen him. Do you really think Thom's capable of masterminding a plot to kill anyone?"

It was an excellent point. Sadie thought back to Jane's comment about Thom not being able to tie his own shoes. It wasn't difficult to imagine that was true.

"Not without help, maybe," Eric threw out. "Someone had to go to great lengths to pull this off. Who else would have a motive as good as Thom's? Ogreski was his secret keeper, and it was destroying him."

Josh was shaking his head before Eric finished talking. "I'm sure Thom and I aren't the only people Mark's screwed over in his life. It wouldn't surprise me at all to find out he was involved in something far more sinister than a plagiarized book. Men like Mark Ogreski don't just make an enemy or two—they have dozens. And Thom couldn't, and wouldn't, do this. Mark was still the most important person in Thom's life even though he knew he had to get away from him." He shook his head. "It's hard to explain, but it's kind of like those abused women who finally leave their husbands but still say they love them."

"But who would kill Mr. Ogreski like *this?*" Sadie questioned. "He was killed with the same kind of gun Damon used, in the same town Thom had lived in when Damon died. Why would someone else make those types of connections? Besides that, whoever did it had to know that the police would pull out all the stops to figure it out and they would see those same connections."

"Those very things lend credibility to the fact that it wasn't Thom and it wasn't me," Josh said. "We're both knee-deep in this mess. We'd be the first people the police would look into. Maybe someone set it up to make Thom look guilty."

"Who?" Sadie and Eric said in tandem.

"I don't know," Josh said, sounding discouraged.

"The two of you together could have pulled this off without leaving an obvious trail," Eric said, leaning back in his chair as he appraised Josh, obviously unwilling to give up the idea that Josh was more involved than he'd admitted thus far. "And you've lied for each other before. What's one more deception?"

He put his hands behind his head and Sadie noticed a little tear in the elbow of his shirt. She could mend that in two minutes flat. Another time of course.

Josh looked at Eric and rolled his eyes toward the ceiling; Sadie found it rather remarkable that he wasn't *more* defensive. "Besides everything else I've told you, you think I'm going to work this hard at a future to throw it away on someone like Mark Ogreski?" He snorted and shook his head. "I might not be proud of some of the things I've done, and I might have plenty of reasons to *want* Mark dead, but I didn't kill him. I didn't need to. His power over Thom was almost over."

Sadie lined that tidbit up with some of the other details she'd learned tonight. It was like a kaleidoscope, turning it a little bit one way or another presented a totally new picture. "Is there any way Mr. Ogreski knew Thom was leaving?"

"I don't think so," Josh said, shaking his head. "Thom was terrified of Mark finding out, so I'm sure he was careful. Why?"

"When you were taking pictures," Sadie started, "I was looking at a copy of *Devilish Details* that had been left backstage. Inside the front cover were the words 'I'm sorry.' Gayle, my friend who helped set up the backup microphone, said the book was on the podium when they brought it on stage. She gave the book to Mr. Ogreski to give to Thom right before he came up to the podium."

"It said, 'I'm sorry'?" Josh repeated, pulling his eyebrows together. "Who wrote it?"

"I have no idea," Sadie said with a shrug as she leaned back in the chair. The pain in her shoulder was getting worse, and she tried to find a better position for it but refused to let it throw her off. "But Mr. Ogreski had also set up an appointment to meet with a reporter after the presentation—presumably to tell her the truth. The reporter found a letter Mrs. Veeter wrote before her death claiming to have proof that Thom hadn't written the book."

Josh looked stunned, his blue eyes almost vacant. Then he slowly shook his head. "Who told you about this meeting?" he asked.

"The reporter," Sadie said, realizing she hadn't introduced Jane and Josh. Maybe that was a good thing. "She's been working several angles of this story for a few weeks, and when she confronted Mr. Ogreski about Damon's book, he agreed to meet with her after tonight's event. She believed he was going to confirm her suspicions."

Josh shook his head. "I don't believe it. She's making it up. Mark would go to his grave before he'd admit to any of this."

"Maybe he did," Eric said.

Sadie and Josh both turned to look at him.

"What?" Sadie said, thinking she must not have heard him correctly.

Eric looked at Sadie. "A reporter is making noise about having proof of the fraud, and the book is going out of print." He looked at Josh. "You say Mark didn't know Thom was planning to break ties, but what if he did? He controlled Thom's life, right? And Thom was a drunk. Are you sure he could keep the fact that he was leaving a secret?"

Sadie picked up on the conjecture even though it made her head spin. "If things were coming to a head—what with a reporter close and Thom breaking away—Mr. Ogreski would know he was out of time."

"Especially if everyone found out about Damon's teacher," Eric put in. "He would be facing far more fallout than just losing his job."

Sadie's mind was racing. "And the chances of him silencing both Thom and the reporter—"

"And you," Eric cut in, pointing at Josh. Then he waved Sadie to continue.

Sadie nodded. "Right, and you too, were slim to none. He was losing power, but he may have had just enough time to keep things on his terms. And, given all the medications the police found in his room, he wasn't coping with all of this as well as you may have thought he was."

"Medications?" Josh repeated. "You mean his sleeping pills?"

"And anxiety medication and antidepressants," Sadie added. "He wasn't a well man. What if he thought the bottom of this pseudo life he'd created was being pulled out from under him?"

They all fell silent. Josh looked slightly shell-shocked. "You think Mark could have done this to himself?"

It did seem a bit ridiculous, Sadie realized, reliving that shotgun blast. And yet, was it possible?

"He couldn't have done it alone, though," Eric put in. He looked at Sadie. "Didn't you say Mark and Thom were late for the dinner because they drove up from Denver today? When would he have rigged the gun? Where would he have gotten the gun in the first place?"

Josh's expression turned thoughtful. "Last night . . ."

"What about last night?" Sadie said, looking at Josh intently.

"Thom called me from the hotel," he said. "He was really

nervous about the presentation and couldn't sleep. I told him to ask Mark for a sleeping pill."

Sadie shook her head in censure. The man was an alcoholic and taking other people's prescriptions was never a good idea.

Josh continued. "They had adjoining rooms—you know, the kind with doors in between?"

Sadie nodded.

"Mark had locked the door on his side and didn't answer when Thom knocked. I told Thom to call him, and he did, on both the hotel phone and Mark's cell phone. Mark never answered."

"O-kay," Sadie said, willing Josh to continue. So Mark was a sound sleeper, what else?

"I assumed Mark had taken a sleeping pill too, but what if he wasn't there at all?"

"You mean, what if he came up to Garrison?" Eric put in.

"And rigged up the gun himself?" Sadie added.

"He'd spoken with the hotel extensively," Josh said, leaning forward as much as he could, which wasn't much. "He wanted to know the exact layout of the room and . . ." He trailed off, then looked at Sadie. "Could you please release my arm? It's completely numb."

Sadie glanced at Eric, who shrugged. She looked back at Josh and realized that this was the first request he'd made. And his legs would still be lashed to the chair. Hadn't he also given them a great deal of information?

"Okay," Sadie said. She pushed back from the table, but Eric put his hand on her arm to stop her.

"I'll do it," he said. Sadie looked at the hand on her arm. The man seemed to have a lack of appreciation for personal space, and yet . . . Sadie shut that thought down at warp speed, turning every bit of her focus to Josh. No "and yet"s allowed.

Eric removed his hand and walked around the back of Josh's chair, squatting to undo the belt. A moment later, Eric dropped the belt on the floor and Josh brought his hand around front, wincing as he rubbed his fingers with his other hand.

"Thank you," Josh muttered as he made a fist, then stretched out his fingers before making a fist again.

Sadie had to look away. She felt horrible that he'd been tied up at all and those feelings were increasing in direct proportion to how much information Josh was giving them.

"You were saying Mark had asked the hotel about the layout?" Eric prodded, back to business the second he sat down. He closed his laptop and kept his eyes on Josh.

"Right," Josh said, nodding. He was still opening and closing his fist, his face showing that it was painful. "He wanted to know the exact layout of the room, audio setup, how many people would be there. I mean, he always did that when Thom was going to present somewhere. He always wanted to know exactly what to expect in hopes it would make Thom less nervous."

"The rental car would show the miles, right?" Eric said.

Sadie nodded, thinking that would be a good way to verify the information. Then she was on to the next thought. "Could he get into the hotel?"

Josh shook his head. "I don't know, but someone did, right? Someone got into the hotel and rigged up the gun."

Sadie picked up when Josh paused. "If he drove up from Denver last night, there'd be a smaller staff at the hotel for the night shift, right? Doesn't seem like it would be hard to get in and out."

"Although he would still be dependent on things working out just right," Eric added, looking between the two of them. "I mean, what if someone else messed with the podium?"

Sadie thought back to the pink Post-It Gayle had given her after the shooting had taken place. "There was a note," she said. "It said the mic had already been tested and was ready to use once it was plugged in."

"It's still relying on a lot of luck that whoever was really supposed to test the mic didn't wonder why there was a note there in the first place," Eric suggested.

Josh added his own thoughts as soon as Eric finished. "Unless the backup microphone was something Mark had insisted on and was not standard practice. Then it would be easily discounted or appreciated that it was ready to go, right?"

"But, why?" Sadie cut in, interrupting the pileup of ideas.

Both men paused.

Sadie leaned forward. "So Mr. Ogreski faces up to the fact that everything's about to become common knowledge—why end it like this?" She spread out her one hand as if to encompass all the details. "He could have simply taken too many sleeping pills, or driven his car off a cliff." She paused to remind herself that this was a man's life she was talking about. She didn't want to lose sight of that. "My point is that this particular . . . method took a lot of planning and the details had to fall in place just right. And at the end he was . . . well, dead. So there's no payoff."

They all sat there for a few seconds, looking at the one detail that made everything else look different.

Suddenly, Josh sat up straight. "The key," he said, nodding toward the orange-capped key on the table next to Eric's computer. "Thom called me tonight when they arrived at the hotel, and I went out to take their bags upstairs while they got set up for the presentation. When I got back to the ballroom, Thom was trying to get the wireless mic to work. I tried to help him for a minute, but then a hotel staff member took over. I stepped back, and that's when Mark came up to me and handed me that key." He nodded toward the key again. "He said Thom asked him to give it to me."

"Why didn't Thom give it to you himself?" Sadie asked. Eric had discovered it fit a storage unit here in Garrison. What was in that storage unit?

"I don't know," Josh said, shaking his head. "But things were crazy and tensions were high because they were running late. At the time I thought it was weird—I mean, why not give me the key later if Thom wanted me to have it? Or why didn't Thom give it to me when I was helping him with the wireless microphone? But I didn't think about it too much, just put the key in my pocket and hurried around to the back of the ballroom so I could start lining up my shots. I got back to my equipment, zoomed in on the stage, and then the gun went off. I forgot all about the key in the aftermath. Well, until you showed up with it." He paused again, his expression becoming even more thoughtful. "But what if Thom knew nothing about the key? What if *Mark* was the one who wanted me to have it?"

CHAPTER 43

Things were just starting to sink in when Jane called out from the other room. "Found it!"

"Found what?" Josh asked as both Eric and Sadie stood.

"Diane Veeter's file on Damon," she said, heading toward the den. "I think he must have given her part of the original manuscript, which is the proof she claimed to have."

Within a few steps, Sadie stopped and turned back to look at the man still strapped to the dining room chair. He looked so vulnerable, like a little kid sentenced to time-out. Had he earned his right to freedom yet?

"It really was inevitable, wasn't it?" Josh said, obviously lost in his own thoughts.

"What was inevitable?" Eric asked, also turning.

"The truth was going to come out one way or another." He looked a little overwhelmed by it all. "It's so . . . surreal. After all these years of hiding it, it's suddenly just—there. Everyone will know what Thom did." His voice lowered. "Everyone will know what I did."

Sadie didn't know how to answer, but felt a wave of sympathy wash over her. "Would you mind undoing his feet?" she asked Eric.

Eric seemed to pause, but then he leaned into her. "Can I ask your son to keep a close eye on him?"

Sadie nodded, thinking that was a good idea. Despite the fact that she wanted to believe everything Josh had told them, she had no one to verify any of it.

As Eric moved toward Josh, she realized he had a new smell since the last time she'd been close enough to smell him at all—cologne. It didn't mask the other smells completely, but it was an improvement. Glancing at him from the corner of her eye, she wondered why he'd bothered with cologne in the first place and when?

Shawn appeared in the doorway. "You want to see it or what?" He saw Eric undoing the belts around Josh's legs and stiffened.

"It's okay," Sadie assured her son. "He's on our side now." Well, that might be coloring it a little too pink, she realized. However, he'd condemned himself with his confession, and he didn't have to talk at all. She lowered her voice so that Josh didn't overhear what she said next. "Will you keep an eye on him?"

Shawn wavered for a moment, but then nodded as Josh rose to his feet, lifting one foot and then the other to shake them out. Sadie wondered if they were numb too.

Josh and Eric joined them at the doorway leading to the den. Shawn stared Josh down while Josh tried to pretend he didn't notice.

They entered the den, and Sadie saw that the pile of folders in the middle of the room was mostly depleted. The ones already sorted were stacked nicely against the couch.

Jane had a folder open on her lap and lifted her head to brush her sweeping bangs out of her eyes. She smiled at Sadie. "A bunch of the files were all mixed together," she explained. "And his stuff was actually in a different folder so once we found one with his name on it, but nothing inside, we had to go through each one." She handed the papers to Sadie. "It looks like you were right—Damon did write it."

"Phew, what stinks?" Eric said, crinkling his nose.

"These files weren't the only thing in the garbage can," Jane said, pushing herself to her feet and stretching her legs. "Some of it came along for the ride."

"And you brought them in here?" Eric said.

Sadie took a scan around the mess in the room that had nothing to do with the files. There were diet soda cans on nearly every surface, and newspapers, magazines, and socks were strewn about the floor. And yet, she had to admit it hadn't smelled bad until she'd brought the files in.

"I'll clean your entire house to make up for it," Sadie said, waving her hand to wipe away the topic so that she could direct her attention to the papers.

"Oh," Eric said. "In that case, it's all good."

Sadie tuned everyone out and read the title of the paper in her hands: "Demon Fire." The paper was old enough that it had been printed on a dot matrix printer. The little dots had faded to a light gray over the years but the letters were still legible. Unlike the papers she'd found in Mark Ogreski's file, this one was the original.

In red pen, Diane had written a note across the top of the paper. "Damon, this is incredible. After years of my own attempts, I've never had such voice and fluidity in my own stories. I was at a writer's conference a while ago and there was an agent there who specifically wanted this kind of book. He thinks paranormal thrillers will be the next big thing. You should submit this to him. He could change your life!"

Sadie shook her head ruefully. "He changed Damon's life all right," she muttered under her breath. And Thom's and Diane's and Josh's too.

Finding proof of the fraud was an anticlimactic discovery, since they'd figured that out awhile ago. But it was still good to have the hard evidence. Sadie moved to the couch where she'd put the file on Mr. Ogreski. She put Damon's paper inside, deciding the folder could serve as a kind of portfolio she could take to the police.

Jane cleared her throat and turned to Eric. "Mind if I use the restroom?"

"Uh, sure," Eric said. He had his arms folded over his chest. "It's through the kitchen on the left. Oh, wait, I guess you know where it is."

"Yeah," Jane said with a quick nod that seemed just a little bit sarcastic.

"So, what now?" Shawn asked while Jane slipped away.

Sadie looked up at the three men watching her and closed the folder. "We go to the police," she said, offering them a consolatory smile even as her stomach dropped.

"But we don't know who did it," Shawn said, then looked at Josh and narrowed his eyes. "Or do we?"

Josh shook his head and shoved his hands in his pockets. "You think they'd have untied me if they thought I'd done it?"

"Maybe since you didn't have a sawed-off shotgun in your pocket they thought it was a safe bet," Shawn returned.

"The thing is," Sadie interrupted, "that we're already in loads of trouble and if we keep trying to figure things out, we're only going to get in deeper." She stood up. "I need to call Tina before we go."

"Tina?" all three men said in unison.

"Diane Veeter's daughter." Sadie cringed again at the idea and felt guilty for being too chicken to tell her the truth in person.

"And then we're going to the storage unit, right?" Josh added.

Sadie exchanged looks with Eric and Shawn, both of whom looked instantly in support of that idea. Sadie wasn't so sure. "Maybe it would help us if we gave the police something to figure out," she suggested. "The key *is* evidence."

"But Mark gave it to me," Josh reminded her. "It makes sense for me to figure out why and what it's for. Even the cops can't blame me for that."

"But if we tag along, then we're—"

"Smart enough to not let this guy out of our sight," Shawn interjected, glaring at Josh.

"Shawn has a point," Eric said. "It doesn't make much sense for us to have gotten to this point, only to let Josh go to the unit alone."

"I didn't have anything to do with this!" Josh yelled, throwing up his hands. "I flew in from Virginia last night, and I didn't get in until noon. I spent the afternoon getting my mom's oil changed and tires rotated before picking up my tux and getting ready for the dinner. I can show you the receipts if you want. But I don't own a gun, I don't know the first thing about what it would take to rig it up like it was, and I flat out didn't have time nor reason to put myself at risk. Mark was a bad person, he was, but I didn't kill him. I told you before, I didn't need to because Thom was finally getting away from him." He crossed his arms and stared at them all, mostly Shawn.

"That's a pretty little story and all," Shawn said, "but I—"

"Enough," Sadie interrupted, putting up her hand. She didn't want to admit it, but Josh's defense was pretty convincing. "Can we just focus on what we're going to do next?" she asked.

They all fell silent, which she appreciated.

"What are we hoping to learn from the storage unit?" she asked.

"Mark gave me the key for a reason," Josh said. "We barely speak anymore and for either of us to acknowledge the other one is a big deal. If he really did kill himself—"

"Kill *himself?*" Shawn interrupted. He dropped his hands to his side. "What the heck?"

Sadie placed her hand on Shawn's arm, hoping it would calm him. "It's a theory," she explained. "But we have no real proof."

"I say we go," Eric said, nodding as he spoke. "Mark gave Josh the key. Let's find out why."

"What about Jane?" Sadie lowered her voice to a whisper as she glanced toward the kitchen.

"What about her?" Shawn asked. "She can come."

"Who is she anyway?" Josh asked.

"She's a reporter with the *Denver Post*," Sadie said, wondering if there was any way to keep Jane from coming. She already felt uncomfortable having her involved so much, and she questioned if she had made the right decision to allow Jane to be here at all.

"A reporter!" Josh burst out.

Sadie and Eric both shushed him, but his eyes remained wide. He said, in a much quieter voice, "Is that the lady you said was meeting with Mark?"

Sadie almost didn't dare answer, but finally she nodded.

Josh swore under his breath and raised both his hands to his hair. "You've got to be kidding me!"

Sadie was suddenly defensive. "She's been helping us."

"Yeah," Josh sneered. "More like she's been helping herself. She's not coming. Whatever is in that storage unit is not part of her story."

"I'm not sure how we can leave her behind," Sadie said.

"Slow down at a corner and I'll push her out for you," Josh said.

"Reporters are vampires."

"What makes you say that?" Eric interjected.

Josh looked at him, then turned away. "I don't want to talk about it."

Oh, boy, another mystery. Sadie wasn't sure she was up for any more riddles tonight.

Josh looked hard at Sadie. "She's not going."

"Okay," Sadie said, deciding it was more important to have Josh than Jane. "Let me go talk to her."

Sadie headed for the kitchen, trying to prepare how to break the news to Jane. It wasn't going to be pretty.

At the bathroom door, she took a deep breath and let it out, willing herself to be calm and yet firm. She lifted her hand and knocked. "Jane?" she asked. "I need to talk to you."

Jane didn't respond.

"Jane?" Sadie said louder as she knocked a second time. When Jane still didn't answer, a funny feeling crept up Sadie's neck. She reached for the knob and turned it in her hand. "I'm coming in," she warned, but when she pushed the door open, an empty bathroom greeted her.

She hurried inside. The bathroom was still a mess, but there weren't that many places a grown woman could hide. A rhythmic drip-drip-drip from the shower kept time with her thoughts as she processed the implications. "Oh, my gosh," she said under her breath as she did one last turn in the bathroom and then hurried out.

"She's gone," Sadie hollered. "Jane's not here." She headed for the den, but the three men met her before she could leave the kitchen. She pointed toward the bathroom. "She's not here." And even though in some ways that solved her problem—freeing her from an ugly confrontation—the fact Jane would sneak away was extremely disturbing.

Josh rushed to the table and then turned to look directly at Sadie. "Where's my camera?"

CHAPTER 44

"She took your camera?" Sadie said even as she moved to the table and started looking around.

"It's not here," Josh said, his voice tight with anger.

Sadie looked up from where she'd been inspecting the seat of one of the chairs pushed under the table.

Josh glared at her. "You set me up."

Sadie straightened. "I did not."

"Some reporter just ran off with my photos!" He turned toward the back door, but only made it two steps before Shawn grabbed his upper arm.

"You're not going after her," Shawn said. "For all we know, you're in league with her yourself."

"She left tracks," Eric said, pulling open the door before turning to look at Sadie. "I'll see if I can catch up."

Sadie nodded, offering him a weak smile that was all she could muster by way of giving her blessing. Eric pulled the door shut behind him and quickly disappeared. Sadie never should have trusted that woman. She'd known it from the very start.

Josh pulled his arm out of Shawn's grasp, but didn't head for the door again. He put both hands on his forehead as he took a deep breath. "I can't believe this is happening," he grumbled, pacing back and forth.

Shawn followed his every movement with his eyes, and Sadie recognized the tension in the way he was holding himself. If Josh tried to make a run for it again, Shawn wouldn't hesitate to take him down. In fact, he'd probably enjoy it.

"Eric will get your camera back," Sadie said, hoping she sounded reassuring.

Josh swore again, and Sadie shot him a look, but he wasn't paying her any attention. Sadie didn't know what else to do. She couldn't even think of something she could cook to take the edge off of the insufferable negativity in the room. A song by the Beatles interrupted her thoughts.

Looking surprised, Shawn reached into his shirt pocket. He pulled out Josh's cell phone and pushed a button, silencing the music.

"At least give me my phone back," Josh said, putting out his hand. "I'd prefer to keep track of my own stuff from here on out."

"Sorry, dude," Shawn said, slipping the phone back in his pocket. "I'm keeping the phone."

Josh looked at Sadie. "You're okay with that?" he demanded. "I've told you everything I know, and yet he still gets to treat me like a criminal?"

Without intending to, Josh had given Sadie an idea. Both her kids assigned certain ring tones for different people, and when she realized the tune the phone had played was "Michelle, My Belle," she remembered there was one path she hadn't yet explored with Josh.

"Who just called?" she asked Shawn.

Josh tensed as Shawn reached into his pocket again, extracted the phone, and then pushed a couple buttons. "It says Michele," Shawn said.

"Really?" Sadie replied. She'd guessed right about the ring tones! She turned back to Josh. "I've been meaning to ask how you know Frank's niece."

Josh was suddenly wary.

"She was sitting at my table tonight," Sadie said, watching his every nuance. "She got up to use the ladies' room and never came back. Well, except she picked you up, didn't she?"

"I knew it," Shawn said, jutting out his chin as he nodded. "He's wrapped up in this like a taco." He glared triumphantly at the smaller man.

Sadie put a hand on her son's arm, but kept her eyes on Josh. "How do you know Michele and what's her part in this?"

"I'm not telling you anything else," Josh said, shaking his head. "I was an idiot to tell you as much as I already did."

The idea of Josh withholding information again was horrendous. "I had no idea Jane was going to take your camera," Sadie said, sincerely apologetic. "And I am so sorry, but we had nothing to do with it, I promise."

"I just want to get out of Garrison and go home."

"Michelle, My Belle" started playing from the phone still in Shawn's hand.

"Sounds like she really wants to talk to you," Sadie said pointedly.

Josh glanced at the phone, but his eyes narrowed slightly—and not at Shawn this time.

Shawn hit the button and ended the call.

"Tell you what," Sadie said, intrigued by Josh's reaction to

Michele's calls. "You tell me about Michele, and I'll give you the phone back."

"Give me the phone back first," he challenged.

Sadie looked at the request from all angles. Shawn could take him down if he had to, so what was the risk? "Shawn, give him his phone."

"What?" Shawn said slowly.

Sadie gave him her best "trust me" look. "You can't deny that he's given us very important information."

"*Assuming* he's telling the truth," Shawn said, glaring at Josh again.

Josh shook his head and looked at Sadie, encouraging her to convince Shawn.

"Give him his phone," Sadie said, keeping her tone calm, but assertive.

Shawn sighed and handed the phone to Josh, who looked at it and put it in his pocket.

"So who is Michele to you?" Sadie pushed, trying not to sound too formal, but finding it a difficult balance.

"We used to date," Josh said, trying to sound casual but failing. A whole new tension was draped all over him. Interesting.

"But you don't anymore?" Shawn said, closing one eye slightly and looking skeptical. "So why is she calling you?"

"And why did she pick you up from the hotel?" Sadie added, watching Josh carefully.

Josh growled a little bit in his throat and shook his head as if to say he couldn't believe he was having to do this.

Sadie was reminded that he didn't *have* to, but he was anyway. Another point in the "Josh isn't the murderer" column of the score sheet in her head.

Josh took a breath and started talking. "A couple years ago, Michele contacted me about Damon. She was working on a college paper about teens who kill. Her Uncle Frank lives here in Garrison, so she knew the story pretty well, but she wanted to talk to the people close to Damon. We seemed to hit it off, and when she finished her paper, we kept in touch. And eventually our relationship got serious. But we broke up right before Christmas. I was as surprised as anyone else to see her here tonight."

"But you called her to pick you up from the hotel," Sadie pointed out.

"No," Josh said, shaking his head. "She called *me* and asked what had happened."

"Which she didn't know because she left the ballroom before the shooting," Sadie pointed out. "Doesn't that strike you as bizarre? She leaves right before Thom is supposed to speak."

A look of concern wrinkled Josh's forehead. Apparently he hadn't thought it through.

"Would *she* have a motive to kill Mr. Ogreski?" Shawn asked, but Sadie could tell from his tone that he found that a shaky suggestion.

However, Josh's concerned look deepened, making Sadie seriously consider the possibility. Could Michele have a motive for murder? Sadie pictured the girl she'd met at her table—the piled-up hair, the strapless gown, and the big doe-eyes. She didn't seem the psychopathic type.

"Would she?" Shawn pressed again.

Josh shook his head, but it wasn't convincing. He glanced around nervously before making eye contact with Sadie again as he reached into his pocket.

Shawn grabbed Josh's wrist as soon as he extracted the phone.

"Sheesh," Josh said, after nearly jumping out of his shoes. Shawn was big, but he was fast.

"Who are you calling?" Shawn demanded.

Sadie tried to shoot Josh a sympathetic look. She was actually relieved by Shawn's stubborn suspicion of Josh. It was wise to not become complacent with anyone.

"Michele," Josh said between clenched teeth. He shot a heated look at Shawn before looking at Sadie. "I've told you everything I know, and I have nothing to hide anymore and no reason to hide it." He looked at Shawn pointedly and flipped his bangs out of his eyes. "I'll put her on speaker."

Chapter 45

"Heya," a chipper female voice said on the phone. "Did you make it to Denver okay?"

Sadie and Shawn were leaning over the table where they'd all sat down in preparation to focus on the call, not wanting to miss a single word.

"I haven't left yet," Josh said rather curtly.

There was a pause. "You haven't left yet!" Michele responded. "What are you thinking? You're supposed to catch a flight in less than an hour."

"A flight *you* insisted I take," Josh cut in, that tightness still in his voice. "And where are you?"

Sadie noticed that Josh had balled his hand into a fist on the table. When a girl as cute and perky as Michele was could earn such anger from a guy like Josh, there were serious issues at hand.

"I'm betting you haven't left yet either," Josh said.

"I'm staying one more night," Michele said innocently. "Just to see how things shake down."

"Why did you leave the dinner early?"

Sadie wondered if Michele would pretend not to know what

he was talking about, but she didn't. "I was bored," she said simply. "And the cake was a little dry."

Sadie sat up straight. Dry! It was not dry! Sadie had to clamp her teeth together to keep from defending herself out loud. Josh looked at her strangely, reminding her that he didn't know she'd made the cake. But Shawn did, and he put a calming hand on her arm, smiling as if to say, "Who cares what she thinks?" After a deep breath, she waved Josh to continue and tried to think of beautiful and peaceful thoughts to calm herself down. She suspected some people would think about butterflies or rainbows, but she thought about food and suddenly realized she hadn't gotten any of the Evil Chicken. Would the injustice never end?

"Bull," Josh said to Michele. "Why did you leave early? You came all the way to Garrison and left as soon as Thom showed up on stage."

Michele sighed. "I had to use the ladies' room."

That was the reason she'd given when she excused herself from the table. Not that Sadie believed her anymore. She'd lied about Sadie's cake and therefore couldn't be trusted to tell the truth about anything.

"Where? At Walmart?" Josh said. "The police had the parking lot to the hotel blocked off within minutes, and no one was allowed in or out without police clearance. That's why I had to get picked up—remember? I already know why you were there tonight, Michele, but you'd better tell me why you left."

Sadie held her breath and waited for Michele's answer. For a moment, she feared Michele had hung up, but then the girl started talking.

"I was in the foyer when Thom came out of the ballroom. Everyone was freaking out. He went out to the parking lot, and I followed him. He tried to get in his car, but it was locked and I guess he'd left the key with Mark. I offered him a ride, and he took me up on it."

Sadie opened her mouth to ask where they'd gone, but Shawn put his hand over her mouth and shook his head. How could she forget that she and Shawn were simply eavesdroppers on this conversation?

Josh watched them, giving Sadie a pointed look before turning his attention back to the call. "Where did you take him?" he asked.

"A gas station," Michele said. "We talked for awhile, but then he got kinda nervous and said he wanted to walk. I had what I wanted, so I let him go."

"I guess you finally got the interview you wanted so badly," Josh said, anger dripping from his every word.

"Sure did," Michele said, chipper once again. "No thanks to you."

"I don't make it a habit to use my friends," Josh said. "And I'll be sure to tell Thom exactly what you're up to as soon as I see him next time. I hope you got what you needed because he'll never talk to you again."

"Oh, I got plenty, thanks," Michele said, a chuckle laced through her words. "He was far more forthcoming than I'd have expected him to be."

"You're pathetic," Josh said. He hit the end button on the phone.

Sadie stared at it, then looked up at Josh, stunned. "You hung up on her."

"Yep," Josh said.

"But we weren't done," Sadie said.

Shawn put a calming hand on Sadie's arm, but kept his eyes on Josh. "Why did she want an interview with Thom?"

Oh, good question, Sadie thought, reengaging.

"Michele and I . . ." he began. "We didn't have any secrets when we were together."

It took Sadie a moment to understand what he was saying. She lifted her eyebrows. "She knew the truth?"

Josh nodded. "You can't imagine how good it felt to finally have someone I could talk to about everything."

"How much did she know?" Shawn asked.

"All of it," Josh said. He met Shawn's eyes and for the first time they weren't staring one another down.

Sadie wondered if that meant Shawn's suspicions were dimming.

Josh continued, "I didn't tell her all at once, of course, but little by little I told her every bit of this big, complicated story. And she loved me anyway—or at least I thought she did. We were talking about getting married, so I felt I had no reason *not* to trust her with every part of my life."

Sadie noted the sadness in his expression. Michele had broken his heart, hadn't she?

"A few weeks before Christmas," Josh continued, "Michele suggested I invite Thom to visit for the holidays. She'd never met him, even though I talked about him quite a bit—especially the last six months or so as he seemed to be getting worse.

"I told her that inviting Thom would only make him feel bad that he couldn't come. He rarely left the house, let alone travel to the East Coast. She was determined to meet him, however, so I suggested we go to California instead and she was all over it—too much all over it. I mean, she'd met my mother once and hadn't made a big deal out of it so it bothered me that seeing Thom was so exciting for her, but I blew it off. I figured she was simply intrigued by him being a celebrity, ya know? Then I found out that her parents were planning a Caribbean cruise with her family over the Christmas holiday and she refused to go even though the tickets were nonrefundable."

"Yikes," Sadie said, totally following this line of suspicious behavior Josh was laying out. Turning down a cruise? That was so not normal.

Josh nodded. "I knew there was something funny going on, but I couldn't figure it out. So I told her Thom had changed his mind and that we couldn't go to California after all. She insisted I call him back and find a time that would work. I refused and it led to the only fight we ever had." He snorted again and closed his eyes as though the memory was physically painful. "That's when I met the real Michele for the first time. I'd thought we never fought because we were so well-matched. Turns out, we never fought because Michele was a chameleon who became what I wanted in hopes it would lead her to Thom."

"What for?" Shawn asked. "Was she some kind of obsessed fan?"

"Sort of," Josh said. "More like an obsessed writer. That paper she'd first contacted me about—the one about teens who kill? At some point she decided to turn it into one of those true crime novels about Damon. While I thought I was trusting her with my deepest secrets and insecurities, she was taking notes. Apparently, from the first few e-mails we'd exchanged she sensed I was hiding something. She was very patient and very sly."

Sheesh, Sadie thought. *Does everyone want to write a book?* Damon, Thom, Diane, Jane, and now Michele. It was like a disease or something.

Josh was still talking. "I found the manuscript on her computer. Three hundred pages of information she'd carefully siphoned from me over the years, mingled with enough conjecture and supposition to make a great story—a story that will destroy Thom. I imagine she's already shopping it around by now. When I saw her at the dinner tonight, I knew she was there to talk to Thom. It wouldn't surprise me if she asked him flat-out if *Devilish Details* was Damon's book. She'd love to have his reaction in her book—the final pages where she confronts the man behind it all." Josh shook his head. "It makes me sick, but I'm grateful she and I were over with by the time I learned about Mrs. Veeter. I'm glad she doesn't get to exploit that part."

Sadie thought of Jane, who had come to town specifically for a story she could exploit. The pictures Josh had taken would go a long way toward helping that whole process. How did people live with themselves?

"Did you tell Thom about Michele's book?" Sadie asked. "Did he know his cover was about to be blown?"

Josh shifted in his chair. "I didn't tell him. I didn't know what to do about it except count it as one more reason to push Thom to go to treatment—let him get well before Michele's book hit the market. Thom and I have a good relationship, but I don't know what he's going to think when he learns I told someone else—let alone told someone who went on to write a book about it. He'll be devastated. I'd like to wait until he's sober and has a good therapist before he finds out."

"So, even with all that you let Michele pick you up?" Sadie asked.

"I was in a complete panic. All the doors were blocked, and I couldn't get my rental car out of the lot. That's when I thought of the kitchen. As luck would have it, there were no officers there yet." He paused and held Sadie's eyes while they both relived the event.

Sadie wondered how different things would be if there *had* been a police officer there.

Josh looked away and continued. "When Michele found out I'd taken those pictures, she convinced me I had to get out of town before the police could determine it was me. She said the longer it took them to figure out who I was, the better chance I had to get away. It was stupid for me to agree, since I'd have been abandoning Thom, but she has a funny way of convincing me to do stupid things." He paused. "We went to her uncle's house since he was still at the hotel and changed my flight. I didn't dare call Thom because if the police got his phone and found out that I'd been trying to call him, it could lead them to me." He looked up at Sadie. "After we made the arrangements, we drove back to the hotel to see if I could get my car, but the lot was still blocked off and there were half a dozen news vans out front. That's when I called my mom. She'd been calling me all night. I told her I had to get out of Garrison and asked if I could take her car to the Denver airport. She was going to bring the rental car back tomorrow and return it for me."

"And then we intercepted you," Sadie said.

Josh nodded and let out a breath. "Not that I'm all warm and fuzzy about what's happened tonight, but I am glad I didn't leave. I don't know what Michele's got up her sleeve, but I have no doubt that getting me out of town is part of her plan."

"You mean beyond getting Thom's interview?"

"*She's* still here," Josh reminded them.

Sadie pondered what Michele might have in the works. Maybe she would go to the police and tell them everything. Or, maybe with Josh gone, she'd be the one person Thom felt comfortable with, giving her more opportunity to bleed him for information. Sadie was searching for her next question when the back door burst open. Sadie pushed away from the table while Shawn and Josh both jumped to their feet. By the time Sadie realized it was Eric, he was inside, his hands on his knees, leaning forward in an attempt to catch his breath. He left the door open and the temperature in the kitchen immediately dropped ten degrees.

Sadie hurried toward him once she got over the shock of his dramatic entrance. "Eric, what happened? Are you okay?"

Eric put out a hand, raising one finger to indicate that Sadie wait for him to get properly oxygenated. It only took twenty seconds, but it felt like a long time before Eric stood up, his chest still heaving.

"I couldn't . . . catch her," he said, an apologetic expression on his face as he looked from Sadie to Josh.

Josh closed his eyes and clenched his jaw.

"But we . . . might . . . have even bigger . . . problems," Eric said.

"What?" Sadie asked, her heart speeding up even more.

"There are cops . . . all over the place out there." He nodded toward the open door. "Jane was stopped." He made eye contact with each one of them in turn.

"By the cops?" Sadie asked.

"Did they take my camera from her?" Josh added.

Eric shook his head, his hands still on his knees. "I don't know. . . . I ducked behind a garage . . . but if she tells them where we are . . . we're in trouble. I didn't see anyone following me, so they might . . . not be convinced yet."

Sadie felt frozen. Was she ready to face up to what she'd done tonight? She looked at Shawn, who looked equally surprised, before glancing at Josh, who seemed concerned.

"Well," Sadie said, trying to sound calm, "I guess we've done everything we can do."

"What about . . . the key?" Eric asked.

Sadie looked at him as he reached into his pocket and produced the orange key he'd spent so much time figuring out.

"If we leave now, we might . . . just get there before they catch up," Eric said.

"I don't know," Sadie said, imagining being involved in a high-speed chase or something equally terrifying.

"Let's go," Shawn said decisively. "We've come this far. We should see it through."

Sadie was still unsure, and she looked at Eric one last time. He was staring at her, but didn't seem angry about her hesitation. His understanding helped to calm her.

"Seriously, Sadie, at this point—what do we have to lose?"

CHAPTER 46

Instead of turning right—where they could see a police car parked down the block—Eric made a left and wound through the side roads and backstreets before heading for a main road far enough away from the action that they could breathe normally. The mood in the Jeep was tense and no one spoke. Sadie decided that having time to think was highly overrated. Where was Pete? What was he doing? What was he thinking? And . . . why hadn't he called?

Sadie reached into her pocket. Maybe he *had* called and she hadn't heard it ring. It had been hours since she'd last tried to contact him. The screen was black, so she hit a random button to bring the screen to life. It remained black. Surprised, Sadie pushed another button. Nothing happened. "Huh," she said under her breath.

"What?" Eric asked, glancing at her. Apparently her mutterings were pretty loud in the silent car.

Sadie pressed down on the power button. Maybe she'd somehow turned it off. Again, nothing happened. "My phone won't turn on." She lifted her thumb off the power button for a few seconds before pressing it again.

DEVIL'S FOOD CAKE

"You can use mine," Shawn said, handing his phone up over the seat.

Sadie shook her head. "I don't need to make a call, I was just checking to see if . . . anyone had called me."

"Anyone?" Shawn said, and Sadie could hear the tease in his voice. "You mean Pete?"

Sadie felt her cheeks color, but she wasn't sure why other than she didn't like being the center of attention. She put her phone back in her pocket. She'd worry about it later.

"Is that it?" she said, pointing at a blue and gold sign half a block ahead, grateful for the change of subject.

"I think so," Eric said, leaning forward. One of the lights in the sign for Advanced Storage was flickering as they all got out of the Jeep. A few feet to the left of the main glass door was an oversized garage door. Sadie assumed it was to allow loading and unloading of larger items. She'd never seen an interior storage unit and it seemed quite clever to her. A little classier than the run-of-the-mill, outdoor type.

Eric pulled the key from his pocket and turned it over, typing in the five-digit number written on the back. Everyone held their breath as he pushed the final number. A slight buzz was the only indication that the door was unlocked. Eric smiled and pulled the door open, stepping back to hold it for the rest of them.

"There it is," Josh said a minute later, pointing at a tiny square on the map stuck to the wall that indicated the different units and how to exit the building in case of a fire. "Looks like we make two lefts and follow that hallway nearly to the end."

"He sure found the unit fast, didn't he, Mom?" Shawn commented as they followed Josh down the hallway.

"He was looking at a map," Sadie said. "It wasn't rocket science."

"I'm just sayin' he found it quick," Shawn said, attempting to look innocent. "Maybe he's a map-genius, or . . . maybe he's been here before."

"Found it," Josh said as he and Eric came to a stop in front of a door.

Eric waited until Sadie and Shawn had joined them before inserting the key, turning it, and pulling the door open.

The single light in the center of the twelve foot by twelve foot room was dim when they flipped the switch, but the room slowly lightened. Sadie suspected it was one of those newfangled energy-saving bulbs that were supposed to last for five years, but which Sadie still seemed to change far too often at home. She looked around, squinting into the slowly illuminating corners of the room.

Twin mattresses leaned against the wall directly across from the door and a stuffed and mounted pheasant sat on the floor. Sadie wrinkled her nose. Taxidermy was not her idea of home décor, no wonder it was in storage. The other walls were lined with stacks of Rubbermaid totes as well as a dresser, some laundry baskets full of odds and ends, and a menagerie of miscellaneous household items. The center of the room was mostly clear, offering just enough room for Josh, Sadie, and Shawn to stand and observe. Eric stayed in the doorway.

"Mark left all this here?" Sadie said, picking up a ceramic duck that had been sitting at the top of an open box. The duck was wearing a bow tie, its wings held out, forming a bowl. For candy? Or was it a fancy type of ashtray?

She noted there wasn't much dust. She'd have expected things to be a lot dirtier after ten years in storage. There was something to be said for having an interior unit.

Josh shook his head. "Not Mark. This stuff is Thom's. He went from a house in Garrison to an apartment in Orange County," Josh said, looking around. "When he moved I remember him saying he was going to store some of Damon's stuff until he decided what to do with it. I'm guessing he never came back for it." He picked up a black backpack and stared at it.

Sadie wondered if it was the same backpack Damon had taken to prom. Would the police have returned it to Thom?

"Do you think Thom really told Mark to give the key to you?" Eric said. He wasn't investigating anything, just standing in the doorway, surveying the area with his hands in the front pockets of his jeans.

Framed by the doorway like he was, Sadie noticed he had very nice shoulders.

"I don't know," Josh said, running a hand through his hair as he turned slowly, taking it all in.

Sadie could practically hear his thoughts. *Where do we begin when we don't know what we're looking for, or even if we're supposed to be looking for anything at all?*

"It's *Thom's* storage unit," Eric added pointedly.

"Mark took over Thom's finances along with everything else," Josh said, shooting Eric an unappreciative glance. "I'm sure Mark's kept the key *safe* for a very long time, just like everything else."

"And since he knew he was going to off himself, he thought the key would be safer with Josh?" Shawn said, taking the lid off a shoebox. "Sweet," he said as he reached into the box. "Basketball cards." He looked at Josh. "You didn't tell me he was a collector." He went back to the box, apparently forgetting for the moment that he was still suspicious of Josh.

"Uh, sorry," Josh said dryly. "I was waiting for the right moment."

Shawn began riffling through the cards. "Man!" He pulled out a card. "He's got a Magic Johnson rookie card. Do you have any idea how much this is worth?"

Sadie walked over to her son and picked up the lid he'd set aside. When he saw the lid in her hand he frowned, but took his hands out of the box so Sadie could close it. She gave him a hard look, and he managed to look penitent. What Sadie had hoped to find was something to verify their hypothesis that Mark's death had been suicide. The fact that Mark gave Josh the key seemed like more than a coincidence, but how could they be sure? The one man who could tell them was dead.

Then Sadie noticed something that had been mostly hidden by a stack of Rubbermaid containers beside it. With the light nearly full-bright now, she could get a better look. "What's that?" She pointed toward what looked like a lacquered black, upright freezer wedged into the far corner.

The three men followed her finger. "It's a gun safe," Eric said from the doorway, finally taking a step inside.

"A gun safe?" Sadie repeated.

Josh was already heading toward it since there weren't many things in his way. In fact, there was a cleared path that took them right to it—Josh in the lead, Sadie behind him, Shawn behind her, and Eric bringing up the rear. It took all of five steps to get them across the room.

Sadie's shoes scraped across the floor and she looked down, surprised to see sand on the floor. No dust, but sand?

"Wow," Shawn said as the procession came to a stop, "imagine that. Josh brought us to a storage unit with a gun safe in it."

Josh turned his head slowly and gave Shawn an exasperated look. "Really?" he said. "You think I'm leading you guys around for kicks?" He shook his head and turned back to the safe.

"You said this stuff was mostly Damon's," Sadie said, hoping to keep everyone focused on the task at hand. "Is the gun safe Damon's too?"

Josh shook his head. "No, the gun safe is Thom's. He was an avid hunter before Damon . . . well, before it happened."

"How many shotguns did Thom have?" she asked.

"Just one. But Damon got his own when he turned fourteen." Josh pointed at the pheasant on the cement floor. "He got that with it. Thom was real proud of him and had it mounted. When Damon started having a hard time, though, Thom changed the combination on the safe. What most people don't know is that Thom knew Damon was in trouble and he was trying to get him help. It just . . . wasn't enough."

So instead Thom put his name on his son's book and made millions, Sadie thought, shaking her head. It was hard to reconcile the grieving father with the plagiarizing one. But then, Sadie remembered Thom as he'd looked at Donna Hender's table. He hadn't escaped the consequences of his choices and the world would soon know the truth. While Sadie appreciated Josh's optimistic expectation that Thom would get the help he needed, Sadie couldn't help but wonder if, like his attempts to intervene on Damon's behalf, it would be too little, too late.

"Didn't Damon use his father's gun that night?" Shawn asked. "Why not use his own?"

Josh shrugged. "Who knows what was going on in Damon's head? He somehow got his dad's gun and sawed off the barrel, presumably so it would fit in the backpack. Maybe he didn't plan to kill himself and didn't want to ruin his own gun. I don't know."

Once again, the only person who could answer that question was dead.

"Do you by chance know the combo?" Eric asked.

Josh shook his head.

"Can you break in?" Sadie asked Eric hopefully. He'd gotten her out of handcuffs and found out what the key belonged to. She'd have never guessed how handy a locksmith could be before tonight.

But Eric was shaking his head. "Safe cracking is a whole different ball game," he said. "It's not your basic lock job."

"I bet the police have someone who can bust into it," Shawn said. The comment cast a heavy pall on the group, reminding them how this evening was going to end.

Josh reached for the handle almost as an afterthought. As soon as he grabbed it, however, he paused and looked up in surprise. "It's open."

"It's open?" Shawn, Sadie, and Eric said at the same time.

Josh pulled back on the handle and the door began swinging open.

Shawn nearly trampled Sadie as he pushed forward.

Sadie slid forward, unable to get traction on the sandy floor. She clutched at Josh's arm to keep from falling headfirst into a large laundry basket full of CDs.

"Whoa," Shawn said, grabbing the edge of the door and holding it closed, the muscles of his forearm straining. "We're just going to let this guy open a safe presumably full of guns? He could kill us all."

"He couldn't kill us all," Sadie said in quick defense, eager to see what was inside the safe. "Maybe one or two of us, but not all three."

"Gee, thanks for the vote of confidence," Josh said, shaking his head. "I'm not going to kill anybody." He glared at Shawn who was easily twice his size. "You're freaking paranoid."

Shawn scowled and then let go of the door. He kept his eyes on Josh, though.

DEVIL'S FOOD CAKE

Josh's jaw was tight as he pulled open the door, temporarily blocking Shawn and Eric's view as it swung open. Sadie was close enough to see everything Josh was seeing and she braced herself for what they might, or might not, find. Along the back of the safe were grooves, two of which supported gun barrels—a rifle and a .22, Sadie thought. No shotgun. Above the guns was a shelf, presumably to hold ammunition. However, instead of bullets, the shelf held a large stack of paper and propped against it was a white envelope with a word written on the front. Sadie recognized the handwriting from the copy of *Devilish Details* she'd found on stage. In the book, the words had said "I'm sorry." Now, the same handwriting spelled, "Thom."

CHAPTER 47

"I think this is Damon's original manuscript," Josh said, reaching into the safe and thumbing through the stack of papers. The edges of the paper weren't crisp and squared up like a brand-new ream, rather they were bent and imperfectly aligned.

Shawn swung the door all the way open so he and Eric could see inside too.

Josh hesitated, then reached for the letter. Everyone took a step back, allowing him to turn around in the tiny room that suddenly seemed much smaller. He held the envelope in his hand a moment, then pulled back the flap which, apparently, wasn't sealed.

Sadie watched Josh's methodical movements as he pulled a single sheet of paper from the envelope and unfolded it, the paper sounding unnaturally loud in the tense silence.

His eyes scanned the paper first, and Sadie found his expression difficult to read. Finally, when she was about out of patience, Josh cleared his throat, opened his mouth to speak, but then closed it. After another moment, he handed the letter to Sadie, who took it hesitantly. Unlike Josh, though, she didn't read it to herself before verbalizing what it said.

DEVIL'S FOOD CAKE

The letter was typed, so she couldn't match up the handwriting.

```
Thom,
    It seemed so simple in the beginning,
didn't it? And here we are, ten years later,
broken men who have run out of road. If you
don't know already, you'll know soon enough
that our secrets are secrets no more. I've
spent weeks trying to decide how best to
handle this before coming to the conclusion
that I'd rather not handle it at all. I'm not
proud of what I've done, and what it's done to
you, and I'm not proud of running away from
the choices I've made, but I've never pro-
fessed to be a good man.
    I killed Diane Veeter, Thom. I had to. She
said she could prove you hadn't written the
book. But I was still high on the rush of
success the book was having. I wasn't going to
let her ruin it for me—for us. But now, a re-
porter at the Denver Post has started to put
the pieces together and, although I've had a
hard time living with myself these last few
years as I've watched you sink deeper and as
I've faced my own demons, I'm not willing to
go to prison. Tell the police they can find
information about Diane Veeter in my file at
work. Closing out the rest of my life ought to
be an easy task. I find it a sad reflection to
note that you are the only person I have left
to say good-bye too. The lies have isolated us
so much from the rest of the world. I wonder
if anyone missed us?
    As for you, old friend, I can only say I'm
sorry. I didn't want things to come to this,
but as a final gift, I hope that the atten-
tion created by my "larger than life" exit
```

from mortality will at least breathe new life into your future. What's that say—"Have a scandal and you're sure to have a hit"? I take full responsibility for everything. I took advantage of a weak man and made him even weaker. It is my hope that once the bloodthirsty media is through with this story, <u>Devilish Details</u> will rise like a phoenix from the ashes and remain in print. It is also my hope that the courts will show you the mercy you were never able to show yourself. I beg of you to take what you have left and live a life you can be proud of—finally. I will no longer stand in your way.

To peace.

Sincerely,

Markus F. Ogreski

Sadie finished reading the letter and the silence pressed upon her until she looked up to see the faces of Shawn and Eric registering the same sobering surprise she herself felt. Josh, standing beside her, had his arms folded over his chest as he stared at the floor.

Sadie reached into her pocket and pulled out the letter she'd taken from Thom's jacket. She unfolded it and put it on top of a storage container next to the new letter. She looked at the signatures. "They're a pretty close match," Sadie said, wondering if the ten-year time span could account for the minimal differences.

"He did it for Thom," Josh finally said. He chuckled without humor and shook his head. "He knew the truth was going to come out and he bailed." He looked up, his eyes narrowed in anger. "He left Thom to face it alone. What a coward."

Sadie was hard-pressed to disagree with him and looked back

at the two letters—one written at the beginning of the lie, and one written to end it.

"Public suicide to sell books," Shawn said, sounding dumbfounded. "That's insane."

Sadie agreed wholeheartedly, but found herself distracted by Eric, who was scuffing his shoe on the floor. Sadie could hear the sand under his shoe. He seemed rather intrigued, which of course intrigued Sadie. Eric leaned down and touched the floor before looking up at them. "Metal shavings," he said.

All four of them looked around the room with new intent.

"If Mark sawed off the barrel here, would he have left the hacksaw behind?" Josh asked as he pulled open a box. He paused and Sadie turned to him. Had he found the hacksaw?

What he pulled from the box, however, wasn't a hacksaw. It was a spool of what looked like wire. He looked up at Sadie. "Doesn't this look like the stuff used to wire that gun into the podium?"

Sadie nodded slowly. It looked just like the cable she'd seen tangled around the gun back at the hotel. Josh would have seen it as well, since he was on stage after the shooting. She looked from Josh to Eric just in time to see Eric stiffen and turn quickly to look over his shoulder.

Sadie, startled by his sudden reaction, opened her mouth to ask him what was wrong when a familiar face appeared behind his left shoulder.

"Lady," Officer Malloy said, making eye contact with her across the room. "You can't imagine how much trouble you're in right now."

CHAPTER 48

Ten minutes later, Sadie stood against the front wall of the storage unit with Shawn to her left and Josh and Eric to her right. The three men were in handcuffs; Sadie had simply been instructed to keep her good arm at her side while a police officer stood guard. All of them had been read their rights in regard to the most obvious charge: evading arrest. Sadie suspected charges for kidnapping and interfering with a police investigation weren't far behind. She felt sick. All of them were silent as the reality of what they'd discovered mingled with the equally difficult reality of what lay ahead. Sadie couldn't imagine how much worse things would get when the police learned the manner in which Josh had become part of the crew.

Officer Malloy hadn't come alone. Two police cruisers were parked out front and although Sadie wasn't facing them, the alternating red and blue lights outside reflected off the white walls in front of her. She swore they were making her dizzy, but was open to the possibility that she was just looking for reasons to be unsettled. There were plenty. Jane had identified Eric's Jeep, which was how the police had found them. Sadie wondered if Jane was in trouble or if she'd talked her way out of it.

DEVIL'S FOOD CAKE

Sadie was trying to be calm, but her anxiety was growing and she was finding it difficult to hold it back. What would happen next? Would they all go to jail? What would happen to Shawn? There were other thoughts as well: Where was Thom? How would he handle this? Would the police believe them now? Or would they continue to discount everything Sadie had learned? The knot in her stomach grew by the second, and she tried to anticipate what the rest of this night would be like.

She heard the whooshing of a door being opened and turned her head, stiffening when she saw Pete walk in amid a swirl of snow. The officer who'd been left to guard them moved toward him, but Pete didn't pay any attention to him, heading instead toward Sadie, his eyes frantic.

If she hadn't already been up against the wall, she'd have taken a step backward, unprepared for how to deal with Pete. But he didn't yell or scream; he didn't even look angry. Instead when he reached her, he wrapped his arms around her as if that type of physical affection was something that came easy to them.

Sadie felt herself stiffen even more, holding back a cry of pain as her shoulder protested the embrace. She was hyperaware of Shawn, Josh, and Eric looking on and although part of her just melted to be in Pete's arms, another part was embarrassed. After a few seconds, she raised her good hand and patted him on the back, trying to return what warmth she could.

Only then did Pete pull back, his arms still around her. "Sadie," he said quietly, but not quietly enough. Sadie was well aware of everyone watching them and straining to hear what they said. "I am so sorry."

Sadie was unprepared to hear his apology. "What?"

"I'm sorry," Pete said again sincerely. He seemed to notice the sling for the first time and took a step back. "Are you okay?"

"I-I'll be fine," Sadie said, trying to overcome her surprise at Pete's attention.

They looked at one another, too many things needing to be said and both of them unable to find the words. Finally, Pete dropped his arms, but the soft expression on his face remained. "So much has happened," he finally said.

Sadie nodded. *That* was an understatement.

"Detective Cunningham?"

Pete turned, and Sadie looked past him to Officer Malloy, who'd emerged from the hallway leading to Thom's storage unit. "I thought Dailey was on this case."

"He is," Pete said in a very professional tone. "And he'll be here in a few minutes with CS. I'm here to bring Mrs. Hoffmiller and her son to the station. The captain would like to meet with them."

"What about Josh and Eric?" Sadie said, wanting to do right by them as best she could. She didn't deserve any more special treatment than they did.

Pete glanced at her, then back to Malloy. "I can only transport two," he said. "I'll call Benson to come for the others. You're to stay here and continue gathering evidence."

Malloy did not seem entirely pleased, but nodded his acceptance.

Pete showed Sadie to the passenger seat of his car and Shawn to the backseat. She was really glad her son was here. It made her feel . . . safer for some reason—like she had backup.

Once in the car, Pete turned on the heat, and Sadie tried to relax but found it impossible. She could feel words coming to the surface, but she didn't know how to broach the topics of what had happened since the last time she'd been able to talk to Pete. She'd already given the letters from Mr. Ogreski to the officers at the storage unit. They hadn't seemed surprised by the information, which made Sadie wonder if they'd come to the same conclusion on their part. If that were the case, had everything she'd done tonight been a waste of time?

"What does Jane Seeley look like?" Pete asked, interrupting Sadie's thoughts with a question she wasn't expecting. It took her a second to backtrack in her memory to find the answer.

"Oh, uh, she's tall, with black hair and—"

"Red?" Pete cut in. "Her hair—does it have red in it?"

Sadie nodded, completely confused. "Yes," she confirmed, watching the thoughtful expression on his face. "Why?"

Pete was quiet as he stared ahead. He began tapping the steering wheel with his thumbs. Sadie waited for him to explain why that detail was so important. "After you left the hotel, I put two officers in charge of finding Jane Seeley. We spent an hour looking for her and didn't let any witnesses leave during that time." He turned to look at her. "We never found her."

"She was there, Pete," Sadie said, instantly on the defensive. "And I didn't let—wait, how did you know who you were looking for?"

"We got her picture from the website for the *Post*. It runs next to her column."

"That's not her photo," Sadie said, but she sensed that Pete had already figured that part out. "You thought I lied about her being there."

"I didn't know what to think," Pete said, letting out a breath as he turned on his right blinker. The streets were packed with snow and he was driving cautiously. "But several of the officers had a lot to say about it."

Sadie remembered what Pete had told her about her *reputation* at the police station. She could only imagine how those officers' feelings would be intensified when they thought she'd lied to them.

"The woman we stopped outside of Eric's house said she was Jane Seeley. I remember seeing her at the hotel. She said she was with the catering staff."

Sadie shook her head, wishing she could shake Jane. "That's why I was arrested?" she asked. "Because everyone thought I'd lied about Jane being there?"

Pete nodded.

"All because Jane uses someone else's photo for her column," she said out loud, leaning against the seat.

Suffice it to say Sadie's opinion of Jane was not improved. And yet, Jane wasn't the only one playing a charade. Thom wasn't an award-winning writer, Mark Ogreski wasn't an honest literary agent, Michele wasn't a curious fan, and even Josh wasn't simply a photographer for a magazine back East. Every one of them had been hiding things, parts of their real selves, and yet working so hard to live behind a façade. Sadie wondered if she, too, weren't doing the same thing. She'd lied and manipulated and operated outside of her comfort zone. Why? To be right? To add spice to her own life?

Pete continued. "The captain appointed another detective to the case and sent me back to the station to do some research into Mark Ogreski. I knew nothing about the arrest until the APB was issued. It's all been pretty ugly since then. I kept hoping you'd answer your phone so we could get things resolved. I mean, I understand that—"

"You called?" Sadie cut in.

Pete glanced at her as he slowed down for a red light. "Several times," he said. "You wouldn't take my calls. I thought you . . ." He

DEVIL'S FOOD CAKE

didn't finish, but Sadie knew what he had been about to say. He'd thought the same thing Sadie thought when he'd ignored her calls.

"My phone's dead," Sadie said, wishing they were talking face to face so she could watch his eyes. "But before that, I'd called you, and sent text messages thinking they would be easier for you to respond to."

Pete nodded. "I was in the middle of so many things I couldn't respond right away."

"I had important information, Pete," Sadie said in her own defense. "And you didn't think I was trustworthy enough to listen to me."

Pete looked at her again, his eyes pleading. "I'm so sorry."

Sadie looked away, knowing she couldn't blame him too much. She liked to think the things she'd discovered were the most important details, but was that fair? And she *had* gotten over-involved—finding the book backstage, butting in on Gayle's interview. From Pete's perspective it made sense that he'd question her judgment, but it still hurt. To believe their connection would override all those other things was more romantic than realistic.

"How much trouble are we in?" Sadie asked the dreaded question as they approached the police station and her stomach began fluttering. She glanced over her shoulder at Shawn who'd been listening quietly throughout the drive. He gave her an encouraging smile. Shouldn't she be the one offering encouragement?

"I don't know," Pete said, sympathetically. "If not for the information you, uh, shared about Thom being at Josh Hender's house we might not have found him for a long time."

"You found Thom?" Shawn said from the backseat, leaning forward. "At Josh's?"

Pete nodded, meeting Shawn's eyes in the rearview mirror.

"We've been questioning him for a couple of hours, but he'd been drinking and we haven't made much progress. Still—we found him because of you, Sadie."

Sadie liked knowing that, but she wondered how helpful it would be in the long run.

Pete pulled into a parking space in front of the main entrance. "The grounds for you to have been arrested in the first place were shaky at best. I managed to convince the captain to listen to your side of things before he decides what to do, but that's the only promise I can make. I'll warn you that this case is very complicated and it's going to take a long time to put back together."

"I appreciate you going to bat for us," Sadie said and took a deep calming breath, but the lump that had been forming in her throat ever since Malloy had showed up in the doorway of the storage unit was still growing.

Pete shifted into park and reached for her hand. She took his and he gave it a squeeze. "I should have done it sooner," he said.

Sadie offered him a forgiving smile, then looked back at Shawn who had been content to listen to their exchange. "Well?" she said, trying to be brave. "Are you ready?"

Shawn shook his head. "No. You?"

CHAPTER 49

A few minutes later, Pete formally introduced her to Captain Dresden—the man with the wiry eyebrows who'd ordered Sadie's arrest at the hotel. Awkward, to say the least.

"So," the captain said, looking at her over his cluttered desk. "This interview will not count as your official statement, but I would like to hear how it is that tonight's events came about."

Sadie took a deep breath and reminded herself that while she might not be proud of everything she'd done, there was honor in being honest. "Well," she said, "it started with the devil's food cake. See, I'm on a diet and . . ."

It was after two A.M. when Sadie finished telling her side of the story. Partway through, the captain had started taking notes. Next to his notes was the letter she'd taken from Thom's suit pocket and her cell phone. The captain said he would need to get her call log and messages off of it before he could give it back. Malloy already had the key to the storage unit. Captain Dresden reviewed the notes in front of him and then looked up at her. "Anything else?"

"Diane Veeter's family should know what really happened to her."

"We'll take care of that," the captain said. "I have some things I need to discuss with the district attorney. For that reason, I'd like to have you go to the hospital," he pointed at her shoulder, "and then return home and get some rest. I expect you here tomorrow at ten A.M. to give your official statement. Can I have your word that you'll go home and stay there?"

"Oh, yes, sir," Sadie said, nodding quickly as she imagined how good it would feel to climb into her own bed. "What about my son and Eric?" She realized she still didn't know Eric's last name.

"I'll need to review their statements before I make a definite decision," he said. "But I anticipate they'll meet you back here tomorrow morning."

"And Josh?"

"Josh has some things he still needs to explain to us about not reporting a crime and posing as a crime scene photographer. But I can promise you we'll be fair."

Sadie nodded. "Thank you," she said. "I appreciate, um, everything."

The captain nodded without smiling and moved to the door, pulling it open.

As Sadie exited the room, she scanned the lobby. Shawn was sitting on a chair against the wall opposite the captain's office. She headed in his direction, relieved to be done with the intimidating interview and eager to tell Shawn they would get to go home, for tonight anyway.

"Cunningham," Captain Dresden said from behind her. "Can I speak with you for a moment?"

Pete, who had been talking to another officer a few feet away, nodded, smiling at Sadie as he passed her.

Sadie reached Shawn, leaning into him once she sat down beside him. She quickly filled him in on the things the captain had told her.

DEVIL'S FOOD CAKE

"I told you it'd all turn out okay," Shawn said with a cocky smile. He nodded toward the door to his left. "Eric's in there," he said. "And Josh is in that next room I think."

"Have you seen anyone else?" Sadie asked. "Pete made it sound like they picked Thom up."

Shawn shrugged. "Haven't seen him."

"Jane?"

Shawn shook his head. "Just us."

Sadie nodded and looked at the door to the captain's office. No one had said how she was supposed to get to the hospital, but she was anxious to be there. The more time passed, the stiffer and more painful her shoulder had become. On top of that, she had a massive headache. The sooner she was able to see a doctor, the sooner she could go home and sleep—assuming that once she was surrounded in quiet she could set aside the disturbing information they'd uncovered tonight. Even though her own circumstances had distracted her, the thought of Mr. Ogreski arranging his own violent death was never far from her mind.

"I'm sorry all this happened, Shawn," Sadie said. "I feel horrible that—"

Shawn cut her off by leaning over and kissing the top of her head. "I'm proud of what we did, Mom," he said. "Maybe we—or, well, me anyway—should have done some things differently. But we didn't hurt anyone and we weren't trying to." He shrugged his big shoulders. "Besides that, this is the best time I've had in Garrison since that time Crab and I put Icy Hot on the toilet seats at school."

Sadie snapped her head to the side. "That was you?" she said. It had been quite the scandal—for two weeks unsuspecting students had their rear ends burning after bathroom breaks.

Shawn just smiled.

Sadie looked around, hoping no one had overheard them. "You are *not* allowed to tell anyone else you're responsible for that," she chided him. "I'd never live it down." After tonight, her reputation couldn't withstand *another* black mark.

Shawn laughed, then sobered, looking down at his mom. "You didn't force me into any of this, Mom, and it'll be okay, you'll see."

"But what if it goes on your record? What if it puts your scholarship at risk?"

"My grades are putting my scholarship at risk," Shawn said. "I don't think a police record will make that big a difference."

Sadie's thoughts took a sharp left-hand turn. "What do you mean your grades are putting the scholarship at risk? What's wrong with your grades?"

Shawn patted her arm slightly. "We should probably talk about that another time," he said in a parental tone. "You're under a lot of pressure right now, and we don't want to add to it."

Sadie paused, completely distracted. "That's why you came home this weekend, isn't it? To confess. What classes are you failing? Can't you make it up before the end of the semester?"

"Seriously, Mom," Shawn said. "Let's talk about this later."

Sadie was not going to talk about this later, and she opened her mouth to continue the discussion when she was startled instead by a sound she could only categorize as a wail. Immediately she sat up straight and scanned the room; everyone in the station was equally alert.

"What was that?" Sadie asked as another wail ripped through the air. She looked toward a hallway on the far left of the room. A few officers were moving in that direction as the door to Captain Dresden's office flew open.

Pete came running through the door, his hand inside his jacket. One of the officers turned toward him. "It's Mr. Mortenson," he said.

Pete growled, heading for the hallway while agonizing sobs replaced the wailing. "They weren't supposed to tell him until he sobered up," he yelled, then pointed at two officers and told them to stay where they were.

Both doors to Sadie's left opened—the rooms Shawn said Eric and Josh were in—and both men appeared with an officer beside them.

A moment later, Thom Mortenson appeared around the corner of the hallway, held up by two officers who were attempting to calm him down. His face was red and contorted with agony, his nose was dripping.

"Josh!" he yelled, pushing against the officers trying to help him. With sloppy, heavy steps, he crossed the room, still partially held up by the police who didn't seem to know what to do with him.

Josh took a few steps to meet him, even though he looked unsure of exactly what he was supposed to do.

Thom reached out and grabbed the sleeves of Josh's sweatshirt, holding the fabric in his closed fists. "It's not true," Thom sobbed, looking like a small child rather than a grown man. "Mark wouldn't do this, he wouldn't. Tell them it's not true, none of it is true."

Josh sent the officers a pained look before looking back at Thom. "I'm so sorry, Thom," he said, trying to sound reassuring. "But it's going to be okay, it really is."

Thom threw his head back and wailed again as his legs seemed to turn to jelly. Josh tried to keep his balance despite the two hundred pounds of dead weight now hanging on his arms. The officers quickly pulled Thom to his feet.

Sadie could barely watch. Between the sympathetic sorrow she felt for Thom and the basic embarrassment she felt for the scene he was making, she felt horribly uncomfortable and inadequate since she knew there was nothing she could do to help.

"Back into room seven," Pete barked to the officers holding Thom. Then he pointed at Josh. "You too." Everyone followed his instructions and a few seconds later the hallway was clear. Thom's sobs lost their intensity, but weren't completely silenced by the walls and doors that now separated him from the rest of the police station. Sadie thought back to those mini-bottles lined up on the table. They certainly weren't helping Thom cope with such shocking news.

After a few seconds, the officers went back to talking to one another, but there was a new tension in the room that Sadie doubted would dissipate any time soon. Reluctantly, she and Shawn returned to their seats, and Eric was taken back into the interrogation room he'd been in. Before he disappeared, though, he caught Sadie's eye and offered a very small, very fleeting smile. And yet it made her feel so much better. Just knowing he didn't hold her personally responsible for what was happening to him was a huge relief. It was a few more minutes before Pete came out of room seven, conferred with another officer, and then headed in Sadie's direction.

"Is he going to be okay?" Sadie asked as she stood up and glanced at room seven. She couldn't hear Thom anymore, but she had no doubt things were still very intense inside the room.

Pete looked at the door as well. "I don't know. He's in bad shape." He touched Sadie's elbow. "Are you ready to go to the hospital?" he asked. "You should really get that looked at."

"I think it's in my best interest to do as you say," Sadie said, trying to lighten the mood.

Pete responded with a smile that made his eyes crinkle at the corners. "It would be nice."

CHAPTER 50

Pete shielded her from the wind and snow as best as he could as she slipped into the passenger seat of his undercover police car for the second time that night. Pete closed the door, and Sadie let out a breath she felt she'd been holding for hours. Shawn had chosen to stay at the police station to see how things turned out with Eric, Josh, and Thom, but Sadie suspected he also wanted to give Sadie and Pete a chance to be alone. Sadie didn't know if she wanted alone time quite so much. Of course, she was grateful to know Pete wasn't angry with her, touched by his concern over her welfare, and greatly appreciated him defending her to the captain and the other officers, but she didn't know how to find words to explain all of what she felt, even in her own head. Like Pete had said earlier, a lot of things had happened that night.

Pete drove out of the parking lot and, as soon as the police station was out of sight, pulled over to the curb. Sadie turned to look at him, wondering if he'd forgotten something and needed to go back to the station, but she had no sooner made eye contact with him when his warm hands reached up and cupped her face. After an evening like Sadie had had, her first instinct was to pull away, jump out of the car, and run for cover, but his eyes chased away her feelings of fight or flight with a tenderness she could see in his face. Pete quickly glanced at the side of her face which still bore the bruise from Donna Hender's mad skillet skills and frowned at the injury.

"It's all right," Sadie said before he could find yet another set of words to use to apologize. A volcano of butterflies erupted in her stomach as a new intimacy began filling the space between them. "It certainly isn't your fault things got so out of hand."

"I should have given you the benefit of the doubt tonight, it would have made all the difference."

Sadie smiled and placed her good hand against his cheek. She patted him twice, then slapped him—but not too hard. "There," she said. "We're even."

Pete chuckled. "You're one of a kind, Sadie Hoffmiller. Do you know that?"

"I'm not sure Garrison could handle many more," Sadie answered. *Or wants the one it has,* she added in her own mind. "Thank you for believing in me—in the end, I mean." That didn't come out right. "I mean, I'm glad you came to your senses." That didn't sound right either. She usually had such a way with words. "What I'm trying to say is—"

Pete suddenly leaned toward her while pulling her face closer to his. He was going to kiss her! Sadie had only an instant to prepare for the moment she'd waited for all these months. Pete's lips touched hers without force or awkwardness, and Sadie found herself truly breathless as the blizzard outside disappeared and a new and unfamiliar warmth radiated through her body. Pete had kissed her. He *was* kissing her. Finally!

He paused and Sadie sensed he was waiting for permission

DEVIL'S FOOD CAKE

to move forward, to deepen the kiss. For reasons she didn't fully understand, she pulled back instead.

Surprised by her own reaction, Sadie tried to determine what was in her way now. She'd wanted this moment, ached for this new level of their relationship for so long. Now here it was, and she found herself anxious and feeling strangely threatened but still all tingly inside. "I'm sorry," she finally whispered. "I don't know what's wrong with me, but . . . I guess I just . . ."

"It's okay," Pete said quickly. Was he as hesitant to hear her reasoning as she was to say it? "It's been a long night."

"Yes," Sadie said, nodding as she grabbed onto that excuse with both hands. She wasn't sure it was the right excuse, but she'd take it.

Pete smiled and sat back. As soon as his warm hands left Sadie's face, she wished she could call for a do-over. She wanted Pete—in her life, in her arms. What *was* wrong with her? Why was she acting like this? She felt tears come to her eyes as Pete put the car back into drive and pulled away from the curb. It didn't feel good to be so at odds with her own feelings.

"Depending on what tomorrow brings," Pete said, his tone not showing how he felt about the rejected kiss, "maybe we could go to dinner. I'm guessing you might not be cooking quite so much for awhile."

"Dinner would be wonderful," Sadie said, trying to convince herself that everything was fine between them. She also took it as a good sign that he expected her to be free for dinner tomorrow—and not in jail.

Pete turned a corner. The blue-and-white sign for the Garrison Community Hospital was lit up. "We'll get you fixed up good as new," he said as he pulled into the parking lot.

Sadie smiled, but wished she believed him. Sure, her shoulder would heal, she wasn't too worried about that, but there were so many other things that couldn't be fixed so easily. She worried about the Veeter family, and Josh—even his crazy mother. And how would Thom get well with this hanging over his head? Sadie liked justice, and she believed that the truth was better than living with lies and secrets, but she wished it were a less painful process . . . for everyone.

As Thom helped her inside, she couldn't help but wonder what tomorrow would hold. Would the answers make more sense? Would she feel more peace? She supposed only time would tell.

CHAPTER 51

After a few hours of fitful sleep, Sadie had taken on the challenge of getting herself showered Saturday morning. It had taken three times longer than it should have, and she was dreading the next six weeks when she'd have limited use of her left arm.

A light tapping on the door distracted Sadie from the pain in her shoulder and the buttons on her shirt that were making her want to swear.

"You're sure you're okay if I go pick up your prescription?" Shawn said from the other side of the door. "The pharmacy opens at nine o'clock so I'm hoping I can be first in line."

"I'll be fine," Sadie said. She'd actually thought he'd left while she'd been in the shower, but the pharmacy wouldn't have been open anyway. "You'll be back by a quarter to ten so we can go back to the police station?"

"Yep," Shawn said. "It should only take me half an hour."

"Okay," Sadie said, still struggling to do up the buttons.

"You're sure you're—"

"Good-bye, Shawn!" Sadie cut in.

"Okay," Shawn said. His voice was a little farther away when he said, "Bye."

Sadie turned her attention back to the white shirt with navy pinstripes—the only shirt that matched the navy blue shoulder sling the hospital had given her the night before. When she finally finished with the buttons, she let out a breath and smoothed the shirt over her navy slacks which were too tight to be comfortable. At least the shirt wasn't straining too much. She might have to break down and buy bigger clothes. The thought did not improve her mood.

The pain medication alone should have knocked her out once she finally climbed into bed—she was usually very sensitive to narcotics—but instead, the events of the night played over and over in her mind. When the sun came up—bright now that the storm had passed—she'd pulled herself out of bed and tackled the arduous task of getting herself ready, the thoughts of last night never far from her mind.

After slipping her feet into her hot-pink house slippers, she shifted into the shoulder sling she'd nicknamed "The Contraption" and adjusted the strap around her neck before wrapping the other strap around her rib cage. In addition to the dual straps, there was a cushion several inches thick under her arm which held her shoulder at the appropriate angle. She'd need to make an appointment with a specialist to see if she'd need surgery, physical therapy, or just rest. She was hoping for rest.

Once buckled in, she turned to look at her reflection and scowled. Despite the color coordination of her clothes, and the form fit of the shirt that really did show off her figure nicely, she still looked disabled. Using her fingers, she combed her hair back from her forehead, wondering what, if anything, she could do with it one-handed.

She heard a noise from the other side of the bathroom door and turned her head.

"Shawn?" she asked.

There was no answer, but Sadie felt the slightest flush of discomfort radiate through her chest even as she forced herself to turn back to the mirror. He probably forgot his wallet or something. After last night her nerves were understandably still on high alert. Once Shawn returned to school—hopefully tomorrow so he wouldn't miss any classes—she would be living alone once again. Now was no time to get paranoid.

Just as she turned on the blow-dryer, she heard the phone ring. Shutting off the blow-dryer, she put it on the counter and headed for the door that separated her bedroom from the master bath. With her cell phone in an evidence bag at the police station, it could be Gayle, or Pete, or even Shawn.

She pulled open the door as the phone rang a third time and took one step into the room just as Thom Mortenson spun around to face her. For an instant Sadie was completely frozen, her mind and body sharing in the surprise that made it difficult to process what she was seeing.

Thom Mortenson was in her bedroom?

They held one another's eyes for a split second as the phone rang a fourth time, Thom looking as startled and wide-eyed as Sadie felt. "What are you—"

Before she could verbalize the entire thought, Thom got over his shock and lunged at her. She tried to retreat into the bathroom, but he was too fast—something she couldn't understand. In a flash he crossed the room and took hold of her good arm, pushing her backward with his body until she hit the doorjamb.

White hot pain shot like lightning through her back and

shoulder, but his hand clamped over her mouth before she could get ahold of herself enough to scream. The phone rang one more time and then went silent, the caller sent to voice mail while Sadie tried to make sense of what was happening.

Sadie's heart and mind raced. How was this possible? Thom?

"You should have stayed in there," he said, pressing harder with the hand on her mouth. His face was only inches from her own. Sadie whimpered behind his hand. He was hurting her. "One more minute and I'd have been out of here."

Sadie tried to focus on taking deep breaths as her brain whirled through the possible reasons he was there. She couldn't come up with anything that made sense—at least not when she held it up to the things she'd learned about Thom last night. The last memory she had of Thom was him sobbing like a little boy. And now he was holding her captive in her own home?

After a few more seconds of silent staring, Thom narrowed his eyes slightly. "If I remove my hand, will you promise not to scream?" he asked in a tight voice.

Sadie nodded, even though she had no intention of keeping the promise indefinitely.

Thom waited a few more seconds and then lowered his hand. "Where's the transponder?"

"Th-the what?" Sadie asked, hating the squeak of fear in her voice and yet unable to stop it. She was absolutely terrified and there wasn't really any way to hide it.

"The transponder," Thom repeated. "A small metal disk. Looks a little like a couple of watch batteries glued together."

Sadie immediately knew what he was talking about. She'd forgotten to give it to the police last night, forgotten about it entirely, actually. And it was what Thom had come here for?

DEVIL'S FOOD CAKE

"I don't know what you're talking about," Sadie bluffed.

Thom's eyes narrowed even more, but he eased up on pressing her against the wall and looked around the room. "You were wearing purple," he said, scanning the floor. He saw the jumbled sweat suit in the corner near the bed and took a step toward it, yanking Sadie forward. Escaping his grasp was impossible since it took all her strength to keep her balance. Thom reached the sweat suit and, while keeping hold of her arm with one hand, he used the other to shake and shift first the pants and then the dirty jacket, digging his hand into the pockets.

Sadie held her breath, hoping the watch-battery thing had fallen out or that he wouldn't find it stuffed into the extra-deep pockets. She hadn't run across it in her pocket even once last night after putting it there—maybe she'd lost it. However, a moment later the tightness on his face softened and he removed his hand, looking at the silver disk he held between his thumb and forefinger. Then he turned his attention to Sadie and his smile fell.

"Now we have to take care of you," he said. "You shouldn't have lied to me."

"I don't understand," she said, trying to take deep breaths that would calm her down.

"What's to understand?" Thom said as he stood up, continuing to glare at her. He was so confident, and that confidence was so disconcerting. He was supposed to be a broken man, an alcoholic who didn't even have a driver's license. How was she supposed to reconcile the man in front of her with the man she'd thought him to be a mere sixty seconds ago? And how did he get here? Had the police let him go for some reason?

"You took something that didn't belong to you," Thom said. "That's stealing."

"I'm sorry?" Sadie said, hating that it came out sounding like a question.

"You will be," Thom said. "And so will I. It might be hard to believe, but I don't enjoy doing things like this."

"Like what? What are you going to do to me?" Sadie asked, barely able to get the words out. She glanced down at the disk in his hand, so many questions piling up in her mind. She couldn't help but ask the one that made it to the top of the heap. "What is that?"

He didn't answer her immediately, instead he pulled on her arm and moved toward the bedroom door. She stumbled after him and although she tried to resist, he was much stronger than she was and he didn't even seem to notice her efforts. They exited the room and headed down the hallway toward the main part of Sadie's house. Thom slipped the disk into his pocket. "The scientific name is an electromagnetic transponder. It's used to create a temporary magnetic field, which has a side effect of disabling battery-powered devices at close range."

Devices like the wireless microphone systems? Sadie wondered.

"Josh *was* in on it," she gasped, thinking of how she'd found the transponder in his pocket. He'd lied about everything!

"No," Thom said, sounding almost distracted. They reached the great room area of Sadie's home and he looked around before turning toward the kitchen. "I simply slipped it in his pocket when he was helping me with the already disabled equipment." He made a growling sound low in his throat. "I couldn't risk the police finding it on me, and I felt sure I could get it back before anyone else found it. Unfortunately, last night didn't come together quite the way I planned it."

He came to a stop and looked around the great room, glancing in turn between the table and the kitchen cupboards, his bushy eyebrows pulled together as he continued to talk. "I didn't realize until after I left the hotel that the transponder continued to keep a magnetic charge after being activated. I had it in my pocket with my cell phone for a couple of minutes—maybe five—and when Josh showed up, I got rid of it. When the police took my phone, someone commented on the fact that your phone was dead too. You'd been in Josh's room *and* you'd found the key. It wasn't hard to put two and two together." He turned his attention back to the kitchen. "When the police hadn't seen it, and were still discussing how the wireless microphone had malfunctioned, I knew you had to still have it." He gave her what she thought was supposed to come across as a sincere look. "I didn't think it would come to this, Sadie."

His regret was little relief. "*You* killed Mr. Ogreski," she whispered, undoing all the things she thought she'd learned last night and merging them with what she knew now. Thom Mortenson was not the broken man he'd appeared to be and that fact changed everything. Thom had driven from Denver to Garrison, accessed the storage unit, rigged the podium, and then played his part tonight. Wow. It was hard to even process it.

"Had to," Thom said matter-of-factly. He pulled her forward into the kitchen, grabbing one of Sadie's sturdy kitchen chairs as he did so. He dragged the chair and Sadie behind him until he reached the middle of the tiled floor. Then he swung the chair around and pushed it up against the cabinets next to the sink.

Sadie looked at the chair, trying to determine what he was doing. Everything was happening so fast.

Thom kept talking. "Mark's depression and anxiety were getting worse. For years I'd played the part of the incompetent fool, forcing him to stay close to me—guilt, you know. As long as he felt responsible for what I'd become, I could feel secure that he wouldn't dare unburden himself for fear of what that would do to me. When we found out about the book going out of print he seemed relieved that the whole thing was coming to an end. And then I found a reporter's number on his cell phone. After a little more digging, I found out they were meeting." Thom shook his head and let out a breath. "He was going to tell, and where would that leave me—the poor, sick man who needed him so much?"

"But you're not a sick man," Sadie said, well, not in terms of alcoholism anyway.

"Mark didn't know that," Thom said as anger built behind his eyes. "For all he knew it would destroy me, and he didn't care."

"So you faked a public suicide," Sadie summed up.

"Like he said in the note, it was his way of giving my story new life." He smiled, obviously proud of himself.

"You wrote that note," she said.

"I've had lots of time to practice his signature while Mark was busy running my life."

Sadie had so many other questions—like how he'd gotten in her house in the first place, and how he'd set Mr. Ogreski's affairs in order like the note had said.

"And now I'll go to treatment," Thom continued. He seemed to really like talking, and Sadie wasn't inclined to interrupt in hopes that the more time she had to think would help her come up with a solution. "I'll free myself from the demons of alcohol and lies and emerge a stronger, better person for my trials. I'm guessing by the time I finish my treatment, the publisher will not only have decided not to take the book out of print but it will be on its way to another printing. I'm even thinking of writing a book about my journey from darkness to light. Everyone loves a redemption story, you know."

"That's horrible," Sadie said, disgusted.

Thom snapped his head around to glare at her. "It's not horrible," he spat. "It was necessary. Do you have any idea how hard it is to pretend you have no will of your own? To play the part of a fool? After all those years Mark was going to betray me! It proved to me all over again that a man has to look after himself because no one else will. I have to put myself first, or get trampled under the feet of everyone else rushing to the front of the line."

Which meant that anyone who got in his way would be trampled instead. "*You* killed Diane," Sadie said after a few more seconds of deciphering what he meant.

"She was going to ruin me," Thom said easily, closing the cupboard and moving to the next one. "I should have assumed Damon had help querying agents, but I had no reason to guess it was her. Damon was a dropout—not the typical teacher's pet."

"But she sent the letter to Mr. Ogreski," Sadie said, wanting answers, needing answers. Thom had already admitted that it was his goal to kill her. That would mean no one would be around to accuse him of the truth. If she somehow managed to get out of this, she needed to know those answers.

"And Mark brought it to me. I told him Mrs. Veeter was a crazy woman who'd been obsessed with Damon's death. I told Mark I'd take care of it, and I did."

Where did it end? Or perhaps the better question was, where had it begun?

"And Damon?" she asked, the words nearly sticking in her throat. It suddenly seemed like too much of a coincidence that Damon had killed himself. She looked at Thom in alarm, willing it not to be true.

Thom stopped looking through the cupboards for the moment and met her eyes, his mouth tight.

"I remember your kids, Sadie," Thom said. "Good kids, cute smiles. They'd been raised by a single parent too, and yet they thrived, didn't they? I, on the other hand, was cursed with a child who would not listen to me, would not let me in, would not love me. When his mother died, she took him with her." He looked past Sadie, his thoughts taking him back in time. "Puberty brought it out in him—the unbridled rage, the extreme behavior, and the lack of self-control. I did everything I could do to help him—everything any father would do. And how did he repay me?" His eyes came back to Sadie. "By dropping out of school, stealing from me, lying to me about anything and everything.

"We had a fight the night before the dance, and I told him he couldn't go. I ended up working late only to come home and find him gone. It was the last straw. I was livid and tracked him down—found him up at Pearson's Pond with that girl. I demanded he come home. That's when he pulled my shotgun out of his backpack. That's when he told me about the book. Told me how he was going to make a million dollars and leave me forever. He said I was an old fool—an old fool who would never be anybody."

Every muscle in Sadie's body was frozen and although her instinct told her to beg for mercy, she didn't dare interrupt Thom's confession.

He continued to talk, though his eyes were completely devoid of any feeling at all—not even anger.

"I'm not exactly sure what happened after I went for the gun. I know the girl was shot first. I remember Damon screaming as he came at me . . . and then they were both dead, Damon at close enough range for it to look self-inflicted."

The mantel clock in the living room chimed once to signal it was nine o'clock. It seemed to remind Thom of where he was and what he was doing.

"I need to get back." He closed the cupboard and opened another one. After scanning it for only a second or two, he reached for Sadie's crystal pitcher on the top shelf. "Perfect."

Sadie tried to pull away, thinking he was going to hit her with it, but instead he held it in front of her and released it. It hit the tiled floor in a dazzling explosion, the sun streaming through the window catching the shards of glass as they flew in every direction. A few of those pieces hit her legs, making short work of her slacks in a couple places. Sadie bit her lip to keep from crying out.

"You really shouldn't stand on chairs in your condition," Thom said, looking at the glass on the floor as though pleased with his work so far.

Sadie realized he was going to make it look like an accident, and if he got away with her murder, he'd get away with everything else. She couldn't let that happen!

With a burst of energy, Sadie spun away from him, catching him off guard as she twisted out of his grasp. She ran for the hallway, but didn't make it five feet before he grabbed her around the waist and swung her around, pinning her back against his chest. He immediately grabbed her good wrist so that she was once again rendered incapable of her own defense. She could barely breathe for the pain in her shoulder, and yet she focused on that pain, letting it remind her that she was still here, still alive. If she could harness that pain and feed it with the injustice of everything Thom Mortenson had done, perhaps it would become a strength instead of a weakness. With that in mind, she got control of her breathing, stifled her panic and attempted to clear her mind.

"You think I'd let you get away?" Thom said into her ear, causing goose bumps to run up her arms and legs. "After all these years of work, you're not going to screw it up for me now." He pulled harder against her diaphragm. "See, I did it, Sadie. I made something of myself. I proved them all wrong."

In the next instant Thom pushed her forward, but kept hold of her hand, causing her to spin away from him as though they were dancing. Her slippered feet sent glass shards scattering across the floor. The jolting pull when she reached the length of their connected arms caused a sharp pain in her injured shoulder, but she pushed the pain into her reserves which were building by the second. She narrowed her eyes at him.

"The only reason you're anything is because of Damon. You've proved nothing but—"

"Shut up!" Thom said, pulling her forward and hitting her across the face.

She saw pinpricks of light and feared she might pass out, but as she lifted her head, she caught sight of the pan from last night's Evil Chicken on the stove where Shawn had left it. Sadie looked up at Thom. He hadn't noticed her looking at the pan, had he? She began gathering all her strength and confidence. When she'd taken her self-defense class all those years ago, the instructor had said that even if neglected, the skill would come back in times of panic. She'd felt that before, but would it hold true one more time? Broken as she was?

Eric's words from last night came back to her: "What do we have to lose?"

Thom was studying the chair and the cabinets, planning out how best to make this accident look real, she assumed. Sadie took advantage of his distraction and pulled her arm up and away from her body. His grip on her wrist tightened but as soon as he pulled back, she used his own resistance against him and crossed her hand in front of both their bodies. Before he could compensate for the lack of balance she'd initiated, she twisted around, her arm behind her back, and roundhouse kicked the back of Thom's knees—well, almost. She hit his calves, but the force was enough to cause him to stumble forward while she finished the spin that got her out of his way. She planted a follow-up heel kick to the back of his knees, but he didn't let go of her wrist like she hoped, instead taking her down with him in an awkward pile on the glass-covered floor.

Sadie grunted at the impact when she landed, half on Thom's back and half on the tile. The glass stung her legs, and she immediately tried to pull her hand away from Thom's iron grip. Thom rolled over, throwing her off of him without letting go. The glass had cut his face just below his right eye.

"How . . . are you going to . . . explain that," Sadie gasped as he rolled on top of her. Glass crunched beneath her back, piercing her skin while her shoulder felt as though it were being severed from her body.

He pulled back his fist just as Sadie remembered another move from her class. A move she'd never used before. If ever there was a moment to use it, however, it was now.

As quickly as she could, she snapped her head forward, connecting her forehead with the bridge of his nose. She could feel the cartilage of Thom's nose collapse beneath her skull. Thom screamed. Unfortunately, the move was not painless on her end either and stars burst before her eyes. Thom loosened his grip on her wrist just enough for Sadie to pull her hand out of his grasp. She felt the warm sensation of his blood drip onto her neck. She nearly gagged, but she managed to hit him in the nose with her hand—a kind of half-slap, half-punch move.

Thom made a noise between a growl and a scream, lifting his hand to protect himself. Sadie rolled to the side, causing him to fall off of her.

With no time to waste, Sadie scrambled for the kitchen stove. One hand, and a floor covered in shards of her favorite crystal pitcher, made the going slower and far more painful than she'd have hoped. The palm of her hand stung, but she forced herself forward. The pan was mere feet away when Thom grabbed her ankle, causing her to belly flop on the floor. The glass made traction impossible, so she rolled onto her back and tried kicking Thom's hand. She kicked her own leg as much as she kicked him though.

"Let go!" she screamed as loud as she could, finally finding her voice.

He didn't, so she screamed it again and again.

Thom only seemed to get stronger, and he pulled her leg toward him with incredible force. His nose was mangled, and he sneered at her while blood dripped off his chin.

Sadie felt her stomach churn as she moved closer to him, her heart beating so fast she couldn't feel it anymore. She willed herself to be patient. A few more inches, then, and as soon as she was in range, she lifted her free foot and brought it down hard and fast into his face.

He screamed again and his grip on her ankle loosened.

Sadie took off toward the stove again. The few inches worth of a head start made all the difference. She reached for the pan just as she felt his hand grab at the hem of her pants. With a burst of power, she managed to knock the pan from the stove, then fumbled for the handle as it fell.

Thom's hand tightened like a vise around her ankle again but this time she let him pull her closer, identifying the spot on the side of his head just above the left ear. The spot Donna Hender had caught on Sadie's head last night. It had knocked her unconscious long enough for Josh's mother to leave. She could only hope that she, too, could buy herself a few seconds.

Thom saw the pan, but his eyes simply narrowed into smaller slits.

She lifted the pan over her head and then brought it down with all the force she could muster.

Thom's head snapped to the side, but immediately swung back to the front, his eyes fairly glowing with rage.

Sadie refused to die on her own kitchen floor. She refused to let Shawn find her there. She swung again, and again, and one more time before Thom's eyes rolled to the ceiling and his face fell onto the floor.

Sadie's staccato breathing was the only sound in the overwhelming stillness that descended on the kitchen. Sadie stared at Thom's body in disbelief as she considered who he really was and how close he'd been to getting away with everything. All the lies, all the betrayal, all the lives lost at his hand. She felt the tears well up in her eyes.

She looked at the frying pan in her hand and dropped it as her body began to shake. It slid a few inches on the glass-covered floor. Sadie stared at it while the adrenaline that had made her strong began waning, and the pain and exhaustion caught up. Thoughts began to clutter her mind, which had been so clear moments before. She needed to get to the phone.

Cautiously she rose to her feet and pressed her back against the counter as she limped around Thom's body, watching him closely for any signs of movement. She didn't think he was dead, but she wasn't about to get close enough to find out for sure. She was nearly at the phone when she heard the back door open.

She froze on instinct until the familiar voice of her son called out.

"Mom, I'm back. You ready to go?"

He came around the corner and stopped cold, his eyes instantly wide as he looked first at her and then at Thom Mortenson's body lying on the kitchen floor. Shawn's mouth fell open, but Sadie spoke before he had the chance to ask what had happened.

"I'm okay," she said, well aware of the cuts all over her body. "We need to call the police."

Shawn nodded dumbly and then fumbled for his cell phone, still staring at Thom.

Sadie turned to look at him as well. Had any of this really happened? It seemed so unreal, so . . . wrong. She reached for a chair and lowered herself into it, still staring, still trying to understand all that had happened. As she tried to accept the last fifteen minutes of her life, she was reminded of her first exchange with Josh. "It's about time things came full circle," she murmured to herself.

Who could have guessed that the circle would complete itself on Sadie's kitchen floor.

CHAPTER 52

"Knock, knock?"

Sadie opened her eyes and looked toward the doorway of the hospital room, instant fear rushing up her legs and arms. The resident hospital shrink who'd talked to Sadie earlier in the afternoon had said such a reaction was normal—something about thalamuses and endorphins and stuff. Sadie thought her reaction had more to do with the fact that Thom was recovering in a room one floor below her. Pete had explained that Josh and his mother had given Thom a place to stay the night before and he'd slipped away without anyone noticing. On the one hand, Sadie was shocked that such a simple plan could work, but then again, it hadn't really worked, had it?

If thoughts of Thom weren't enough to stress a woman out, she'd had to leave someone else in charge of cleaning all the glass shards off her kitchen floor. That was not the kind of job Sadie liked to leave to someone else.

She was so wrapped up in the psychology behind her reaction that she forgot what it was she was reacting to until a man poked his head around the curtain. He had a neatly trimmed goatee and slicked-back dark hair. The smell of his cologne nearly canceled out all the medicinal scents of the hospital.

Sadie didn't recognize him for a few seconds, then her eyebrows tried to go up, but the swelling from the beatings to the head she'd withstood the last few days, coupled with the cuts from the glass, made it a painful endeavor.

"Eric?" she asked.

He just smiled wider.

More like Eric's younger, better-looking brother, she thought to herself as he took a few steps closer, revealing that the slicked-back hair was really just his regular hair, but clean and pulled into a ponytail—although she could swear he'd had a trim.

Gayle had come to the hospital earlier and fixed Sadie's hair while Sadie relayed the whole shocking story, but there was nothing to be done about her face and the stupid shoulder sling. Seeing Eric all cleaned up made her feel vulnerable and self-conscious. He held out a handful of daisies. Sadie loved daisies.

"You should wear a name tag," Sadie suggested as she accepted the bouquet. Even his nails were clean. "I almost didn't recognize you."

Eric smiled and did a single shoulder shrug. He was dressed in jeans and a black polo shirt. He looked good in black. Maybe too good.

"So, I went to the station at ten only to hear how you just can't get enough adventure in your life," he said.

"Or adventure can't get enough of me," Sadie said. Once her injuries had been attended to, she'd had two hours of discussion with Pete and the captain, but it had all been focused on what happened this morning rather than the charges from last night. Then the captain had insisted she stay at the hospital overnight for observation and for her home to be properly photographed and cleaned up.

"How did it go with the police?" she asked.

"I'm not in jail," Eric said. "That's a plus. They said it could be weeks before the district attorney decides what to do. I don't think we're supposed to leave the country until they decide."

"Oh," Sadie said, surprised, but in a good way. "I think I can handle that."

They both were quiet for a moment. When Eric spoke, his voice was soft. "Are you okay?"

Sadie nodded. "I will be. I heal incredibly well."

"Glad to hear it," Eric said. He nodded toward the bouquet. "You didn't read my card."

Sadie hadn't even noticed a card. But she turned the bouquet in her hands until she saw the corner of a little pink envelope poking out between the stems. Unfortunately, it was impossible for her to grab the envelope, since she was holding the bouquet with her one good arm. She tried turning the flowers on their side and shaking the card out. When that didn't work, she tried to hold the bouquet low enough that her immobilized hand could help her, but the angle was all wrong.

Eric stepped up and plucked the card out of the flowers with a smile on his face. "Trade," he said, taking the flowers and giving her the little card. He looked around the room. "Is there a bedpan or something I can put these in?"

Sadie managed to laugh even though she'd have gotten after Shawn if he'd said something like that. The card was easier to hold at her side, allowing her to use both hands to open the envelope. It wasn't sealed, which she found rather thoughtful. On the front was a watercolor rendering of a Saint Bernard. The words "Get Well Soon!" were written on the rum barrel around his neck.

"Hello?"

They both turned as Breanna stepped around the curtain, holding a large, flat, multicolored box in her hands. A plastic grocery bag hung from her arm. She'd arrived in Garrison a couple of hours earlier and had been hovering ever since. She'd taken over the position of "woman in charge" seamlessly, something that used to be difficult for her to do. Sadie wasn't sure she liked the bossy Breanna, but had finally convinced her and Shawn to get her some real food. The meatloaf the hospital had served for lunch had been . . . below Sadie's standards.

Breanna put the box on the bedside table as Shawn appeared behind her. He acknowledged Eric with a quick nod, which Eric returned as he moved around the bed to make room for Sadie's children.

"Okay," Breanna said, too intent on her task to be bothered with taking inventory of the room. "We ended up at the ice cream shop down the street. Someone thought you'd like that better than a burger." She eyed Shawn accusingly.

"Tell me you wouldn't choose ice cream cake over McDonalds?" Shawn challenged, raising his eyebrows. He looked at his sister and grinned. "Tell her what it's called."

Breanna shook her head as she opened the lid of the box. Then she glanced over at Sadie. "Died and Gone to Heaven cake," she said as though disappointed in herself for going along with any of this. "Totally inappropriate." She pulled down the sides of the box, revealing the cake inside.

Sadie blinked and stared. The cake was at least four inches tall, and from where Sadie sat, it had several layers that included Oreos, ice cream, hot fudge, and whipping cream.

"It's awesome," Shawn said. He helped Bre lower the table so that Sadie could see the top of the cake. Hot fudge letters spelled out "Congratulations."

"Congratulations?" Sadie said. Her children were so strange sometimes.

"Yeah, for not being dead," Shawn said. "That's why it's so funny."

DEVIL'S FOOD CAKE

A Died and Gone to Heaven cake to celebrate that you're still alive. Get it?"

"I get it," she finally said, shaking her head at her son's warped sense of humor, but smiling all the same. "But it's huge. How are we going to eat it all before it melts?"

"You're about to become the nurses' favorite patient," Breanna said. She dug through the plastic bag and pulled out a package of paper plates and some plastic utensils. She finally looked up at Eric. "Oh, hi," she said. Her hair, as usual, was pulled into a ponytail, not too different from Eric's hairstyle. She had no makeup on and was wearing worn-out jeans and a plain red hooded sweatshirt—her typical uniform of everyday life. And yet, she was nothing less than stunning. "You must be Eric."

Sadie looked at her daughter in surprise. How did she know that was Eric? Sadie had talked about him when she relayed the last twenty-four hours, of course, but not in enough detail for Breanna to identify him so quickly. Had Shawn been talking about him? If so, what had he said?

"I'm Breanna," she said with a welcoming smile. "Sadie's daughter."

Eric smiled back. "Pleased to meet you," he said politely.

Sadie couldn't tell if he was ill at ease with her children or not.

"Me too," she said. As she turned back to the cake, she looked at Sadie and raised her eyebrows quickly two times.

What did that mean?

"Want some?" Shawn asked, holding out a plate of cake to Eric.

"Oh yeah," Eric said, quickly abandoning the flowers on a chair in the corner in order to take the proffered cake.

"Here Mom," Bre said a minute later, putting a plate on Sadie's lap. "What's that?" She nodded toward the card Sadie was still holding.

"Oh," Sadie said, "Eric brought me flowers." She fumbled trying to open the card and nearly dropped it in her cake.

"Let me help," Shawn said, taking the card before Sadie could stop him.

Sadie glanced at Eric, whose cheeks suddenly went red as he hurried to swallow the cake. "Uh," he said once he could speak, but it was too late. Shawn had already opened the card and read what was written inside, his mouth turning up in a slow smile.

Sadie looked between Shawn and Eric, suddenly very nervous. She put out her hand. "I believe it was given to me," she said.

"Sure was," Shawn said as yet another voice joined the crowd.

"Hello?"

They all turned to see Pete come around the curtain. He nodded a greeting to everyone, but came to Sadie and kissed her on the top of her head. "How are you doing?" he asked as he stepped back, a sympathetic smile on his handsome face.

"I'm good," she said, smiling. The room fell suddenly silent, and she looked at the three people standing behind Pete, none of whom were smiling. As soon as she looked at them, however, all three of them went back to what they were doing: Eric took another bite, Shawn went about cutting himself a huge piece of cake, and Breanna pulled another plate out of the plastic bag.

"Want some cake?" Sadie offered to Pete.

"We're celebrating Mom not being dead," Shawn said.

"Oh, well that's certainly something worth celebrating," Pete said, though he looked a little taken aback.

Sadie just smiled. What else could she do? The room went silent again, and Sadie decided to fill her mouth and her thoughts with cake.

"This is really good," Pete said as he cut off a second bite.

DEVIL'S FOOD CAKE

"Mom could make a better one," Shawn said, causing Sadie to look up at him.

"I've never made an ice cream cake," she said, looking at the cake with new eyes. It was just layers of yummy stuff. Let's see, if she started with an Oreo crust, and adapted her hot fudge sauce recipe . . .

"So," Pete said after a minute, "when I left the station Dresden was still talking to the district attorney." He glanced at Shawn. "I think they're going to let you go home tomorrow so you don't miss any classes, but you'll have to come back during your school's spring break." He turned to Sadie. "The longer we can postpone anyone pressing charges the better it will be for all of you." He included Eric in the look he cast around the room.

Shawn scrunched up his face. "I was kinda hoping they'd make me stay here for a few more days. I've got a killer test in my Orthophysiology class on Monday."

"What happened with Josh?" Sadie asked.

"And that Jane woman," Shawn added, his mouth full of cake.

Sadie shot him a look and he shrugged.

"Josh has been asked to stay in town. In light of these newest discoveries, his version of events is even more important. He's cooperating fully." Pete paused to take another bite, leaving the rest of them to wait until he swallowed to finish the update. "Jane was released; we had nothing to hold her on once the camera was returned. I suspect she'll have the feature story in tomorrow's paper."

Sadie shook her head. It seemed so unfair that Jane should benefit from all her shenanigans.

"So until the district attorneys make a decision," Eric said, "we just go about our normal lives?"

Pete nodded. "And stay out of trouble." He looked at Sadie and winked. "The fact is that we jumped the gun with your first arrest," he said. "And we wouldn't have found Thom without your help. It's hard to ignore that. And then with all this . . ." He waved one hand through the air. "Well, we'll just have to see how they balance it all out."

"Yet it seems hard to imagine they'd ignore it completely," Sadie said, thinking specifically of Josh. Kidnapping and lashing someone to a kitchen chair didn't seem like a swept-under-the-rug type of charge.

"I'll let you know what I hear," Pete said with a shrug. "But so far I think we can count it as good news."

"Well," Eric said a moment later, drawing Sadie's attention back to him, "I guess I better go." His plate was empty and he walked toward the bed so he could drop it in the trash.

Sadie watched him closely. The cake was wonderful, but she hated that it had interrupted their conversation. She had all kinds of things she wanted to say to him, like "Thank you," and "I'm sorry," and even "When will I see you again?" But they all seemed difficult to say in front of her current audience. Still, she had to say something.

"I plan to make good on my promise to clean your house," she said. "I just need a few weeks to recover, okay?" It wasn't until she finished talking that she realized everyone was listening. She felt her cheeks heat up, not wanting to draw any more attention to herself than she already had.

Eric smiled. He really did have a nice smile. "It's a date," he said.

Sadie felt her face fall. A date? That wasn't what she meant.

Eric's eyes flickered to Pete, who was suddenly watching the other man with a bit more caution. Eric said his good-byes, and Sadie took another bite of cake thoughtfully. A *date?*

After taking her last bite, she looked up to see Shawn watching her, his arms folded in that imposing stance that came so easily to him. "Oh, look," he suddenly said, exaggerating the act of opening his eyes wide as he unfolded his arms. "Here's that card."

DEVIL'S FOOD CAKE

Now? Sadie thought, casting a glance at a curious Pete.

Shawn leaned forward and handed her the card, taking her now empty plate.

"Card?" Pete asked.

Sadie wanted to ignore the question, but not answering seemed like a poor choice. "Oh, Eric brought me some flowers." She waved toward the abandoned bouquet on the chair.

"Oh," Pete said, turning to look. He still had that thoughtful look on his face when he turned around again.

"I should put those in water," Breanna said, picking up the flowers.

"And we should probably take the rest of this cake out to the nurses' station before it melts," Shawn said, putting his plate on the end of Sadie's bed to free his hands. He looked at Pete. "Could you help me get it out there? I don't want to spill it or anything."

Shawn needed Pete's help? Sadie wondered. She was so confused.

"Oh," Pete said, setting down his plate next to Shawn's. "Sure."

Shawn glanced at his mom quickly before taking one end of the bed table. "We can just wheel this whole thing out there," he said.

Sadie finally understood. He was creating an opportunity for her to be alone.

Moments later Breanna had disappeared into the bathroom, Shawn and Pete were rolling the cake down the hall, and Sadie was alone. She picked up the card again and flipped it open, ignoring the butterflies she felt for reasons she couldn't define.

BONNIE,
THANKS FOR THE BEST TIME I'VE HAD IN YEARS.
I'M HOPING THERE ARE EVEN BETTER TIMES AHEAD.
SINCERELY,
CLYDE

Josi S. Kilpack

Died and Gone to Heaven Cake

8 ounces Hershey's chocolate syrup
1 can Eagle Brand sweetened condensed milk
⅓ cup butter
½ teaspoon vanilla
½ gallon vanilla ice cream (softened)*
24 Oreo cookies
¼ cup butter
8 ounces Cool Whip
2 ounces pecans, chopped

In a medium saucepan, bring chocolate syrup, milk, and butter to a boil. Reduce heat and simmer for 5 minutes. Stir constantly until the mixture becomes thick, like hot fudge sauce. Add vanilla. Remove chocolate sauce from heat and allow to cool completely.

Place ice cream in a large bowl and allow to soften.

Crush 24 Oreos into a graham-cracker crust consistency. (Put the cookies in a zip-top bag and smash them with a rolling pin. Whatever it takes to get the crumbs as fine as possible.) Melt ¼ cup butter and mix into the crushed cookies. Pat into a 9x13 pan. Put in freezer for 10 minutes.

When ice cream has softened to the texture of thick icing, spread it with a knife over the Oreo cookie crust. Freeze for 30 minutes.

Pour cooled chocolate sauce over ice cream. Freeze for 30 minutes.

Add a layer of Cool Whip and top with pecans. Cover with foil and freeze for an additional 4 to 6 hours.

Serves 12.

*Shawn would like me to try this with Starlight Mint ice cream.

ACKNOWLEDGMENTS

Writing this series has presented me with new challenges I didn't see coming; good challenges, but challenges all the same. I am indebted to some key people who helped Sadie stay Sadie and who kept me from repeating the same twists and turns I've used in other books. My writer's group has been my first line of defense for many books, and once again they did not let me down. Much thanks goes out to each of them: Becki Clayson, Jody Durfee, Ronda Hinrichsen, and the late Anne Craeger, who lost her battle with cancer before this book was finished. These four women patiently helped me shape this story in ways I could never have done on my own and I am so grateful to each of them for the influence they have on my writing and on my life.

Sadie's Test Kitchen is a closed blog that tests out all the recipes included in the series, and several cooks have also allowed me to use their own recipes. Their assistance was priceless for this book; I could not have done it without them. Bear-hug thanks to Don, Sandra, Laree, Annie, Barbara, Shirley, Michelle, Whit, and Danyelle.

Julie Wright did a turbo read through at the midnight hour

Acknowledgments

after convincing me that I could not send it to my publisher without anyone reading the whole book start to finish. She was, of course, right and caught things that definitely needed to be caught. Lisa Mangum, my editor and friend, and Rachel Ann Nunes also read the book en route and gave me good feedback that helped to smooth my story. The end result was a story I could be proud of, but I would never have reached that point without the help of generous friends.

After the creation portion, comes the production process and I am grateful to Shauna Gibby for yet another fabulous cover, Rachael Ward for typesetting, Lisa Mangum for her editorial prowess, and Jana Erickson for organizing all the details. Big thanks to the marketing staff at Deseret Book, specifically Roberta Stout who makes organizing an event look so easy, even though I know it is not.

And yet behind all these people and behind every scene I write is my real life, which is brimming with wonderful kids, an amazing husband, and friends, fans, and family who cheer me on, push me forward, and remind me that the best things in life do not happen on paper. I thank the Lord every day for all the goodness he has given me and hope that in some small way I give a little bit back through the pages of my stories.

Enjoy this sneak peek of

Key Lime Pie

Coming Fall 2010

Chapter 1

"Hey."

Sadie Hoffmiller looked up from where she was planting marigolds in the courthouse flower beds as part of the community service she'd been sentenced to after an unfortunate situation she'd been involved in a few months earlier.

The April sun blinded her; she lifted a gloved hand to shield her eyes even though she knew the voice.

Eric Burton. She'd met him quite by accident during that same unfortunate situation for which she now found herself working to erase from her police record. It was almost impossible to believe that she, Sadie Hoffmiller, had a record, but there it was. At least it was only community service. The judge could have been much harder on both of them. "Hi there," Sadie responded, sitting back on her heels and attempting to smooth her hair before realizing her glove was covered in dirt and therefore made whatever state her hair was in even worse. "I thought you'd finished up your community service on Monday."

"And how would you know that?" he asked, giving her a playful smile. "Have you been asking about me?"

Sadie felt her cheeks heat up for no good reason and went back to her flowers. "Actually I was looking forward to having a little peace and quiet around here. I've been counting down your hours more than I've been counting down my own." Sadie knew Eric had made short work of his three hundred hours, sometimes doing up to twenty hours a week. Sadie had tried to keep up, but she still had a dozen hours left.

Eric laughed out loud, making it impossible for Sadie to feign her offense at his banter. He lowered himself to the mottled green and brown grass beside her and laid on his back, supporting his weight with his elbows and lifting his face to the sun that was almost directly overhead. Eric's long hair was pulled into its usual ponytail at the base of his neck and he was wearing jeans and a gray, long-sleeved shirt with a green alien head on the front.

Sadie watched him out of the corner of her eye as she went back to her marigolds. Sometimes he was flirty, and now and again he was downright brazen in his attention toward her, and yet he back-pedaled quickly when those moments came around, always leaving a bewildered Sadie in his wake.

"I told Tami I'd help with Wednesday's food deliveries until someone else breaks the law and gets court ordered to take my place," Eric said, interrupting her thoughts. "Apparently Garrison doesn't have enough of us fringe citizens."

Us? He wasn't calling Sadie a fringe citizen, was he? She glanced at him quickly and realized he probably was. And he'd think it was a compliment. "It's generous of you to keep helping her out," Sadie said.

"It was generous of you to give her the cookies. She insisted I have one," Eric said after a few seconds.

Sadie felt him watching her, and she imagined his blue eyes were even brighter than usual in the sunshine. But she didn't allow herself to look and instead became even more intent on reaching for another flower.

When she didn't answer, Eric spoke again. "What kind of cookies were they?"

She still didn't answer.

"I'm not leaving until you tell me, so you may as well fess up."

Sadie narrowed her eyes at him as she sat back on her heels and let out a breath. "No one was supposed to know they were from me," she said quietly, embarrassed to be found out. "They were an anonymous thank-you gift. I didn't want Tami to feel indebted."

"If it makes you feel better, she hasn't figured it out yet," Eric said with a wry grin. "I'll keep your secret if you give me the recipe."

Not since Sadie's late husband, Neil, had she met a man who preferred the kitchen to the La-Z-Boy, and while Eric insisted that he loved to cook, Sadie had seen his house and had a hard time believing he could cook in such a mess. She didn't want to doubt him, but there were just so many ways that Eric confused her. Cooking was only one of them.

"So?"

Sadie blinked. "What?"

"The recipe," Eric said, shaking his head slightly. "Are you going to give it to me or do I have to tell Tami to find a way to thank you for the thank-you."

"You're impossible." In some ways Eric was like a younger brother, teasing and goading her all the time, and yet . . . in other ways he was nothing like a brother at all. Not one little bit.

"They're my Kickin' Craisin cookies," Sadie said in surrender.

"Kickin' Craisin, huh," Eric said thoughtfully. "Where's the kick come from?"

"Cayenne pepper," Sadie said, unable to hide a smile. She loved people's reactions when she told them the secret ingredient.

Eric's eyebrows shot up. "In a cookie?"

Sadie smiled even wider. "But just a little. You want zing, not zoiks."

Eric threw his head back and laughed.

"Am I interrupting something?"

Sadie looked up as Eric's laugh cut off. Pete Cunningham, her kinda-sorta-maybe-boyfriend was blocking the sun while looking down on them. She smiled, but felt as though she'd been caught doing something she shouldn't have been. "Pete," she said, hoping that by making her voice sound lighter she could cover up her discomfort. "Is it four already?"

"Almost," Pete said. Then he looked at Eric. "Mr. Burton," he said with a polite nod. Too polite.

"Detective," Eric said just as coolly. He pushed himself up to a sitting position while Sadie patted another flower into place.

"I didn't realize it was so late," Sadie said, moving faster. "It's going to get cold again so I'd like to get these last few flowers in the ground before the weather turns."

"I can finish up for you, if you'd like," Eric said to Sadie, his tone suspiciously formal.

Sadie looked at him in surprise.

"If I hadn't been distracting you, you wouldn't be running late."

Sadie sighed and gave him a reproachful look. His gallantry was only a ploy to make the point that *he'd* been distracting her from the date she had with *Pete*. However, she chose to take him at his word. To do anything else would open an opportunity for him to make even more uncomfortable comments.

"That would be great," she said, brushing off her gloves before removing them and handing them to Eric with a smug grin.

He frowned slightly—clearly he'd hoped to draw this conversation out a little longer—but he took the proffered gloves.

Sadie pushed herself up, cringing at the cramps in her knees from kneeling so long. Pete reached down to help her and she raised her left hand toward him.

Eric put a hand on her arm. "Your shoulder?"

"Oh, right," Sadie said, lifting her other hand instead. She'd torn a ligament in her shoulder a few months back—another part of the unfortunate situation. Her shoulder had improved a great deal over the last several weeks but it was still tender. Why was it that Eric had remembered her injury and Pete hadn't?

"I just need a couple minutes to clean up and I'll be ready," she said to Pete when she got to her feet, untying the apron she'd worn to protect her clothes. She and Pete were going to Baxter's for an early dinner and then planned to catch a movie at the Capitol Theatre that played classics on Wednesday nights. Tonight they were featuring *Out of Africa*. Sadie hadn't seen it for years and, of course, a DVD couldn't compare to the big screen anyway.

"That's fine," Pete said, smiling at her with those hazel eyes she liked so much. Pete was wonderful: kind, smart, supportive, and stable—everything she wanted. And yet, there was something about him that was either too much or too little. Their relationship hadn't progressed much over the last few months, but they were in a comfortable place and they both seemed okay with that for now. "I've got a few phone calls to make," Pete continued, leaning in to kiss her on the cheek. "I'll wait for you in the car if that's okay."

Sadie nodded and Pete headed toward the parking lot. "I appreciate your help finishing up," she said to Eric, who had been oddly quiet. She felt bad he was digging in the dirt even though it wasn't her fault—he'd offered to do it.

"I'll just bet you do," Eric said darkly.

"What?" Sadie questioned, sure she'd misinterpreted his tone.

Eric sat back, put his hands on his thighs, and glanced briefly at Pete's retreating back before looking at Sadie. "Is that really the kind of guy you want to be with?"

Sadie was instantly defensive. "Obviously," she answered, folding her arms over her chest.

Eric looked at her thoughtfully for a moment before turning back to the flower bed, stabbing the trowel into the dirt. "Huh."

Sadie knew she should turn around and leave. She didn't. "Huh, what?"

Eric shrugged and then jammed a poor marigold into the hole he'd just dug. "I pegged you to want someone who was a little more real, a little more, I don't know, fun."

"Pete's real," Sadie said even though she wasn't sure what that meant. "And he's . . . fun."

Eric paused, then put down his trowel and stood slowly. Sadie watched every movement until he reached his feet. "Is he?" Eric asked, hooking his thumbs into the belt loops of his jeans. His tone had changed dramatically. It was no longer hard, it was now whispery and . . . almost intimate. He took a step toward her so that they were only a foot apart. His nearness forced Sadie to look up, but only a little since he was only a few inches taller than she was.

She knew she *should* take a step backward, but she didn't want to so she didn't.

"You deserve more than a safe bet, Sadie," he said. His breath smelled like cinnamon, with a hint of cayenne. "You deserve someone who will enjoy life *with* you rather than just live it by your side."

KEY LIME PIE

Sadie knew that behind Eric's words was the statement that *he* was the kind of man she'd enjoy life with and it brought to the forefront of her mind all the thoughts she'd tried not to think about him but had a very hard time avoiding. All of a sudden it was impossible to ignore that she was attracted to this man.

It made her feel utterly ridiculous.

"I'm older than you are," she said before realizing she'd opened her mouth. Her face instantly burned. Did she seriously just say that! Out loud?

"Am I?" he asked.

Sadie narrowed her eyes. "You know you are."

Eric made an innocent face and shrugged. "I don't know any such thing."

"I'm fifty-six," Sadie said in an attempt to convince him. The words almost stuck in her throat. It was not normal for a woman to admit her age, but this was an emergency. She watched his face, but he showed no reaction at all. "How old are you?"

Eric shook his head. "It doesn't matter."

"It *does* matter." He was younger than she was! She knew it!

"Not to me," he said. "Is that your only reason for choosing him over me?"

Sadie cast a look over her shoulder; Pete was only twenty yards away. His car must be on the other side of the parking lot, though. She couldn't see it. Which meant he couldn't see them either.

Eric took her chin in his hand and turned her face toward his. He didn't say anything, just lifted his eyebrows expectantly as he dropped his hand.

Sadie's head was still spinning, but there didn't seem to be any option other than answering.

"I—uh . . ." She stumbled to find another reason but somehow could only focus on the things she *couldn't* say. She was a professional; he was a locksmith. She was organized; he was a slob. And she was older than he was!

She had to say something. "You have longer hair than I do."

Eric smiled. "I'll cut it."

This was not happening! And yet it was. She was not having this conversation! And yet she was. She didn't know what to say. And yet she spoke because it had to be said. "We're too different."

"Not really," Eric said and took another tiny step toward her. She could feel the toe of his boot against the toe of her shoe. "You just have a hard time admitting that I'm the kind of guy you really want to be with."

Sadie stared into Eric's blue eyes and when he leaned into her, she found herself steeling herself expectantly. He was going to kiss her.

And she was totally going to let him.

Inches from making contact, however, Eric paused. "Mark my words, Sadie Hoffmiller, the first time our lips meet, it will be *you* kissing *me*."

He stepped back while Sadie tried to make sense of what he'd just said—and what he *hadn't* done. Her eyes snapped to meet his laughing ones. The expression on his face told her in no uncertain terms that she'd just proved something he'd suspected all along.

Sadie opened her mouth but could find no words. She wasn't used to being made a fool of and felt instant heat rush up her spine. She was saved from responding, however, by the ringing of his cell phone—some heavy metal song she didn't want to know the title of. AC/DC, she thought. He winked at her while digging the phone from his pocket.

"This is Eric," he said into the phone a moment later, turning away from Sadie who stood with her hands balled into fists at her sides. How dare he trick her into saying things she shouldn't have said; into feeling things she shouldn't be feeling.

She waited for him to get off the phone so she could tell him what she *really* thought of him, but then she noticed his face turn pale and his eyes go wide.

"What?" he breathed before going silent again. He made eye contact with Sadie, a pleading, scared look on his face that drained her of all her anger. "Yes," he continued. "I can fax them to you in about ten minutes." He pulled the phone away from his ear and stared at it for a moment before turning it off.

"Eric?" Sadie said as he turned back to face her, a frightened expression on his face that caused Sadie's heart to race. "What's happened?"

"They found a body in Florida," he said. "They think it might be my Megan."

About the Author

Josi S. Kilpack was born and raised in Salt Lake City, graduated from Olympus High, made an appearance at Salt Lake Community College, and then jumped headfirst into life as a grown-up. She married Lee Kilpack in 1993 and they welcomed their first daughter a year later. Josi began writing her first novel in 1998, and has followed that with ten more novels. She currently lives in Willard, Utah, with her husband, four kids, a dog, and a varying number of chickens.

For more information about Josi, or to read the first chapter of any of her books, go to her website www.josiskilpack.com